Baroness Orczy's

Old Man in the Corner

Baroness Orczy's
Old Man in the Corner

The Old Man in the Corner

The Case of Miss Elliott

The Glasgow Mystery

Coachwhip Publications
Landisville, Pennsylvania

The Old Man in the Corner first published 1908. (Individual stories date several years earlier.)
The Case of Miss Elliott first published 1905.
"The Glasgow Mystery" first published in the *Royal Magazine* in 1901.

ISBN 1-61646-015-6
ISBN-13 978-1-61646-015-0

Cover Image: Noose © Gary Woodard

CoachwhipBooks.com

Contents

The Old Man in the Corner

The Case of Miss Elliott

The Glasgow Mystery

The Old Man in the Corner

1
The Fenchurch Street Mystery

I.

The man in the corner pushed aside his glass, and leant across the table.

"Mysteries!" he commented. "There is no such thing as a mystery in connection with any crime, provided intelligence is brought to bear upon its investigation."

Very much astonished Polly Burton looked over the top of her newspaper, and fixed a pair of very severe, coldly inquiring brown eyes upon him.

She had disapproved of the man from the instant when he shuffled across the shop and sat down opposite to her, at the same marble-topped table which already held her large coffee (3d.), her roll and butter (2d.), and plate of tongue (6d.).

Now this particular corner, this very same table, that special view of the magnificent marble hall—known as the Norfolk Street branch of the Aërated Bread Company's depôts—were Polly's own corner, table, and view. Here she had partaken of eleven pennyworth of luncheon and one pennyworth of daily information ever since that glorious never-to-be-forgotten day when she was enrolled on the staff of the *Evening Observer* (we'll call it that, if you please), and became a member of that illustrious and world-famed organization known as the British Press.

She was a personality, was Miss Burton of the *Evening Observer*. Her cards were printed thus:

MISS MARY J. BURTON.

Evening Observer.

She had interviewed Miss Ellen Terry and the Bishop of Madagascar, Mr. Seymour Hicks and the Chief Commissioner of Police. She had been present at the last Marlborough House garden party—in the cloak-room, that is to say, where she caught sight of Lady Thingummy's hat, Miss What-you-may-call's sunshade, and of various other things modistical or fashionable, all of which were duly described under the heading "Royalty and Dress" in the early afternoon edition of the *Evening Observer*.

(The article itself is signed M.J.B., and is to be found in the files of that leading halfpennyworth.)

For these reasons—and for various others, too—Polly felt irate with the man in the corner, and told him so with her eyes, as plainly as any pair of brown eyes can speak.

She had been reading an article in the *Daily Telegraph*. The article was palpitatingly interesting. Had Polly been commenting audibly upon it? Certain it is that the man over there had spoken in direct answer to her thoughts.

She looked at him and frowned; the next moment she smiled. Miss Burton (of the *Evening Observer)* had a keen sense of humour, which two years' association with the British Press had not succeeded in destroying, and the appearance of the man was sufficient to tickle the most ultra-morose fancy. Polly thought to herself that she had never seen any one so pale, so thin, with such funny light-coloured hair, brushed very smoothly across the top of a very obviously bald crown. He looked so timid and nervous as he fidgeted incessantly with a piece of string; his long, lean, and trembling fingers tying and untying it into knots of wonderful and complicated proportions.

Having carefully studied every detail of the quaint personality Polly felt more amiable.

"And yet," she remarked kindly but authoritatively, "this article, in an otherwise well-informed journal, will tell you that, even within the last year, no fewer than six crimes have completely baffled the police, and the perpetrators of them are still at large."

"Pardon me," he said gently, "I never for a moment ventured to suggest that there were no mysteries to the *police*; I merely remarked that there were none where intelligence was brought to bear upon the investigation of crime."

"Not even in the Fenchurch Street *mystery*. I suppose," she asked sarcastically.

"Least of all in the so-called Fenchurch Street *mystery*," he replied quietly.

Now the Fenchurch Street mystery, as that extraordinary crime had popularly been called, had puzzled—as Polly well knew—the brains of every thinking man and woman for the last twelve months. It had puzzled her not inconsiderably; she had been interested, fascinated; she had studied the case, formed her own theories, thought about it all often and often, had even written one or two letters to the Press on the subject—suggesting, arguing, hinting at possibilities and probabilities, adducing proofs which other amateur detectives were equally ready to refute. The attitude of that timid man in the corner, therefore, was peculiarly exasperating, and she retorted with sarcasm destined to completely annihilate her self-complacent interlocutor.

"What a pity it is, in that case, that you do not offer your priceless services to our misguided though well-meaning police."

"Isn't it?" he replied with perfect good-humour. "Well, you know, for one thing I doubt if they would accept them; and in the second place my inclinations and my duty would—were I to become an active member of the detective force—nearly always be in direct conflict. As often as not my sympathies go to the criminal who is clever and astute enough to lead our entire police force by the nose.

"I don't know how much of the case you remember," he went on quietly. "It certainly, at first, began even to puzzle me. On the 12th of last December a woman, poorly dressed, but with an unmistakable air of having seen better days, gave information at Scotland Yard of the disappearance of her husband, William Kershaw, of no occupation, and apparently of no fixed abode. She was accompanied by a friend—a fat, oily-looking German—and between them they told a tale which set the police immediately on the move.

"It appears that on the 10th of December, at about three o'clock in the afternoon, Karl Müller, the German, called on his friend, William Kershaw, for the purpose of collecting a small debt—some ten pounds or so—which the latter owed him. On arriving at the squalid lodging in Charlotte Street, Fitzroy Square, he found William Kershaw in a wild state of excitement, and his wife in tears. Müller attempted to state the object of his visit, but Kershaw, with wild gestures, waved him aside, and—in his own words—flabbergasted him by asking him point-blank for another loan of two pounds, which sum, he declared, would be the means of a speedy fortune for himself and the friend who would help him in his need.

"After a quarter of an hour spent in obscure hints, Kershaw, finding the cautious German obdurate, decided to let him into the secret plan, which, he averred, would place thousands into their hands."

Instinctively Polly had put down her paper; the mild stranger, with his nervous air and timid, watery eyes, had a peculiar way of telling his tale, which somehow fascinated her.

"I don't know," he resumed, "if you remember the story which the German told to the police, and which was corroborated in every detail by the wife or widow. Briefly it was this: Some thirty years previously, Kershaw, then twenty years of age, and a medical student at one of the London hospitals, had a chum named Barker, with whom he roomed, together with another.

"The latter, so it appears, brought home one evening a very considerable sum of money, which he had won on the turf, and the following morning he was found murdered in his bed. Kershaw, fortunately for himself, was able to prove a conclusive *alibi*; he had spent the night on duty at the hospital; as for Barker, he had disappeared, that is to say, as far as the police were concerned, but not as far as the watchful eyes of his friend Kershaw were able to spy—at least, so the latter said. Barker very cleverly contrived to get away out of the country, and, after sundry vicissitudes, finally settled down at Vladivostok, in Eastern Siberia, where, under the assumed name of Smethurst, he built up an enormous fortune by trading in furs.

"Now, mind you, every one knows Smethurst, the Siberian millionaire. Kershaw's story that he had once been called Barker, and had committed a murder thirty years ago, was never proved, was it? I am merely telling you what Kershaw said to his friend the German and to his wife on that memorable afternoon of December the 10th.

"According to him Smethurst had made one gigantic mistake in his clever career—he had on four occasions written to his late friend, William Kershaw. Two of these letters had no bearing on the case, since they were written more than twenty-five years ago, and Kershaw, moreover, had lost them—so he said—long ago. According to him, however, the first of these letters was written when Smethurst, alias Barker, had spent all the money he had obtained from the crime, and found himself destitute in New York.

"Kershaw, then in fairly prosperous circumstances, sent him a £10 note for the sake of old times. The second, when the tables had turned, and Kershaw had begun to go downhill, Smethurst, as he then already called himself, sent his whilom friend £50. After that, as Müller gathered, Kershaw had made sundry demands on Smethurst's ever-increasing purse, and had accompanied these demands by various threats, which, considering the distant country in which the millionaire lived, were worse than futile.

"But now the climax had come, and Kershaw, after a final moment of hesitation, handed over to his German friend the two last letters purporting to have been written by Smethurst, and which, if you remember, played such an important part in the mysterious story of this extraordinary crime. I have a copy of both these letters here," added the man in the corner, as he took out a piece of paper from a very worn-out pocket-book, and, unfolding it very deliberately, he began to read:—

"'Sir,—Your preposterous demands for money are wholly unwarrantable. I have already helped you quite as much as you deserve. However, for the sake of old times, and because you once helped me when I was in a terrible difficulty, I am willing to once more let you impose upon my good nature. A friend of mine here, a Russian merchant, to whom I have sold my business, starts in a few days for an extended tour to many European and Asiatic ports in his yacht, and has invited me to accompany him as far as England. Being tired of foreign parts, and desirous of seeing the old country once again after thirty years' absence, I have decided to accept his invitation. I don't know when we may actually be in Europe, but I promise you that as soon as we touch a suitable port I will write to you again, making an appointment for you to see me in London. But remember that if your demands are too preposterous I will not for a moment listen to them, and that I am the last man in the world to submit to persistent and unwarrantable blackmail.

'I am, sir,

'Yours truly,

'Francis Smethurst.'

"The second letter was dated from Southampton," continued the old man in the corner calmly, "and, curiously enough, was the only letter which Kershaw professed to have received from Smethurst of which he had kept the envelope, and which was dated.

It was quite brief," he added, referring once more to his piece of paper.

> "'Dear Sir,—Referring to my letter of a few weeks ago, I wish to inform you that the *Tsarskoe Selo* will touch at Tilbury on Tuesday next, the 10th. I shall land there, and immediately go up to London by the first train I can get. If you like, you may meet me at Fenchurch Street Station, in the first-class waiting-room, in the late afternoon. Since I surmise that after thirty years' absence my face may not be familiar to you, I may as well tell you that you will recognize me by a heavy Astrakhan fur coat, which I shall wear, together with a cap of the same. You may then introduce yourself to me, and I will personally listen to what you may have to say.
>
> 'Yours faithfully,
>
> 'Francis Smethurst.'

"It was this last letter which had caused William Kershaw's excitement and his wife's tears. In the German's own words, he was walking up and down the room like a wild beast, gesticulating wildly, and muttering sundry exclamations. Mrs. Kershaw, however, was full of apprehension. She mistrusted the man from foreign parts—who, according to her husband's story, had already one crime upon his conscience—who might, she feared, risk another, in order to be rid of a dangerous enemy. Woman-like, she thought the scheme a dishonourable one, for the law, she knew, is severe on the blackmailer.

"The assignation might be a cunning trap, in any case it was a curious one; why, she argued, did not Smethurst elect to see Kershaw at his hotel the following day? A thousand whys and wherefores made her anxious, but the fat German had been won over by Kershaw's visions of untold gold, held tantalisingly before his eyes. He had lent the necessary £2, with which his friend intended to tidy himself up a bit before he went to meet his friend the millionaire. Half an hour afterwards Kershaw had left his lodgings, and that was the last the unfortunate woman saw of her husband, or Müller, the German, of his friend.

"Anxiously his wife waited that night, but he did not return; the next day she seems to have spent in making purposeless and futile inquiries about the neighbourhood of Fenchurch Street; and on the 12th she went to Scotland Yard, gave what particulars she knew, and placed in the hands of the police the two letters written by Smethurst."

II.

The man in the corner had finished his glass of milk. His watery blue eyes looked across at Miss Polly Burton's eager little face, from which all traces of severity had now been chased away by an obvious and intense excitement.

"It was only on the 31st," he resumed after a while, "that a body, decomposed past all recognition, was found by two lightermen in the bottom of a disused barge. She had been moored at one time at the foot of one of those dark flights of steps which lead down between tall warehouses to the river in the East End of London. I have a photograph of the place here," he added, selecting one out of his pocket, and placing it before Polly.

"The actual barge, you see, had already been removed when I took this snapshot, but you will realize what a perfect place this alley is for the purpose of one man cutting another's throat in comfort, and without fear of detection. The body, as I said, was decomposed beyond all recognition; it had probably been there eleven days, but sundry articles, such as a silver ring and a tie pin, were recognizable, and were identified by Mrs. Kershaw as belonging to her husband.

"She, of course, was loud in denouncing Smethurst, and the police had no doubt a very strong case against him, for two days after the discovery of the body in the barge, the Siberian millionaire, as he was already popularly called by enterprising interviewers, was arrested in his luxurious suite of rooms at the Hotel Cecil.

"To confess the truth, at this point I was not a little puzzled. Mrs. Kershaw's story and Smethurst's letters had both found their way into the papers, and following my usual method—mind you, I am only an amateur, I try to reason out a case for the love of the thing—I sought about for a motive for the crime, which the police declared Smethurst had committed. To effectually get rid of a dangerous blackmailer was the generally accepted theory. Well! did it ever strike you how paltry that motive really was?"

Miss Polly had to confess, however, that it had never struck her in that light.

"Surely a man who had succeeded in building up an immense fortune by his own individual efforts, was not the sort of fool to believe that he had anything to fear from a man like Kershaw. He must have *known* that Kershaw held no damning proofs against him—not enough to hang him, anyway. Have you ever seen Smethurst?" he added, as he once more fumbled in his pocket-book.

Polly replied that she had seen Smethurst's picture in the illustrated papers at the time. Then he added, placing a small photograph before her:

"What strikes you most about the face?"

"Well, I think its strange, astonished expression, due to the total absence of eyebrows, and the funny foreign cut of the hair."

"So close that it almost looks as if it had been shaved. Exactly. That is what struck me most when I elbowed my way into the court that morning and first caught sight of the millionaire in the dock. He was a tall, soldierly-looking man, upright in stature, his face very bronzed and tanned. He wore neither moustache nor beard, his hair was cropped quite close to his head, like a Frenchman's; but, of course, what was so very remarkable about him was that total absence of eyebrows and even eyelashes, which gave the face such a peculiar appearance—as you say, a perpetually astonished look.

"He seemed, however, wonderfully calm; he had been accommodated with a chair in the dock—being a millionaire—and chatted pleasantly with his lawyer, Sir Arthur Inglewood, in the intervals between the calling of the several witnesses for the prosecution;

whilst during the examination of these witnesses he sat quite placidly, with his head shaded by his hand.

"Müller and Mrs. Kershaw repeated the story which they had already told to the police. I think you said that you were not able, owing to pressure of work, to go to the court that day, and hear the case, so perhaps you have no recollection of Mrs. Kershaw. No? Ah, well! Here is a snapshot I managed to get of her once. That is her. Exactly as she stood in the box—over-dressed—in elaborate crape, with a bonnet which once had contained pink roses, and to which a remnant of pink petals still clung obtrusively amidst the deep black.

"She would not look at the prisoner, and turned her head resolutely towards the magistrate. I fancy she had been fond of that vagabond husband of hers: an enormous wedding-ring encircled her finger, and that, too, was swathed in black. She firmly believed that Kershaw's murderer sat there in the dock, and she literally flaunted her grief before him.

"I was indescribably sorry for her. As for Müller, he was just fat, oily, pompous, conscious of his own importance as a witness; his fat fingers, covered with brass rings, gripped the two incriminating letters, which he had identified. They were his passports, as it were, to a delightful land of importance and notoriety. Sir Arthur Inglewood, I think, disappointed him by stating that he had no questions to ask of him. Müller had been brimful of answers, ready with the most perfect indictment, the most elaborate accusations against the bloated millionaire who had decoyed his dear friend Kershaw, and murdered him in Heaven knows what an out-of-the-way corner of the East End.

"After this, however, the excitement grew apace. Müller had been dismissed, and had retired from the court altogether, leading away Mrs. Kershaw, who had completely broken down.

"Constable D 21 was giving evidence as to the arrest in the meanwhile. The prisoner, he said, had seemed completely taken by surprise, not understanding the cause or history of the accusation against him; however, when put in full possession of the facts, and realizing, no doubt, the absolute futility of any resistance, he had quietly enough followed the constable into the cab. No one at the fashionable and crowded Hotel Cecil had even suspected that anything unusual had occurred.

"Then a gigantic sigh of expectancy came from every one of the spectators. The 'fun' was about to begin. James Buckland, a porter at Fenchurch Street railway station, had just sworn to tell all the truth, etc. After all, it did not amount to much. He said that at six o'clock in the afternoon of December the 10th, in the midst of one of the densest fogs he ever remembers, the 5.5 from Tilbury steamed into the station, being just about an hour late. He was on the arrival platform, and was hailed by a passenger in a first-class carriage. He could see very little of him beyond an enormous black fur coat and a travelling cap of fur also.

"The passenger had a quantity of luggage, all marked F.S., and he directed James Buckland to place it all upon a four-wheel cab, with the exception of a small hand-bag, which he carried himself. Having seen that all his luggage was safely bestowed, the stranger in the fur coat paid the porter, and, telling the cabman to wait until he returned, he walked away in the direction of the waiting-rooms, still carrying his small hand-bag.

"'I stayed for a bit,' added James Buckland, 'talking to the driver about the fog and that; then I went about my business, seein' that the local from Southend 'ad been signalled.'

"The prosecution insisted most strongly upon the hour when the stranger in the fur coat, having seen to his luggage, walked away towards the waiting-rooms. The porter was emphatic. 'It was not a minute later than 6.15,' he averred.

"Sir Arthur Inglewood still had no questions to ask, and the driver of the cab was called.

"He corroborated the evidence of James Buckland as to the hour when the gentleman in the fur coat had engaged him, and having filled his cab in and out with luggage, had told him to wait. And cabby did wait. He waited in the dense fog—until he was tired, until he seriously thought of depositing all the luggage in the lost property office, and of looking out for another fare—waited until at last, at a quarter before nine, whom should he see walking hurriedly towards his cab but the gentleman in the fur coat and cap, who got in quickly and told the driver to take him at once to the Hotel Cecil. This, cabby declared, had occurred at a quarter before nine. Still Sir Arthur Inglewood made no comment, and Mr. Francis Smethurst, in the crowded, stuffy court, had calmly dropped to sleep.

"The next witness, Constable Thomas Taylor, had noticed a shabbily dressed individual, with shaggy hair and beard, loafing about the station and waiting-rooms in the afternoon of December the 10th. He seemed to be watching the arrival platform of the Tilbury and Southend trains.

"Two separate and independent witnesses, cleverly unearthed by the police, had seen this same shabbily dressed individual stroll into the first-class waiting-room at about 6.15 on Wednesday, December the 10th, and go straight up to a gentleman in a heavy fur coat and cap, who had also just come into the room. The two talked together for a while; no one heard what they said, but presently they walked off together. No one seemed to know in which direction.

"Francis Smethurst was rousing himself from his apathy; he whispered to his lawyer, who nodded with a bland smile of encouragement. The employés of the Hotel Cecil gave evidence as to the arrival of Mr. Smethurst at about 9.30 P.M. on Wednesday, December the 10th, in a cab, with a quantity of luggage; and this closed the case for the prosecution.

"Everybody in that court already *saw* Smethurst mounting the gallows. It was uninterested curiosity which caused the elegant audience to wait and hear what Sir Arthur Inglewood had to say. He, of course, is the most fashionable man in the law at the present moment. His lolling attitudes, his drawling speech, are quite the rage, and imitated by the gilded youth of society.

"Even at this moment, when the Siberian millionaire's neck literally and metaphorically hung in the balance, an expectant titter went round the fair spectators as Sir Arthur stretched out his long loose limbs and lounged across the table. He waited to make his effect—Sir Arthur is a born actor—and there is no doubt that he made it, when in his slowest, most drawly tones he said quietly:

"'With regard to this alleged murder of one William Kershaw, on Wednesday, December the 10th, between 6.15 and 8.45 P.M., your Honour, I now propose to call two witnesses, who saw this same William Kershaw alive on Tuesday afternoon, December the 16th, that is to say, six days after the supposed murder.'

"It was as if a bombshell had exploded in the court. Even his Honour was aghast, and I am sure the lady next to me only recovered from the shock of the surprise in order to wonder whether she need put off her dinner party after all.

"As for me," added the man in the corner, with that strange mixture of nervousness and self-complacency which had set Miss Polly Burton wondering, "well, you see, *I* had made up my mind long ago where the hitch lay in this particular case, and I was not so surprised as some of the others.

"Perhaps you remember the wonderful development of the case, which so completely mystified the police—and in fact everybody except myself. Torriani and a waiter at his hotel in the Commercial Road both deposed that at about 3.30 P.M. on December the 10th a shabbily dressed individual lolled into the coffee-room and ordered some tea. He was pleasant enough and talkative, told the waiter that his name was William Kershaw, that very soon all London would be talking about him, as he was about, through an unexpected stroke of good fortune, to become a very rich man, and so on, and so on, nonsense without end.

"When he had finished his tea he lolled out again, but no sooner had he disappeared down a turning of the road than the waiter discovered an old umbrella, left behind accidentally by the shabby, talkative individual. As is the custom in his highly respectable restaurant, Signor Torriani put the umbrella carefully away in his office, on the chance of his customer calling to claim it when he had discovered his loss. And sure enough nearly a week later, on Tuesday, the 16th, at about 1 P.M., the same shabbily dressed individual called and asked for his umbrella. He had some lunch, and chatted once again to the waiter. Signor Torriani and the waiter gave a description of William Kershaw, which coincided exactly with that given by Mrs. Kershaw of her husband.

"Oddly enough he seemed to be a very absent-minded sort of person, for on this second occasion, no sooner had he left than the waiter found a pocket-book in the coffee-room, underneath the table. It contained sundry letters and bills, all addressed to William Kershaw. This pocket-book was produced, and Karl Müller, who had returned to the court, easily identified it as having belonged to his dear and lamented friend 'Villiam.'

"This was the first blow to the case against the accused. It was a pretty stiff one, you will admit. Already it had begun to collapse like a house of cards. Still, there was the assignation, and the undisputed meeting between Smethurst and Kershaw, and those two and a half hours of a foggy evening to satisfactorily account for."

The man in the corner made a long pause, keeping the girl on tenterhooks. He had fidgeted with his bit of string till there was not an inch of it free from the most complicated and elaborate knots.

"I assure you," he resumed at last, "that at that very moment the whole mystery was, to me, as clear as daylight. I only marvelled how his Honour could waste his time and mine by putting what he thought were searching questions to the accused relating to his past. Francis Smethurst, who had quite shaken off his somnolence, spoke with a curious nasal twang, and with an almost imperceptible soupçon of foreign accent, He calmly denied Kershaw's version of his past; declared that he had never been called Barker, and had certainly never been mixed up in any murder case thirty years ago.

"'But you knew this man Kershaw,' persisted his Honour, 'since you wrote to him?'

"'Pardon me, your Honour,' said the accused quietly, 'I have never, to my knowledge, seen this man Kershaw, and I can swear that I never wrote to him.'

"'Never wrote to him?' retorted his Honour warningly. 'That is a strange assertion to make when I have two of your letters to him in my hands at the present moment.'

"'I never wrote those letters, your Honour,' persisted the accused quietly, 'they are not in my handwriting.'

"'Which we can easily prove,' came in Sir Arthur Inglewood's drawly tones, as he handed up a packet to his Honour; 'here are a number of letters written by my client since he has landed in this country, and some of which were written under my very eyes.'

"As Sir Arthur Inglewood had said, this could be easily proved, and the prisoner, at his Honour's request, scribbled a few lines, together with his signature, several times upon a sheet of note-paper. It was easy to read upon the magistrate's astounded countenance, that there was not the slightest similarity in the two hand-writings.

"A fresh mystery had cropped up. Who, then, had made the assignation with William Kershaw at Fenchurch Street railway station? The prisoner gave a fairly satisfactory account of the employment of his time since his landing in England.

"'I came over on the *Tsarskoe Selo*,' he said, 'a yacht belonging to a friend of mine. When we arrived at the mouth of the Thames there was such a dense fog that it was twenty-four hours before it was thought safe for me to land. My friend, who is a Russian, would not land at all; he was regularly frightened at this land of fogs. He was going on to Madeira immediately.

"'I actually landed on Tuesday, the 10th, and took a train at once for town. I did see to my luggage and a cab, as the porter and driver told your Honour; then I tried to find my way to a refreshment-room, where I could get a glass of wine. I drifted into the waiting-room, and there I was accosted by a shabbily dressed individual, who began telling me a piteous tale. Who he was I do not know. He *said* he was an old soldier who had served his country faithfully, and then been left to starve. He begged of me to accompany him to his lodgings, where I could see his wife and starving children, and verify the truth and piteousness of his tale.

"'Well, your Honour,' added the prisoner with noble frankness, 'it was my first day in the old country. I had come back after thirty years with my pockets full of gold, and this was the first sad tale I had heard; but I am a business man, and did not want to be exactly "done" in the eye. I followed my man through the fog, out into the streets. He walked silently by my side for a time. I had not a notion where I was.

"'Suddenly I turned to him with some question, and realized in a moment that my gentleman had given me the slip. Finding, probably, that I would not part with my money till I *had* seen the starving wife and children, he left me to my fate, and went in search of more willing bait.

"'The place where I found myself was dismal and deserted. I could see no trace of cab or omnibus. I retraced my steps and tried to find my way back to the station, only to find myself in worse and more deserted neighbourhoods. I became hopelessly lost and fogged. I don't wonder that two and a half hours elapsed while I thus wandered on in the dark and deserted streets; my sole astonishment is that I ever found the station at all that night, or rather close to it a policeman, who showed me the way.'

"'But how do you account for Kershaw knowing all your movements?' still persisted his Honour, 'and his knowing the exact date of your arrival in England? How do you account for these two letters, in fact?'

"'I cannot account for it or them, your Honour,' replied the prisoner quietly. 'I have proved to you, have I not, that I never wrote those letters, and that the man—er—Kershaw is his name?—was not murdered by me?'

"'Can you tell me of anyone here or abroad who might have heard of your movements, and of the date of your arrival?'

"'My late employés at Vladivostok, of course, knew of my departure, but none of them could have written these letters, since none of them know a word of English.'

"'Then you can throw no light upon these mysterious letters? You cannot help the police in any way towards the clearing up of this strange affair?'

"'The affair is as mysterious to me as to your Honour, and to the police of this country.'

"Francis Smethurst was discharged, of course; there was no semblance of evidence against him sufficient to commit him for trial. The two overwhelming points of his defence which had completely routed the prosecution were, firstly, the proof that he had never written the letters making the assignation, and secondly, the fact that the man supposed to have been murdered on the 10th was seen to be alive and well on the 16th. But then, who in the world was the mysterious individual who had apprised Kershaw of the movements of Smethurst, the millionaire?"

III.

The man in the corner cocked his funny thin head on one side and looked at Polly; then he took up his beloved bit of string and deliberately untied every knot he had made in it. When it was quite smooth he laid it out upon the table.

"I will take you, if you like, point by point along the line of reasoning which I followed myself, and which will inevitably lead you, as it led me, to the only possible solution of the mystery.

"First take this point," he said with nervous restlessness, once more taking up his bit of string, and forming with each point raised a series of knots which would have shamed a navigating instructor, "obviously it was *impossible* for Kershaw not to have been acquainted with Smethurst, since he was fully apprised of the latter's arrival in England by two letters. Now it was clear to me from the first that *no one* could have written those two letters except Smethurst. You will argue that those letters were proved not to have been written by the man in the dock. Exactly. Remember, Kershaw was a careless man—he had lost both envelopes. To him they were insignificant. Now it was never *disproved* that those letters were written by Smethurst."

"But—" suggested Polly.

"Wait a minute," he interrupted, while knot number two appeared upon the scene, "it was proved that six days after the murder, William Kershaw was alive, and visited the Torriani Hotel, where already he was known, and where he conveniently left a pocket-book behind, so that there should be no mistake as to his identity; but it was never questioned where Mr. Francis Smethurst, the millionaire, happened to spend that very same afternoon."

"Surely, you don't mean?" gasped the girl.

"One moment, please," he added triumphantly. "How did it come about that the landlord of the Torriani Hotel was brought into court at all? How did Sir Arthur Inglewood, or rather his client, know that William Kershaw had on those two memorable occasions visited the hotel, and that its landlord could bring such convincing evidence forward that would for ever exonerate the millionaire from the imputation of murder?"

"Surely," I argued, "the usual means, the police—"

"The police had kept the whole affair very dark until the arrest at the Hotel Cecil. They did not put into the papers the usual: 'If anyone happens to know of the whereabouts, etc. etc'. Had the landlord of that hotel heard of the disappearance of Kershaw through the usual channels, he would have put himself in communication with the police. Sir Arthur Inglewood produced him. How did Sir Arthur Inglewood come on his track?"

"Surely, you don't mean?"

"Point number four," he resumed imperturbably, "Mrs. Kershaw was never requested to produce a specimen of her husband's handwriting. Why? Because the police, clever as you say they are, never started on the right tack. They believed William Kershaw to have been murdered; they looked for William Kershaw.

"On December the 31st, what was presumed to be the body of William Kershaw was found by two lightermen: I have shown you a photograph of the place where it was found. Dark and deserted it is in all conscience, is it not? Just the place where a bully and a coward would decoy an unsuspecting stranger, murder him first, then rob him of his valuables, his papers, his very identity, and leave him there to rot. The body was found in a disused barge which had been moored some time against the wall, at the foot of these steps. It was in the last stages of decomposition, and, of course, could not be identified; but the police would have it that it was the body of William Kershaw.

"It never entered their heads that it was the body of *Francis Smethurst, and that William Kershaw was his murderer.*

"Ah! it was cleverly, artistically conceived! Kershaw is a genius. Think of it all! His disguise! Kershaw had a shaggy beard, hair, and moustache. He shaved up to his very eyebrows! No wonder that even his wife did not recognize him across the court; and remember she never saw much of his face while he stood in the dock. Kershaw was shabby, slouchy, he stooped. Smethurst, the millionaire, might have served in the Prussian army.

"Then that lovely trait about going to revisit the Torriani Hotel. Just a few days' grace, in order to purchase moustache and beard and wig, exactly similar to what he had himself shaved off. Making up to look like himself! Splendid! Then leaving the pocket-book behind! He! he! he! Kershaw was not murdered! Of course not. He called at the Torriani Hotel six days after the murder, whilst Mr. Smethurst, the millionaire, hobnobbed in the park with duchesses! Hang such a man! Fie!"

He fumbled for his hat. With nervous, trembling fingers he held it deferentially in his hand whilst he rose from the table. Polly watched him as he strode up to the desk, and paid twopence for his glass of milk and his bun. Soon he disappeared through the shop, whilst she still found herself hopelessly bewildered, with a number of snap-shot photographs before her, still staring at a long piece of string, smothered from end to end in a series of knots, as bewildering, as irritating, as puzzling as the man who had lately sat in the corner.

2
The Robbery in Phillimore Terrace

I.

Whether Miss Polly Burton really did expect to see the man in the corner that Saturday afternoon, 'twere difficult to say; certain it is that when she found her way to the table close by the window and realized that he was not there, she felt conscious of an overwhelming sense of disappointment. And yet during the whole of the week she had, with more pride than wisdom, avoided this particular A.B.C. shop.

"I thought you would not keep away very long," said a quiet voice close to her ear.

She nearly lost her balance—where in the world had he come from? She certainly had not heard the slightest sound, and yet there he sat, in the corner, like a veritable Jack-in-the-box, his mild blue eyes staring apologetically at her, his nervous fingers toying with the inevitable bit of string.

The waitress brought him his glass of milk and a cheese-cake. He ate it in silence, while his piece of string lay idly beside him on the table. When he had finished he fumbled in his capacious pockets, and drew out the inevitable pocket-book.

Placing a small photograph before the girl, he said quietly:

"That is the back of the houses in Phillimore Terrace, which overlook Adam and Eve Mews."

She looked at the photograph, then at him, with a kindly look of indulgent expectancy.

"You will notice that the row of back gardens have each an exit into the mews. These mews are built in the shape of a capital F. The photograph is taken looking straight down the short horizontal line, which ends, as you see, in a *cul-de-sac*. The bottom of the vertical line turns into Phillimore Terrace, and the end of the upper long horizontal line into High Street, Kensington. Now, on that particular night, or rather early morning, of January 15th, Constable D 21, having turned into the mews from Phillimore Terrace, stood for a moment at the angle formed by the long vertical artery of the mews and the short horizontal one which, as I observed before, looks on to the back gardens of the Terrace houses, and ends in a *cul-de-sac*.

"How long D 21 stood at that particular corner he could not exactly say, but he thinks it must have been three or four minutes before he noticed a suspicious-looking individual shambling along under the shadow of the garden walls. He was working his way cautiously in the direction of the *cul-de-sac*, and D 21, also keeping well within the shadow, went noiselessly after him.

"He had almost overtaken him—was, in fact, not more than thirty yards from him—when from out of one of the two end houses—No. 22, Phillimore Terrace, in fact—a man, in nothing but his night-shirt, rushed out excitedly, and, before D 21 had time to intervene, literally threw himself upon the suspected individual, rolling over and over with him on the hard cobble-stones, and frantically shrieking, 'Thief! Thief! Police!'

"It was some time before the constable succeeded in rescuing the tramp from the excited grip of his assailant, and several minutes before he could make himself heard.

"'There! there! that'll do!' he managed to say at last, as he gave the man in the shirt a vigorous shove, which silenced him for the moment. 'Leave the man alone now, you mustn't make that noise this time o' night, wakin' up all the folks.' The unfortunate tramp, who in the meanwhile had managed to got on to his feet again, made no attempt to get away; probably he thought he would stand but a poor chance. But the man in the shirt had partly recovered his power of speech, and was now blurting out jerky, half—intelligible sentences:

"'I have been robbed—robbed—I—that is—my master—Mr. Knopf. The desk is open—the diamonds gone—all in my charge—and—now they are stolen! That's the thief—I'll swear—I heard him—not three minutes ago—rushed downstairs—the door into the garden was smashed—I ran across the garden—he was sneaking about here still—Thief! Thief! Police! Diamonds! Constable, don't let him go—I'll make you responsible if you let him go—'

"'Now then—that'll do!' admonished D 21 as soon as he could get a word in, 'stop that row, will you?'

"The man in the shirt was gradually recovering from his excitement.

"'Can I give this man in charge?' he asked.

"'What for?'

"'Burglary and housebreaking. I heard him, I tell you. He must have Mr. Knopf's diamonds about him at this moment.'

"'Where is Mr. Knopf?'

"'Out of town,' groaned the man in the shirt. 'He went to Brighton last night, and left me in charge, and now this thief has been and—'

"The tramp shrugged his shoulders and suddenly, without a word, he quietly began taking off his coat and waistcoat. These he handed across to the constable. Eagerly the man in the shirt fell on them, and turned the ragged pockets inside out. From one of the windows a hilarious voice made some facetious remark, as the tramp with equal solemnity began divesting himself of his nether garments.

"'Now then, stop that nonsense,' pronounced D 21 severely, 'what were you doing here this time o' night, anyway?'

"'The streets o' London is free to the public, ain't they?' queried the tramp.

"'This don't lead nowhere, my man.'

"'Then I've lost my way, that's all,' growled the man surlily, 'and p'raps you'll let me get along now.'

"By this time a couple of constables had appeared upon the scene. D 21 had no intention of losing sight of his friend the tramp, and the man in the shirt had again made a dash for the latter's collar at the bare idea that he should be allowed to 'get along.'

"I think D 21 was alive to the humour of the situation. He suggested that Robertson (the man in the night-shirt) should go in and get some clothes on, whilst he himself would wait for the inspector and the detective, whom D 15 would send round from the station immediately.

"Poor Robertson's teeth were chattering with cold. He had a violent fit of sneezing as D 21 hurried him into the house. The latter, with another constable, remained to watch the burglared premises both back and front, and D 15 took the wretched tramp to the station with a view to sending an inspector and a detective round immediately.

"When the two latter gentlemen arrived at No. 22, Phillimore Terrace, they found poor old Robertson in bed, shivering, and still quite blue. He had got himself a hot drink, but his eyes were streaming and his voice was terribly husky. D 21 had stationed himself in the dining-room, where Robertson had pointed the desk out to him, with its broken lock and scattered contents.

"Robertson, between his sneezes, gave what account he could of the events which happened immediately before the robbery.

"His master, Mr. Ferdinand Knopf, he said, was a diamond merchant, and a bachelor. He himself had been in Mr. Knopf's employ over fifteen years, and was his only indoor servant. A charwoman came every day to do the housework.

"Last night Mr. Knopf dined at the house of Mr. Shipman, at No. 26, lower down. Mr. Shipman is the great jeweller who has his place of business in South Audley Street. By the last post there came a letter with the Brighton postmark, and marked 'urgent,' for Mr. Knopf, and he (Robertson) was just wondering if he should run over to No. 26 with it, when his master returned. He gave one glance at the contents of the letter, asked for his A.B.C. Railway Guide, and ordered him (Robertson) to pack his bag at once and fetch him a cab.

"'I guessed what it was,' continued Robertson after another violent fit of sneezing. 'Mr. Knopf has a brother, Mr. Emile Knopf, to whom he is very much attached, and who is a great invalid. He generally goes about from one seaside place to another. He is now at Brighton, and has recently been very ill.

"'If you will take the trouble to go downstairs I think you will still find the letter lying on the hall table.

"'I read it after Mr. Knopf left; it was not from his brother, but from a gentleman who signed himself J. Collins, M.D. I don't remember the exact words, but, of course, you'll be able to read the letter—Mr. J. Collins said he had been called in very suddenly to see Mr. Emile Knopf, who, he added, had not many hours to live, and had begged of the doctor to communicate at once with his brother in London.

"'Before leaving, Mr. Knopf warned me that there were some valuables in his desk—diamonds mostly, and told me to be particularly careful about locking up the house. He often has left me like this in charge of his premises, and usually there have been diamonds in his desk, for Mr. Knopf has no regular City office as he is a commercial traveller.'

"This, briefly, was the gist of the matter which Robertson related to the inspector with many repetitions and persistent volubility.

"The detective and inspector, before returning to the station with their report, thought they would call at No. 26, on Mr. Shipman, the great jeweller.

"You remember, of course," added the man in the corner, dreamily contemplating his bit of string, "the exciting developments of this extraordinary case. Mr. Arthur Shipman is the head of the firm of Shipman and Co., the wealthy jewellers. He is a widower, and lives very quietly by himself in his own old-fashioned way in the small Kensington house, leaving it to his two married sons to keep up the style and swagger befitting the representatives of so wealthy a firm.

"'I have only known Mr. Knopf a very little while,' he explained to the detectives. 'He sold me two or three stones once or twice, I think; but we are both single men, and we have often dined together. Last night he dined with me. He had that afternoon received a very fine consignment of Brazilian diamonds, as he told me, and knowing how beset I am with callers at my business place, he had brought the stones with him, hoping, perhaps, to do a bit of trade over the nuts and wine.

"'I bought £25,000 worth of him,' added the jeweller, as if he were speaking of so many farthings, 'and gave him a cheque across the dinner table for that amount. I think we were both pleased with our bargain, and we had a final bottle of '48 port over it together. Mr. Knopf left me at about 9.30, for he knows I go very early to bed, and I took my new stock upstairs with me, and locked it up in the safe. I certainly heard nothing of the noise in the mews last night. I sleep on the second floor, in the front of the house, and this is the first I have heard of poor Mr. Knopf's loss—'

"At this point of his narrative Mr. Shipman very suddenly paused, and his face became very pale. With a hasty word of excuse he unceremoniously left the room, and the detective heard him running quickly upstairs.

"Less than two minutes later Mr. Shipman returned. There was no need for him to speak; both the detective and the inspector guessed the truth in a moment by the look upon his face.

"'The diamonds!' he gasped. 'I have been robbed.'"

II.

"Now I must tell you," continued the man in the corner, "that after I had read the account of the double robbery, which appeared in the early afternoon papers, I set to work and had a good think—yes!" he added with a smile, noting Polly's look at the bit of string, on which he was still at work, "yes! aided by this small adjunct to continued thought—I made notes as to how I should proceed to discover the clever thief, who had carried off a small fortune in a single night. Of course, my methods are not those of a London detective; he has his own way of going to work. The one who was conducting this case questioned the unfortunate jeweller very closely about his servants and his household generally.

"'I have three servants,' explained Mr. Shipman, two of whom have been with me for many years; one, the housemaid, is a fairly new comer—she has been here about six months. She came recommended by a friend, and bore an excellent character. She and the parlourmaid room together. The cook, who knew me when I was a schoolboy, sleeps alone; all three servants sleep on the floor above. I locked the jewels up in the safe which stands in the dressing-room. My keys and watch I placed, as usual, beside my bed. As a rule, I am a fairly light sleeper.

"'I cannot understand how it could have happened—but—you had better come up and have a look at the safe. The key must have been abstracted from my bedside, the safe opened, and the keys replaced—all while I was fast asleep. Though I had no occasion to look into the safe until just now, I should have discovered my loss before going to business, for I intended to take the diamonds away with me—'

"The detective and the inspector went up to have a look at the safe. The lock had in no way been tampered with—it had been opened with its own key. The detective spoke of chloroform, but Mr. Shipman declared that when he woke in the morning at about half-past seven there was no smell of chloroform in the room. However, the proceedings of the daring thief certainly pointed to the use of an anaesthetic. An examination of the premises brought to light the fact that the burglar had, as in Mr. Knopf's house, used the glass-panelled door from the garden as a means of entrance, but in this instance he had carefully cut out the pane of glass with a diamond, slipped the bolts, turned the key, and walked in.

"'Which among your servants knew that you had the diamonds in your house last night, Mr. Shipman?' asked the detective.

"'Not one, I should say,' replied the jeweller, 'though, perhaps, the parlourmaid, whilst waiting at table, may have heard me and Mr. Knopf discussing our bargain.'

"'Would you object to my searching all your servants' boxes?'

"'Certainly not. They would not object, either, I am sure. They are perfectly honest.'

"The searching of servants' belongings is invariably a useless proceeding," added the man in the corner, with a shrug of the shoulders. "No one, not even a latter-day domestic, would be fool enough to keep stolen property in the house. However, the usual farce was gone through, with more or less protest on the part of Mr. Shipman's servants, and with the usual result.

"The jeweller could give no further information; the detective and inspector, to do them justice, did their work of investigation minutely and, what is more, intelligently. It seemed evident, from their deductions, that the burglar had commenced proceedings on No. 26, Phillimore Terrace, and had then gone on, probably climbing over the garden walls between the houses to No. 22, where he was almost caught in the act by Robertson. The facts were simple enough, but the mystery remained as to the individual who had managed to glean the information of the presence of the diamonds in both the houses, and the means which he had adopted to get that information. It was obvious that the thief or thieves knew more about Mr. Knopf's affairs than Mr. Shipman's, since they had known how to use Mr. Emile Knopf's name in order to get his brother out of the way.

"It was now nearly ten o'clock, and the detectives, having taken leave of Mr. Shipman, went back to No. 22, in order to ascertain whether Mr. Knopf had come back; the door was opened by the old charwoman, who said that her master had returned, and was having some breakfast in the dining-room.

"Mr. Ferdinand Knopf was a middle-aged man, with sallow complexion, black hair and beard, of obviously Hebrew extraction. He spoke with a marked foreign accent, but very courteously, to the two officials, who, he begged, would excuse him if he went on with his breakfast.

"'I was fully prepared to hear the bad news,' he explained, 'which my man Robertson told me when I arrived. The letter I got last night was a bogus one; there is no such person as J. Collins, M.D. My brother had never felt better in his life. You will, I am sure, very soon trace the cunning writer of that epistle—ah! but I was in a rage, I can tell you, when I got to the Metropole at

Brighton, and found that Emile, my brother, had never heard of any Doctor Collins.

"'The last train to town had gone, although I raced back to the station as hard as I could. Poor old Robertson, he has a terrible cold. Ah yes! my loss! it is for me a very serious one; if I had not made that lucky bargain with Mr. Shipman last night I should, perhaps, at this moment be a ruined man.

"'The stones I had yesterday were, firstly, some magnificent Brazilians; these I sold to Mr. Shipman mostly. Then I had some very good Cape diamonds—all gone; and some quite special Parisians, of wonderful work and finish, entrusted to me for sale by a great French house. I tell you, sir, my loss will be nearly £10,000 altogether. I sell on commission, and, of course, have to make good the loss.'

"He was evidently trying to bear up manfully, and as a business man should, under his sad fate. He refused in any way to attach the slightest blame to his old and faithful servant Robertson, who had caught, perhaps, his death of cold in his zeal for his absent master. As for any hint of suspicion falling even remotely upon the man, the very idea appeared to Mr. Knopf absolutely preposterous.

"With regard to the old charwoman, Mr. Knopf certainly knew nothing about her, beyond the fact that she had been recommended to him by one of the tradespeople in the neighbourhood, and seemed perfectly honest, respectable, and sober.

"About the tramp Mr. Knopf knew still less, nor could he imagine how he, or in fact anybody else, could possibly know that he happened to have diamonds in his house that night.

"This certainly seemed the great hitch in the case.

"Mr. Ferdinand Knopf, at the instance of the police, later on went to the station and had a look at the suspected tramp. He declared that he had never set eyes on him before.

"Mr. Shipman, on his way home from business in the afternoon, had done likewise, and made a similar statement.

"Brought before the magistrate, the tramp gave but a poor account of himself. He gave a name and address, which latter, of course, proved to be false. After that he absolutely refused to speak. He seemed not to care whether he was kept in custody or not. Very soon even the police realized that, for the present, at any rate, nothing could be got out of the suspected tramp.

"Mr. Francis Howard, the detective, who had charge of the case, though he would not admit it even to himself, was at his wits' ends. You must remember that the burglary, through its very simplicity, was an exceedingly mysterious affair. The constable, D 21, who had stood in Adam and Eve Mews, presumably while Mr. Knopf's house was being robbed, had seen no one turn out from the *cul-de-sac* into the main passage of the mews.

"The stables, which immediately faced the back entrance of the Phillimore Terrace houses, were all private ones belonging to residents in the neighbourhood. The coachmen, their families, and all the grooms who slept in the stablings were rigidly watched and questioned. One and all had seen nothing, heard nothing, until Robertson's shrieks had roused them from their sleep.

"As for the letter from Brighton, it was absolutely commonplace, and written upon note-paper which the detective, with Machiavellian cunning, traced to a stationer's shop in West Street. But the trade at that particular shop was a very brisk one; scores of people had bought note-paper there, similar to that on which the supposed doctor had written his tricky letter. The handwriting was cramped, perhaps a disguised one; in any case, except under very exceptional circumstances, it could afford no clue to the identity of the thief. Needless to say, the tramp, when told to write his name, wrote a totally different and absolutely uneducated hand.

"Matters stood, however, in the same persistently mysterious state when a small discovery was made, which suggested to Mr. Francis Howard an idea, which, if properly carried out, would, he hoped, inevitably bring the cunning burglar safely within the grasp of the police.

"That was the discovery of a few of Mr. Knopf's diamonds," continued the man in the corner after a slight pause, "evidently trampled into the ground by the thief whilst making his hurried exit through the garden of No. 22, Phillimore Terrace.

"At the end of this garden there is a small studio which had been built by a former owner of the house, and behind it a small piece of waste ground about seven feet square which had once been a rockery, and is still filled with large loose stones, in the shadow of which earwigs and woodlice innumerable have made a happy hunting ground.

"It was Robertson who, two days after the robbery, having need of a large stone, for some household purpose or other, dislodged one from that piece of waste ground, and found a few shining pebbles beneath it. Mr. Knopf took them round to the police-station himself immediately, and identified the stones as some of his Parisian ones.

"Later on the detective went to view the place where the find had been made, and there conceived the plan upon which he built big cherished hopes.

"Acting upon the advice of Mr. Francis Howard, the police decided to let the anonymous tramp out of his safe retreat within the station, and to allow him to wander whithersoever he chose. A good idea, perhaps—the presumption being that, sooner or later, if the man was in any way mixed up with the cunning thieves, he would either rejoin his comrades or even lead the police to where the remnant of his hoard lay hidden; needless to say, his footsteps were to be literally dogged.

"The wretched tramp, on his discharge, wandered out of the yard, wrapping his thin coat round his shoulders, for it was a bitterly cold afternoon. He began operations by turning into the Town Hall Tavern for a good feed and a copious drink. Mr. Francis Howard noted that he seemed to eye every passer-by with suspicion, but he seemed to enjoy his dinner, and sat some time over his bottle of wine.

"It was close upon four o'clock when he left the tavern, and then began for the indefatigable Mr. Howard one of the most wearisome and uninteresting chases, through the mazes of the London streets, he ever remembers to have made. Up Notting Hill, down the slums of Notting Dale, along the High Street, beyond Hammersmith, and through Shepherd's Bush did that anonymous tramp lead the unfortunate detective, never hurrying himself, stopping every now and then at a public-house to get a drink, whither Mr. Howard did not always care to follow him.

"In spite of his fatigue, Mr. Francis Howard's hopes rose with every half-hour of this weary tramp. The man was obviously striving to kill time; he seemed to feel no weariness, but walked on and on, perhaps suspecting that he was being followed.

"At last, with a beating heart, though half perished with cold, and with terribly sore feet, the detective began to realize that the tramp was gradually working his way back towards Kensington. It was then close upon eleven o'clock at night; once or twice the man had walked up and down the High Street, from St. Paul's School to Derry and Toms' shops and back again, he had looked down one or two of the side streets and—at last—he turned into Phillimore Terrace. He seemed in no hurry, he oven stopped once in the middle of the road, trying to light a pipe, which, as there was a high east wind, took him some considerable time. Then he leisurely sauntered down the street, and turned into Adam and Eve Mews, with Mr. Francis Howard now close at his heels.

"Acting upon the detective's instructions, there were several men in plain clothes ready to his call in the immediate neighbourhood. Two stood within the shadow of the steps of the Congregational Church at the corner of the mews, others were stationed well within a soft call.

"Hardly, therefore, had the hare turned into the *cul-de-sac* at the back of Phillimore Terrace than, at a slight sound from Mr. Francis Howard, every egress was barred to him, and he was caught like a rat in a trap.

"As soon as the tramp had advanced some thirty yards or so (the whole length of this part of the mews is about one hundred yards) and was lost in the shadow, Mr. Francis Howard directed four or five of his men to proceed cautiously up the mews, whilst the same number were to form a line all along the front of Phillimore Terrace between the mews and the High Street.

"Remember, the back-garden walls threw long and dense shadows, but the silhouette of the man would be clearly outlined if he made any attempt at climbing over them. Mr. Howard felt quite sure that the thief was bent on recovering the stolen goods, which, no doubt, he had hidden in the rear of one of the houses. He would be caught *in flagrante delicto*, and, with a heavy sentence hovering over him, he would probably be induced to name his accomplice. Mr. Francis Howard was thoroughly enjoying himself.

"The minutes sped on; absolute silence, in spite of the presence of so many men, reigned in the dark and deserted mews.

"Of course, this night's adventure was never allowed to get into the papers," added the man in the corner with his mild smile. "Had the plan been successful, we should have heard all about it, with a long eulogistic article as to the astuteness of our police; but as it was—well, the tramp sauntered up the mews—and—there he remained for aught Mr. Francis Howard or the other constables could ever explain. The earth or the shadows swallowed him up. No one saw him climb one of the garden walls, no one heard him break open a door; he had retreated within the shadow of the garden walls, and was seen or heard of no more."

"One of the servants in the Phillimore Terrace houses must have belonged to the gang," said Polly with quick decision.

"Ah, yes! but which?" said the man in the corner, making a beautiful knot in his bit of string. "I can assure you that the police left not a stone unturned once more to catch sight of that tramp whom they had had in custody for two days, but not a trace of him could they find, nor of the diamonds, from that day to this."

III.

"The tramp was missing," continued the man in the corner, "and Mr. Francis Howard tried to find the missing tramp. Going round to the front, and seeing the lights at No. 26 still in, he called upon Mr. Shipman. The jeweller had had a few friends to dinner, and was giving them whiskies-and-sodas before saying good night. The servants had just finished washing up, and were waiting to go to bed; neither they nor Mr. Shipman nor his guests had seen or heard anything of the suspicious individual.

"Mr. Francis Howard went on to see Mr. Ferdinand Knopf. This gentleman was having his warm bath, preparatory to going to bed.

So Robertson told the detective. However, Mr. Knopf insisted on talking to Mr. Howard through his bath-room door. Mr. Knopf thanked him for all the trouble he was taking, and felt sure that he and Mr. Shipman would soon recover possession of their diamonds, thanks to the persevering detective.

"He! he! he!" laughed the man in the corner. "Poor Mr. Howard. He persevered—but got no farther; no, nor anyone else, for that matter. Even I might not be able to convict the thieves if I told all I knew to the police.

"Now, follow my reasoning, point by point," he added eagerly.

"Who knew of the presence of the diamonds in the house of Mr. Shipman and Mr. Knopf? Firstly," he said, putting up an ugly claw-like finger, "Mr. Shipman, then Mr. Knopf, then, presumably, the man Robertson."

"And the tramp?" said Polly.

"Leave the tramp alone for the present since he has vanished, and take point number two. Mr. Shipman was drugged. That was pretty obvious; no man under ordinary circumstances would, without waking, have his keys abstracted and then replaced at his own bedside. Mr. Howard suggested that the thief was armed with some anaesthetic; but how did the thief get into Mr. Shipman's room without waking him from his natural sleep? Is it not simpler to suppose that the thief had taken the precaution to drug the jeweller *before* the latter went to bed?"

"But—"

"Wait a moment, and take point number three. Though there was every proof that Mr. Shipman had been in possession of £25,000 worth of goods since Mr. Knopf had a cheque from him for that amount, there was no proof that in Mr. Knopf's house there was even an odd stone worth a sovereign.

"And then again," went on the scarecrow, getting more and more excited, "did it ever strike you, or anybody else, that at *no* time, while the tramp was in custody, while all that searching examination was being gone on with, no one ever saw Mr. Knopf and his man Robertson together at the same time?

"Ah!" he continued, whilst suddenly the young girl seemed to see the whole thing as in a vision, "they did not forget a single detail—follow them with me, point by point. Two cunning scoundrels—geniuses they should be called—well provided with some ill-gotten funds—but determined on a grand *coup*. They play at respectability, for six months, say. One is the master, the other the servant; they take a house in the same street as their intended victim, make friends with him, accomplish one or two creditable but very small business transactions, always drawing on the reserve funds, which might even have amounted to a few hundreds—and a bit of credit.

"Then the Brazilian diamonds, and the Parisians—which, remember, were so perfect that they required chemical testing to be detected. The Parisian stones are sold—not in business, of course—in the evening, after dinner and a good deal of wine. Mr. Knopf's Brazilians were beautiful; perfect! Mr. Knopf was a well-known diamond merchant.

"Mr. Shipman bought—but with the morning would have come sober sense, the cheque stopped before it could have been presented, the swindler caught. No! those exquisite Parisians were never intended to rest in Mr. Shipman's safe until the morning. That last bottle of '48 port, with the aid of a powerful soporific, ensured that Mr. Shipman would sleep undisturbed during the night.

"Ah! remember all the details, they were so admirable! the letter posted in Brighton by the cunning rogue to himself, the smashed desk, the broken pane of glass in his own house. The man Robertson on the watch, while Knopf himself in ragged clothing found his way into No. 26. If Constable D 21 had not appeared upon the scene that exciting comedy in the early morning would not have been enacted. As it was, in the supposed fight, Mr. Shipman's diamonds passed from the hands of the tramp into those of his accomplice.

"Then, later on, Robertson, ill in bed, while his master was supposed to have returned—by the way, it never struck anybody that no one saw Mr. Knopf come home, though he surely would have driven up in a cab. Then the double part played by one man for the next two days. It certainly never struck either the police or the inspector. Remember they only saw Robertson when in bed with a streaming cold. But Knopf had to be got out of gaol as soon as possible; the dual *rôle* could not have been kept up for long. Hence the story of the diamonds found in the garden of No. 22. The cunning rogues guessed that the usual plan would be acted upon, and the suspected thief allowed to visit the scene where his hoard lay hidden.

"It had all been foreseen, and Robertson must have been constantly on the watch. The tramp stopped, mind you, in Phillimore Terrace for some moments, lighting a pipe. The accomplice, then, was fully on the alert; he slipped the bolts of the back garden gate. Five minutes later Knopf was in the house, in a hot bath, getting rid of the disguise of our friend the tramp. Remember that again here the detective did not actually see him.

"The next morning Mr. Knopf, black hair and beard and all, was himself again. The whole trick lay in one simple art, which those two cunning rascals knew to absolute perfection, the art of impersonating one another.

"They are brothers, presumably—twin brothers, I should say."

"But Mr. Knopf—" suggested Polly.

"Well, look in the Trades' Directory; you will see F. Knopf & Co., diamond merchants, of some City address. Ask about the firm among the trade; you will hear that it is firmly established on a sound financial basis. He! he! he! and it deserves to be," added the man in the corner, as, calling for the waitress, he received his ticket, and taking up his shabby hat, took himself and his bit of string rapidly out of the room.

3
The York Mystery

I.

The man in the corner looked quite cheerful that morning; he had had two glasses of milk and had even gone to the extravagance of an extra cheese-cake. Polly knew that he was itching to talk police and murders, for he cast furtive glances at her from time to time, produced a bit of string, tied and untied it into scores of complicated knots, and finally, bringing out his pocket-book, he placed two or three photographs before her.

"Do you know who that is?" he asked, pointing to one of these.

The girl looked at the face on the picture. It was that of a woman, not exactly pretty, but very gentle and childlike, with a strange pathetic look in the large eyes which was wonderfully appealing.

"That was Lady Arthur Skelmerton," he said, and in a flash there flitted before Polly's mind the weird and tragic history which had broken this loving woman's heart. Lady Arthur Skelmerton! That name recalled one of the most bewildering, most mysterious passages in the annals of undiscovered crimes.

"Yes. It was sad, wasn't it?" he commented, in answer to Polly's thoughts. "Another case which but for idiotic blunders on the part of the police must have stood clear as daylight before the public and satisfied general anxiety. Would you object to my recapitulating its preliminary details?"

She said nothing, so he continued without waiting further for a reply.

"It all occurred during the York racing week, a time which brings to the quiet cathedral city its quota of shady characters, who congregate wherever money and wits happen to fly away from their owners. Lord Arthur Skelmerton, a very well-known figure in London society and in racing circles, had rented one of the fine houses which overlook the racecourse. He had entered Peppercorn, by St. Armand—Notre Dame, for the Great Ebor Handicap. Peppercorn was the winner of the Newmarket, and his chances for the Ebor were considered a practical certainty.

"If you have ever been to York you will have noticed the fine houses which have their drive and front entrances in the road called 'The Mount,' and the gardens of which extend as far as the racecourse, commanding a lovely view over the entire track. It was one of these houses, called 'The Elms,' which Lord Arthur Skelmerton had rented for the summer.

"Lady Arthur came down some little time before the racing week with her servants—she had no children; but she had many relatives and friends in York, since she was the daughter of old Sir John Etty, the cocoa manufacturer, a rigid Quaker, who, it was generally said, kept the tightest possible hold on his own purse-strings and looked with marked disfavour upon his aristocratic son-in-law's fondness for gaming tables and betting books.

"As a matter of fact, Maud Etty had married the handsome young lieutenant in the Hussars, quite against her father's wishes. But she was an only child, and after a good deal of demur and grumbling, Sir John, who idolized his daughter, gave way to her whim, and a reluctant consent to the marriage was wrung from him.

"But, as a Yorkshireman, he was far too shrewd a man of the world not to know that love played but a very small part in persuading a Duke's son to marry the daughter of a cocoa manufacturer, and as long as he lived he determined that since his daughter was being wed because of her wealth, that wealth should at least secure her own happiness. He refused to give Lady Arthur any capital, which, in spite of the most carefully worded settlements, would inevitably, sooner or later, have found its way into the pockets of Lord Arthur's racing friends. But he made his daughter a very handsome allowance, amounting to over £3000 a year, which enabled her to keep up an establishment befitting her new rank.

"A great many of these facts, intimate enough as they are, leaked out, you see, during that period of intense excitement which followed the murder of Charles Lavender, and when the public eye was fixed searchingly upon Lord Arthur Skelmerton, probing all the inner details of his idle, useless life.

"It soon became a matter of common gossip that poor little Lady Arthur continued to worship her handsome husband in spite of his obvious neglect, and not having as yet presented him with an heir, she settled herself down into a life of humble apology for her plebeian existence, atoning for it by condoning all his faults and forgiving all his vices, even to the extent of cloaking them before the prying eyes of Sir John, who was persuaded to look upon his son-in-law as a paragon of all the domestic virtues and a perfect model of a husband.

"Among Lord Arthur Skelmerton's many expensive tastes there was certainly that for horseflesh and cards. After some successful betting at the beginning of his married life, he had started a racing-stable which it was generally believed—as he was very lucky—was a regular source of income to him.

"Peppercorn, however, after his brilliant performances at Newmarket did not continue to fulfil his master's expectations. His collapse at York was attributed to the hardness of the course and to various other causes, but its immediate effect was to put Lord Arthur Skelmerton in what is popularly called a tight place, for he had backed his horse for all he was worth, and must have stood to lose considerably over £5000 on that one day.

"The collapse of the favourite and the grand victory of King Cole, a rank outsider, on the other hand, had proved a golden harvest for the bookmakers, and all the York hotels were busy with dinners and suppers given by the confraternity of the Turf to celebrate the happy occasion. The next day was Friday, one of few important racing events, after which the brilliant and the shady throng which had flocked into the venerable city for the week would fly to more congenial climes, and leave it, with its fine old Minster and its ancient walls, as sleepy, as quiet as before.

"Lord Arthur Skelmerton also intended to leave York on the Saturday, and on the Friday night he gave a farewell bachelor dinner party at 'The Elms,' at which Lady Arthur did not appear. After dinner the gentlemen settled down to bridge, with pretty stiff points, you may be sure. It had just struck eleven at the Minster Tower, when constables McNaught and Murphy, who were patrolling the racecourse, were startled by loud cries of 'murder' and 'police.'

"Quickly ascertaining whence these cries proceeded, they hurried on at a gallop, and came up—quite close to the boundary of Lord Arthur Skelmerton's grounds—upon a group of three men, two of whom seemed to be wrestling vigorously with one another, whilst the third was lying face downwards on the ground. As soon as the constables drew near, one of the wrestlers shouted more vigorously, and with a certain tone of authority:

"'Here, you fellows, hurry up, sharp; the brute is giving me the slip!'

"But the brute did not seem inclined to do anything of the sort; he certainly extricated himself with a violent jerk from his assailant's grasp, but made no attempt to run away. The constables had quickly dismounted, whilst he who had shouted for help originally added more quietly:

"'My name is Skelmerton. This is the boundary of my property. I was smoking a cigar at the pavilion over there with a friend when I heard loud voices, followed by a cry and a groan. I hurried down the steps, and saw this poor fellow lying on the ground, with a knife sticking between his shoulder-blades, and his murderer,' he added, pointing to the man who stood quietly by with Constable McNaught's firm grip upon his shoulder, 'still stooping over the body of his victim. I was too late, I fear, to save the latter, but just in time to grapple with the assassin—'

"'It's a lie!' here interrupted the man hoarsely. 'I didn't do it, constable; I swear I didn't do it. I saw him fall—I was coming along a couple of hundred yards away, and I tried to see if the poor fellow was dead. I swear I didn't do it.'

"'You'll have to explain that to the inspector presently, my man,' was Constable McNaught's quiet comment, and, still vigorously protesting his innocence, the accused allowed himself to be led away, and the body was conveyed to the station, pending fuller identification.

"The next morning the papers were full of the tragedy; a column and a half of the *York Herald* was devoted to an account of Lord Arthur Skelmerton's plucky capture of the assassin. The latter had continued to declare his innocence, but had remarked, it appears, with grim humour, that he quite saw he was in a tight place, out of which, however, he would find it easy to extricate himself. He had stated to the police that the deceased's name was Charles Lavender, a well-known bookmaker, which fact was soon verified, for many of the murdered man's 'pals' were still in the city.

"So far the most pushing of newspaper reporters had been unable to glean further information from the police; no one doubted, however, but that the man in charge, who gave his name as George Higgins, had killed the bookmaker for purposes of robbery. The inquest had been fixed for the Tuesday after the murder.

"Lord Arthur had been obliged to stay in York a few days, as his evidence would be needed. That fact gave the case, perhaps, a certain amount of interest as far as York and London 'society' were concerned. Charles Lavender, moreover, was well known on the turf; but no bombshell exploding beneath the walls of the ancient cathedral city could more have astonished its inhabitants than the news which, at about five in the afternoon on the day of the inquest, spread like wildfire throughout the town. That news was that the inquest had concluded at three o'clock with a verdict of 'Wilful murder against some person or persons unknown,' and that two hours later the police had arrested Lord Arthur Skelmerton at his private residence, 'The Elms,' and charged him on a warrant with the murder of Charles Lavender, the bookmaker."

II.

"The police, it appears, instinctively feeling that some mystery lurked round the death of the bookmaker and his supposed murderer's quiet protestations of innocence, had taken a very considerable amount of trouble in collecting all the evidence they could for the inquest which might throw some light upon Charles Lavender's life, previous to his tragic end. Thus it was that a very large array of witnesses was brought before the coroner, chief among whom was, of course, Lord Arthur Skelmerton.

"The first witnesses called were the two constables, who deposed that, just as the church clocks in the neighbourhood were striking eleven, they had heard the cries for help, had ridden to the spot whence the sounds proceeded, and had found the prisoner in the tight grasp of Lord Arthur Skelmerton, who at once accused the man of murder, and gave him in charge. Both constables gave the same version of the incident, and both were positive as to the time when it occurred.

"Medical evidence went to prove that the deceased had been stabbed from behind between the shoulder-blades whilst he was walking, that the wound was inflicted by a large hunting knife, which was produced, and which had been left sticking in the wound.

"Lord Arthur Skelmerton was then called and substantially repeated what he had already told the constables. He stated, namely, that on the night in question he had some gentlemen friends to dinner, and afterwards bridge was played. He himself was not playing much, and at a few minutes before eleven he strolled out with a cigar as far as the pavilion at the end of his garden; he then heard the voices, the cry and the groan previously described by him, and managed to hold the murderer down until the arrival of the constables.

"At this point the police proposed to call a witness, James Terry by name and a bookmaker by profession, who had been chiefly instrumental in identifying the deceased, a 'pal' of his. It was his evidence which first introduced that element of sensation into the case which culminated in the wildly exciting arrest of a Duke's son upon a capital charge.

"It appears that on the evening after the Ebor, Terry and Lavender were in the bar of the Black Swan Hotel having drinks.

"'I had done pretty well over Peppercorn's fiasco,' he explained, 'but poor old Lavender was very much down in the dumps; he had held only a few very small bets against the favourite, and the rest of the day had been a poor one with him. I asked him if he had any bets with the owner of Peppercorn, and he told me that he only held one for less than £500.

"'I laughed and said that if he held one for £5000 it would make no difference, as from what I had heard from the other fellows, Lord Arthur Skelmerton must be about stumped. Lavender seemed terribly put out at this, and swore he would get that £500 out of Lord Arthur, if no one else got another penny from him.

"'It's the only money I've made to-day,' he says to me. 'I mean to get it.'

"'You won't,' I says.

"'I will,' he says.

"'You will have to look pretty sharp about it then,' I says, 'for every one will be wanting to get something, and first come first served.'

"'Oh! He'll serve me right enough, never you mind!' says Lavender to me with a laugh. 'If he don't pay up willingly, I've got that in my pocket which will make him sit up and open my lady's eyes and Sir John Etty's too about their precious noble lord.'

"'Then he seemed to think he had gone too far, and wouldn't say anything more to me about that affair. I saw him on the course the next day. I asked him if he had got his £500. He said: "No, but I shall get it to-day."'

"Lord Arthur Skelmerton, after having given his own evidence, had left the court; it was therefore impossible to know how he would take this account, which threw so serious a light upon an association with the dead man, of which he himself had said nothing.

"Nothing could shake James Terry's account of the facts he had placed before the jury, and when the police informed the coroner that they proposed to place George Higgins himself in the witness-box, as his evidence would prove, as it were, a complement and corollary of that of Terry, the jury very eagerly assented.

"If James Terry, the bookmaker, loud, florid, vulgar, was an unprepossessing individual, certainly George Higgins, who was still under the accusation of murder, was ten thousand times more so.

"None too clean, slouchy, obsequious yet insolent, he was the very personification of the cad who haunts the racecourse and who lives not so much by his own wits as by the lack of them in others. He described himself as a turf commission agent, whatever that may be.

"He stated that at about six o'clock on the Friday afternoon, when the racecourse was still full of people, all hurrying after the day's excitements, he himself happened to be standing close to the hedge which marks the boundary of Lord Arthur Skelmerton's grounds. There is a pavilion there at the end of the garden, he explained, on slightly elevated ground, and he could hear and see a group of ladies and gentlemen having tea. Some steps lead down a little to the left of the garden on to the course, and presently he noticed at the bottom of these steps Lord Arthur Skelmerton and Charles Lavender standing talking together. He knew both gentlemen by sight, but he could not see them very well as they were both partly hidden by the hedge. He was quite sure that the gentlemen had not seen him, and he could not help overhearing some of their conversation.

"'That's my last word, Lavender,' Lord Arthur was saying very quietly. 'I haven't got the money and I can't pay you now. You'll have to wait.'

"'Wait? I can't wait,' said old Lavender in reply. 'I've got my engagements to meet, same as you. I'm not going to risk being posted up as a defaulter while you hold £500 of my money. You'd better give it me now or—'

"But Lord Arthur interrupted him very quietly, and said:

"'Yes, my good man ... or?'

"'Or I'll let Sir John have a good look at that little bill I had of yours a couple of years ago. If you'll remember, my lord, it has got at the bottom of it Sir John's signature in *your* handwriting.

Perhaps Sir John, or perhaps my lady, would pay me something for that little bill. If not, the police can have a squint at it. I've held my tongue long enough, and—'

"'Look here, Lavender,' said Lord Arthur, 'do you know what this little game of yours is called in law?'

"'Yes, and I don't care,' says Lavender. 'If I don't have that £500 I am a ruined man. If you ruin me I'll do for you, and we shall be quits. That's my last word.'

"He was talking very loudly, and I thought some of Lord Arthur's friends up in the pavilion must have heard. He thought so, too, I think, for he said quickly:

"'If you don't hold your confounded tongue, I'll give you in charge for blackmail this instant.'

"'You wouldn't dare,' says Lavender, and he began to laugh. But just then a lady from the top of the steps said: 'Your tea is getting cold,' and Lord Arthur turned to go; but just before he went Lavender says to him: 'I'll come back to-night. You'll have the money then.'

"George Higgins, it appears, after he had heard this interesting conversation, pondered as to whether he could not turn what he knew into some sort of profit. Being a gentleman who lives entirely by his wits, this type of knowledge forms his chief source of income. As a preliminary to future moves, he decided not to lose sight of Lavender for the rest of the day.

"'Lavender went and had dinner at The Black Swan,' explained Mr. George Higgins, 'and I, after I had had a bite myself, waited outside till I saw him come out. At about ten o'clock I was rewarded for my trouble. He told the hall porter to get him a fly and he jumped into it. I could not hear what direction he gave the driver, but the fly certainly drove off towards the racecourse.

"'Now, I was interested in this little affair,' continued the witness, 'and I couldn't afford a fly. I started to run. Of course, I couldn't keep up with it, but I thought I knew which way my gentleman had gone. I made straight for the racecourse, and for the hedge at the bottom of Lord Arthur Skelmerton's grounds.

"'It was rather a dark night and there was a slight drizzle. I couldn't see more than about a hundred yards before me. All at once it seemed to me as if I heard Lavender's voice talking loudly in the distance. I hurried forward, and suddenly saw a group of two figures—mere blurs in the darkness—for one instant, at a distance of about fifty yards from where I was.

"'The next moment one figure had fallen forward and the other had disappeared. I ran to the spot, only to find the body of the murdered man lying on the ground. I stooped to see if I could be of any use to him, and immediately I was collared from behind by Lord Arthur himself.'

"You may imagine," said the man in the corner, "how keen was the excitement of that moment in court. Coroner and jury alike literally hung breathless on every word that shabby, vulgar individual uttered. You see, by itself his evidence would have been worth very little, but coming on the top of that given by James Terry, its significance—more, its truth—had become glaringly apparent. Closely cross-examined, he adhered strictly to his statement; and having finished his evidence, George Higgins remained in charge of the constables, and the next witness of importance was called up.

"This was Mr. Chipps, the senior footman in the employment of Lord Arthur Skelmerton. He deposed that at about 10.30 on the Friday evening a 'party' drove up to 'The Elms' in a fly, and asked to see Lord Arthur. On being told that his lordship had company he seemed terribly put out.

"'I hasked the party to give me 'is card,' continued Mr. Chipps, 'as I didn't know, perhaps, that 'is lordship might wish to see 'im, but I kept 'im standing at the 'all door, as I didn't altogether like his looks. I took the card in. His lordship and the gentlemen was playin' cards in the smoking-room, and as soon as I could do so without disturbing 'is lordship, I give him the party's card.'

"'What name was there on the card?' here interrupted the coroner.

"'I couldn't say now, sir,' replied Mr. Chipps; 'I don't really remember. It was a name I had never seen before. But I see so many visiting cards one way and the other in 'is lordship's 'all that I can't remember all the names.'

"'Then, after a few minutes' waiting, you gave his lordship the card? What happened then?'

"''Is lordship didn't seem at all pleased,' said Mr. Chipps with much guarded dignity; 'but finally he said: "Show him into the library, Chipps, I'll see him," and he got up from the card table, saying to the gentlemen: "Go on without me; I'll be back in a minute or two."

"'I was about to open the door for 'is lordship when my lady came into the room, and then his lordship suddenly changed his mind like, and said to me: "Tell that man I'm busy and can't see him," and 'e sat down again at the card table. I went back to the 'all, and told the party 'is lordship wouldn't see 'im. 'E said: "Oh! it doesn't matter," and went away quite quiet like.'

"'Do you recollect at all at what time that was?' asked one of the jury.

"'Yes, sir, while I was waiting to speak to 'is lordship I looked at the clock, sir; it was twenty past ten, sir.'

"There was one more significant fact in connection with the case, which tended still more to excite the curiosity of the public at the time, and still further to bewilder the police later on, and that fact was mentioned by Chipps in his evidence. The knife, namely, with which Charles Lavender had been stabbed, and which, remember, had been left in the wound, was now produced in court. After a little hesitation Chipps identified it as the property of his master, Lord Arthur Skelmerton.

"Can you wonder, then, that the jury absolutely refused to bring in a verdict against George Higgins? There was really, beyond Lord Arthur Skelmerton's testimony, not one particle of evidence against him, whilst, as the day wore on and witness after witness was called up, suspicion ripened in the minds of all those present that the murderer could be no other than Lord Arthur Skelmerton himself.

"The knife was, of course, the strongest piece of circumstantial evidence, and no doubt the police hoped to collect a great deal more now that they held a clue in their hands. Directly after the verdict, therefore, which was guardedly directed against some person unknown, the police obtained a warrant and later on arrested Lord Arthur in his own house."

"The sensation, of course, was tremendous. Hours before he was brought up before the magistrate the approach to the court was thronged. His friends, mostly ladies, were all eager, you see, to watch the dashing society man in so terrible a position. There was universal sympathy for Lady Arthur, who was in a very precarious state of health. Her worship of her worthless husband was well known; small wonder that his final and awful misdeed had practically broken her heart. The latest bulletin issued just after his arrest stated that her ladyship was not expected to live. She was then in a comatose condition, and all hope had perforce to be abandoned.

"At last the prisoner was brought in. He looked very pale, perhaps, but otherwise kept up the bearing of a high-bred gentleman. He was accompanied by his solicitor, Sir Marmaduke Ingersoll, who was evidently talking to him in quiet, reassuring tones.

"Mr. Buchanan prosecuted for the Treasury, and certainly his indictment was terrific. According to him but one decision could be arrived at, namely, that the accused in the dock had, in a moment of passion, and perhaps of fear, killed the blackmailer who threatened him with disclosures which might for ever have ruined him socially, and, having committed the deed and fearing its consequences, probably realizing that the patrolling constables might catch sight of his retreating figure, he had availed himself of George Higgins's presence on the spot to loudly accuse him of the murder.

"Having concluded his able speech, Mr. Buchanan called his witnesses, and the evidence, which on second hearing seemed more damning than ever, was all gone through again.

"Sir Marmaduke had no question to ask of the witnesses for the prosecution; he stared at them placidly through his gold-rimmed spectacles. Then he was ready to call his own for the defence. Colonel McIntosh, R.A., was the first. He was present at the bachelors' party given by Lord Arthur the night of the murder. His evidence tended at first to corroborate that of Chipps the footman with regard to Lord Arthur's orders to show the visitor into the library, and his counter-order as soon as his wife came into the room.

"'Did you not think it strange, Colonel?' asked Mr. Buchanan, 'that Lord Arthur should so suddenly have changed his mind about seeing his visitor?'

"'Well, not exactly strange,' said the Colonel, a fine, manly, soldierly figure who looked curiously out of his element in the witness-box. 'I don't think that it is a very rare occurrence for racing men to have certain acquaintances whom they would not wish their wives to know anything about.'

"'Then it did not strike you that Lord Arthur Skelmerton had some reason for not wishing his wife to know of that particular visitor's presence in his house?'

"'I don't think that I gave the matter the slightest serious consideration,' was the Colonel's guarded reply.

"Mr. Buchanan did not press the point, and allowed the witness to conclude his statements.

"'I had finished my turn at bridge,' he said, 'and went out into the garden to smoke a cigar. Lord Arthur Skelmerton joined me a few minutes later, and we were sitting in the pavilion when I heard a loud and, as I thought, threatening voice from the other side of the hedge.

"'I did not catch the words, but Lord Arthur said to me: "There seems to be a row down there. I'll go and have a look and see what it is." I tried to dissuade him, and certainly made no attempt to follow him, but not more than half a minute could have elapsed before I heard a cry and a groan, then Lord Arthur's footsteps hurrying down the wooden stairs which lead on to the racecourse.'

"You may imagine," said the man in the corner, "what severe cross-examination the gallant Colonel had to undergo in order that his assertions might in some way be shaken by the prosecution, but with military precision and frigid calm he repeated his important statements amidst a general silence, through which you could have heard the proverbial pin.

"He had heard the threatening voice *while* sitting with Lord Arthur Skelmerton; then came the cry and groan, and, *after that*, Lord Arthur's steps down the stairs. He himself thought of following to see what had happened, but it was a very dark night and he did not know the grounds very well. While trying to find his way to the garden steps he heard Lord Arthur's cry for help, the tramp of the patrolling constables' horses, and subsequently the whole scene between Lord Arthur, the man Higgins, and the constables. When he finally found his way to the stairs, Lord Arthur was returning in order to send a groom for police assistance.

"The witness stuck to his points as he had to his guns at Beckfontein a year ago; nothing could shake him, and Sir Marmaduke looked triumphantly across at his opposing colleague.

"With the gallant Colonel's statements the edifice of the prosecution certainly began to collapse. You see, there was not a particle of evidence to show that the accused had met and spoken to the deceased after the latter's visit at the front door of 'The Elms.' He told Chipps that he wouldn't see the visitor, and Chipps went into the hall directly and showed Lavender out the way he came. No assignation could have been made, no hint could have been given by the murdered man to Lord Arthur that he would go round to the back entrance and wished to see him there.

"Two other guests of Lord Arthur's swore positively that after Chipps had announced the visitor, their host stayed at the card-table until a quarter to eleven, when evidently he went out to join Colonel McIntosh in the garden. Sir Marmaduke's speech was clever in the extreme. Bit by bit he demolished that tower of strength, the case against the accused, basing his defence entirely upon the evidence of Lord Arthur Skelmerton's guests that night.

"Until 10.45 Lord Arthur was playing cards; a quarter of an hour later the police were on the scene, and the murder had been committed. In the meanwhile Colonel McIntosh's evidence proved conclusively that the accused had been sitting with him, smoking a cigar. It was obvious, therefore, clear as daylight, concluded the great lawyer, that his client was entitled to a full discharge; nay, more, he thought that the police should have been more careful before they harrowed up public feeling by arresting a high-born gentleman on such insufficient evidence as they had brought forward.

"The question of the knife remained certainly, but Sir Marmaduke passed over it with guarded eloquence, placing that strange question in the category of those inexplicable coincidences which tend to puzzle the ablest detectives, and cause them to commit such unpardonable blunders as the present one had been. After all, the footman may have been mistaken. The pattern of that knife was not an exclusive one, and he, on behalf of his client, flatly denied that it had ever belonged to him.

"Well," continued the man in the corner, with the chuckle peculiar to him in moments of excitement, "the noble prisoner was discharged. Perhaps it would be invidious to say that he left the court without a stain on his character, for I daresay you know from experience that the crime known as the York Mystery has never been satisfactorily cleared up.

"Many people shook their heads dubiously when they remembered that, after all, Charles Lavender was killed with a knife which one witness had sworn belonged to Lord Arthur; others, again, reverted to the original theory that George Higgins was the murderer, that he and James Terry had concocted the story of Lavender's attempt at blackmail on Lord Arthur, and that the murder had been committed for the sole purpose of robbery.

"Be that as it may, the police have not so far been able to collect sufficient evidence against Higgins or Terry, and the crime has been classed by press and public alike in the category of so-called impenetrable mysteries."

III.

The man in the corner called for another glass of milk, and drank it down slowly before he resumed:

"Now Lord Arthur lives mostly abroad," he said. "His poor, suffering wife died the day after he was liberated by the magistrate. She never recovered consciousness even sufficiently to hear the joyful news that the man she loved so well was innocent after all.

"Mystery!" he added as if in answer to Polly's own thoughts. "The murder of that man was never a mystery to me. I cannot understand how the police could have been so blind when every one of the witnesses, both for the prosecution and defence, practically pointed all the time to the one guilty person. What do you think of it all yourself?"

"I think the whole case so bewildering," she replied, "that I do not see one single clear point in it."

"You don't?" he said excitedly, while the bony fingers fidgeted again with that inevitable bit of string. "You don't see that there is one point clear which to me was the key of the whole thing?

"Lavender was murdered, wasn't he? Lord Arthur did not kill him. He had, at least, in Colonel McIntosh an unimpeachable witness to prove that he could not have committed that murder—and yet," he added with slow, excited emphasis, marking each sentence with a knot, "and yet he deliberately tries to throw the guilt upon a man who obviously was also innocent. Now why?"

"He may have thought him guilty."

"Or wished to shield or cover the retreat of *one he knew to be guilty*."

"I don't understand."

"Think of someone," he said excitedly, "someone whose desire would be as great as that of Lord Arthur to silence a scandal round that gentleman's name. Someone who, unknown perhaps to Lord Arthur, had overheard the same conversation which George Higgins related to the police and the magistrate, someone who, whilst Chipps was taking Lavender's card in to his master, had a few minutes' time wherein to make an assignation with Lavender, promising him money, no doubt, in exchange for the compromising bills."

"Surely you don't mean—" gasped Polly.

"Point number one," he interrupted quietly, "utterly missed by the police. George Higgins in his deposition stated that at the most animated stage of Lavender's conversation with Lord Arthur, and when the bookmaker's tone of voice became loud and threatening, a voice from the top of the steps interrupted that conversation, saying: 'Your tea is getting cold.'"

"Yes—but—" she argued.

"Wait a moment, for there is point number two. That voice was a lady's voice. Now, I did exactly what the police should have done, but did not do. I went to have a look from the racecourse side at those garden steps which to my mind are such important factors in the discovery of this crime. I found only about a dozen rather low steps; anyone standing on the top must have heard every word Charles Lavender uttered the moment he raised his voice."

"Even then—"

"Very well, you grant that," he said excitedly. "Then there was the great, the all-important point which, oddly enough, the prosecution never for a moment took into consideration. When Chipps, the footman, first told Lavender that Lord Arthur could not see him the bookmaker was terribly put out; Chipps then goes to speak to his master; a few minutes elapse, and when the footman once again tells Lavender that his lordship won't see him, the latter says 'Very well,' and seems to treat the matter with complete indifference.

"Obviously, therefore, something must have happened in between to alter the bookmaker's frame of mind. Well! What had happened? Think over all the evidence, and you will see that one thing only had occurred in the interval, namely, Lady Arthur's advent into the room.

"In order to go into the smoking-room she must have crossed the hall; she must have seen Lavender. In that brief interval she must have realized that the man was persistent, and therefore a living danger to her husband. Remember, women have done strange things; they are a far greater puzzle to the student of human nature than the sterner, less complex sex has ever been. As I argued before—as the police should have argued all along—why did Lord Arthur deliberately accuse an innocent man of murder if not to shield the guilty one?

"Remember, Lady Arthur may have been discovered; the man, George Higgins, may have caught sight of her before she had time to make good her retreat. His attention, as well us that of the constables, had to be diverted. Lord Arthur acted on the blind impulse of saving his wife at any cost."

"She may have been met by Colonel McIntosh," argued Polly.

"Perhaps she was," he said. "Who knows? The gallant colonel had to swear to his friend's innocence. He could do that in all conscience—after that his duty was accomplished. No innocent man was suffering for the guilty. The knife which had belonged to Lord Arthur would always save George Higgins. For a time it had pointed to the husband; fortunately never to the wife. Poor thing, she died probably of a broken heart, but women when they love, think only of one object on earth—the one who is beloved.

"To me the whole thing was clear from the very first. When I read the account of the murder—the knife! stabbing!—bah! Don't I know enough of *English* crime not to be certain at once that no English*man*, be he ruffian from the gutter or be he Duke's son, ever stabs his victim in the back. Italians, French, Spaniards do it, if you will, and women of most nations. An Englishman's instinct is to strike and not to stab. George Higgins or Lord Arthur Skelmerton would have knocked their victim down; the woman only would lie in wait till the enemy's back was turned. She knows her weakness, and she does not mean to miss.

"Think it over. There is not one flaw in my argument, but the police never thought the matter out—perhaps in this case it was as well."

He had gone and left Miss Polly Burton still staring at the photograph of a pretty, gentle-looking woman, with a decided, wilful curve round the mouth, and a strange, unaccountable look in the large pathetic eyes; and the little journalist felt quite thankful that in this case the murder of Charles Lavender the bookmaker—cowardly, wicked as it was—had remained a mystery to the police and the public.

4
The Mysterious Death on the Underground Railway

I.

It was all very well for Mr. Richard Frobisher (of the *London Mail*) to cut up rough about it. Polly did not altogether blame him.

She liked him all the better for that frank outburst of manlike ill-temper which, after all said and done, was only a very flattering form of masculine jealousy.

Moreover, Polly distinctly felt guilty about the whole thing. She had promised to meet Dickie—that is Mr. Richard Frobisher—at two o'clock sharp outside the Palace Theatre, because she wanted to go to a Maud Allan *matinée*, and because he naturally wished to go with her.

But at two o'clock sharp she was still in Norfolk Street, Strand, inside an A.B.C. shop, sipping cold coffee opposite a grotesque old man who was fiddling with a bit of string.

How could she be expected to remember Maud Allan or the Palace Theatre, or Dickie himself for a matter of that? The man in the corner had begun to talk of that mysterious death on the underground railway, and Polly had lost count of time, of place, and circumstance.

She had gone to lunch quite early, for she was looking forward to the *matinée* at the Palace.

The old scarecrow was sitting in his accustomed place when she came into the A.B.C. shop, but he had made no remark all the time that the young girl was munching her scone and butter. She was just busy thinking how rude he was not even to have said "Good morning," when an abrupt remark from him caused her to look up.

"Will you be good enough," he said suddenly, "to give me a description of the man who sat next to you just now, while you were having your cup of coffee and scone."

Involuntarily Polly turned her head towards the distant door, through which a man in a light overcoat was even now quickly passing. That man had certainly sat at the next table to hers, when she first sat down to her coffee and scone: he had finished his luncheon—whatever it was—moment ago, had paid at the desk and gone out. The incident did not appear to Polly as being of the slightest consequence.

Therefore she did not reply to the rude old man, but shrugged her shoulders, and called to the waitress to bring her bill.

"Do you know if he was tall or short, dark or fair?" continued the man in the corner, seemingly not the least disconcerted by the young girl's indifference. "Can you tell me at all what he was like?"

"Of course I can," rejoined Polly impatiently, "but I don't see that my description of one of the customers of an A.B.C. shop can have the slightest importance."

He was silent for a minute, while his nervous fingers fumbled about in his capacious pockets in search of the inevitable piece of string. When he had found this necessary "adjunct to thought," he viewed the young girl again through his half-closed lids, and added maliciously:

"But supposing it were of paramount importance that you should give an accurate description of a man who sat next to you for half an hour to-day, how would you proceed?"

"I should say that he was of medium height—"

"Five foot eight, nine, or ten?" he interrupted quietly.

"How can one tell to an inch or two?" rejoined Polly crossly. "He was between colours."

"What's that?" he inquired blandly.

"Neither fair nor dark—his nose—"

"Well, what was his nose like? Will you sketch it?"

"I am not an artist. His nose was fairly straight—his eyes—"

"Were neither dark nor light—his hair had the same striking peculiarity—he was neither short nor tall—his nose was neither aquiline nor snub—" he recapitulated sarcastically.

"No," she retorted; "he was just ordinary looking."

"Would you know him again—say to-morrow, and among a number of other men who were 'neither tall nor short, dark nor fair, aquiline nor snub-nosed,' etc.?"

"I don't know—I might—he was certainly not striking enough to be specially remembered."

"Exactly," he said, while he leant forward excitedly, for all the world like a Jack-in-the-box let loose. "Precisely; and you are a journalist—call yourself one, at least—and it should be part of your business to notice and describe people. I don't mean only the wonderful personage with the clear Saxon features, the fine blue eyes, the noble brow and classic face, but the ordinary person—the person who represents ninety out of every hundred of his own kind—the average Englishman, say, of the middle classes, who is neither very tall nor very short, who wears a moustache which is neither fair nor dark, but which masks his mouth, and a top hat which hides the shape of his head and brow, a man, in fact, who dresses like hundreds of his fellow-creatures, moves like them, speaks like them, has no peculiarity.

"Try to describe *him*, to recognize him, say a week hence, among his other eighty-nine doubles; worse still, to swear his life away, if he happened to be implicated in some crime, wherein *your* recognition of him would place the halter round his neck.

"Try that, I say, and having utterly failed you will more readily understand how one of the greatest scoundrels unhung is still at large, and why the mystery on the Underground Railway was never cleared up.

"I think it was the only time in my life that I was seriously tempted to give the police the benefit of my own views upon the matter. You see, though I admire the brute for his cleverness, I did not see that his being unpunished could possibly benefit any one.

"In these days of tubes and motor traction of all kinds, the old-fashioned 'best, cheapest, and quickest route to City and West End' is often deserted, and the good old Metropolitan Railway carriages cannot at any time be said to be overcrowded. Anyway, when that particular train steamed into Aldgate at about 4 P.M. on March 18th last, the first-class carriages were all but empty.

"The guard marched up and down the platform looking into all the carriages to see if anyone had left a halfpenny evening paper behind for him, and opening the door of one of the first-class compartments, he noticed a lady sitting in the further corner, with her head turned away towards the window, evidently oblivious of the fact that on this line Aldgate is the terminal station.

"'Where are you for, lady?' he said.

"The lady did not move, and the guard stepped into the carriage, thinking that perhaps the lady was asleep. He touched her arm lightly and looked into her face. In his own poetic language, he was 'struck all of a 'eap.' In the glassy eyes, the ashen colour of the cheeks, the rigidity of the head, there was the unmistakable look of death.

"Hastily the guard, having carefully locked the carriage door, summoned a couple of porters, and sent one of them off to the police-station, and the other in search of the station-master.

"Fortunately at this time of day the up platform is not very crowded, all the traffic tending westward in the afternoon. It was only when an inspector and two police constables, accompanied by a detective in plain clothes and a medical officer, appeared upon the scene, and stood round a first-class railway compartment, that a few idlers realized that something unusual had occurred, and crowded round, eager and curious.

"Thus it was that the later editions of the evening papers, under the sensational heading, 'Mysterious Suicide on the Underground Railway,' had already an account of the extraordinary event. The medical officer had very soon come to the decision that the guard had not been mistaken, and that life was indeed extinct.

"The lady was young, and must have been very pretty before the look of fright and horror had so terribly distorted her features. She was very elegantly dressed, and the more frivolous papers were able to give their feminine readers a detailed account of the unfortunate woman's gown, her shoes, hat, and gloves.

"It appears that one of the latter, the one on the right hand, was partly off, leaving the thumb and wrist bare. That hand held a small satchel, which the police opened, with a view to the possible identification of the deceased, but which was found to contain only a little loose silver, some smelling-salts, and a small empty bottle, which was handed over to the medical officer for purposes of analysis.

"It was the presence of that small bottle which had caused the report to circulate freely that the mysterious case on the Underground Railway was one of suicide. Certain it was that neither about the lady's person, nor in the appearance of the railway carriage, was there the slightest sign of struggle or even of resistance. Only the look in the poor woman's eyes spoke of sudden terror, of the rapid vision of an unexpected and violent death, which probably only lasted an infinitesimal fraction of a second, but which had left its indelible mark upon the face, otherwise so placid and so still."

"The body of the deceased was conveyed to the mortuary. So far, of course, not a soul had been able to identify her, or to throw the slightest light upon the mystery which hung around her death.

"Against that, quite a crowd of idlers—genuinely interested or not—obtained admission to view the body, on the pretext of having lost or mislaid a relative or a friend. At about 8.30 P.M. a young man, very well dressed, drove up to the station in a hansom, and sent in his card to the superintendent. It was Mr. Hazeldene, shipping agent, of 11, Crown Lane, E.C., and No. 19, Addison Row, Kensington.

"The young man looked in a pitiable state of mental distress; his hand clutched nervously a copy of the *St. James's Gazette*, which contained the fatal news. He said very little to the superintendent except that a person who was very dear to him had not returned home that evening.

"He had not felt really anxious until half an hour ago, when suddenly he thought of looking at his paper. The description of the deceased lady, though vague, had terribly alarmed him. He had jumped into a hansom, and now begged permission to view the body, in order that his worst fears might be allayed.

"You know what followed, of course," continued the man in the corner, "the grief of the young man was truly pitiable. In the woman lying there in a public mortuary before him, Mr. Hazeldene had recognized his wife.

"I am waxing melodramatic," said the man in the corner, who looked up at Polly with a mild and gentle smile, while his nervous fingers vainly endeavoured to add another knot on the scrappy bit of string with which he was continually playing, "and I fear that the whole story savours of the penny novelette, but you must admit, and no doubt you remember, that it was an intensely pathetic and truly dramatic moment.

"The unfortunate young husband of the deceased lady was not much worried with questions that night. As a matter of fact, he was not in a fit condition to make any coherent statement. It was at the coroner's inquest on the following day that certain facts came to light, which for the time being seemed to clear up the mystery surrounding Mrs. Hazeldene's death, only to plunge that same mystery, later on, into denser gloom than before.

"The first witness at the inquest was, of course, Mr. Hazeldene himself. I think every one's sympathy went out to the young man as he stood before the coroner and tried to throw what light he could upon the mystery. He was well dressed, as he had been the day before, but he looked terribly ill and worried, and no doubt the fact that he had not shaved gave his face a careworn and neglected air.

"It appears that he and the deceased had been married some six years or so, and that they had always been happy in their married life. They had no children. Mrs. Hazeldene seemed to enjoy the best of health till lately, when she had had a slight attack of influenza, in which Dr. Arthur Jones had attended her. The doctor was present at this moment, and would no doubt explain to the coroner and the jury whether he thought that Mrs. Hazeldene had the slightest tendency to heart disease, which might have had a sudden and fatal ending.

"The coroner was, of course, very considerate to the bereaved husband. He tried by circumlocution to get at the point he wanted, namely, Mrs. Hazeldene's mental condition lately. Mr. Hazeldene seemed loath to talk about this. No doubt he had been warned as to the existence of the small bottle found in his wife's satchel.

"'It certainly did seem to me at times,' he at last reluctantly admitted, 'that my wife did not seem quite herself. She used to be very gay and bright, and lately I often saw her in the evening sitting, as if brooding over some matters, which evidently she did not care to communicate to me.'

"Still the coroner insisted, and suggested the small bottle.

"'I know, I know,' replied the young man, with a short, heavy sigh. 'You mean—the question of suicide—I cannot understand it at all—it seems so sudden and so terrible—she certainly had seemed listless and troubled lately—but only at times—and yesterday morning, when I went to business, she appeared quite herself again, and I suggested that we should go to the opera in the evening. She was delighted, I know, and told me she would do some shopping, and pay a few calls in the afternoon.'

"'Do you know at all where she intended to go when she got into the Underground Railway?'

"'Well, not with certainty. You see, she may have meant to get out at Baker Street, and go down to Bond Street to do her shopping. Then, again, she sometimes goes to a shop in St. Paul's Churchyard, in which case she would take a ticket to Aldersgate Street; but I cannot say.'

"'Now, Mr. Hazeldene,' said the coroner at last very kindly, 'will you try to tell me if there was anything in Mrs. Hazeldene's life which you know of, and which might in some measure explain the cause of the distressed state of mind, which you yourself had noticed? Did there exist any financial difficulty which might have preyed upon Mrs. Hazeldene's mind; was there any friend—to whose intercourse with Mrs. Hazeldene—you—er—at any time took exception? In fact,' added the coroner, as if thankful that he had got over an unpleasant moment, 'can you give me the slightest indication which would tend to confirm the suspicion that the unfortunate lady, in a moment of mental anxiety or derangement, may have wished to take her own life?'

"There was silence in the court for a few moments. Mr. Hazeldene seemed to every one there present to be labouring under some terrible moral doubt. He looked very pale and wretched, and twice attempted to speak before he at last said in scarcely audible tones:

"'No; there were no financial difficulties of any sort. My wife had an independent fortune of her own—she had no extravagant tastes—'

"'Nor any friend you at any time objected to?' insisted the coroner.

"'Nor any friend, I—at any time objected to,' stammered the unfortunate young man, evidently speaking with an effort.

"I was present at the inquest," resumed the man in the corner, after he had drunk a glass of milk and ordered another, "and I can assure you that the most obtuse person there plainly realized that Mr. Hazeldene was telling a lie. It was pretty plain to the meanest intelligence that the unfortunate lady had not fallen into a state of morbid dejection for nothing, and that perhaps there existed a third person who could throw more light on her strange and sudden death than the unhappy, bereaved young widower.

"That the death was more mysterious even than it had at first appeared became very soon apparent. You read the case at the time, no doubt, and must remember the excitement in the public mind caused by the evidence of the two doctors. Dr. Arthur Jones, the lady's usual medical man, who had attended her in a last very slight illness, and who had seen her in a professional capacity fairly recently, declared most emphatically that Mrs. Hazeldene suffered from no organic complaint which could possibly have been the cause of sudden death. Moreover, he had assisted Mr. Andrew Thornton, the district medical officer, in making a postmortem examination, and together they had come to the conclusion that death was due to the action of prussic acid, which had caused instantaneous failure of the heart, but how the drug had been administered neither he nor his colleague were at present able to state.

"'Do I understand, then, Dr. Jones, that the deceased died, poisoned with prussic acid?'

"'Such is my opinion,' replied the doctor.

"'Did the bottle found in her satchel contain prussic acid?'

"'It had contained some at one time, certainly.'

"'In your opinion, then, the lady caused her own death by taking a dose of that drug?'

"'Pardon me, I never suggested such a thing; the lady died poisoned by the drug, but how the drug was administered we cannot say. By injection of some sort, certainly. The drug certainly was not swallowed; there was not a vestige of it in the stomach.'

"'Yes,' added the doctor in reply to another question from the coroner, 'death had probably followed the injection in this case almost immediately; say within a couple of minutes, or perhaps three. It was quite possible that the body would not have more than one quick and sudden convulsion, perhaps not that; death in such cases is absolutely sudden and crushing.'

"I don't think that at the time any one in the room realized how important the doctor's statement was, a statement which, by the way, was confirmed in all its details by the district medical officer, who had conducted the postmortem. Mrs. Hazeldene had died suddenly from an injection of prussic acid, administered no one knew how or when. She had been travelling in a first-class railway carriage in a busy time of the day. That young and elegant woman must have had singular nerve and coolness to go through the process of a self-inflicted injection of a deadly poison in the presence of perhaps two or three other persons.

"Mind you, when I say that no one there realized the importance of the doctor's statement at that moment, I am wrong; there were three persons, who fully understood at once the gravity of the situation, and the astounding development which the case was beginning to assume.

"Of course, I should have put myself out of the question," added the weird old man, with that inimitable self-conceit peculiar to himself. "I guessed then and there in a moment where the police were going wrong, and where they would go on going wrong until the mysterious death on the Underground Railway had sunk into oblivion, together with the other cases which they mismanage from time to time.

"I said there were three persons who understood the gravity of the two doctors' statements—the other two were, firstly, the detective who had originally examined the railway carriage, a young man of energy and plenty of misguided intelligence, the other was Mr. Hazeldene.

"At this point the interesting element of the whole story was first introduced into the proceedings, and this was done through the humble channel of Emma Funnel, Mrs. Hazeldene's maid, who, as far as was known then, was the last person who had seen the unfortunate lady alive and had spoken to her.

"'Mrs. Hazeldene lunched at home,' explained Emma, who was shy, and spoke almost in a whisper; 'she seemed well and cheerful. She went out at about half-past three, and told me she was going to Spence's, in St. Paul's Churchyard, to try on her new tailor-made gown. Mrs. Hazeldene had meant to go there in the morning, but was prevented as Mr. Errington called.'

"'Mr. Errington?' asked the coroner casually. 'Who is Mr. Errington?'

"But this Emma found difficult to explain. Mr. Errington was—Mr. Errington, that's all.

"'Mr. Errington was a friend of the family. He lived in a flat in the Albert Mansions. He very often came to Addison Row, and generally stayed late.'

"Pressed still further with questions, Emma at last stated that latterly Mrs. Hazeldene had been to the theatre several times with Mr. Errington, and that on those nights the master looked very gloomy, and was very cross.

"Recalled, the young widower was strangely reticent. He gave forth his answers very grudgingly, and the coroner was evidently absolutely satisfied with himself at the marvellous way in which, after a quarter of an hour of firm yet very kind questionings, he had elicited from the witness what information he wanted.

"Mr. Errington was a friend of his wife. He was a gentleman of means, and seemed to have a great deal of time at his command. He himself did not particularly care about Mr. Errington, but he certainly had never made any observations to his wife on the subject.

"'But who is Mr. Errington?' repeated the coroner once more. 'What does he do? What is his business or profession?'

"'He has no business or profession.

"'What is his occupation, then?

"He has no special occupation. He has ample private means. But he has a great and very absorbing hobby.'

"'What is that?'

"'He spends all his time in chemical experiments, and is, I believe, as an amateur, a very distinguished toxicologist.'"

II.

"Did you ever see Mr. Errington, the gentleman so closely connected with the mysterious death on the Underground Railway?" asked the man in the corner as he placed one or two of his little snap-shot photos before Miss Polly Burton.

"There he is, to the very life. Fairly good-looking, a pleasant face enough, but ordinary, absolutely ordinary.

"It was this absence of any peculiarity which very nearly, but not quite, placed the halter round Mr. Errington's neck.

"But I am going too fast, and you will lose the thread.

"The public, of course, never heard how it actually came about that Mr. Errington, the wealthy bachelor of Albert Mansions, of the Grosvenor, and other young dandies' clubs, one fine day found himself before the magistrates at Bow Street, charged with being concerned in the death of Mary Beatrice Hazeldene, late of No. 19, Addison Row.

"I can assure you both press and public were literally flabbergasted. You see, Mr. Errington was a well-known and very popular member of a certain smart section of London society. He was a constant visitor at the opera, the racecourse, the Park, and the Carlton, he had a great many friends, and there was consequently quite a large attendance at the police court that morning.

"What had transpired was this:

"After the very scrappy bits of evidence which came to light at the inquest, two gentlemen bethought themselves that perhaps they had some duty to perform towards the State and the public generally. Accordingly they had come forward, offering to throw what light they could upon the mysterious affair on the Underground Railway.

"The police naturally felt that their information, such as it was, came rather late in the day, but as it proved of paramount importance, and the two gentlemen, moreover, were of undoubtedly good position in the world, they were thankful for what they could get, and acted accordingly; they accordingly brought Mr. Errington up before the magistrate on a charge of murder.

"The accused looked pale and worried when I first caught sight of him in the court that day, which was not to be wondered at, considering the terrible position in which he found himself.

"He had been arrested at Marseilles, where he was preparing to start for Colombo.

"I don't think he realized how terrible his position really was until later in the proceedings, when all the evidence relating to the arrest had been heard, and Emma Funnel had repeated her statement as to Mr. Errington's call at 19, Addison Row, in the morning, and Mrs. Hazeldene starting off for St. Paul's Churchyard at 3.30 in the afternoon.

"Mr. Hazeldene had nothing to add to the statements he had made at the coroner's inquest. He had last seen his wife alive on the morning of the fatal day. She had seemed very well and cheerful.

"I think every one present understood that he was trying to say as little as possible that could in any way couple his deceased wife's name with that of the accused.

"And yet, from the servant's evidence, it undoubtedly leaked out that Mrs. Hazeldene, who was young, pretty, and evidently fond of admiration, had once or twice annoyed her husband by her somewhat open, yet perfectly innocent, flirtation with Mr. Errington.

"I think every one was most agreeably impressed by the widower's moderate and dignified attitude. You will see his photo there, among this bundle. That is just how he appeared in court. In deep black, of course, but without any sign of ostentation in his mourning. He had allowed his beard to grow lately, and wore it closely cut in a point.

"After his evidence, the sensation of the day occurred. A tall, dark-haired man, with the word 'City' written metaphorically all over him, had kissed the book, and was waiting to tell the truth, and nothing but the truth.

"He gave his name as Andrew Campbell, head of the firm of Campbell & Co., brokers, of Throgmorton Street.

"In the afternoon of March 18th Mr. Campbell, travelling on the Underground Railway, had noticed a very pretty woman in the same carriage as himself. She had asked him if she was in the right train for Aldersgate. Mr. Campbell replied in the affirmative, and then buried himself in the Stock Exchange quotations of his evening paper.

"At Gower Street, a gentleman in a tweed suit and bowler hat got into the carriage, and took a seat opposite the lady.

"She seemed very much astonished at seeing him, but Mr. Andrew Campbell did not recollect the exact words she said.

"The two talked to one another a good deal, and certainly the lady appeared animated and cheerful. Witness took no notice of them; he was very much engrossed in some calculations, and finally got out at Farringdon Street. He noticed that the man in the tweed suit also got out close behind him, having shaken hands with the lady, and said in a pleasant way: '*Au revoir*! Don't be late tonight.' Mr. Campbell did not hear the lady's reply, and soon lost sight of the man in the crowd.

"Every one was on tenter-hooks, and eagerly waiting for the palpitating moment when witness would describe and identify the man who last had seen and spoken to the unfortunate woman, within five minutes probably of her strange and unaccountable death.

"Personally I knew what was coming before the Scotch stockbroker spoke.

"I could have jotted down the graphic and lifelike description he would give of a probable murderer. It would have fitted equally well the man who sat and had luncheon at this table just now; it would certainly have described five out of every ten young Englishmen you know.

"The individual was of medium height, he wore a moustache which was not very fair nor yet very dark, his hair was between colours. He wore a bowler hat, and a tweed suit—and—and—that was all—Mr. Campbell might perhaps know him again, but then again, he might not—he was not paying much attention—the gentleman was sitting on the same side of the carriage as himself—and he had his hat on all the time. He himself was busy with his newspaper—yes—he might know him again—but he really could not say.

"Mr. Andrew Campbell's evidence was not worth very much, you will say. No, it was not in itself, and would not have justified any arrest were it not for the additional statements made by Mr. James Verner, manager of Messrs. Rodney & Co., colour printers.

"Mr. Verner is a personal friend of Mr. Andrew Campbell, and it appears that at Farringdon Street, where he was waiting for his train, he saw Mr. Campbell get out of a first-class railway carriage. Mr. Verner spoke to him for a second, and then, just as the train was moving off, he stepped into the same compartment which had just been vacated by the stockbroker and the man in the tweed suit. He vaguely recollects a lady sitting in the opposite corner to his own, with her face turned away from him, apparently asleep, but he paid no special attention to her. He was like nearly all business men when they are travelling—engrossed in his paper. Presently a special quotation interested him; he wished to make a note of it, took out a pencil from his waistcoat pocket, and seeing a clean piece of paste-board on the floor, he picked it up, and scribbled on it the memorandum, which he wished to keep. He then slipped the card into his pocket-book.

"'It was only two or three days later,' added Mr. Verner in the midst of breathless silence, 'that I had occasion to refer to these same notes again.

"'In the meanwhile the papers had been full of the mysterious death on the Underground Railway, and the names of those connected with it were pretty familiar to me. It was, therefore, with much astonishment that on looking at the paste-board which I had casually picked up in the railway carriage I saw the name on it, "Frank Errington."'

"There was no doubt that the sensation in court was almost unprecedented. Never since the days of the Fenchurch Street mystery, and the trial of Smethurst, had I seen so much excitement. Mind you, I was not excited—I knew by now every detail of that crime as if I had committed it myself. In fact, I could not have done it better, although I have been a student of crime for many years now. Many people there—his friends, mostly—believed that Errington was doomed. I think he thought so, too, for I could see that his face was terribly white, and he now and then passed his tongue over his lips, as if they were parched.

"You see he was in the awful dilemma—a perfectly natural one, by the way—of being absolutely incapable of *proving* an *alibi*. The crime—if crime there was—had been committed three weeks ago. A man about town like Mr. Frank Errington might remember that he spent certain hours of a special afternoon at his club, or in the Park, but it is very doubtful in nine cases out of ten if he can find a friend who could positively swear as to having seen him there. No! no! Mr. Errington was in a tight corner, and he knew it. You see, there were—besides the evidence—two or three circumstances which did not improve matters for him. His hobby in the direction of toxicology, to begin with. The police had found in his room every description of poisonous substances, including prussic acid.

"Then, again, that journey to Marseilles, the start for Colombo, was, though perfectly innocent, a very unfortunate one. Mr. Errington had gone on an aimless voyage, but the public thought that he had fled, terrified at his own crime. Sir Arthur Inglewood, however, here again displayed his marvellous skill on behalf of his client by the masterly way in which he literally turned all the witnesses for the Crown inside out.

"Having first got Mr. Andrew Campbell to state positively that in the accused he certainly did *not* recognize the man in the tweed suit, the eminent lawyer, after twenty minutes' cross-examination, had so completely upset the stockbroker's equanimity that it is very likely he would not have recognized his own office-boy.

"But through all his flurry and all his annoyance Mr. Andrew Campbell remained very sure of one thing; namely, that the lady was alive and cheerful, and talking pleasantly with the man in the tweed suit up to the moment when the latter, having shaken hands with her, left her with a pleasant '*Au revoir*! Don't be late to-night.' He had heard neither scream nor struggle, and in his opinion, if the individual in the tweed suit had administered a dose of poison to his companion, it must have been with her own knowledge and free will; and the lady in the train most emphatically neither looked nor spoke like a woman prepared for a sudden and violent death.

"Mr. James Verner, against that, swore equally positively that he had stood in full view of the carriage door from the moment that Mr. Campbell got out until he himself stepped into the compartment, that there was no one else in that carriage between Farringdon Street and Aldgate, and that the lady, to the best of his belief, had made no movement during the whole of that journey.

"No; Frank Errington was *not* committed for trial on the capital charge," said the man in the corner with one of his sardonic smiles, "thanks to the cleverness of Sir Arthur Inglewood, his lawyer. He absolutely denied his identity with the man in the tweed suit, and swore he had not seen Mrs. Hazeldene since eleven o'clock in the morning of that fatal day. There was no *proof* that he had; moreover, according to Mr. Campbell's opinion, the man in the tweed suit was in all probability not the murderer. Common sense would not admit that a woman could have a deadly poison injected into her without her knowledge, while chatting pleasantly to her murderer.

"Mr. Errington lives abroad now. He is about to marry. I don't think any of his real friends for a moment believed that he committed the dastardly crime. The police think they know better. They do know this much, that it could not have been a case of suicide, that if the man who undoubtedly travelled with Mrs. Hazeldene on that fatal afternoon had no crime upon his conscience he would long ago have come forward and thrown what light he could upon the mystery.

"As to who that man was, the police in their blindness have not the faintest doubt. Under the unshakable belief that Errington is guilty they have spent the last few months in unceasing labour to try and find further and stronger proofs of his guilt. But they won't find them, because there are none. There are no positive proofs against the actual murderer, for he was one of those clever blackguards who think of everything, foresee every eventuality, who know human nature well, and can foretell exactly what evidence will be brought against them, and act accordingly.

"This blackguard from the first kept the figure, the personality, of Frank Errington before his mind. Frank Errington was the dust which the scoundrel threw metaphorically in the eyes of the police, and you must admit that he succeeded in blinding them—to the extent even of making them entirely forget the one simple little sentence, overheard by Mr. Andrew Campbell, and which was, of course, the clue to the whole thing—the only slip the cunning rogue made— '*Au revoir*! Don't be late to-night.' Mrs. Hazeldene was going that night to the opera with her husband—

"You are astonished?" he added with a shrug of the shoulders, "you do not see the tragedy yet, as I have seen it before me all along. The frivolous young wife, the flirtation with the friend?—all a blind, all pretence. I took the trouble which the police should have taken immediately, of finding out something about the finances of the Hazeldene *ménage*. Money is in nine cases out of ten the keynote to a crime.

"I found that the will of Mary Beatrice Hazeldene had been proved by the husband, her sole executor, the estate being sworn at £15,000. I found out, moreover, that Mr. Edward Sholto Hazeldene was a poor shipper's clerk when he married the daughter of a wealthy builder in Kensington—and then I made note of the fact that the disconsolate widower had allowed his beard to grow since the death of his wife.

"There's no doubt that he was a clever rogue," added the strange creature, leaning excitedly over the table, and peering into Polly's face. "Do you know how that deadly poison was injected into the poor woman's system? By the simplest of all means, one known to every scoundrel in Southern Europe. A ring—yes! a ring, which has a tiny hollow needle capable of holding a sufficient quantity of prussic acid to have killed two persons instead of one. The man in the tweed suit shook hands with his fair companion—probably she hardly felt the prick, not sufficiently in any case to make her utter a scream. And, mind you, the scoundrel had every facility, through his friendship with Mr. Errington, of procuring what poison he required, not to mention his friend's visiting card. We cannot gauge how many months ago he began to try and copy Frank Errington in his style of dress, the cut of his moustache, his general appearance, making the change probably so gradual, that no one in his own *entourage* would notice it. He selected for his model a man his own height and build, with the same coloured hair."

"But there was the terrible risk of being identified by his fellow-traveller in the Underground," suggested Polly.

"Yes, there certainly was that risk; he chose to take it, and he was wise. He reckoned that several days would in any case elapse before that person, who, by the way, was a business man absorbed in his newspaper, would actually see him again. The great secret of successful crime is to study human nature," added the man in the corner, as he began looking for his hat and coat. "Edward Hazeldene knew it well."

"But the ring?"

"He may have bought that when he was on his honeymoon," he suggested with a grim chuckle; "the tragedy was not planned in a week, it may have taken years to mature. But you will own that there goes a frightful scoundrel unhung. I have left you his photograph as he was a year ago, and as he is now. You will see he has shaved his beard again, but also his moustache. I fancy he is a friend now of Mr. Andrew Campbell."

He left Miss Polly Burton wondering, not knowing what to believe.

And that is why she missed her appointment with Mr. Richard Frobisher (of the *London Mail*) to go and see Maud Allan dance at the Palace Theatre that afternoon.

5
The Liverpool Mystery

I.

"A title—a foreign title, I mean—is always very useful for purposes of swindles and frauds," remarked the man in the corner to Polly one day. "The cleverest robberies of modern times were perpetrated lately in Vienna by a man who dubbed himself Lord Seymour; whilst over here the same class of thief calls himself Count Something ending in 'o,' or Prince the other, ending in 'off.'"

"Fortunately for our hotel and lodging-house keepers over here," she replied, "they are beginning to be more alive to the ways of foreign swindlers, and look upon all titled gentry who speak broken English as possible swindlers or thieves."

"The result sometimes being exceedingly unpleasant to the real *grands seigneurs* who honour this country at times with their visits," replied the man in the corner. "Now, take the case of Prince Semionicz, a man whose sixteen quarterings are duly recorded in Gotha, who carried enough luggage with him to pay for the use of every room in an hotel for at least a week, whose gold cigarette case with diamond and turquoise ornament was actually stolen without his taking the slightest trouble to try and recover it; that same man was undoubtedly looked upon with suspicion by the manager of the Liverpool North-Western Hotel from the moment that his secretary—a dapper, somewhat vulgar little Frenchman—bespoke on behalf of his employer, with himself and a valet, the best suite of rooms the hotel contained.

"Obviously those suspicions were unfounded, for the little secretary, as soon as Prince Semionicz had arrived, deposited with the manager a pile of bank notes, also papers and bonds, the value of which would exceed tenfold the most outrageous bill that could possibly be placed before the noble visitor. Moreover, M. Albert Lambert explained that the Prince, who only meant to stay in Liverpool a few days, was on his way to Chicago, where he wished to visit Princess Anna Semionicz, his sister, who was married to Mr. Girwan, the great copper king and multi-millionaire.

"Yet, as I told you before, in spite of all these undoubted securities, suspicion of the wealthy Russian Prince lurked in the minds of most Liverpudlians who came in business contact with him. He had been at the North-Western two days when he sent his secretary to Window and Vassall, the jewellers of Bold Street, with a request that they would kindly send a representative round to the hotel with some nice pieces of jewellery, diamonds and pearls chiefly, which he was desirous of taking as a present to his sister in Chicago.

"Mr. Winslow took the order from M. Albert with a pleasant bow. Then he went to his inner office and consulted with his partner, Mr. Vassall, as to the best course to adopt. Both the gentlemen were desirous of doing business, for business had been very slack lately: neither wished to refuse a possible customer, or to offend Mr. Pettitt, the manager of the North-Western, who had recommended them to the Prince. But that foreign title and the vulgar little French secretary stuck in the throats of the two pompous and worthy Liverpool jewellers, and together they agreed, firstly, that no credit should be given; and, secondly, that if a cheque or even a banker's draft were tendered, the jewels were not to be given up until that cheque or draft was cashed.

"Then came the question as to who should take the jewels to the hotel. It was altogether against business etiquette for the senior partners to do such errands themselves; moreover, it was thought that it would be easier for a clerk to explain, without giving undue offence, that he could not take the responsibility of a cheque or draft, without having cashed it previously to giving up the jewels.

"Then there was the question of the probable necessity of conferring in a foreign tongue. The head assistant, Charles Needham, who had been in the employ of Winslow and Vassall for over twelve years, was, in true British fashion, ignorant of any language save his own; it was therefore decided to dispatch Mr. Schwarz, a young German clerk lately arrived, on the delicate errand.

"Mr. Schwarz was Mr. Winslow's nephew and godson, a sister of that gentleman having married the head of the great German firm of Schwarz & Co., silversmiths, of Hamburg and Berlin.

"The young man had soon become a great favourite with his uncle, whose heir he would presumably be, as Mr. Winslow had no children.

"At first Mr. Vassall made some demur about sending Mr. Schwarz with so many valuable jewels alone in a city which he had not yet had the time to study thoroughly; but finally he allowed himself to be persuaded by his senior partner, and a fine selection of necklaces, pendants, bracelets, and rings, amounting in value to over £16,000, having been made, it was decided that Mr. Schwarz should go to the North-Western in a cab the next day at about three o'clock in the afternoon. This he accordingly did, the following day being a Thursday.

"Business went on in the shop as usual under the direction of the head assistant, until about seven o'clock, when Mr. Winslow returned from his club, where he usually spent an hour over the papers every afternoon, and at once asked for his nephew. To his astonishment Mr. Needham informed him that Mr. Schwarz had not yet returned. This seemed a little strange, and Mr. Winslow, with a slightly anxious look in his face, went into the inner office in order to consult his junior partner. Mr. Vassall offered to go round to the hotel and interview Mr. Pettitt.

"'I was beginning to get anxious myself,' he said, 'but did not quite like to say so. I have been in over half an hour, hoping every moment that you would come in, and that perhaps you could give me some reassuring news. I thought that perhaps you had met Mr. Schwarz, and were coming back together.'

"However, Mr. Vassall walked round to the hotel and interviewed the hall porter. The latter perfectly well remembered Mr. Schwarz sending in his card to Prince Semionicz.

"'At what time was that?' asked Mr. Vassall.

"'About ten minutes past three, sir, when he came; it was about an hour later when he left.'

"'When he left?' gasped, more than said, Mr. Vassall.

"'Yes, sir. Mr. Schwarz left here about a quarter before four, sir.'

"'Are you quite sure?'

"'Quite sure. Mr. Pettitt was in the hall when he left, and he asked him something about business. Mr. Schwarz laughed and said, "not bad." I hope there's nothing wrong, sir,' added the man.

"'Oh—er—nothing—thank you. Can I see Mr. Pettitt?'

"'Certainly, sir.'

"Mr. Pettitt, the manager of the hotel, shared Mr. Vassall's anxiety, immediately he heard that the young German had not yet returned home.

"'I spoke to him a little before four o'clock. We had just switched on the electric light, which we always do these winter months at that hour. But I shouldn't worry myself, Mr. Vassall; the young man may have seen to some business on his way home. You'll probably find him in when you go back.'

"Apparently somewhat reassured, Mr. Vassall thanked Mr. Pettitt and hurried back to the shop, only to find that Mr. Schwarz had not returned, though it was now close on eight o'clock.

"Mr. Winslow looked so haggard and upset that it would have been cruel to heap reproaches upon his other troubles or to utter so much as the faintest suspicion that young Schwarz's permanent disappearance with £16,000 in jewels and money was within the bounds of probability.

"There was one chance left, but under the circumstances a very slight one indeed. The Winslows' private house was up the Birkenhead end of the town. Young Schwarz had been living with them ever since his arrival in Liverpool, and he may have—either not feeling well or for some other reason—gone straight home without calling at the shop. It was unlikely, as valuable jewellery was never kept at the private house, but—it just might have happened.

"It would be useless," continued the man in the corner, "and decidedly uninteresting, were I to relate to you Messrs. Winslow's and Vassall's further anxieties with regard to the missing young man. Suffice it to say that on reaching his private house Mr. Winslow found that his godson had neither returned nor sent any telegraphic message of any kind.

"Not wishing to needlessly alarm his wife, Mr. Winslow made an attempt at eating his dinner, but directly after that he hurried back to the North-Western Hotel, and asked to see Prince Semionicz. The Prince was at the theatre with his secretary, and probably would not be home until nearly midnight.

"Mr. Winslow, then, not knowing what to think, nor yet what to fear, and in spite of the horror he felt of giving publicity to his nephew's disappearance, thought it his duty to go round to the police-station and interview the inspector. It is wonderful how quickly news of that type travels in a large city like Liverpool. Already the morning papers of the following day were full of the latest sensation: 'Mysterious disappearance of a well-known tradesman.'

"Mr. Winslow found a copy of the paper containing the sensational announcement on his breakfast-table. It lay side by side with a letter addressed to him in his nephew's handwriting, which had been posted in Liverpool.

"Mr. Winslow placed that letter, written to him by his nephew, into the hands of the police. Its contents, therefore, quickly became public property. The astounding statements made therein by Mr. Schwarz created, in quiet, businesslike Liverpool, a sensation which has seldom been equalled.

"It appears that the young fellow did call on Prince Semionicz at a quarter past three on Wednesday, December 10th, with a bag full of jewels, amounting in value to some £16,000. The Prince duly admired, and finally selected from among the ornaments a necklace, pendant, and bracelet, the whole being priced by Mr. Schwarz, according to his instructions, at £10,500. Prince Semionicz was most prompt and businesslike in his dealings.

"'You will require immediate payment for these, of course,' he said in perfect English, 'and I know you business men prefer solid cash to cheques, especially when dealing with foreigners. I always provide myself with plenty of Bank of England notes in consequence,' he added with a pleasant smile, 'as £10,500 in gold would perhaps be a little inconvenient to carry. If you will kindly make out the receipt, my secretary, M. Lambert, will settle all business matters with you.'

"He thereupon took the jewels he had selected and locked them up in his dressing-case, the beautiful silver fillings of which Mr. Schwarz just caught a short glimpse of. Then, having been accommodated with paper and ink, the young jeweller made out the account and receipt, whilst M. Lambert, the secretary, counted out before him 105 crisp Bank of England notes of £100 each. Then, with a final bow to his exceedingly urbane and eminently satisfactory customer, Mr. Schwarz took his leave. In the hall he saw and spoke to Mr. Pettitt, and then he went out into the street.

"He had just left the hotel and was about to cross towards St. George's Hall when a gentleman, in a magnificent fur coat, stepped quickly out of a cab which had been stationed near the kerb, and, touching him lightly upon the shoulder, said with an unmistakable air of authority, at the same time handing him a card:

"'That is my name. I must speak with you immediately."

"Schwarz glanced at the card, and by the light of the arc lamps above his head read on it the name of 'Dimitri Slaviansky Burgreneff, de la IIIe Section de la Police Imperial de S.M. le Czar.'

"Quickly the owner of the unpronounceable name and the significant title pointed to the cab from which he had just alighted, and Schwarz, whose every suspicion with regard to his princely customer bristled up in one moment, clutched his bag and followed his imposing interlocutor; as soon as they were both comfortably seated in the cab the latter began, with courteous apology in broken but fluent English:

"'I must ask your pardon, sir, for thus trespassing upon your valuable time, and I certainly should not have done so but for the certainty that our interests in a certain matter which I have in hand are practically identical, in so far that we both should wish to outwit a clever rogue.'

"Instinctively, and his mind full of terrible apprehension, Mr. Schwarz's hand wandered to his pocket-book, filled to overflowing with the bank-notes which he had so lately received from the Prince.

"'Ah, I see,' interposed the courteous Russian with a smile, 'he has played the confidence trick on you, with the usual addition of so many so-called bank-notes.'

"'So-called,' gasped the unfortunate young man.

"'I don't think I often err in my estimate of my own countrymen,' continued M. Burgreneff; 'I have vast experience, you must remember. Therefore, I doubt if I am doing M.—er—what does he call himself?—Prince something—an injustice if I assert, even without handling those crisp bits of paper you have in your pocket-book, that no bank would exchange them for gold.'

"Remembering his uncle's suspicions and his own, Mr. Schwarz cursed himself for his blindness and folly in accepting notes so easily without for a moment imagining that they might be false. Now, with every one of those suspicions fully on the alert, he felt the bits of paper with nervous, anxious fingers, while the imperturbable Russian calmly struck a match.

"'See here,' he said, pointing to one of the notes, 'the shape of that "w" in the signature of the chief cashier. I am not an English police officer, but I could pick out that spurious "w" among a thousand genuine ones. You see, I have seen a good many.'

"Now, of course, poor young Schwarz had not seen very many Bank of England notes. He could not have told whether one 'w' in Mr. Bowen's signature is better than another, but, though he did not speak English nearly as fluently as his pompous interlocutor, he understood every word of the appalling statement the latter had just made.

"'Then that Prince,' he said, 'at the hotel—'

"'Is no more Prince than you and I, my dear sir,' concluded the gentleman of His Imperial Majesty's police calmly.

"'And the jewels? Mr. Winslow's jewels?'

"'With the jewels there may be a chance—oh! a mere chance. These forged bank-notes, which you accepted so trustingly, may prove the means of recovering your property.'

"'How?'

"'The penalty of forging and circulating spurious bank-notes is very heavy. You know that. The fear of seven years' penal servitude will act as a wonderful sedative upon the—er—Prince's joyful mood. He will give up the jewels to me all right enough, never you fear. He knows,' added the Russian officer grimly, 'that there are plenty of old scores to settle up, without the additional one of forged bank-notes. Our interests, you see, are identical. May I rely on your co-operation?'

"'Oh, I will do as you wish,' said the delighted young German. 'Mr. Winslow and Mr. Vassall, they trusted me, and I have been such a fool. I hope it is not too late.'

"'I think not,' said M. Burgreneff, his hand already on the door of the cab. 'Though I have been talking to you I have kept an eye on the hotel, and our friend the Prince has not yet gone out. We are accustomed, you know, to have eyes everywhere, we of the Russian secret police. I don't think that I will ask you to be present at the confrontation. Perhaps you will wait for me in the cab. There is a nasty fog outside, and you will be more private. Will you give me those beautiful bank-notes? Thank you! Don't be anxious. I won't be long.'

"He lifted his hat, and slipped the notes into the inner pocket of his magnificent fur coat. As he did so, Mr. Schwarz caught sight of a rich uniform and a wide sash, which no doubt was destined to carry additional moral weight with the clever rogue upstairs.

"Then His Imperial Majesty's police officer stepped quickly out of the cab, and Mr. Schwarz was left alone."

II.

"Yes, left severely alone," continued the man in the corner with a sarcastic chuckle. "So severely alone, in fact, that one quarter of an hour after another passed by and still the magnificent police officer in the gorgeous uniform did not return. Then, when it was too late, Schwarz cursed himself once again for the double-dyed idiot that he was. He had been only too ready to believe that Prince Semionicz was a liar and a rogue, and under these unjust suspicions he had fallen an all too easy prey to one of the most cunning rascals he had ever come across.

"An inquiry from the hall porter at the North-Western elicited the fact that no such personage as Mr. Schwarz described had entered the hotel. The young man asked to see Prince Semionicz, hoping against hope that all was not yet lost. The Prince received him most courteously; he was dictating some letters to his secretary, while the valet was in the next room preparing his master's evening clothes. Mr. Schwarz found it very difficult to explain what he actually did want.

"There stood the dressing-case in which the Prince had locked up the jewels, and there the bag from which the secretary had taken the bank-notes. After much hesitation on Schwarz's part and much impatience on that of the Prince, the young man blurted out the whole story of the so-called Russian police officer whose card he still held in his hand.

"The Prince, it appears, took the whole thing wonderfully good-naturedly; no doubt he thought the jeweller a hopeless fool. He showed him the jewels, the receipt he held, and also a large bundle of bank-notes similar to those Schwarz had with such culpable folly given up to the clever rascal in the cab.

"'I pay all my bills with Bank of England notes, Mr. Schwarz. It would have been wiser, perhaps, if you had spoken to the manager of the hotel about me before you were so ready to believe any cock-and-bull story about my supposed rogueries.'

"Finally he placed a small 16mo volume before the young jeweller, and said with a pleasant smile:

"'If people in this country who are in a large way of business, and are therefore likely to come in contact with people of foreign nationality, were to study these little volumes before doing business with any foreigner who claims a title, much disappointment and a great loss would often be saved. Now in this case had you looked up page 797 of this little volume of Gotha's Almanach you would have seen my name in it and known from the first that the so-called Russian detective was a liar.'

"There was nothing more to be said, and Mr. Schwarz left the hotel. No doubt, now that he had been hopelessly duped he dared not go home, and half hoped by communicating with the police that they might succeed in arresting the thief before he had time to leave Liverpool. He interviewed Detective-Inspector Watson, and was at once confronted with the awful difficulty which would make the recovery of the bank-notes practically hopeless. He had never had the time or opportunity of jotting down the numbers of the notes.

"Mr. Winslow, though terribly wrathful against his nephew, did not wish to keep him out of his home. As soon as he had received Schwarz's letter, he traced him, with Inspector Watson's help, to his lodgings in North Street, where the unfortunate young man meant to remain hidden until the terrible storm had blown over, or perhaps until the thief had been caught red-handed with the booty still in his hands.

"This happy event, needless to say, never did occur, though the police made every effort to trace the man who had decoyed Schwarz into the cab. His appearance was such an uncommon one; it seemed most unlikely that no one in Liverpool should have noticed him after he left that cab. The wonderful fur coat, the long beard, all must have been noticeable, even though it was past four o'clock on a somewhat foggy December afternoon.

"But every investigation proved futile; no one answering Schwarz's description of the man had been seen anywhere. The papers continued to refer to the case as 'the Liverpool Mystery.' Scotland Yard sent Mr. Fairburn down—the celebrated detective—

at the request of the Liverpool police, to help in the investigations, but nothing availed.

"Prince Semionicz, with his suite, left Liverpool, and he who had attempted to blacken his character, and had succeeded in robbing Messrs. Winslow and Vassall of £10,500, had completely disappeared."

The man in the corner readjusted his collar and necktie, which, during the narrative of this interesting mystery, had worked its way up his long, crane-like neck under his large flappy ears. His costume of checked tweed of a peculiarly loud pattern had tickled the fancy of some of the waitresses, who were standing gazing at him and giggling in one corner. This evidently made him nervous. He gazed up very meekly at Polly, looking for all the world like a bald-headed adjutant dressed for a holiday.

"Of course, all sorts of theories of the theft got about at first. One of the most popular, and at the same time most quickly exploded, being that young Schwarz had told a cock-and-bull story, and was the actual thief himself.

"However, as I said before, that was very quickly exploded, as Mr. Schwarz senior, a very wealthy merchant, never allowed his son's carelessness to be a serious loss to his kind employers. As soon as he thoroughly grasped all the circumstances of the extraordinary case, he drew a cheque for £10,500 and remitted it to Messrs. Winslow and Vassall. It was just, but it was also high-minded.

"All Liverpool knew of the generous action, as Mr. Winslow took care that it should; and any evil suspicion regarding young Mr. Schwarz vanished as quickly as it had come.

"Then, of course, there was the theory about the Prince and his suite, and to this day I fancy there are plenty of people in Liverpool, and also in London, who declare that the so-called Russian police officer was a confederate. No doubt that theory was very plausible, and Messrs. Winslow and Vassall spent a good deal of money in trying to prove a case against the Russian Prince.

"Very soon, however, that theory was also bound to collapse. Mr. Fairburn, whose reputation as an investigator of crime waxes in direct inverted ratio to his capacities, did hit upon the obvious course of interviewing the managers of the larger London and Liverpool *agents de change*. He soon found that Prince Semionicz had converted a great deal of Russian and French money into English bank-notes since his arrival in this country. More than £30,000 in good solid, honest money was traced to the pockets of the gentleman with the sixteen quarterings. It seemed, therefore, more than improbable that a man who was obviously fairly wealthy would risk imprisonment and hard labour, if not worse, for the sake of increasing his fortune by £10,000.

"However, the theory of the Prince's guilt has taken firm root in the dull minds of our police authorities. They have had every information with regard to Prince Semionicz's antecedents from Russia; his position, his wealth, have been placed above suspicion, and yet they suspect and go on suspecting him or his secretary. They have communicated with the police of every European capital; and while they still hope to obtain sufficient evidence against those they suspect, they calmly allow the guilty to enjoy the fruit of his clever roguery."

"The guilty?" said Polly. "Who do you think—"

"Who do I think knew at that moment that young Schwarz had money in his possession?" he said excitedly, wriggling in his chair like a Jack-in-the-box. "Obviously some one was guilty of that theft who knew that Schwarz had gone to interview a rich Russian, and would in all probability return with a large sum of money in his possession?"

"Who, indeed, but the Prince and his secretary?" she argued. "But just now you said—"

"Just now I said that the police were determined to find the Prince and his secretary guilty; they did not look further than their own stumpy noses. Messrs. Winslow and Vassall spent money with a free hand in those investigations. Mr. Winslow, as the senior partner, stood to lose over £9000 by that robbery. Now, with Mr. Vassall it was different.

"When I saw how the police went on blundering in this case I took the trouble to make certain inquiries, the whole thing interested me so much, and I learnt all that I wished to know. I found out, namely, that Mr. Vassall was very much a junior partner in the firm, that he only drew ten per cent of the profits, having been promoted lately to a partnership from having been senior assistant.

"Now, the police did not take the trouble to find that out."

"But you don't mean that—"

"I mean that in all cases where robbery affects more than one person the first thing to find out is whether it affects the second party equally with the first. I proved that to you, didn't I, over that robbery in Phillimore Terrace? There, as here, one of the two parties stood to lose very little in comparison with the other—"

"Even then—" she began.

"Wait a moment, for I found out something more. The moment I had ascertained that Mr. Vassall was not drawing more than about £500 a year from the business profits I tried to ascertain at what rate he lived and what were his chief vices. I found that he kept a fine house in Albert Terrace. Now, the rents of those houses are £250 a year. Therefore speculation, horse-racing or some sort of gambling, must help to keep up that establishment. Speculation and most forms of gambling are synonymous with debt and ruin. It is only a question of time. Whether Mr. Vassall was in debt or not at the time, that I cannot say, but this I do know, that ever since that unfortunate loss to him of about £1000 he has kept his house in nicer style than before, and he now has a good banking account at the Lancashire and Liverpool bank, which he opened a year after his 'heavy loss.'"

"But it must have been very difficult—" argued Polly.

"What?" he said. "To have planned out the whole thing? For carrying it out was mere child's play. He had twenty-four hours in which to put his plan into execution. Why, what was there to do? Firstly, to go to a local printer in some out-of-the-way part of the town and get him to print a few cards with the high-sounding name. That, of course, is done 'while you wait.' Beyond that there was the purchase of a good second-hand uniform, fur coat, and a beard and a wig from a costumier's.

"No, no, the execution was not difficult; it was the planning of it all, the daring that was so fine. Schwarz, of course, was a foreigner; he had only been in England a little over a fortnight. Vassall's broken English misled him; probably he did not know the junior partner very intimately. I have no doubt that but for his uncle's absurd British prejudice and suspicions against the Russian Prince, Schwarz would not have been so ready to believe in the latter's roguery. As I said, it would be a great boon if English tradesmen studied Gotha more; but it was clever, wasn't it? I couldn't have done it much better myself."

That last sentence was so characteristic. Before Polly could think of some plausible argument against his theory he was gone, and she was trying vainly to find another solution to the Liverpool mystery.

6
The Edinburgh Mystery

I.

The man in the corner had not enjoyed his lunch. Miss Polly Burton could see that he had something on his mind, for, even before he began to talk that morning, he was fidgeting with his bit of string, and setting all her nerves on the jar.

"Have you ever felt real sympathy with a criminal or a thief?" he asked her after a while.

"Only once, I think," she replied, "and then I am not quite sure that the unfortunate woman who did enlist my sympathies was the criminal you make her out to be."

"You mean the heroine of the York mystery?" he replied blandly. "I know that you tried very hard that time to discredit the only possible version of that mysterious murder, the version which is my own. Now, I am equally sure that you have at the present moment no more notion as to who killed and robbed poor Lady Donaldson in Charlotte Square, Edinburgh, than the police have themselves, and yet you are fully prepared to pooh-pooh my arguments, and to disbelieve my version of the mystery. Such is the lady journalist's mind."

"If you have some cock-and-bull story to explain that extraordinary case," she retorted, "of course I shall disbelieve it. Certainly, if you are going to try and enlist my sympathies on behalf of Edith Crawford, I can assure you you won't succeed."

"Well, I don't know that that is altogether my intention. I see you are interested in the case, but I dare say you don't remember all the circumstances. You must forgive me if I repeat that which you know already. If you have ever been to Edinburgh at all, you will have heard of Graham's bank, and Mr. Andrew Graham, the present head of the firm, is undoubtedly one of the most prominent notabilities of 'modern Athens.'"

The man in the corner took two or three photos from his pocket-book and placed them before the young girl; then, pointing at them with his long bony finger—

"That," he said, "is Mr. Elphinstone Graham, the eldest son, a typical young Scotchman, as you see, and this is David Graham, the second son."

Polly looked more closely at this last photo, and saw before her a young face, upon which some lasting sorrow seemed already to have left its mark. The face was delicate and thin, the features pinched, and the eyes seemed almost unnaturally large and prominent.

"He was deformed," commented the man in the corner in answer to the girl's thoughts, "and, as such, an object of pity and even of repugnance to most of his friends. There was also a good deal of talk in Edinburgh society as to his mental condition, his mind, according to many intimate friends of the Grahams, being at times decidedly unhinged. Be that as it may, I fancy that his life must have been a very sad one; he had lost his mother when quite a baby, and his father seemed, strangely enough, to have an almost unconquerable dislike towards him.

"Every one got to know presently of David Graham's sad position in his father's own house, and also of the great affection lavished upon him by his godmother, Lady Donaldson, who was a sister of Mr. Graham's.

"She was a lady of considerable wealth, being the widow of Sir George Donaldson, the great distiller; but she seems to have been decidedly eccentric. Latterly she had astonished all her family—who were rigid Presbyterians—by announcing her intention of embracing the Roman Catholic faith, and then retiring to the convent of St. Augustine's at Newton Abbot in Devonshire.

"She had sole and absolute control of the vast fortune which a doting husband had bequeathed to her. Clearly, therefore, she was at liberty to bestow it upon a Devonshire convent if she chose. But this evidently was not altogether her intention.

"I told you how fond she was of her deformed godson, did I not? Being a bundle of eccentricities, she had many hobbies, none more pronounced than the fixed determination to see—before retiring from the world altogether—David Graham happily married.

"Now, it appears that David Graham, ugly, deformed, half-demented as he was, had fallen desperately in love with Miss Edith Crawford, daughter of the late Dr. Crawford, of Prince's Gardens. The young lady, however—very naturally, perhaps—fought shy of David Graham, who, about this time, certainly seemed very queer and morose, but Lady Donaldson, with characteristic determination, seems to have made up her mind to melt Miss Crawford's heart towards her unfortunate nephew.

"On October the 2nd last, at a family party given by Mr. Graham in his fine mansion in Charlotte Square, Lady Donaldson openly announced her intention of making over, by deed of gift, to her nephew, David Graham, certain property, money, and shares, amounting in total value to the sum of £100,000, and also her magnificent diamonds, which were worth £50,000, for the use of the said David's wife. Keith Macfinlay, a lawyer of Prince's Street, received the next day instructions for drawing up the necessary deed of gift, which she pledged herself to sign the day of her godson's wedding.

"A week later *The Scotsman* contained the following paragraph:—

> "'A marriage is arranged and will shortly take place between David, younger son of Andrew Graham, Esq., of Charlotte Square, Edinburgh, and Dochnakirk, Perthshire, and Edith Lillian, only surviving daughter of the late Dr. Kenneth Crawford, of Prince's Gardens.'

"In Edinburgh society comments were loud and various upon the forthcoming marriage, and, on the whole, these comments were far from complimentary to the families concerned. I do not think that the Scotch are a particularly sentimental race, but there was such obvious buying, selling, and bargaining about this marriage that Scottish chivalry rose in revolt at the thought.

"Against that the three people most concerned seemed perfectly satisfied. David Graham was positively transformed; his moroseness was gone from him, he lost his queer ways and wild manners, and became gentle and affectionate in the midst of this great and unexpected happiness. Miss Edith Crawford ordered her trousseau, and talked of the diamonds to her friends, and Lady Donaldson was only waiting for the consummation of this marriage—her heart's desire—before she finally retired from the world, at peace with it and with herself.

"The deed of gift was ready for signature on the wedding day, which was fixed for November 7th, and Lady Donaldson took up her abode temporarily in her brother's house in Charlotte Square.

"Mr. Graham gave a large ball on October 23rd. Special interest is attached to this ball, from the fact that for this occasion Lady Donaldson insisted that David's future wife should wear the magnificent diamonds which were soon to become hers.

"They were, it seems, superb, and became Miss Crawford's stately beauty to perfection. The ball was a brilliant success, the last guest leaving at four A.M. The next day it was the universal topic of conversation, and the day after that, when Edinburgh unfolded the late editions of its morning papers, it learned with horror and dismay that Lady Donaldson had been found murdered in her room, and that the celebrated diamonds had been stolen.

"Hardly had the beautiful little city, however, recovered from this awful shock, than its newspapers had another thrilling sensation ready for their readers.

"Already all Scotch and English papers had mysteriously hinted at 'startling information' obtained by the Procurator Fiscal, and at an 'impending sensational arrest.'

"Then the announcement came, and every one in Edinburgh read, horror-struck and aghast, that the 'sensational arrest' was none other than that of Miss Edith Crawford, for murder and robbery, both so daring and horrible that reason refused to believe that a young lady, born and bred in the best social circle, could have conceived, much less executed, so heinous a crime. She had been arrested in London at the Midland Hotel, and brought to Edinburgh, where she was judicially examined, bail being refused."

II.

"Little more than a fortnight after that, Edith Crawford was duly committed to stand her trial before the High Court of Justiciary. She had pleaded 'Not Guilty' at the pleading diet, and her defence was entrusted to Sir James Fenwick, one of the most eminent advocates at the Criminal Bar.

"Strange to say," continued the man in the corner after a while, "public opinion from the first went dead against the accused. The public is absolutely like a child, perfectly irresponsible and wholly illogical; it argued that since Miss Crawford had been ready to contract a marriage with a half-demented, deformed creature for the sake of his £100,000 she must have been equally ready to murder and rob an old lady for the sake of £50,000 worth of jewellery, without the encumbrance of so undesirable a husband.

"Perhaps the great sympathy aroused in the popular mind for David Graham had much to do with this ill-feeling against the accused. David Graham had, by this cruel and dastardly murder, lost the best—if not the only—friend he possessed. He had also lost at one fell swoop the large fortune which Lady Donaldson had been about to assign to him.

"The deed of gift had never been signed, and the old lady's vast wealth, instead of enriching her favourite nephew, was distributed—since she had made no will—amongst her heirs-at-law. And now to crown this long chapter of sorrow David Graham saw the girl he loved accused of the awful crime which had robbed him of friend and fortune.

"It was, therefore, with an unmistakable thrill of righteous satisfaction that Edinburgh society saw this 'mercenary girl' in so terrible a plight.

"I was immensely interested in the case, and journeyed down to Edinburgh in order to get a good view of the chief actors in the thrilling drama which was about to be unfolded there.

"I succeeded—I generally do—in securing one of the front seats among the audience, and was already comfortably installed in my place in court when through the trap door I saw the head of the prisoner emerge. She was very becomingly dressed in deep black, and, led by two policemen, she took her place in the dock. Sir James Fenwick shook hands with her very warmly, and I could almost hear him instilling words of comfort into her.

"The trial lasted six clear days, during which time more than forty persons were examined for the prosecution, and as many for the defence. But the most interesting witnesses were certainly the two doctors, the maid Tremlett, Campbell, the High Street jeweller, and David Graham.

"There was, of course, a great deal of medical evidence to go through. Poor Lady Donaldson had been found with a silk scarf tied tightly round her neck, her face showing even to the inexperienced eye every symptom of strangulation.

"Then Tremlett, Lady Donaldson's confidential maid, was called. Closely examined by Crown Counsel, she gave an account of the ball at Charlotte Square on the 23rd, and the wearing of the jewels by Miss Crawford on that occasion.

"'I helped Miss Crawford on with the tiara over her hair,' she said; 'and my lady put the two necklaces round Miss Crawford's neck herself. There were also some beautiful brooches, bracelets, and earrings. At four o'clock in the morning when the ball was over, Miss Crawford brought the jewels back to my lady's room. My lady had already gone to bed, and I had put out the electric light, as I was going, too. There was only one candle left in the room, close to the bed.

"'Miss Crawford took all the jewels off, and asked Lady Donaldson for the key of the safe, so that she might put them away. My lady gave her the key and said to me, "You can go to bed, Tremlett, you must be dead tired." I was glad to go, for I could hardly stand up—I was so tired. I said "Good night!" to my lady and also to Miss Crawford, who was busy putting the jewels away. As I was going out of the room I heard Lady Donaldson saying: "Have you managed it, my dear?" Miss Crawford said: "I have put everything away very nicely."'

"In answer to Sir James Fenwick, Tremlett said that Lady Donaldson always carried the key of her jewel safe on a ribbon round her neck, and had done so the whole day preceding her death.

"'On the night of the 24th,' she continued, 'Lady Donaldson still seemed rather tired, and went up to her room directly after dinner, and while the family were still sitting in the dining-room. She made me dress her hair, then she slipped on her dressing-gown and sat in the arm-chair with a book. She told me that she then felt strangely uncomfortable and nervous, and could not account for it.

"'However, she did not want me to sit with her, so I thought that the best thing I could do was to tell Mr. David Graham that her ladyship did not seem very cheerful. Her ladyship was so fond of Mr. David; it always made her happy to have him with her. I then went to my room, and at half-past eight Mr. David called me. He said: "Your mistress does seem a little restless to-night. If I were you I would just go and listen at her door in about an hour's time, and if she has not gone to bed I would go in and stay with her until she has." At about ten o'clock I did as Mr. David suggested, and listened at her ladyship's door. However, all was quiet in the room, and, thinking her ladyship had gone to sleep, I went back to bed.

"'The next morning at eight o'clock, when I took in my mistress's cup of tea, I saw her lying on the floor, her poor dear face all purple and distorted. I screamed, and the other servants came rushing along. Then Mr. Graham had the door locked and sent for the doctor and the police.'

"The poor woman seemed to find it very difficult not to break down. She was closely questioned by Sir James Fenwick, but had nothing further to say. She had last seen her mistress alive at eight o'clock on the evening of the 24th.

"'And when you listened at her door at ten o'clock,' asked Sir James, 'did you try to open it?'

"'I did, but it was locked,' she replied.

"'Did Lady Donaldson usually lock her bedroom at night?'

"'Nearly always.'

"'And in the morning when you took in the tea?'

"'The door was open. I walked straight in.'

"'You are quite sure?' insisted Sir James.

"'I swear it,' solemnly asserted the woman.

"After that we were informed by several members of Mr. Graham's establishment that Miss Crawford had been in to tea at Charlotte Square in the afternoon of the 24th, that she told every one she was going to London by the night mail, as she had some special shopping she wished to do there. It appears that Mr. Graham and David both tried to persuade her to stay to dinner, and then to go by the 9.10 P.M. from the Caledonian Station. Miss Crawford however had refused, saying she always preferred to go from the Waverley Station. It was nearer to her own rooms, and she still had a good deal of writing to do.

"In spite of this, two witnesses saw the accused in Charlotte Square later on in the evening. She was carrying a bag which seemed heavy, and was walking towards the Caledonian Railway Station.

"But the most thrilling moment in that sensational trial was reached on the second day, when David Graham, looking wretchedly ill, unkempt, and haggard, stepped into the witness-box. A murmur of sympathy went round the audience at sight of him, who was the second, perhaps, most deeply stricken victim of the Charlotte Square tragedy.

"David Graham, in answer to Crown Counsel, gave an account of his last interview with Lady Donaldson.

"'Tremlett had told me that she seemed anxious and upset, and I went to have a chat with her; she soon cheered up and....'

"There the unfortunate young man hesitated visibly, but after a while resumed with an obvious effort.

"'She spoke of my marriage, and of the gift she was about to bestow upon me. She said the diamonds would be for my wife, and after that for my daughter, if I had one. She also complained that Mr. Macfinlay had been so punctilious about preparing the deed of gift, and that it was a great pity the £100,000 could not just pass from her hands to mine without so much fuss.

"'I stayed talking with her for about half an hour; then I left her, as she seemed ready to go to bed; but I told her maid to listen at the door in about an hour's time.'

"There was deep silence in the court for a few moments, a silence which to me seemed almost electrical. It was as if, some time before it was uttered, the next question put by Crown Counsel to the witness had hovered in the air.

"'You were engaged to Miss Edith Crawford at one time, were you not?'

"One felt, rather than heard, the almost inaudible 'Yes' which escaped from David Graham's compressed lips.

"'Under what circumstances was that engagement broken off?'

"Sir James Fenwick had already risen in protest, but David Graham had been the first to speak.

"'I do not think that I need answer that question.'

"'I will put it in a different form, then,' said Crown Counsel urbanely— 'one to which my learned friend cannot possibly take exception. Did you or did you not on October 27th receive a letter from the accused, in which she desired to be released from her promise of marriage to you?'

"Again David Graham would have refused to answer, and he certainly gave no audible reply to the learned counsel's question; but every one in the audience there present—aye, every member of the jury and of the bar—read upon David Graham's pale countenance and large, sorrowful eyes that ominous 'Yes!' which had failed to reach his trembling lips."

III.

"There is no doubt," continued the man in the corner, "that what little sympathy the young girl's terrible position had aroused in the public mind had died out the moment that David Graham left the witness-box on the second day of the trial. Whether Edith Crawford was guilty of murder or not, the callous way in which she had accepted a deformed lover, and then thrown him over, had set every one's mind against her.

"It was Mr. Graham himself who had been the first to put the Procurator Fiscal in possession of the fact that the accused had written to David from London, breaking off her engagement. This information had, no doubt, directed the attention of the Fiscal to Miss Crawford, and the police soon brought forward the evidence which had led to her arrest.

"We had a final sensation on the third day, when Mr. Campbell, jeweller, of High Street, gave his evidence. He said that on October 25th a lady came to his shop and offered to sell him a pair of diamond earrings. Trade had been very bad, and he had refused the bargain, although the lady seemed ready to part with the earrings for an extraordinarily low sum, considering the beauty of the stones.

"In fact it was because of this evident desire on the lady's part to sell at *any* cost that he had looked at her more keenly than he otherwise would have done. He was now ready to swear that the lady that offered him the diamond earrings was the prisoner in the dock.

"I can assure you that as we all listened to this apparently damnatory evidence, you might have heard a pin drop amongst the audience in that crowded court. The girl alone, there in the dock, remained calm and unmoved. Remember that for two days we had heard evidence to prove that old Dr. Crawford had died leaving his daughter penniless, that having no mother she had been brought up by a maiden aunt, who had trained her to be a governess, which occupation she had followed for years, and that certainly she had never been known by any of her friends to be in possession of solitaire diamond earrings.

"The prosecution had certainly secured an ace of trumps, but Sir James Fenwick, who during the whole of that day had seemed to take little interest in the proceedings, here rose from his seat, and I knew at once that he had got a tit-bit in the way of a 'point' up his sleeve. Gaunt, and unusually tall, and with his beak-like nose, he always looks strangely impressive when he seriously tackles a witness. He did it this time with a vengeance, I can tell you. He was all over the pompous little jeweller in a moment.

"'Had Mr. Campbell made a special entry in his book, as to the visit of the lady in question?'

"'No.'

"'Had he any special means of ascertaining when that visit did actually take place?'

"'No—but—'

"'What record had he of the visit?'

"Mr. Campbell had none. In fact, after about twenty minutes of cross-examination, he had to admit that he had given but little thought to the interview with the lady at the time, and certainly not in connection with the murder of Lady Donaldson, until he had read in the papers that a young lady had been arrested.

"Then he and his clerk talked the matter over, it appears, and together they had certainly recollected that a lady had brought some beautiful earrings for sale on a day which *must have been* the very morning after the murder. If Sir James Fenwick's object was to discredit this special witness, he certainly gained his point.

"All the pomposity went out of Mr. Campbell, he became flurried, then excited, then he lost his temper. After that he was allowed to leave the court, and Sir James Fenwick resumed his seat, and waited like a vulture for its prey.

"It presented itself in the person of Mr. Campbell's clerk, who, before the Procurator Fiscal, had corroborated his employer's evidence in every respect. In Scotland no witness in any one case is present in court during the examination of another, and Mr. Macfarlane, the clerk, was, therefore, quite unprepared for the pitfalls which Sir James Fenwick had prepared for him. He tumbled into them, head foremost, and the eminent advocate turned him inside out like a glove.

"Mr. Macfarlane did not lose his temper; he was of too humble a frame of mind to do that, but he got into a hopeless quagmire of mixed recollections, and he too left the witness-box quite unprepared to swear as to the day of the interview with the lady with the diamond earrings.

"I dare say, mind you," continued the man in the corner with a chuckle, "that to most people present, Sir James Fenwick's cross-questioning seemed completely irrelevant. Both Mr. Campbell and his clerk were quite ready to swear that they had had an interview concerning some diamond earrings with a lady, of whose identity with the accused they were perfectly convinced, and to the casual observer the question as to the time or even the day when that interview took place could make but little difference in the ultimate issue.

"Now I took in, in a moment, the entire drift of Sir James Fenwick's defence of Edith Crawford. When Mr. Macfarlane left the witness-box, the second victim of the eminent advocate's caustic tongue, I could read as in a book the whole history of that crime, its investigation, and the mistakes made by the police first and the Public Prosecutor afterwards.

"Sir James Fenwick knew them, too, of course, and he placed a finger upon each one, demolishing—like a child who blows upon a house of cards—the entire scaffolding erected by the prosecution.

"Mr. Campbell's and Mr. Macfarlane's identification of the accused with the lady who, on some date—admitted to be uncertain—had tried to sell a pair of diamond earrings, was the first point. Sir James had plenty of witnesses to prove that on the 25th, the day after the murder, the accused was in London, whilst, the day before, Mr. Campbell's shop had been closed long before the family circle had seen the last of Lady Donaldson. Clearly the jeweller and his clerk must have seen some other lady, whom their vivid imagination had pictured as being identical with the accused.

"Then came the great question of time. Mr. David Graham had been evidently the last to see Lady Donaldson alive. He had spoken to her as late as 8.30 P.M. Sir James Fenwick had called two porters at the Caledonian Railway Station who testified to Miss Crawford having taken her seat in a first-class carriage of the 9.10 train, some minutes before it started.

"'Was it conceivable, therefore,' argued Sir James, 'that in the space of half an hour the accused—a young girl—could have found her way surreptitiously into the house, at a time when the entire household was still astir, that she should have strangled Lady Donaldson, forced open the safe, and made away with the jewels? A man—an experienced burglar might have done it, but I contend that the accused is physically incapable of accomplishing such a feat.

"'With regard to the broken engagement,' continued the eminent counsel with a smile, 'it may have seemed a little heartless, certainly, but heartlessness is no crime in the eyes of the law. The accused has stated in her declaration that at the time she wrote to Mr. David Graham, breaking off her engagement, she had heard nothing of the Edinburgh tragedy.

"'The London papers had reported the crime very briefly. The accused was busy shopping; she knew nothing of Mr. David Graham's altered position. In no case was the breaking off of the engagement a proof that the accused had obtained possession of the jewels by so foul a deed.'

"It is, of course, impossible for me," continued the man in the corner apologetically, "to give you any idea of the eminent advocate's eloquence and masterful logic. It struck every one, I think, just as it did me, that he chiefly directed his attention to the fact that there was absolutely no *proof* against the accused.

"Be that as it may, the result of that remarkable trial was a verdict of 'Non Proven.' The jury was absent forty minutes, and it appears that in the mind of every one of them there remained, in spite of Sir James' arguments, a firmly rooted conviction—call it instinct, if you like—that Edith Crawford had done away with Lady Donaldson in order to become possessed of those jewels, and that in spite of the pompous jeweller's many contradictions, she had offered him some of those diamonds for sale. But there was not enough proof to convict, and she was given the benefit of the doubt.

"I have heard English people argue that in England she would have been hanged. Personally I doubt that. I think that an English jury, not having the judicial loophole of 'Non Proven,' would have been bound to acquit her. What do you think?"

IV.

There was a moment's silence, for Polly did not reply immediately, and he went on making impossible knots in his bit of string. Then she said quietly—

"I think that I agree with those English people who say that an English jury would have condemned her.... I have no doubt that she was guilty. She may not have committed that awful deed herself. Some one in the Charlotte Square house may have been her accomplice and killed and robbed Lady Donaldson while Edith Crawford waited outside for the jewels. David Graham left his godmother at 8.30 P.M. If the accomplice was one of the servants in the house, he or she would have had plenty of time for any amount of villainy, and Edith Crawford could have yet caught the 9.10 P.M. train from the Caledonian Station."

"Then who, in your opinion," he asked sarcastically, and cocking his funny birdlike head on one side, "tried to sell diamond earrings to Mr. Campbell, the jeweller?"

"Edith Crawford, of course," she retorted triumphantly; "he and his clerk both recognized her."

"When did she try to sell them the earrings?"

"Ah, that is what I cannot quite make out, and there to my mind lies the only mystery in this case. On the 25th she was certainly in London, and it is not very likely that she would go back to Edinburgh in order to dispose of the jewels there, where they could most easily be traced."

"Not very likely, certainly," he assented drily.

"And," added the young girl, "on the day before she left for London, Lady Donaldson was alive."

"And pray," he said suddenly, as with comic complacency he surveyed a beautiful knot he had just twisted up between his long fingers, "what has that fact got to do with it?"

"But it has everything to do with it!" she retorted.

"Ah, there you go," he sighed with comic emphasis. "My teachings don't seem to have improved your powers of reasoning. You are as bad as the police. Lady Donaldson has been robbed and murdered, and you immediately argue that she was robbed and murdered by the same person."

"But—" argued Polly.

"There is no but," he said, getting more and more excited. "See how simple it is. Edith Crawford wears the diamonds one night, then she brings them back to Lady Donaldson's room. Remember the maid's statement: 'My lady said: "Have you put them back, my dear?"—a simple statement, utterly ignored by the prosecution. But what did it mean? That Lady Donaldson could not see for herself whether Edith Crawford had put back the jewels or not, *since she asked the question*."

"Then you argue—"

"I never argue," he interrupted excitedly; "I state undeniable facts. Edith Crawford, who wanted to steal the jewels, took them then and there, when she had the opportunity. Why in the world should she have waited? Lady Donaldson was in bed, and Tremlett, the maid, had gone.

"The next day—namely, the 25th—she tries to dispose of a pair of earrings to Mr. Campbell; she fails, and decides to go to London, where she has a better chance. Sir James Fenwick did not think it desirable to bring forward witnesses to prove what I have since ascertained is a fact, namely, that on the 27th of October, three days before her arrest, Miss Crawford crossed over to Belgium, and came back to London the next day. In Belgium, no doubt, Lady Donaldson's diamonds, taken out of their settings, calmly repose at this moment, while the money derived from their sale is safely deposited in a Belgian bank."

"But then, who murdered Lady Donaldson, and why?" gasped Polly.

"Cannot you guess?" he queried blandly. "Have I not placed the case clearly enough before you? To me it seems so simple. It was a daring, brutal murder, remember. Think of one who, not being the thief himself, would, nevertheless, have the strongest of all motives to shield the thief from the consequences of her own misdeed: aye! and the power too—since it would be absolutely illogical, nay, impossible, that he should be an accomplice."

"Surely—"

"Think of a curious nature, warped morally, as well as physically—do you know how those natures feel? A thousand times more strongly than the even, straight natures in everyday life. Then think of such a nature brought face to face with this awful problem.

"Do you think that such a nature would hesitate a moment before committing a crime to save the loved one from the consequences of that deed? Mind you, I don't assert for a moment that David Graham had any *intention* of murdering Lady Donaldson. Tremlett tells him that she seems strangely upset; he goes to her room and finds that she has discovered that she has been robbed. She naturally suspects Edith Crawford, recollects the incidents of the other night, and probably expresses her feelings to David Graham, and threatens immediate prosecution, scandal, what you will.

"I repeat it again, I dare say he had no wish to kill her. Probably he merely threatened to. A medical gentleman who spoke of sudden heart failure was no doubt right. Then imagine David Graham's remorse, his horror and his fears. The empty safe probably is the first object that suggested to him the grim tableau of robbery and murder, which he arranges in order to ensure his own safety.

"But remember one thing: no miscreant was seen to enter or leave the house surreptitiously; the murderer left no signs of entrance, and none of exit. An armed burglar would have left some trace—*some one* would have heard *something*. Then who locked and unlocked Lady Donaldson's door that night while she herself lay dead?

"Some one in the house, I tell you—some one who left no trace—some one against whom there could be no suspicion—some one who killed without apparently the slightest premeditation, and without the slightest motive. Think of it—I know I am right—and then tell me if I have at all enlisted your sympathies in the author of the Edinburgh Mystery."

He was gone. Polly looked again at the photo of David Graham. Did a crooked mind really dwell in that crooked body, and were there in the world such crimes that were great enough to be deemed sublime?

7
The Theft at the English Provident Bank

I.

"That question of motive is a very difficult and complicated one at times," said the man in the corner, leisurely pulling off a huge pair of flaming dog-skin gloves from his meagre fingers. "I have known experienced criminal investigators declare, as an infallible axiom, that to find the person interested in the committal of the crime is to find the criminal.

"Well, that may be so in most cases, but my experience has proved to me that there is one factor in this world of ours which is the mainspring of human actions, and that factor is human passions. For good or evil passions rule this poor humanity of ours. Remember, there are the women! French detectives, who are acknowledged masters in their craft, never proceed till after they have discovered the feminine element in a crime; whether in theft, murder, or fraud, according to their theory, there is always a woman.

"Perhaps the reason why the Phillimore Terrace robbery was never brought home to its perpetrators is because there was no woman in any way connected with it, and I am quite sure, on the other hand, that the reason why the thief at the English Provident Bank is still unpunished is because a clever woman has escaped the eyes of our police force."

He had spoken at great length and very dictatorially. Miss Polly Burton did not venture to contradict him, knowing by now that whenever he was irritable he was invariably rude, and she then had the worst of it.

"When I am old," he resumed, "and have nothing more to do, I think I shall take professionally to the police force; they have much to learn."

Could anything be more ludicrous than the self-satisfaction, the abnormal conceit of this remark, made by that shrivelled piece of mankind, in a nervous, hesitating tone of voice? Polly made no comment, but drew from her pocket a beautiful piece of string, and knowing his custom of knotting such an article while unravelling his mysteries, she handed it across the table to him. She positively thought that he blushed.

"As an adjunct to thought," she said, moved by a conciliatory spirit.

He looked at the invaluable toy which the young girl had tantalisingly placed close to his hand: then he forced himself to look all round the coffee-room: at Polly, at the waitresses, at the piles of pallid buns upon the counter. But, involuntarily, his mild blue eyes wandered back lovingly to the long piece of string, on which his playful imagination no doubt already saw a series of knots which would be equally tantalising to tie and to untie.

"Tell me about the theft at the English Provident Bank," suggested Polly condescendingly.

He looked at her, as if she had proposed some mysterious complicity in an unheard-of crime. Finally his lean fingers sought the end of the piece of string, and drew it towards him. His face brightened up in a moment.

"There was an element of tragedy in that particular robbery," he began, after a few moments of beatified knotting, "altogether different to that connected with most crimes; a tragedy which, as far as I am concerned, would seal my lips for ever, and forbid them to utter a word, which might lead the police on the right track."

"Your lips," suggested Polly sarcastically, "are, as far as I can see, usually sealed before our long-suffering, incompetent police and—"

"And you should be the last to grumble at this," he quietly interrupted, "for you have spent some very pleasant half-hours already, listening to what you have termed my 'cock-and-bull' stories. You know the English Provident Bank, of course, in Oxford Street; there were plenty of sketches of it at the time in the illustrated papers. Here is a photo of the outside. I took it myself some time ago, and only wish I had been cheeky or lucky enough to get a snap-shot of the interior. But you see that the office has a separate entrance from the rest of the house, which was, and still is, as is usual in such cases, inhabited by the manager and his family.

"Mr. Ireland was the manager then; it was less than six months ago. He lived over the bank, with his wife and family, consisting of a son, who was clerk in the business, and two or three younger children. The house is really smaller than it looks on this photo, for it has no depth, and only one set of rooms on each floor looking out into the street, the back of the house being nothing but the staircase. Mr. Ireland and his family, therefore, occupied the whole of it.

"As for the business premises, they were, and, in fact, are, of the usual pattern; an office with its rows of desks, clerks, and cashiers, and beyond, through a glass door, the manager's private room, with the ponderous safe, and desk, and so on.

"The private room has a door into the hall of the house, so that the manager is not obliged to go out into the street in order to go to business. There are no living-rooms on the ground floor, and the house has no basement.

"I am obliged to put all these architectural details before you, though they may sound rather dry and uninteresting, but they are really necessary in order to make my argument clear.

"At night, of course, the bank premises are barred and bolted against the street, and as an additional precaution there is always a night watchman in the office. As I mentioned before, there is only a glass door between the office and the manager's private room. This, of course, accounted for the fact that the night watchman heard all that he did hear, on that memorable night, and so helped further to entangle the thread of that impenetrable mystery.

"Mr. Ireland as a rule went into his office every morning a little before ten o'clock, but on that particular morning, for some reason which he never could or would explain, he went down before having his breakfast at about nine o'clock. Mrs. Ireland stated subsequently that, not hearing him return, she sent the servant down to tell the master that breakfast was getting cold. The girl's shrieks were the first intimation that something alarming had occurred.

"Mrs. Ireland hastened downstairs. On reaching the hall she found the door of her husband's room open, and it was from there that the girl's shrieks proceeded.

"'The master, mum—the poor master—he is dead, mum—I am sure he is dead!'—accompanied by vigorous thumps against the glass partition, and not very measured language on the part of the watchman from the outer office, such as— 'Why don't you open the door instead of making that row?'

"Mrs. Ireland is not the sort of woman who, under any circumstances, would lose her presence of mind. I think she proved that throughout the many trying circumstances connected with the investigation of the case. She gave only one glance at the room and realized the situation. On the arm-chair, with head thrown back and eyes closed, lay Mr. Ireland, apparently in a dead faint; some terrible shock must have very suddenly shattered his nervous system, and rendered him prostrate for the moment. What that shock had been it was pretty easy to guess.

"The door of the safe was wide open, and Mr. Ireland had evidently tottered and fainted before some awful fact which the open safe had revealed to him; he had caught himself against a chair which lay on the floor, and then finally sunk, unconscious, into the arm-chair.

"All this, which takes some time to describe," continued the man in the corner, "took, remember, only a second to pass like a flash through Mrs. Ireland's mind; she quickly turned the key of the glass door, which was on the inside, and with the help of James Fairbairn, the watchman, she carried her husband upstairs to his room, and immediately sent both for the police and for a doctor.

"As Mrs. Ireland had anticipated, her husband had received a severe mental shock which had completely prostrated him. The doctor prescribed absolute quiet, and forbade all worrying questions for the present. The patient was not a young man; the shock had been very severe—it was a case, a very slight one, of cerebral congestion—and Mr. Ireland's reason, if not his life, might be gravely jeopardised by any attempt to recall before his enfeebled mind the circumstances which had preceded his collapse.

"The police therefore could proceed but slowly in their investigations. The detective who had charge of the case was necessarily handicapped, whilst one of the chief actors concerned in the drama was unable to help him in his work.

"To begin with, the robber or robbers had obviously not found their way into the manager's inner room through the bank premises. James Fairbairn had been on the watch all night, with the electric light full on, and obviously no one could have crossed the outer office or forced the heavily barred doors without his knowledge.

"There remained the other access to the room, that is, the one through the hall of the house. The hall door, it appears, was always barred and bolted by Mr. Ireland himself when he came home, whether from the theatre or his club. It was a duty he never allowed any one to perform but himself. During his annual holiday, with his wife and family, his son, who usually had the sub-manager to stay with him on those occasions, did the bolting and barring—but with the distinct understanding that this should be done by ten o'clock at night.

"As I have already explained to you, there is only a glass partition between the general office and the manager's private room, and, according to James Fairbairn's account, this was naturally always left wide open so that he, during his night watch, would of necessity hear the faintest sound. As a rule there was no light left in the manager's room, and the other door—that leading into the hall—was bolted from the inside by James Fairbairn the moment he had satisfied himself that the premises were safe, and he had begun his night-watch. An electric bell in both the offices communicated with Mr. Ireland's bedroom and that of his son, Mr. Robert Ireland, and there was a telephone installed to the nearest district messengers' office, with an understood signal which meant 'Police.'

"At nine o'clock in the morning it was the night watchman's duty, as soon as the first cashier had arrived, to dust and tidy the manager's room, and to undo the bolts; after that he was free to go home to his breakfast and rest.

"You will see, of course, that James Fairbairn's position in the English Provident Bank is one of great responsibility and trust; but then in every bank and business house there are men who hold similar positions. They are always men of well-known and tried characters, often old soldiers with good-conduct records behind them. James Fairbairn is a fine, powerful Scotchman; he had been night watchman to the English Provident Bank for fifteen years, and was then not more than forty-three or forty-four years old. He is an ex-guardsman, and stands six feet three inches in his socks.

"It was his evidence, of course, which was of such paramount importance, and which somehow or other managed, in spite of the utmost care exercised by the police, to become public property, and to cause the wildest excitement in banking and business circles.

"James Fairbairn stated that at eight o'clock in the evening of March 25th, having bolted and barred all the shutters and the door of the back premises, he was about to lock the manager's door as usual, when Mr. Ireland called to him from the floor above, telling him to leave that door open, as he might want to go into the office again for a minute when he came home at eleven o'clock. James Fairbairn asked if he should leave the light on, but Mr. Ireland said: 'No, turn it out. I can switch it on if I want it.'

"The night watchman at the English Provident Bank has permission to smoke, he also is allowed a nice fire, and a tray consisting of a plate of substantial sandwiches and one glass of ale, which he can take when he likes. James Fairbairn settled himself in front of the fire, lit his pipe, took out his newspaper, and began to read. He thought he had heard the street door open and shut at about a quarter to ten; he supposed that it was Mr. Ireland going out to his club, but at ten minutes to ten o'clock the watchman heard the door of the manager's room open, and some one enter, immediately closing the glass partition door and turning the key.

"He naturally concluded it was Mr. Ireland himself.

"From where he sat he could not see into the room, but he noticed that the electric light had not been switched on, and that the manager seemingly had no light but an occasional match.

"'For the minute,' continued James Fairbairn, 'a thought did just cross my mind that something might perhaps be wrong, and I put my newspaper aside and went to the other end of the room towards the glass partition. The manager's room was still quite dark, and I could not clearly see into it, but the door into the hall was open, and there was, of course, a light through there. I had got quite close to the partition, when I saw Mrs. Ireland standing in the doorway, and heard her saying in a very astonished tone of voice: 'Why, Lewis, I thought you had gone to your club ages ago. What in the world are you doing here in the dark?'

"'Lewis is Mr. Ireland's Christian name,' was James Fairbairn's further statement. 'I did not hear the manager's reply, but quite satisfied now that nothing was wrong, I went back to my pipe and my newspaper. Almost directly afterwards I heard the manager leave his room, cross the hall and go out by the street door. It was only after he had gone that I recollected that he must have forgotten to unlock the glass partition and that I could not therefore bolt the door into the hall the same as usual, and I suppose that is how those confounded thieves got the better of me.'"

II.

"By the time the public had been able to think over James Fairbairn's evidence, a certain disquietude and unrest had begun to make itself felt both in the bank itself and among those of our detective force who had charge of the case. The newspapers spoke of the matter with very obvious caution, and warned all their readers to await the further development of this sad case.

"While the manager of the English Provident Bank lay in such a precarious condition of health, it was impossible to arrive at any definite knowledge as to what the thief had actually made away with. The chief cashier, however, estimated the loss at about £5000 in gold and notes of the bank money—that was, of course, on the assumption that Mr. Ireland had no private money or valuables of his own in the safe.

"Mind you, at this point public sympathy was much stirred in favour of the poor man who lay ill, perhaps dying, and yet whom, strangely enough, suspicion had already slightly touched with its poisoned wing.

"Suspicion is a strong word, perhaps, to use at this point in the story. No one suspected anybody at present. James Fairbairn had told his story, and had vowed that some thief with false keys must have sneaked through the house into the inner office.

"Public excitement, you will remember, lost nothing by waiting. Hardly had we all had time to wonder over the night watchman's singular evidence, and, pending further and fuller detail, to check our growing sympathy for the man who was ill, than the sensational side of this mysterious case culminated in one extraordinary, absolutely unexpected fact. Mrs. Ireland, after a twenty-four hours' untiring watch beside her husband's sick bed, had at last been approached by the detective, and been asked to reply to a few simple questions, and thus help to throw some light on the mystery which had caused Mr. Ireland's illness and her own consequent anxiety.

"She professed herself quite ready to reply to any questions put to her, and she literally astounded both inspector and detective when she firmly and emphatically declared that James Fairbairn must have been dreaming or asleep when he thought he saw her in the doorway at ten o'clock that night, and fancied he heard her voice.

"She may or may not have been down in the hall at that particular hour, for she usually ran down herself to see if the last post had brought any letters, but most certainly she had neither seen nor spoken to Mr. Ireland at that hour, for Mr. Ireland had gone out an hour before, she herself having seen him to the front door. Never for a moment did she swerve from this extraordinary statement. She spoke to James Fairbairn in the presence of the detective, and told him he *must* absolutely have been mistaken, that she had *not* seen Mr. Ireland, and that she had *not* spoken to him.

"One other person was questioned by the police, and that was Mr. Robert Ireland, the manager's eldest son. It was presumed that he would know something of his father's affairs; the idea having now taken firm hold of the detective's mind that perhaps grave financial difficulties had tempted the unfortunate manager to appropriate some of the firm's money.

"Mr. Robert Ireland, however, could not say very much. His father did not confide in him to the extent of telling him all his private affairs, but money never seemed scarce at home certainly, and Mr. Ireland had, to his son's knowledge, not a single extravagant habit. He himself had been dining out with a friend on that memorable evening, and had gone on with him to the Oxford Music Hall. He met his father on the doorstep of the bank at about 11.30 P.M. and they went in together. There certainly was nothing remarkable about Mr. Ireland then, his son averred; he appeared in no way excited, and bade his son good night quite cheerfully.

"There was the extraordinary, the remarkable hitch," continued the man in the corner, waxing more and more excited every moment. "The public—who is at times very dense—saw it clearly nevertheless: of course, every one at once jumped to the natural conclusion that Mrs. Ireland was telling a lie—a noble lie, a self-sacrificing lie, a lie endowed with all the virtues if you like, but still a lie.

"She was trying to save her husband, and was going the wrong way to work. James Fairbairn, after all, could not have dreamt quite all that he declared he had seen and heard. No one suspected James Fairbairn; there was no occasion to do that; to begin with he was a great heavy Scotchman with obviously no powers of invention, such as Mrs. Ireland's strange assertion credited him with; moreover, the theft of the bank-notes could not have been of the slightest use to him.

"But, remember, there was the hitch; without it the public mind would already have condemned the sick man upstairs, without hope of rehabilitation. This fact struck every one.

"Granting that Mr. Ireland had gone into his office at ten minutes to ten o'clock at night for the purpose of extracting £5000 worth of notes and gold from the bank safe, whilst giving the theft the appearance of a night burglary; granting that he was disturbed in his nefarious project by his wife, who, failing to persuade him to make restitution, took his side boldly, and very clumsily attempted to rescue him out of his difficult position—why should he, at nine o'clock the following morning, fall in a dead faint and get cerebral congestion at sight of a defalcation he knew had occurred? One might simulate a fainting fit, but no one can assume a high temperature and a congestion, which the most ordinary practitioner who happened to be called in would soon see were non-existent.

"Mr. Ireland, according to James Fairbairn's evidence, must have gone out soon after the theft, come in again with his son an hour and a half later, talked to him, gone quietly to bed, and waited for nine hours before he fell ill at sight of his own crime. It was not logical, you will admit. Unfortunately, the poor man himself was unable to give any explanation of the night's tragic adventures.

"He was still very weak, and though under strong suspicion, he was left, by the doctor's orders, in absolute ignorance of the heavy charges which were gradually accumulating against him. He had made many anxious inquiries from all those who had access to his bedside as to the result of the investigation, and the probable speedy capture of the burglars, but every one had strict orders to inform him merely that the police so far had no clue of any kind.

"You will admit, as every one did, that there was something very pathetic about the unfortunate man's position, so helpless to defend himself, if defence there was, against so much overwhelming evidence. That is why I think public sympathy remained with him. Still, it was terrible to think of his wife presumably knowing him to be guilty, and anxiously waiting whilst dreading the moment when, restored to health, he would have to face the doubts, the suspicions, probably the open accusations, which were fast rising up around him."

III.

"It was close on six weeks before the doctor at last allowed his patient to attend to the grave business which had prostrated him for so long.

"In the meantime, among the many people who directly or indirectly were made to suffer in this mysterious affair, no one, I think, was more pitied, and more genuinely sympathised with, than Robert Ireland, the manager's eldest son.

"You remember that he had been clerk in the bank? Well, naturally, the moment suspicion began to fasten on his father his position in the business became untenable. I think every one was very kind to him. Mr. Sutherland French, who was made acting manager 'during Mr. Lewis Ireland's regrettable absence,' did everything in his power to show his goodwill and sympathy to the young man, but I don't think that he or any one else was much astonished when, after Mrs. Ireland's extraordinary attitude in the case had become public property, he quietly intimated to the acting manager that he had determined to sever his connection with the bank.

"The best of recommendations was, of course, placed at his disposal, and it was finally understood that, as soon as his father was completely restored to health and would no longer require his presence in London, he would try to obtain employment somewhere abroad. He spoke of the new volunteer corps organized for the military policing of the new colonies, and, truth to tell, no one could blame him that he should wish to leave far behind him all London banking connections. The son's attitude certainly did not tend to ameliorate the father's position. It was pretty evident that his own family had ceased to hope in the poor manager's innocence.

"And yet he was absolutely innocent. You must remember how that fact was clearly demonstrated as soon as the poor man was able to say a word for himself. And he said it to some purpose, too.

"Mr. Ireland was, and is, very fond of music. On the evening in question, while sitting in his club, he saw in one of the daily papers the announcement of a peculiarly attractive programme at the Queen's Hall concert. He was not dressed, but nevertheless felt an irresistible desire to hear one or two of these attractive musical items, and he strolled down to the Hall. Now, this sort of alibi is usually very difficult to prove, but Dame Fortune, oddly enough, favoured Mr. Ireland on this occasion, probably to compensate him for the hard knocks she had been dealing him pretty freely of late.

"It appears that there was some difficulty about his seat, which was sold to him at the box office, and which he, nevertheless, found wrongfully occupied by a determined lady, who refused to move. The management had to be appealed to; the attendants also remembered not only the incident, but also the face and appearance of the gentleman who was the innocent cause of the altercation.

"As soon as Mr. Ireland could speak for himself he mentioned the incident and the persons who had been witness to it. He was identified by them, to the amazement, it must be confessed, of police and public alike, who had comfortably decided that no one *could* be guilty save the manager of the Provident Bank himself. Moreover, Mr. Ireland was a fairly wealthy man, with a good balance at the Union Bank, and plenty of private means, the result of years of provident living.

"He had but to prove that if he really had been in need of an immediate £5000—which was all the amount extracted from the bank safe that night—he had plenty of securities on which he could, at an hour's notice, have raised twice that sum. His life insurances had been fully paid up; he had not a debt which a £5 note could not easily have covered.

"On the fatal night he certainly did remember asking the watchman not to bolt the door to his office, as he thought he might have one or two letters to write when he came home, but later on he had forgotten all about this. After the concert he met his son in Oxford Street, just outside the house, and thought no more about the office, the door of which was shut, and presented no unusual appearance.

"Mr. Ireland absolutely denied having been in his office at the hour when James Fairbairn positively asserted he heard Mrs. Ireland say in an astonished tone of voice: 'Why, Lewis, what in the world are you doing here?' It became pretty clear therefore that

James Fairbairn's view of the manager's wife had been a mere vision.

"Mr. Ireland gave up his position as manager of the English Provident: both he and his wife felt no doubt that on the whole, perhaps, there had been too much talk, too much scandal connected with their name, to be altogether advantageous to the bank. Moreover, Mr. Ireland's health was not so good as it had been. He has a pretty house now at Sittingbourne, and amuses himself during his leisure hours with amateur horticulture, and I, who alone in London besides the persons directly connected with this mysterious affair, know the true solution of the enigma, often wonder how much of it is known to the ex-manager of the English Provident Bank."

The man in the corner had been silent for some time. Miss Polly Burton, in her presumption, had made up her mind, at the commencement of his tale, to listen attentively to every point of the evidence in connection with the case which he recapitulated before her, and to follow the point, in order to try and arrive at a conclusion of her own, and overwhelm the antediluvian scarecrow with her sagacity.

She said nothing, for she had arrived at no conclusion; the case puzzled every one, and had amazed the public in its various stages, from the moment when opinion began to cast doubt on Mr. Ireland's honesty to that when his integrity was proved beyond a doubt. One or two people had suspected Mrs. Ireland to have been the actual thief, but that idea had soon to be abandoned.

Mrs. Ireland had all the money she wanted; the theft occurred six months ago, and not a single bank-note was ever traced to her pocket; moreover, she must have had an accomplice, since some one else was in the manager's room that night; and if that some one else was her accomplice, why did she risk betraying him by speaking loudly in the presence of James Fairbairn, when it would have been so much simpler to turn out the light and plunge the hall into darkness?

"You are altogether on the wrong track," sounded a sharp voice in direct answer to Polly's thoughts— "altogether wrong. If you want to acquire my method of induction, and improve your reasoning power, you must follow my system. First think of the one absolutely undisputed, positive fact. You must have a starting-point, and not go wandering about in the realms of suppositions."

"But there are no positive facts," she said irritably.

"You don't say so?" he said quietly. "Do you not call it a positive fact that the bank safe was robbed of £5000 on the evening of March 25th before 11.30 P.M."

"Yes, that is all which is positive and—"

"Do you not call it a positive fact," he interrupted quietly, "that the lock of the safe not being picked, it must have been opened by its own key?"

"I know that," she rejoined crossly, "and that is why every one agreed that James Fairbairn could not possibly—"

"And do you not call it a positive fact, then, that James Fairbairn could not possibly, etc., etc., seeing that the glass partition door was locked from the inside; Mrs. Ireland herself let James Fairbairn into her husband's office when she saw him lying fainting before the open safe. Of course that was a positive fact, and so was the one that proved to any thinking mind that if that safe was opened with a key, it could only have been done by a person having access to that key."

"But the man in the private office—"

"Exactly! the man in the private office. Enumerate his points, if you please," said the funny creature, marking each point with one of his favourite knots. "He was a man who might that night have had access to the key of the safe, unsuspected by the manager or even his wife, and a man for whom Mrs. Ireland was willing to tell a downright lie. Are there many men for whom a woman of the better middle class, and an Englishwoman, would be ready to perjure herself? Surely not! She might do it for her husband. The public thought she had. It never struck them that she might have done it for her son!"

"Her son!" exclaimed Polly.

"Ah! she was a clever woman," he ejaculated enthusiastically, "one with courage and presence of mind, which I don't think I have ever seen equalled. She runs downstairs before going to bed in order to see whether the last post has brought any letters. She sees the door of her husband's office ajar, she pushes it open, and there, by the sudden flash of a hastily struck match she realizes in a moment that a thief stands before the open safe, and in that thief she has already recognized her son. At that very moment she hears the watchman's step approaching the partition. There is no time to warn her son; she does not know the glass door is locked; James Fairbairn may switch on the electric light and see the young man in the very act of robbing his employers' safe.

"One thing alone can reassure the watchman. One person alone had the right to be there at that hour of the night, and without hesitation she pronounces her husband's name.

"Mind you, I firmly believe that at the time the poor woman only wished to gain time, that she had every hope that her son had not yet had the opportunity to lay so heavy a guilt upon his conscience.

"What passed between mother and son we shall never know, but this much we do know, that the young villain made off with his booty, and trusted that his mother would never betray him. Poor woman! what a night of it she must have spent; but she was clever and far-seeing. She knew that her husband's character could not suffer through her action. Accordingly, she took the only course open to her to save her son even from his father's wrath, and boldly denied James Fairbairn's statement.

"Of course, she was fully aware that her husband could easily clear himself, and the worst that could be said of her was that she had thought him guilty and had tried to save him. She trusted to the future to clear her of any charge of complicity in the theft.

"By now every one has forgotten most of the circumstances; the police are still watching the career of James Fairbairn and Mrs. Ireland's expenditure. As you know, not a single note, so far, has been traced to her. Against that, one or two of the notes have found their way back to England. No one realizes how easy it is to cash English bank-notes at the smaller *agents de change* abroad. The *changeurs* are only too glad to get them; what do they care where they come from as long as they are genuine? And a week or two later *M. le Changeur* could not swear who tendered him any one particular note.

"You see, young Robert Ireland went abroad, he will come back some day having made a fortune. There's his photo. And this is his mother—a clever woman, wasn't she?"

And before Polly had time to reply he was gone. She really had never seen any one move across a room so quickly. But he always left an interesting trail behind: a piece of string knotted from end to end and a few photos.

8

The Dublin Mystery

I.

"I always thought that the history of that forged will was about as interesting as any I had read," said the man in the corner that day. He had been silent for some time, and was meditatively sorting and looking through a packet of small photographs in his pocket-book. Polly guessed that some of these would presently be placed before her for inspection—and she had not long to wait.

"That is old Brooks," he said, pointing to one of the photographs, "Millionaire Brooks, as he was called, and these are his two sons, Percival and Murray. It was a curious case, wasn't it? Personally I don't wonder that the police were completely at sea. If a member of that highly estimable force happened to be as clever as the clever author of that forged will, we should have very few undetected crimes in this country."

"That is why I always try to persuade you to give our poor ignorant police the benefit of your great insight and wisdom," said Polly, with a smile.

"I know," he said blandly, "you have been most kind in that way, but I am only an amateur. Crime interests me only when it resembles a clever game of chess, with many intricate moves which all tend to one solution, the checkmating of the antagonist—the detective force of the country. Now, confess that, in the Dublin mystery, the clever police there were absolutely checkmated."

"Absolutely."

"Just as the public was. There were actually two crimes committed in one city which have completely baffled detection: the murder of Patrick Wethered the lawyer, and the forged will of Millionaire Brooks. There are not many millionaires in Ireland; no wonder old Brooks was a notability in his way, since his business—bacon curing, I believe it is—is said to be worth over £2,000,000 of solid money.

"His younger son Murray was a refined, highly educated man, and was, moreover, the apple of his father's eye, as he was the spoilt darling of Dublin society; good-looking, a splendid dancer, and a perfect rider, he was the acknowledged 'catch' of the matrimonial market of Ireland, and many a very aristocratic house was opened hospitably to the favourite son of the millionaire.

"Of course, Percival Brooks, the eldest son, would inherit the bulk of the old man's property and also probably the larger share in the business; he, too, was good-looking, more so than his brother; he, too, rode, danced, and talked well, but it was many years ago that mammas with marriageable daughters had given up all hopes of Percival Brooks as a probable son-in-law. That young man's infatuation for Maisie Fortescue, a lady of undoubted charm but very doubtful antecedents, who had astonished the London and Dublin music-halls with her extravagant dances, was too well known and too old-established to encourage any hopes in other quarters.

"Whether Percival Brooks would ever marry Maisie Fortescue was thought to be very doubtful. Old Brooks had the full disposal of all his wealth, and it would have fared ill with Percival if he introduced an undesirable wife into the magnificent Fitzwilliam Place establishment.

"That is how matters stood," continued the man in the corner, "when Dublin society one morning learnt, with deep regret and dismay, that old Brooks had died very suddenly at his residence after only a few hours' illness. At first it was generally understood that he had had an apoplectic stroke; anyway, he had been at business hale and hearty as ever the day before his death, which occurred late on the evening of February 1st.

"It was the morning papers of February 2nd which told the sad news to their readers, and it was those selfsame papers which on that eventful morning contained another even more startling piece of news, that proved the prelude to a series of sensations such as tranquil, placid Dublin had not experienced for many years. This was, that on that very afternoon which saw the death of Dublin's greatest millionaire, Mr. Patrick Wethered, his solicitor, was murdered in Phoenix Park at five o'clock in the afternoon while actually walking to his own house from his visit to his client in Fitzwilliam Place.

"Patrick Wethered was as well known as the proverbial town pump; his mysterious and tragic death filled all Dublin with dismay. The lawyer, who was a man sixty years of age, had been struck on the back of the head by a heavy stick, garrotted, and subsequently robbed, for neither money, watch, or pocket-book were found upon his person, whilst the police soon gathered from Patrick Wethered's household that he had left home at two o'clock that afternoon, carrying both watch and pocket-book, and undoubtedly money as well.

"An inquest was held, and a verdict of wilful murder was found against some person or persons unknown.

"But Dublin had not exhausted its stock of sensations yet. Millionaire Brooks had been buried with due pomp and magnificence, and his will had been proved (his business and personalty being estimated at £2,500,000) by Percival Gordon Brooks, his eldest son and sole executor. The younger son, Murray, who had devoted the best years of his life to being a friend and companion to his father, while Percival ran after ballet-dancers and music-hall stars—Murray, who had avowedly been the apple of his father's eye in consequence—was left with a miserly pittance of £300 a year, and no share whatever in the gigantic business of Brooks & Sons, bacon curers, of Dublin.

"Something had evidently happened within the precincts of the Brooks' town mansion, which the public and Dublin society tried in vain to fathom. Elderly mammas and blushing *débutantes* were already thinking of the best means whereby next season they might more easily show the cold shoulder to young Murray Brooks, who had so suddenly become a hopeless 'detrimental' in the marriage market, when all these sensations terminated in one gigantic, overwhelming bit of scandal, which for the next three months furnished food for gossip in every drawing-room in Dublin.

"Mr. Murray Brooks, namely, had entered a claim for probate of a will, made by his father in 1891, declaring that the later will made the very day of his father's death and proved by his brother as sole executor, was null and void, that will being a forgery."

II.

"The facts that transpired in connection with this extraordinary case were sufficiently mysterious to puzzle everybody. As I told you before, all Mr. Brooks' friends never quite grasped the idea that the old man should so completely have cut off his favourite son with the proverbial shilling.

"You see, Percival had always been a thorn in the old man's flesh. Horse-racing, gambling, theatres, and music-halls were, in the old pork-butcher's eyes, so many deadly sins which his son committed every day of his life, and all the Fitzwilliam Place household could testify to the many and bitter quarrels which had arisen between father and son over the latter's gambling or racing debts. Many people asserted that Brooks would sooner have left his money to charitable institutions than seen it squandered upon the brightest stars that adorned the music-hall stage.

"The case came up for hearing early in the autumn. In the meanwhile Percival Brooks had given up his racecourse associates, settled down in the Fitzwilliam Place mansion, and conducted his father's business, without a manager, but with all the energy and forethought which he had previously devoted to more unworthy causes.

"Murray had elected not to stay on in the old house; no doubt associations were of too painful and recent a nature; he was boarding with the family of a Mr. Wilson Hibbert, who was the late Patrick Wethered's, the murdered lawyer's, partner. They were quiet, homely people, who lived in a very pokey little house in

Kilkenny Street, and poor Murray must, in spite of his grief, have felt very bitterly the change from his luxurious quarters in his father's mansion to his present tiny room and homely meals.

"Percival Brooks, who was now drawing an income of over a hundred thousand a year, was very severely criticised for adhering so strictly to the letter of his father's will, and only paying his brother that paltry £300 a year, which was very literally but the crumbs off his own magnificent dinner table.

"The issue of that contested will case was therefore awaited with eager interest. In the meanwhile the police, who had at first seemed fairly loquacious on the subject of the murder of Mr. Patrick Wethered, suddenly became strangely reticent, and by their very reticence aroused a certain amount of uneasiness in the public mind, until one day the *Irish Times* published the following extraordinary, enigmatic paragraph:

"'We hear on authority which cannot be questioned, that certain extraordinary developments are expected in connection with the brutal murder of our distinguished townsman Mr. Wethered; the police, in fact, are vainly trying to keep it secret that they hold a clue which is as important as it is sensational, and that they only await the impending issue of a well-known litigation in the probate court to effect an arrest.'

"The Dublin public flocked to the court to hear the arguments in the great will case. I myself journeyed down to Dublin. As soon as I succeeded in fighting my way to the densely crowded court, I took stock of the various actors in the drama, which I as a spectator was prepared to enjoy. There were Percival Brooks and Murray his brother, the two litigants, both good-looking and well dressed, and both striving, by keeping up a running conversation with their lawyer, to appear unconcerned and confident of the issue. With Percival Brooks was Henry Oranmore, the eminent Irish K.C., whilst Walter Hibbert, a rising young barrister, the son of Wilson Hibbert, appeared for Murray.

"The will of which the latter claimed probate was one dated 1891, and had been made by Mr. Brooks during a severe illness which threatened to end his days. This will had been deposited in the hands of Messrs. Wethered and Hibbert, solicitors to the deceased, and by it Mr. Brooks left his personalty equally divided between his two sons, but had left his business entirely to his youngest son, with a charge of £2000 a year upon it, payable to Percival. You see that Murray Brooks therefore had a very deep interest in that second will being found null and void.

"Old Mr. Hibbert had very ably instructed his son, and Walter Hibbert's opening speech was exceedingly clever. He would show, he said, on behalf of his client, that the will dated February 1st, 1908, could never have been made by the late Mr. Brooks, as it was absolutely contrary to his avowed intentions, and that if the late Mr. Brooks did on the day in question make any fresh will at all, it certainly was *not* the one proved by Mr. Percival Brooks, for that was absolutely a forgery from beginning to end. Mr. Walter Hibbert proposed to call several witnesses in support of both these points.

"On the other hand, Mr. Henry Oranmore, K.C., very ably and courteously replied that he too had several witnesses to prove that Mr. Brooks certainly did make a will on the day in question, and that, whatever his intentions may have been in the past, he must have modified them on the day of his death, for the will proved by Mr. Percival Brooks was found after his death under his pillow, duly signed and witnessed and in every way legal.

"Then the battle began in sober earnest. There were a great many witnesses to be called on both sides, their evidence being of more or less importance—chiefly less. But the interest centred round the prosaic figure of John O'Neill, the butler at Fitzwilliam Place, who had been in Mr. Brooks' family for thirty years.

"'I was clearing away my breakfast things,' said John, 'when I heard the master's voice in the study close by. Oh my, he was that angry! I could hear the words "disgrace," and "villain," and "liar," and "ballet-dancer," and one or two other ugly words as applied to some female lady, which I would not like to repeat. At first I did not take much notice, as I was quite used to hearing my poor dear master having words with Mr. Percival. So I went downstairs carrying my breakfast things; but I had just started cleaning my silver when the study bell goes ringing violently, and I hear Mr. Percival's voice shouting in the hall: "John! quick! Send for Dr. Mulligan at once. Your master is not well! Send one of the men, and you come up and help me to get Mr. Brooks to bed."

"'I sent one of the grooms for the doctor,' continued John, who seemed still affected at the recollection of his poor master, to whom he had evidently been very much attached, 'and I went up to see Mr. Brooks. I found him lying on the study floor, his head supported in Mr. Percival's arms. "My father has fallen in a faint," said the young master; "help me to get him up to his room before Dr. Mulligan comes."

"'Mr. Percival looked very white and upset, which was only natural; and when we had got my poor master to bed, I asked if I should not go and break the news to Mr. Murray, who had gone to business an hour ago. However, before Mr. Percival had time to give me an order the doctor came. I thought I had seen death plainly writ in my master's face, and when I showed the doctor out an hour later, and he told me that he would be back directly, I knew that the end was near.

"'Mr. Brooks rang for me a minute or two later. He told me to send at once for Mr. Wethered, or else for Mr. Hibbert, if Mr. Wethered could not come. "I haven't many hours to live, John," he says to me— "my heart is broke, the doctor says my heart is broke. A man shouldn't marry and have children, John, for they will sooner or later break his heart." I was so upset I couldn't speak; but I sent round at once for Mr. Wethered, who came himself just about three o'clock that afternoon.

"'After he had been with my master about an hour I was called in, and Mr. Wethered said to me that Mr. Brooks wished me and one other of us servants to witness that he had signed a paper which was on a table by his bedside. I called Pat Mooney, the head footman, and before us both Mr. Brooks put his name at the bottom of that paper. Then Mr. Wethered give me the pen and told me to write my name as a witness, and that Pat Mooney was to do the same. After that we were both told that we could go.'

"The old butler went on to explain that he was present in his late master's room on the following day when the undertakers, who had come to lay the dead man out, found a paper underneath his pillow. John O'Neill, who recognized the paper as the one to which he had appended his signature the day before, took it to Mr. Percival, and gave it into his hands.

"In answer to Mr. Walter Hibbert, John asserted positively that he took the paper from the undertaker's hand and went straight with it to Mr. Percival's room.

"'He was alone,' said John; 'I gave him the paper. He just glanced at it, and I thought he looked rather astonished, but he said nothing, and I at once left the room.'

"'When you say that you recognized the paper as the one which you had seen your master sign the day before, how did you actually recognize that it was the same paper?' asked Mr. Hibbert amidst breathless interest on the part of the spectators. I narrowly observed the witness's face.

"'It looked exactly the same paper to me, sir,' replied John, somewhat vaguely.

"'Did you look at the contents, then?'

"'No, sir; certainly not.'

"'Had you done so the day before?'

"'No, sir, only at my master's signature.'

"'Then you only thought by the *outside* look of the paper that it was the same?'

"'It looked the same thing, sir,' persisted John obstinately.

"You see," continued the man in the corner, leaning eagerly forward across the narrow marble table, "the contention of Murray Brooks' adviser was that Mr. Brooks, having made a will and hidden it—for some reason or other under his pillow—that will had fallen, through the means related by John O'Neill, into the hands of Mr. Percival Brooks, who had destroyed it and substituted a forged one in its place, which adjudged the whole of Mr. Brooks' millions to himself. It was a terrible and very daring accusation directed against a gentleman who, in spite of his many wild oats sowed in early youth, was a prominent and important figure in Irish high life.

"All those present were aghast at what they heard, and the whispered comments I could hear around me showed me that public opinion, at least, did not uphold Mr. Murray Brooks' daring accusation against his brother.

"But John O'Neill had not finished his evidence, and Mr. Walter Hibbert had a bit of sensation still up his sleeve. He had, namely, produced a paper, the will proved by Mr. Percival Brooks, and had asked John O'Neill if once again he recognized the paper.

"'Certainly, sir,' said John unhesitatingly, 'that is the one the undertaker found under my poor dead master's pillow, and which I took to Mr. Percival's room immediately.'

"Then the paper was unfolded and placed before the witness.

"'Now, Mr. O'Neill, will you tell me if that is your signature?'

"John looked at it for a moment; then he said: 'Excuse me, sir,' and produced a pair of spectacles which he carefully adjusted before he again examined the paper. Then he thoughtfully shook his head.

"'It don't look much like my writing, sir,' he said at last. 'That is to say,' he added, by way of elucidating the matter, 'it does look like my writing, but then I don't think it is.'

"There was at that moment a look in Mr. Percival Brooks' face," continued the man in the corner quietly, "which then and there gave me the whole history of that quarrel, that illness of Mr. Brooks, of the will, aye! and of the murder of Patrick Wethered too.

"All I wondered at was how every one of those learned counsel on both sides did not get the clue just the same as I did, but went on arguing, speechifying, cross-examining for nearly a week, until they arrived at the one conclusion which was inevitable from the very first, namely, that the will *was* a forgery—a gross, clumsy, idiotic forgery, since both John O'Neill and Pat Mooney, the two witnesses, absolutely repudiated the signatures as their own. The only successful bit of caligraphy the forger had done was the signature of old Mr. Brooks.

"It was a very curious fact, and one which had undoubtedly aided the forger in accomplishing his work quickly, that Mr. Wethered the lawyer having, no doubt, realized that Mr. Brooks had not many moments in life to spare, had not drawn up the usual engrossed, magnificent document dear to the lawyer heart, but had used for his client's will one of those regular printed forms which can be purchased at any stationer's.

"Mr. Percival Brooks, of course, flatly denied the serious allegation brought against him. He admitted that the butler had brought him the document the morning after his father's death, and that he certainly, on glancing at it, had been very much astonished to see that that document was his father's will. Against that he declared that its contents did not astonish him in the slightest degree, that he himself knew of the testator's intentions, but that he certainly thought his father had entrusted the will to the care of Mr. Wethered, who did all his business for him.

"'I only very cursorily glanced at the signature,' he concluded, speaking in a perfectly calm, clear voice; 'you must understand that the thought of forgery was very far from my mind, and that my father's signature is exceedingly well imitated, if, indeed, it is not his own, which I am not at all prepared to believe. As for the two witnesses' signatures, I don't think I had ever seen them before. I took the document to Messrs. Barkston and Maud, who had often done business for me before, and they assured me that the will was in perfect form and order.'

"Asked why he had not entrusted the will to his father's solicitors, he replied:

"'For the very simple reason that exactly half an hour before the will was placed in my hands, I had read that Mr. Patrick Wethered had been murdered the night before. Mr. Hibbert, the junior partner, was not personally known to me.'

"After that, for form's sake, a good deal of expert evidence was heard on the subject of the dead man's signature. But that was quite unanimous, and merely went to corroborate what had already been established beyond a doubt, namely, that the will dated February 1st, 1908, was a forgery, and probate of the will dated 1891 was therefore granted to Mr. Murray Brooks, the sole executor mentioned therein."

III.

"Two days later the police applied for a warrant for the arrest of Mr. Percival Brooks on a charge of forgery.

"The Crown prosecuted, and Mr. Brooks had again the support of Mr. Oranmore, the eminent K.C. Perfectly calm, like a man conscious of his own innocence and unable to grasp the idea that justice does sometimes miscarry, Mr. Brooks, the son of the millionaire, himself still the possessor of a very large fortune under the former will, stood up in the dock on that memorable day in October, 1908, which still no doubt lives in the memory of his many friends.

"All the evidence with regard to Mr. Brooks' last moments and the forged will was gone through over again. That will, it was the contention of the Crown, had been forged so entirely in favour of the accused, cutting out every one else, that obviously no one but the beneficiary under that false will would have had any motive in forging it.

"Very pale, and with a frown between his deep-set, handsome Irish eyes, Percival Brooks listened to this large volume of evidence piled up against him by the Crown.

"At times he held brief consultations with Mr. Oranmore, who seemed as cool as a cucumber. Have you ever seen Oranmore in court? He is a character worthy of Dickens. His pronounced brogue, his fat, podgy, clean-shaven face, his not always immaculately clean large hands, have often delighted the caricaturist. As it very soon transpired during that memorable magisterial inquiry, he relied for a verdict in favour of his client upon two main points, and he had concentrated all his skill upon making these two points as telling as he possibly could.

"The first point was the question of time, John O'Neill, cross-examined by Oranmore, stated without hesitation that he had given the will to Mr. Percival at eleven o'clock in the morning. And now the eminent K.C. brought forward and placed in the witness-box the very lawyers into whose hands the accused had then immediately placed the will. Now, Mr. Barkston, a very well-known solicitor of King Street, declared positively that Mr. Percival Brooks was in his office at a quarter before twelve; two of his clerks testified to the same time exactly, and it was *impossible*, contended Mr. Oranmore, that within three-quarters of an hour Mr. Brooks could have gone to a stationer's, bought a will form, copied Mr. Wethered's writing, his father's signature, and that of John O'Neill and Pat Mooney.

"Such a thing might have been planned, arranged, practised, and ultimately, after a great deal of trouble, successfully carried out, but human intelligence could not grasp the other as a possibility.

"Still the judge wavered. The eminent K.C. had shaken but not shattered his belief in the prisoner's guilt. But there was one point more, and this Oranmore, with the skill of a dramatist, had reserved for the fall of the curtain.

"He noted every sign in the judge's face, he guessed that his client was not yet absolutely safe, then only did he produce his last two witnesses.

"One of them was Mary Sullivan, one of the housemaids in the Fitzwilliam mansion. She had been sent up by the cook at a quarter past four o'clock on the afternoon of February 1st with some hot water, which the nurse had ordered, for the master's room. Just as she was about to knock at the door Mr. Wethered was coming out of the room. Mary stopped with the tray in her hand, and at the door Mr. Wethered turned and said quite loudly: 'Now, don't fret, don't be anxious; do try and be calm. Your will is safe in my pocket, nothing can change it or alter one word of it but yourself.'

"It was, of course, a very ticklish point in law whether the housemaid's evidence could be accepted. You see, she was quoting the words of a man since dead, spoken to another man also dead. There is no doubt that had there been very strong evidence on the other side against Percival Brooks, Mary Sullivan's would have counted for nothing; but, as I told you before, the judge's belief in the prisoner's guilt was already very seriously shaken, and now the final blow aimed at it by Mr. Oranmore shattered his last lingering doubts.

"Dr. Mulligan, namely, had been placed by Mr. Oranmore into the witness-box. He was a medical man of unimpeachable authority, in fact, absolutely at the head of his profession in Dublin. What he said practically corroborated Mary Sullivan's testimony. He had gone in to see Mr. Brooks at half-past four, and understood from him that his lawyer had just left him.

"Mr. Brooks certainly, though terribly weak, was calm and more composed. He was dying from a sudden heart attack, and Dr. Mulligan foresaw the almost immediate end. But he was still conscious and managed to murmur feebly: 'I feel much easier in my mind now, doctor—have made my will—Wethered has been—he's got it in his pocket—it is safe there—safe from that—' But the words died on his lips, and after that he spoke but little. He saw his two sons before he died, but hardly knew them or even looked at them.

"You see," concluded the man in the corner, "you see that the prosecution was bound to collapse. Oranmore did not give it a leg to stand on. The will was forged, it is true, forged in the favour of Percival Brooks and of no one else, forged for him and for his benefit. Whether he knew and connived at the forgery was never proved or, as far as I know, even hinted, but it was impossible to go against all the evidence, which pointed that, as far as the act itself was concerned, he at least was innocent. You see, Dr. Mulligan's evidence was not to be shaken. Mary Sullivan's was equally strong.

"There were two witnesses swearing positively that old Brooks' will was in Mr. Wethered's keeping when that gentleman left the Fitzwilliam mansion at a quarter past four. At five o'clock in the afternoon the lawyer was found dead in Phoenix Park. Between a quarter past four and eight o'clock in the evening Percival Brooks never left the house—that was subsequently proved by Oranmore up to the hilt and beyond a doubt. Since the will found under old Brooks' pillow was a forged will, where then was the will he did make, and which Wethered carried away with him in his pocket?"

"Stolen, of course," said Polly, "by those who murdered and robbed him; it may have been of no value to them, but they naturally would destroy it, lest it might prove a clue against them."

"Then you think it was mere coincidence?" he asked excitedly.

"What?"

"That Wethered was murdered and robbed at the very moment that he carried the will in his pocket, whilst another was being forged in its place?"

"It certainly would be very curious, if it *were* a coincidence," she said musingly.

"Very," he repeated with biting sarcasm, whilst nervously his bony fingers played with the inevitable bit of string. "Very curious indeed. Just think of the whole thing. There was the old man with all his wealth, and two sons, one to whom he is devoted, and the other with whom he does nothing but quarrel. One day there is another of these quarrels, but more violent, more terrible than any that have previously occurred, with the result that the father, heart-broken by it all, has an attack of apoplexy and practically dies of a broken heart. After that he alters his will, and subsequently a will is proved which turns out to be a forgery.

"Now everybody—police, press, and public alike—at once jump to the conclusion that, as Percival Brooks benefits by that forged will, Percival Brooks must be the forger."

"Seek for him whom the crime benefits, is your own axiom," argued the girl.

"I beg your pardon?"

"Percival Brooks benefited to the tune of £2,000,000."

"I beg your pardon. He did nothing of the sort. He was left with less than half the share that his younger brother inherited."

"Now, yes; but that was a former will and—"

"And that forged will was so clumsily executed, the signature so carelessly imitated, that the forgery was bound to come to light. Did *that* never strike you?"

"Yes, but—"

"There is no but," he interrupted. "It was all as clear as daylight to me from the very first. The quarrel with the old man, which broke his heart, was not with his eldest son, with whom he was used to quarrelling, but with the second son whom he idolised, in whom he believed. Don't you remember how John O'Neill heard the words 'liar' and 'deceit'? Percival Brooks had never deceived his father. His sins were all on the surface. Murray had led a quiet life, had pandered to his father, and fawned upon him, until, like most hypocrites, he at last got found out. Who knows what ugly gambling debt or debt of honour, suddenly revealed to old Brooks, was the cause of that last and deadly quarrel?

"You remember that it was Percival who remained beside his father and carried him up to his room. Where was Murray throughout that long and painful day, when his father lay dying—he, the idolised son, the apple of the old man's eye? You never hear his name mentioned as being present there all that day. But he knew that he had offended his father mortally, and that his father meant to cut him off with a shilling. He knew that Mr. Wethered had been sent for, that Wethered left the house soon after four o'clock.

"And here the cleverness of the man comes in. Having lain in wait for Wethered and knocked him on the back of the head with a stick, he could not very well make that will disappear altogether. There remained the faint chance of some other witnesses knowing that Mr. Brooks had made a fresh will, Mr. Wethered's partner, his clerk, or one of the confidential servants in the house. Therefore *a* will must be discovered after the old man's death.

"Now, Murray Brooks was not an expert forger, it takes years of training to become that. A forged will executed by himself would be sure to be found out—yes, that's it, sure to be found out. The forgery will be palpable—let it be palpable, and then it will be found out, branded as such, and the original will of 1891, so favourable to the young blackguard's interests, would be held as valid. Was it devilry or merely additional caution which prompted Murray to pen that forged will so glaringly in Percival's favour? It is impossible to say.

"Anyhow, it was the cleverest touch in that marvellously devised crime. To plan that evil deed was great, to execute it was easy enough. He had several hours' leisure in which to do it. Then at night it was simplicity itself to slip the document under the dead man's pillow. Sacrilege causes no shudder to such natures as Murray Brooks. The rest of the drama you know already—"

"But Percival Brooks?"

"The jury returned a verdict of 'Not guilty.' There was no evidence against him."

"But the money? Surely the scoundrel does not have the enjoyment of it still?"

"No; he enjoyed it for a time, but he died, about three months ago, and forgot to take the precaution of making a will, so his brother Percival has got the business after all. If you ever go to Dublin, I should order some of Brooks' bacon if I were you. It is very good."

9

An Unparalleled Outrage

I.

"Do you care for the seaside?" asked the man in the corner when he had finished his lunch. "I don't mean the seaside at Ostend or Trouville, but honest English seaside with nigger minstrels, three-shilling excursionists, and dirty, expensive furnished apartments, where they charge you a shilling for lighting the hall gas on Sundays and sixpence on other evenings. Do you care for that?"

"I prefer the country."

"Ah! perhaps it is preferable. Personally I only liked one of our English seaside resorts once, and that was for a week, when Edward Skinner was up before the magistrate, charged with what was known as the 'Brighton Outrage.' I don't know if you remember the memorable day in Brighton, memorable for that elegant town, which deals more in amusements than mysteries, when Mr. Francis Morton, one of its most noted residents, disappeared. Yes! disappeared as completely as any vanishing lady in a music-hall. He was wealthy, had a fine house, servants, a wife and children, and he disappeared. There was no getting away from that.

"Mr. Francis Morton lived with his wife in one of the large houses in Sussex Square at the Kemp Town end of Brighton. Mrs. Morton was well known for her Americanisms, her swagger dinner parties, and beautiful Paris gowns. She was the daughter of one of the many American millionaires (I think her father was a Chicago pork-butcher), who conveniently provide wealthy wives for English gentlemen; and she had married Mr. Francis Morton a few years ago and brought him her quarter of a million, for no other reason but that she fell in love with him. He was neither good-looking nor distinguished, in fact, he was one of those men who seem to have CITY stamped all over their person.

"He was a gentleman of very regular habits, going up to London every morning on business and returning every afternoon by the 'husband's train.' So regular was he in these habits that all the servants at the Sussex Square house were betrayed into actual gossip over the fact that on Wednesday, March 17th, the master was not home for dinner. Hales, the butler, remarked that the mistress seemed a bit anxious and didn't eat much food. The evening wore on and Mr. Morton did not appear. At nine o'clock the young footman was dispatched to the station to make inquiries whether his master had been seen there in the afternoon, or whether—which Heaven forbid—there had been an accident on the line. The young man interviewed two or three porters, the bookstall boy, and ticket clerk; all were agreed that Mr. Morton did not go up to London during the day; no one had seen him within the precincts of the station. There certainly had been no accident reported either on the up or down line.

"But the morning of the 18th came, with its initial postman's knock, but neither Mr. Morton nor any sign or news from him. Mrs. Morton, who evidently had spent a sleepless night, for she looked sadly changed and haggard, sent a wire to the hall porter at the large building in Cannon Street, where her husband had his office. An hour later she had the reply: 'Not seen Mr. Morton all day yesterday, not here to-day.' By the afternoon every one in Brighton knew that a fellow-resident had mysteriously disappeared from or in the city.

"A couple of days, then another, elapsed, and still no sign of Mr. Morton. The police were doing their best. The gentleman was so well known in Brighton—as he had been a resident two years—that it was not difficult to firmly establish the one fact that he had not left the city, since no one saw him in the station on the morning of the 17th, nor at any time since then. Mild excitement prevailed throughout the town. At first the newspapers took the matter somewhat jocosely. 'Where is Mr. Morton?' was the usual placard on the evening's contents bills, but after three days had gone by and the worthy Brighton resident was still missing, while Mrs. Morton was seen to look more haggard and careworn every day, mild excitement gave place to anxiety.

"There were vague hints now as to foul play. The news had leaked out that the missing gentleman was carrying a large sum of money on the day of his disappearance. There were also vague rumours of a scandal not unconnected with Mrs. Morton herself and her own past history, which in her anxiety for her husband she had been forced to reveal to the detective-inspector in charge of the case.

"Then on Saturday the news which the late evening papers contained was this:

"'Acting on certain information received, the police to-day forced an entrance into one of the rooms of Russell House, a high-class furnished apartment on the King's Parade, and there they discovered our missing distinguished townsman, Mr. Francis Morton, who had been robbed and subsequently locked up in that room since Wednesday, the 17th. When discovered he was in the last stages of inanition; he was tied into an arm-chair with ropes, a thick wool shawl had been wound round his mouth, and it is a positive marvel that, left thus without food and very little air, the unfortunate gentleman survived the horrors of these four days of incarceration.

"'He has been conveyed to his residence in Sussex Square, and we are pleased to say that Doctor Mellish, who is in attendance, has declared his patient to be out of serious danger, and that with care and rest he will be soon quite himself again.

"'At the same time our readers will learn with unmixed satisfaction that the police of our city, with their usual acuteness and activity, have already discovered the identity and whereabouts of the cowardly ruffian who committed this unparalleled outrage.'"

II.

"I really don't know," continued the man in the corner blandly, "what it was that interested me in the case from the very first. Certainly it had nothing very out of the way or mysterious about it, but I journeyed down to Brighton nevertheless, as I felt that something deeper and more subtle lay behind that extraordinary assault, following a robbery, no doubt.

"I must tell you that the police had allowed it to be freely circulated abroad that they held a clue. It had been easy enough to ascertain who the lodger was who had rented the furnished room in Russell House. His name was supposed to be Edward Skinner, and he had taken the room about a fortnight ago, but had gone away ostensibly for two or three days on the very day of Mr. Morton's mysterious disappearance. It was on the 20th that Mr. Morton was found, and thirty-six hours later the public were gratified to hear that Mr. Edward Skinner had been traced to London and arrested on the charge of assault upon the person of Mr. Francis Morton and of robbing him of the sum of £10,000.

"Then a further sensation was added to the already bewildering case by the startling announcement that Mr. Francis Morton refused to prosecute.

"Of course, the Treasury took up the case and subpoenaed Mr. Morton as a witness, so that gentleman—if he wished to hush the matter up, or had been in any way terrorised into a promise of doing so—gained nothing by his refusal, except an additional amount of curiosity in the public mind and further sensation around the mysterious case.

"It was all this, you see, which had interested me and brought me down to Brighton on March 23rd to see the prisoner Edward Skinner arraigned before the beak. I must say that he was a very ordinary-looking individual. Fair, of ruddy complexion, with snub nose and the beginning of a bald place on the top of his head, he, too, looked the embodiment of a prosperous, stodgy 'City gent.'

"I took a quick survey of the witnesses present, and guessed that the handsome, stylish woman sitting next to Mr. Reginald Pepys, the noted lawyer for the Crown, was Mrs. Morton.

"There was a large crowd in court, and I heard whispered comments among the feminine portion thereof as to the beauty of Mrs. Morton's gown, the value of her large picture hat, and the magnificence of her diamond rings.

"The police gave all the evidence required with regard to the finding of Mr. Morton in the room at Russell House and also to the arrest of Skinner at the Langham Hotel in London. It appears that the prisoner seemed completely taken aback at the charge preferred against him, and declared that though he knew Mr. Francis Morton slightly in business he knew nothing as to his private life.

"'Prisoner stated,' continued Inspector Buckle, 'that he was not even aware Mr. Morton lived in Brighton, but I have evidence here, which I will place before your Honour, to prove that the prisoner was seen in the company of Mr. Morton at 9.30 o'clock on the morning of the assault.'

"Cross-examined by Mr. Matthew Quiller, the detective-inspector admitted that prisoner merely said that he did not know that Mr. Morton was a *resident* of Brighton—he never denied having met him there.

"The witness, or rather witnesses, referred to by the police were two Brighton tradesmen who knew Mr. Morton by sight and had seen him on the morning of the 17th walking with the accused.

"In this instance Mr. Quiller had no question to ask of the witnesses, and it was generally understood that the prisoner did not wish to contradict their statement.

"Constable Hartrick told the story of the finding of the unfortunate Mr. Morton after his four days' incarceration. The constable had been sent round by the chief inspector, after certain information given by Mrs. Chapman, the landlady of Russell House. He had found the door locked and forced it open. Mr. Morton was in an arm-chair, with several yards of rope wound loosely round him; he was almost unconscious, and there was a thick wool shawl tied round his mouth which must have deadened any cry or groan the poor gentleman might have uttered. But, as a matter of fact, the constable was under the impression that Mr. Morton had been either drugged or stunned in some way at first, which had left him weak and faint and prevented him from making himself heard or extricating himself from his bonds, which were very clumsily, evidently very hastily, wound round his body.

"The medical officer who was called in, and also Dr. Mellish who attended Mr. Morton, both said that he seemed dazed by some stupefying drug, and also, of course, terribly weak and faint with the want of food.

"The first witness of real importance was Mrs. Chapman, the proprietress of Russell House, whose original information to the police led to the discovery of Mr. Morton. In answer to Mr. Pepys, she said that on March 1st the accused called at her house and gave his name as Mr. Edward Skinner.

"'He required, he said, a furnished room at a moderate rental for a permanency, with full attendance when he was in, but he added that he would often be away for two or three days, or even longer, at a time.

"'He told me that he was a traveller for a tea-house,' continued Mrs. Chapman, 'and I showed him the front room on the third floor, as he did not want to pay more than twelve shillings a week. I asked him for a reference, but he put three sovereigns in my hand, and said with a laugh that he supposed paying for his room a month in advance was sufficient reference; if I didn't like him after that, I could give him a week's notice to quit.'

"'You did not think of asking him the name of the firm for which he travelled?' asked Mr. Pepys.

"'No, I was quite satisfied as he paid me for the room. The next day he sent in his luggage and took possession of the room. He went out most mornings on business, but was always in Brighton for Saturday and Sunday. On the 16th he told me that he was going to Liverpool for a couple of days; he slept in the house that night, and went off early on the 17th, taking his portmanteau with him.'

"'At what time did he leave?' asked Mr. Pepys.

"'I couldn't say exactly,' replied Mrs. Chapman with some hesitation. 'You see this is the off season here. None of my rooms are let, except the one to Mr. Skinner, and I only have one servant. I keep four during the summer, autumn, and winter season,' she added with conscious pride, fearing that her former statement might prejudice the reputation of Russell House. 'I thought I had heard Mr. Skinner go out about nine o'clock, but about an hour later the girl and I were both in the basement, and we heard the front door open and shut with a bang, and then a step in the hall.

"'"That's Mr. Skinner," said Mary. "So it is," I said, "why, I thought he had gone an hour ago." "He did go out then," said Mary, "for he left his bedroom door open and I went in to do his bed and tidy his room." "Just go and see if that's him, Mary," I said, and Mary ran up to the hall and up the stairs, and came back to tell me that that was Mr. Skinner all right enough; he had gone straight up to his room. Mary didn't see him, but he had another gentleman with him, as she could hear them talking in Mr. Skinner's room.'

"'Then you can't tell us at what time the prisoner left the house finally?'

"'No, that I can't. I went out shopping soon after that. When I came in it was twelve o'clock. I went up to the third floor and found that Mr. Skinner had locked his door and taken the key with him. As I knew Mary had already done, the room I did not trouble more about it, though I did think it strange for a gentleman to look up his room and not leave the key with me.'

"'And, of course, you heard no noise of any kind in the room then?'

"'No. Not that day or the next, but on the third day Mary and I both thought we heard a funny sound. I said that Mr. Skinner had left his window open, and it was the blind flapping against the window-pane; but when we heard that funny noise again I put my ear to the keyhole and I thought I could hear a groan. I was very frightened, and sent Mary for the police.'

"Mrs. Chapman had nothing more of interest to say. The prisoner certainly was her lodger. She had last seen him on the evening of the 16th going up to his room with his candle. Mary the servant had much the same story to relate as her mistress.

"'I think it was 'im, right enough,' said Mary guardedly. 'I didn't see 'im, but I went up to 'is landing and stopped a moment outside 'is door. I could 'ear loud voices in the room—gentlemen talking.'

"'I suppose you would not do such a thing as to listen, Mary?' queried Mr. Pepys with a smile.

"'No, sir,' said Mary with a bland smile, 'I didn't catch what the gentlemen said, but one of them spoke so loud I thought they must be quarrelling.'

"'Mr. Skinner was the only person in possession of a latch-key, I presume. No one else could have come in without ringing at the door?'

"'Oh no, sir.'

"That was all. So far, you see, the case was progressing splendidly for the Crown against the prisoner. The contention, of course, was that Skinner had met Mr. Morton, brought him home with him, assaulted, drugged, then gagged and bound him, and finally robbed him of whatever money he had in his possession, which, according to certain affidavits which presently would be placed before the magistrate, amounted to £10,000 in notes.

"But in all this there still remained the great element of mystery for which the public and the magistrate would demand an explanation: namely, what were the relationships between Mr. Morton and Skinner, which had induced the former to refuse the prosecution of the man who had not only robbed him, but had so nearly succeeded in leaving him to die a terrible and lingering death?

"Mr. Morton was too ill as yet to appear in person. Dr. Mellish had absolutely forbidden his patient to undergo the fatigue and excitement of giving evidence himself in court that day. But his depositions had been taken at his bedside, were sworn to by him, and were now placed before the magistrate by the prosecuting counsel, and the facts they revealed were certainly as remarkable as they were brief and enigmatical.

"As they were read by Mr. Pepys, an awed and expectant hush seemed to descend over the large crowd gathered there, and all necks were strained eagerly forward to catch a glimpse of a tall, elegant woman, faultlessly dressed and wearing exquisite jewellery, but whose handsome face wore, as the prosecuting counsel read her husband's deposition, a more and more ashen hue.

"'This, your Honour, is the statement made upon oath by Mr. Francis Morton,' commenced Mr. Pepys in that loud, sonorous voice of his which sounds so impressive in a crowded and hushed court. '"I was obliged, for certain reasons which I refuse to disclose, to make a payment of a large sum of money to a man whom I did not know and have never seen. It was in a matter of which my wife was cognisant and which had entirely to do with her own affairs. I was merely the go-between, as I thought it was not fit that she should see to this matter herself. The individual in question had made certain demands, of which she kept me in ignorance as long as she could, not wishing to unnecessarily worry me. At last she decided to place the whole matter before me, and I agreed with her that it would be best to satisfy the man's demands.

"'"I then wrote to that individual whose name I do not wish to disclose, addressing the letter, as my wife directed me to do, to the Brighton post office, saying that I was ready to pay the £10,000 to him, at any place or time and in what manner he might appoint. I received a reply which bore the Brighton postmark, and which desired me to be outside Furnival's, the drapers, in West Street, at 9.30 on the morning of March 17th, and to bring the money (£10,000) in Bank of England notes.

"'"On the 16th my wife gave me a cheque for the amount and I cashed it at her bank—Bird's in Fleet Street. At half-past nine the following morning I was at the appointed place. An individual wearing a grey overcoat, bowler hat, and red tie accosted me by name and requested me to walk as far as his lodgings in the King's Parade. I followed him. Neither of us spoke. He stopped at a house which bore the name 'Russell House,' and which I shall be able to swear to as soon as I am able to go out. He let himself in with a latch-key, and asked me to follow him up to his room on the third floor. I thought I noticed when we were in the room that he locked the door; however, I had nothing of any value about me except the

£10,000, which I was ready to give him. We had not exchanged the slightest word.

"'"I gave him the notes, and he folded them and put them in his pocket-book. Then I turned towards the door, and, without the slightest warning, I felt myself suddenly gripped by the shoulder, while a handkerchief was pressed to my nose and mouth. I struggled as best I could, but the handkerchief was saturated with chloroform, and I soon lost consciousness. I hazily remember the man saying to me in short, jerky sentences, spoken at intervals while I was still weakly struggling:

"'"'What a fool you must think me, my dear sir! Did you really think that I was going to let you quietly walk out of here, straight to the police-station, eh? Such dodges have been done before, I know, when a man's silence has to be bought for money. Find out who he is, see where he lives, give him the money, then inform against him. No you don't! not this time. I am off to the Contain-ing with this £10,000, and I can get to Newhaven in time for the midday boat, so you'll have to keep quiet until I am the other side of the Channel, my friend. You won't be much inconvenienced; my landlady will hear your groans presently and release you, so you'll be all right. There, now, drink this—that's better.' He forced some-thing bitter down my throat, then I remember nothing more.

"'"When I regained consciousness I was sitting in an arm-chair with some rope tied round me and a wool shawl round my mouth. I hadn't the strength to make the slightest effort to disentangle myself or to utter a scream. I felt terribly sick and faint."'

"Mr. Reginald Pepys had finished reading, and no one in that crowded court had thought of uttering a sound; the magistrate's eyes were fixed upon the handsome lady in the magnificent gown, who was mopping her eyes with a dainty lace handkerchief.

"The extraordinary narrative of the victim of so daring an out-rage had kept every one in suspense; one thing was still expected to make the measure of sensation as full as it had ever been over any criminal case, and that was Mrs. Morton's evidence. She was called by the prosecuting counsel, and slowly, gracefully, she entered the witness-box. There was no doubt that she had felt keenly the tortures which her husband had undergone, and also the humiliation of seeing her name dragged forcibly into this ugly, blackmailing scandal.

"Closely questioned by Mr. Reginald Pepys, she was forced to admit that the man who blackmailed her was connected with her early life in a way which would have brought terrible disgrace upon her and upon her children. The story she told, amidst many tears and sobs, and much use of her beautiful lace handkerchief and beringed hands, was exceedingly pathetic.

"It appears that when she was barely seventeen she was inveigled into a secret marriage with one of those foreign adventurers who swarm in every country, and who styled himself Comte Armand de la Tremouille. He seems to have been a blackguard of unusually low pattern, for, after he had extracted from her some £200 of her pin money and a few diamond brooches, he left her one fine day with a laconic word to say that he was sailing for Europe by the *Argentina*, and would not be back for some time. She was in love with the brute, poor young soul, for when, a week later, she read that the *Argentina* was wrecked, and presumably every soul on board had perished, she wept very many bitter tears over her early widowhood.

"Fortunately her father, a very wealthy pork-butcher of Chicago, had known nothing of his daughter's culpable foolishness. Four years later he took her to London, where she met Mr. Francis Morton and married him. She led six or seven years of very happy married life when one day, like a thunderbolt from a clear, blue sky, she received a typewritten letter, signed 'Armand de la Tremouille,' full of protestations of undying love, telling a long and pathetic tale of years of suffering in a foreign land, whither he had drifted after having been rescued almost miraculously from the wreck of the *Argentina*, and where he never had been able to scrape a sufficient amount of money to pay for his passage home. At last fate had favoured him. He had, after many vicissitudes, found the whereabouts of his dear wife, and was now ready to forgive all that was past and take her to his loving arms once again.

"What followed was the usual course of events when there is a blackguard and a fool of a woman. She was terrorised and did not dare to tell her husband for some time; she corresponded with the Comte de la Tremouille, begging him for her sake and in memory of the past not to attempt to see her. She found him amenable to reason in the shape of several hundred pounds which passed through the Brighton post office into his hands. At last one day, by accident, Mr. Morton came across one of the Comte de la Tremouille's interesting letters. She confessed everything, throwing herself upon her husband's mercy.

"Now, Mr. Francis Morton was a business man, who viewed life practically and soberly. He liked his wife, who kept him in luxury, and wished to keep her, whereas the Comte de la Tremouille seemed willing enough to give her up for a consideration. Mrs. Morton, who had the sole and absolute control of her fortune, on the other hand, was willing enough to pay the price and hush up the scandal, which she believed—since she was a bit of a fool—would land her in prison for bigamy. Mr. Francis Morton wrote to the Comte de la Tremouille that his wife was ready to pay him the sum of £10,000 which he demanded in payment for her absolute liberty and his own complete disappearance out of her life now and for ever. The appointment was made, and Mr. Morton left his house at 9 A.M. on March 17th with the £10,000 in his pocket.

"The public and the magistrate had hung breathless upon her words. There was nothing but sympathy felt for this handsome woman, who throughout had been more sinned against than sinning, and whose gravest fault seems to have been a total lack of intelligence in dealing with her own life. But I can assure you of one thing, that in no case within my recollection was there ever such a sensation in a court as when the magistrate, after a few minutes' silence, said gently to Mrs. Morton:

"'And now, Mrs. Morton, will you kindly look at the prisoner, and tell me if in him you recognize your former husband?'

"And she, without even turning to look at the accused, said quietly:

"'Oh no! your Honour! of course that man is *not* the Comte de la Tremouille.'"

III.

"I can assure you that the situation was quite dramatic," continued the man in the corner, whilst his funny, claw-like hands took up a bit of string with renewed feverishness.

"In answer to further questions from the magistrate, she declared that she had never seen the accused; he might have been the go-between, however, that she could not say. The letters she received were all typewritten, but signed 'Armand de la Tremouille,' and certainly the signature was identical with that on the letters she used to receive from him years ago, all of which she had kept.

"'And did it *never* strike you,' asked the magistrate with a smile, 'that the letters you received might be forgeries?'

"'How could they be?' she replied decisively; 'no one knew of my marriage to the Comte de la Tremouille, no one in England certainly. And, besides, if some one did know the Comte intimately enough to forge his handwriting and to blackmail me, why should that some one have waited all these years? I have been married seven years, your Honour.'

"That was true enough, and there the matter rested as far as she was concerned. But the identity of Mr. Francis Morton's assailant had to be finally established, of course, before the prisoner was committed for trial. Dr. Mellish promised that Mr. Morton would be allowed to come to court for half an hour and identify the accused on the following day, and the case was adjourned until then. The accused was led away between two constables, bail being refused, and Brighton had perforce to moderate its impatience until the Wednesday.

"On that day the court was crowded to overflowing; actors, playwrights, literary men of all sorts had fought for admission to study for themselves the various phases and faces in connection with the case. Mrs. Morton was not present when the prisoner, quiet and self-possessed, was brought in and placed in the dock. His solicitor was with him, and a sensational defence was expected.

"Presently there was a stir in the court, and that certain sound, half rustle, half sigh, which preludes an expected palpitating event. Mr. Morton, pale, thin, wearing yet in his hollow eyes the stamp of those five days of suffering, walked into court leaning on the arm of his doctor—Mrs. Morton was not with him.

"He was at once accommodated with a chair in the witness-box, and the magistrate, after a few words of kindly sympathy, asked him if he had anything to add to his written statement. On Mr. Morton replying in the negative, the magistrate added:

"'And now, Mr. Morton, will you kindly look at the accused in the dock and tell me whether you recognize the person who took you to the room in Russell House and then assaulted you?'

"Slowly the sick man turned towards the prisoner and looked at him; then he shook his head and replied quietly:

"'No, sir, that certainly was not the man.'

"'You are quite sure?' asked the magistrate in amazement, while the crowd literally gasped with wonder.

"'I swear it,' asserted Mr. Morton.

"'Can you describe the man who assaulted you?'

"'Certainly. He was dark, of swarthy complexion, tall, thin, with bushy eyebrows and thick black hair and short beard. He spoke English with just the faintest suspicion of a foreign accent.'

"The prisoner, as I told you before, was English in every feature. English in his ruddy complexion, and absolutely English in his speech.

"After that the case for the prosecution began to collapse. Every one had expected a sensational defence, and Mr. Matthew Quiller, counsel for Skinner, fully justified all these expectations. He had no fewer than four witnesses present who swore positively that at 9.45 A.M. on the morning of Wednesday, March 17th, the prisoner was in the express train leaving Brighton for Victoria.

"Not being endowed with the gift of being in two places at once, and Mr. Morton having added the whole weight of his own evidence in Mr. Edward Skinner's favour, that gentleman was once more remanded by the magistrate, pending further investigation by the police, bail being allowed this time in two sureties of £50 each."

IV.

"Tell me what you think of it," said the man in the corner, seeing that Polly remained silent and puzzled.

"Well," she replied dubiously, "I suppose that the so-called Armand de la Tremouille's story was true in substance. That he did not perish on the *Argentina*, but drifted home, and blackmailed his former wife."

"Doesn't it strike you that there are at least two very strong points against that theory?" he asked, making two gigantic knots in his piece of string.

"Two?"

"Yes. In the first place, if the blackmailer was the 'Comte de la Tremouille' returned to life, why should he have been content to take £10,000 from a lady who was his lawful wife, and who could keep him in luxury for the rest of his natural life upon her large fortune, which was close upon a quarter of a million? The real Comte de la Tremouille, remember, had never found it difficult to get money out of his wife during their brief married life, whatever Mr. Morton's subsequent experience in the same direction might have been. And, secondly, why should he have typewritten his letters to his wife?"

"Because—"

"That was a point which, to my mind, the police never made the most of. Now, my experience in criminal cases has invariably been that when a typewritten letter figures in one, that letter is a forgery. It is not very difficult to imitate a signature, but it is a jolly sight more difficult to imitate a handwriting throughout an entire letter."

"Then, do you think—"

"I think, if you will allow me," he interrupted excitedly, "that we will go through the points—the sensible, tangible points of the case. Firstly: Mr. Morton disappears with £10,000 in his pocket for four entire days; at the end of that time he is discovered loosely tied to an arm-chair, and a wool shawl round his mouth. Secondly: A man named Skinner is accused of the outrage. Mr. Morton, although he himself is able, mind you, to furnish the best defence possible for Skinner, by denying his identity with the man who assaulted him, refuses to prosecute. Why?"

"He did not wish to drag his wife's name into the case."

"He must have known that the Crown would take up the case. Then, again, how is it no one saw him in the company of the swarthy foreigner he described?"

"Two witnesses did see Mr. Morton in company with Skinner," argued Polly.

"Yes, at 9.20 in West Street; that would give Edward Skinner time to catch the 9.45 at the station, and to entrust Mr. Morton with the latch-key of Russell House," remarked the man in the corner dryly.

"What nonsense!" Polly ejaculated.

"Nonsense, is it?" he said, tugging wildly at his bit of string; "is it nonsense to affirm that if a man wants to make sure that his victim shall not escape, he does not usually wind rope 'loosely' round his figure, nor does he throw a wool shawl lightly round his mouth. The police were idiotic beyond words; they themselves discovered that Morton was so 'loosely' fastened to his chair that very little movement would have disentangled him, and yet it never struck them that nothing was easier for that particular type of scoundrel to sit down in an arm-chair and wind a few yards of rope round himself, then, having wrapped a wool shawl round his throat, to slip his two arms inside the ropes."

"But what object would a man in Mr. Morton's position have for playing such extraordinary pranks?"

"Ah, the motive! There you are! What do I always tell you? Seek the motive! Now, what was Mr. Morton's position? He was the husband of a lady who owned a quarter of a million of money, not one penny of which he could touch without her consent, as it was settled on herself, and who, after the terrible way in which she had been plundered and then abandoned in her early youth, no doubt kept a very tight hold upon the purse-strings. Mr. Morton's subsequent life has proved that he had certain expensive, not altogether avowable, tastes. One day he discovers the old love letters of the 'Comte Armand de la Tremouille.'

"Then he lays his plans. He typewrites a letter, forges the signature of the erstwhile Count, and awaits events. The fish does rise to the bait. He gets sundry bits of money, and his success makes him daring. He looks round him for an accomplice—clever, unscrupulous, greedy—and selects Mr. Edward Skinner, probably some former pal of his wild oats days.

"The plan was very neat, you must confess. Mr. Skinner takes the room in Russell House, and studies all the manners and customs of his landlady and her servant. He then draws the full attention of the police upon himself. He meets Morton in West Street, then disappears ostensibly after the 'assault.' In the meanwhile Morton goes to Russell House. He walks upstairs, talks loudly in the room, then makes elaborate preparations for his comedy."

"Why! he nearly died of starvation!"

"That, I dare say, was not a part of his reckoning. He thought, no doubt, that Mrs. Chapman or the servant would discover and rescue him pretty soon. He meant to appear just a little faint, and endured quietly the first twenty-four hours of inanition. But the excitement and want of food told on him more than he expected. After twenty-four hours he turned very giddy and sick, and, falling from one fainting fit into another, was unable to give the alarm.

"However, he is all right again now, and concludes his part of a downright blackguard to perfection. Under the plea that his conscience does not allow him to live with a lady whose first husband is still alive, he has taken a bachelor flat in London, and only pays afternoon calls on his wife in Brighton. But presently he will tire of his bachelor life, and will return to his wife. And I'll guarantee that the Comte de la Tremouille will never be heard of again."

And that afternoon the man in the corner left Miss Polly Burton alone with a couple of photos of two uininteresting, stodgy, quiet-looking men—Morton and Skinner—who, if the old scarecrow was right in his theories, were a pair of the finest blackguards unhung.

10
The Regent's Park Murder

I.

By this time Miss Polly Burton had become quite accustomed to her extraordinary *vis-á-vis* in the corner.

He was always there, when she arrived, in the selfsame corner, dressed in one of his remarkable check tweed suits; he seldom said good morning, and invariably when she appeared he began to fidget with increased nervousness, with some tattered and knotty piece of string.

"Were you ever interested in the Regent's Park murder?" he asked her one day.

Polly replied that she had forgotten most of the particulars connected with that curious murder, but that she fully remembered the stir and flutter it had caused in a certain section of London Society.

"The racing and gambling set, particularly, you mean," he said. "All the persons implicated in the murder, directly or indirectly, were of the type commonly called 'Society men,' or 'men about town,' whilst the Harewood Club in Hanover Square, round which centred all the scandal in connection with the murder, was one of the smartest clubs in London.

"Probably the doings of the Harewood Club, which was essentially a gambling club, would for ever have remained 'officially' absent from the knowledge of the police authorities but for the murder in the Regent's Park and the revelations which came to light in connection with it.

"I dare say you know the quiet square which lies between Portland Place and the Regent's Park and is called Park Crescent at its south end, and subsequently Park Square East and West. The Marylebone Road, with all its heavy traffic, cuts straight across the large square and its pretty gardens, but the latter are connected together by a tunnel under the road; and of course you must remember that the new tube station in the south portion of the Square had not yet been planned.

"February 6th, 1907, was a very foggy night, nevertheless Mr. Aaron Cohen, of 30, Park Square West, at two o'clock in the morning, having finally pocketed the heavy winnings which he had just swept off the green table of the Harewood Club, started to walk home alone. An hour later most of the inhabitants of Park Square West were aroused from their peaceful slumbers by the sounds of a violent altercation in the road. A man's angry voice was heard shouting violently for a minute or two, and was followed immediately by frantic screams of 'Police' and 'Murder.' Then there was the double sharp report of firearms, and nothing more.

"The fog was very dense, and, as you no doubt have experienced yourself, it is very difficult to locate sound in a fog. Nevertheless, not more than a minute or two had elapsed before Constable F 18, the point policeman at the corner of Marylebone Road, arrived on the scene, and, having first of all whistled for any of his comrades on the beat, began to grope his way about in the fog, more confused than effectually assisted by contradictory directions from the inhabitants of the houses close by, who were nearly falling out of the upper windows as they shouted out to the constable.

"'By the railings, policeman.'

"'Higher up the road.'

"'No, lower down.'

"'It was on this side of the pavement I am sure.'

"No, the other.'

"At last it was another policeman, F 22, who, turning into Park Square West from the north side, almost stumbled upon the body of a man lying on the pavement with his head against the railings of the Square. By this time quite a little crowd of people from the different houses in the road had come down, curious to know what had actually happened.

"The policeman turned the strong light of his bull's-eye lantern on the unfortunate man's face.

"'It looks as if he had been strangled, don't it?' he murmured to his comrade.

"And he pointed to the swollen tongue, the eyes half out of their sockets, bloodshot and congested, the purple, almost black, hue of the face.

"At this point one of the spectators, more callous to horrors, peered curiously into the dead man's face. He uttered an exclamation of astonishment.

"'Why, surely, it's Mr. Cohen from No. 30!'

"The mention of a name familiar down the length of the street had caused two or three other men to come forward and to look more closely into the horribly distorted mask of the murdered man.

"'Our next-door neighbour, undoubtedly,' asserted Mr. Ellison, a young barrister, residing at No. 31.

"'What in the world was he doing this foggy night all alone, and on foot?' asked somebody else.

"'He usually came home very late. I fancy he belonged to some gambling club in town. I dare say he couldn't get a cab to bring him out here. Mind you, I don't know much about him. We only knew him to nod to.'

"'Poor beggar! it looks almost like an old-fashioned case of garroting.'

"'Anyway, the blackguardly murderer, whoever he was, wanted to make sure he had killed his man!' added Constable F 18, as he picked up an object from the pavement. 'Here's the revolver, with two cartridges missing. You gentlemen heard the report just now?'

"'He don't seem to have hit him though. The poor bloke was strangled, no doubt.'

"'And tried to shoot at his assailant, obviously,' asserted the young barrister with authority.

"'If he succeeded in hitting the brute, there might be a chance of tracing the way he went.'

"'But not in the fog.'

"Soon, however, the appearance of the inspector, detective, and medical officer, who had quickly been informed of the tragedy, put an end to further discussion.

"The bell at No. 30 was rung, and the servants—all four of them women—were asked to look at the body.

"Amidst tears of horror and screams of fright, they all recognized in the murdered man their master, Mr. Aaron Cohen. He was therefore conveyed to his own room pending the coroner's inquest.

"The police had a pretty difficult task, you will admit; there were so very few indications to go by, and at first literally no clue.

"The inquest revealed practically nothing. Very little was known in the neighbourhood about Mr. Aaron Cohen and his affairs. His female servants did not even know the name or whereabouts of the various clubs he frequented.

"He had an office in Throgmorton Street and went to business every day. He dined at home, and sometimes had friends to dinner. When he was alone he invariably went to the club, where he stayed until the small hours of the morning.

"The night of the murder he had gone out at about nine o'clock. That was the last his servants had seen of him. With regard to the revolver, all four servants swore positively that they had never seen it before, and that, unless Mr. Cohen had bought it that very day, it did not belong to their master.

"Beyond that, no trace whatever of the murderer had been found, but on the morning after the crime a couple of keys linked together by a short metal chain were found close to a gate at the opposite end of the Square, that which immediately faced Portland Place. These were proved to be, firstly, Mr. Cohen's latch-key, and, secondly, his gate-key of the Square.

"It was therefore presumed that the murderer, having accomplished his fell design and ransacked his victim's pockets, had found the keys and made good his escape by slipping into the Square, cutting under the tunnel, and out again by the further gate. He then took the precaution not to carry the keys with him any further, but threw them away and disappeared in the fog.

"The jury returned a verdict of wilful murder against some person or persons unknown, and the police were put on their mettle to discover the unknown and daring murderer. The result of their investigations, conducted with marvellous skill by Mr. William Fisher, led, about a week after the crime, to the sensational arrest of one of London's smartest young bucks.

"The case Mr. Fisher had got up against the accused briefly amounted to this:

"On the night of February 6th, soon after midnight, play began to run very high at the Harewood Club, in Hanover Square. Mr. Aaron Cohen held the bank at roulette against some twenty or thirty of his friends, mostly young fellows with no wits and plenty of money. 'The Bank' was winning heavily, and it appears that this was the third consecutive night on which Mr. Aaron Cohen had gone home richer by several hundreds than he had been at the start of play.

"Young John Ashley, who is the son of a very worthy county gentleman who is M.F.H. somewhere in the Midlands, was losing heavily, and in his case also it appears that it was the third consecutive night that Fortune had turned her face against him.

"Remember," continued the man in the corner, "that when I tell you all these details and facts, I am giving you the combined evidence of several witnesses, which it took many days to collect and to classify.

"It appears that young Mr. Ashley, though very popular in society, was generally believed to be in what is vulgarly termed 'low water'; up to his eyes in debt, and mortally afraid of his dad, whose younger son he was, and who had on one occasion threatened to ship him off to Australia with a £5 note in his pocket if he made any further extravagant calls upon his paternal indulgence.

"It was also evident to all John Ashley's many companions that the worthy M.F.H. held the purse-strings in a very tight grip. The young man, bitten with the desire to cut a smart figure in the circles in which he moved, had often recourse to the varying fortunes which now and again smiled upon him across the green tables in the Harewood Club.

"Be that as it may, the general consensus of opinion at the Club was that young Ashley had changed his last 'pony' before he sat down to a turn of roulette with Aaron Cohen on that particular night of February 6th.

"It appears that all his friends, conspicuous among whom was Mr. Walter Hatherell, tried their very best to dissuade him from pitting his luck against that of Cohen, who had been having a most unprecedented run of good fortune. But young Ashley, heated with wine, exasperated at his own bad luck, would listen to no one; he tossed one £5 note after another on the board, he borrowed from those who would lend, then played on parole for a while. Finally, at half-past one in the morning, after a run of nineteen on the red, the young man found himself without a penny in his pockets, and owing a debt—gambling debt—a debt of honour of £1500 to Mr. Aaron Cohen.

"Now we must render this much maligned gentleman that justice which was persistently denied to him by press and public alike; it was positively asserted by all those present that Mr. Cohen himself repeatedly tried to induce young Mr. Ashley to give up playing. He himself was in a delicate position in the matter, as he was the winner, and once or twice the taunt had risen to the young man's lips, accusing the holder of the bank of the wish to retire on a competence before the break in his luck.

"Mr. Aaron Cohen, smoking the best of Havanas, had finally shrugged his shoulders and said: 'As you please!'

"But at half-past one he had had enough of the player, who always lost and never paid—never could pay, so Mr. Cohen probably believed. He therefore at that hour refused to accept Mr. John Ashley's 'promissory' stakes any longer. A very few heated words ensued, quickly checked by the management, who are ever on the alert to avoid the least suspicion of scandal.

"In the meanwhile Mr. Hatherell, with great good sense, persuaded young Ashley to leave the Club and all its temptations and go home; if possible to bed.

"The friendship of the two young men, which was very well known in society, consisted chiefly, it appears, in Walter Hatherell being the willing companion and helpmeet of John Ashley in his mad and extravagant pranks. But to-night the latter, apparently tardily sobered by his terrible and heavy losses, allowed himself to be led away by his friend from the scene of his disasters. It was then about twenty minutes to two.

"Here the situation becomes interesting," continued the man in the corner in his nervous way. "No wonder that the police interrogated at least a dozen witnesses before they were quite satisfied that every statement was conclusively proved.

"Walter Hatherell, after about ten minutes' absence, that is to say at ten minutes to two, returned to the club room. In reply to several inquiries, he said that he had parted with his friend at the corner of New Bond Street, since he seemed anxious to be alone, and that Ashley said he would take a turn down Piccadilly before going home—he thought a walk would do him good.

"At two o'clock or thereabouts Mr. Aaron Cohen, satisfied with his evening's work, gave up his position at the bank and, pocketing his heavy winnings, started on his homeward walk, while Mr. Walter Hatherell left the club half an hour later.

"At three o'clock precisely the cries of 'Murder' and the report of fire-arms were heard in Park Square West, and Mr. Aaron Cohen was found strangled outside the garden railings."

II.

"Now at first sight the murder in the Regent's Park appeared both to police and public as one of those silly, clumsy crimes, obviously the work of a novice, and absolutely purposeless, seeing that it could but inevitably lead its perpetrators, without any difficulty, to the gallows.

"You see, a motive had been established. 'Seek him whom the crime benefits,' say our French *confrères*. But there was something more than that.

"Constable James Funnell, on his beat, turned from Portland Place into Park Crescent a few minutes after he had heard the clock at Holy Trinity Church, Marylebone, strike half-past two. The fog at that moment was perhaps not quite so dense as it was later on in the morning, and the policeman saw two gentlemen in overcoats and top-hats leaning arm in arm against the railings of the Square, close to the gate. He could not, of course, distinguish their faces because of the fog, but he heard one of them saying to the other:

"'It is but a question of time, Mr. Cohen. I know my father will pay the money for me, and you will lose nothing by waiting.'

"To this the other apparently made no reply, and the constable passed on; when he returned to the same spot, after having walked over his beat, the two gentlemen had gone, but later on it was near this very gate that the two keys referred to at the inquest had been found.

"Another interesting fact," added the man in the corner, with one of those sarcastic smiles of his which Polly could not quite explain, "was the finding of the revolver upon the scene of the crime. That revolver, shown to Mr. Ashley's valet, was sworn to by him as being the property of his master.

"All these facts made, of course, a very remarkable, so far quite unbroken, chain of circumstantial evidence against Mr. John Ashley. No wonder, therefore, that the police, thoroughly satisfied with Mr. Fisher's work and their own, applied for a warrant against the young man, and arrested him in his rooms in Clarges Street exactly a week after the committal of the crime.

"As a matter of fact, you know, experience has invariably taught me that when a murderer seems particularly foolish and clumsy, and proofs against him seem particularly damning, that is the time when the police should be most guarded against pitfalls.

"Now in this case, if John Ashley had indeed committed the murder in Regent's Park in the manner suggested by the police, he would have been a criminal in more senses than one, for idiocy of that kind is to my mind worse than many crimes.

"The prosecution brought its witnesses up in triumphal array one after another. There were the members of the Harewood Club—who had seen the prisoner's excited condition after his heavy gambling losses to Mr. Aaron Cohen; there was Mr. Hatherell, who, in spite of his friendship for Ashley, was bound to admit that he had parted from him at the corner of Bond Street at twenty minutes to two, and had not seen him again till his return home at five A.M.

"Then came the evidence of Arthur Chipps, John Ashley's valet. It proved of a very sensational character.

"He deposed that on the night in question his master came home at about ten minutes to two. Chipps had then not yet gone to bed. Five minutes later Mr. Ashley went out again, telling the valet not to sit up for him. Chipps could not say at what time either of the young gentlemen had come home.

"That short visit home—presumably to fetch the revolver—was thought to be very important, and Mr. John Ashley's friends felt that his case was practically hopeless.

"The valet's evidence and that of James Funnell, the constable, who had overheard the conversation near the park railings, were certainly the two most damning proofs against the accused. I assure you I was having a rare old time that day. There were two faces in court to watch which was the greatest treat I had had for many a day. One of these was Mr. John Ashley's.

"Here's his photo—short, dark, dapper, a little 'racy' in style, but otherwise he looks a son of a well-to-do farmer. He was very quiet and placid in court, and addressed a few words now and again to his solicitor. He listened gravely, and with an occasional shrug of the shoulders, to the recital of the crime, such as the police had reconstructed it, before an excited and horrified audience.

"Mr. John Ashley, driven to madness and frenzy by terrible financial difficulties, had first of all gone home in search of a weapon, then waylaid Mr. Aaron Cohen somewhere on that gentleman's way home. The young man had begged for delay. Mr. Cohen perhaps was obdurate; but Ashley followed him with his importunities almost to his door.

"There, seeing his creditor determined at last to cut short the painful interview, he had seized the unfortunate man at an unguarded moment from behind, and strangled him; then, fearing that his dastardly work was not fully accomplished, he had shot twice at the already dead body, missing it both times from sheer nervous excitement. The murderer then must have emptied his victim's pockets, and, finding the key of the garden, thought that it would be a safe way of evading capture by cutting across the squares, under the tunnel, and so through the more distant gate which faced Portland Place.

"The loss of the revolver was one of those unforeseen accidents which a retributive Providence places in the path of the miscreant, delivering him by his own act of folly into the hands of human justice.

"Mr. John Ashley, however, did not appear the least bit impressed by the recital of his crime. He had not engaged the services of one of the most eminent lawyers, expert at extracting contradictions from witnesses by skilful cross-examinations—oh, dear me, no! he had been contented with those of a dull, prosy, very second-rate limb of the law, who, as he called his witnesses, was completely innocent of any desire to create a sensation.

"He rose quietly from his seat, and, amidst breathless silence, called the first of three witnesses on behalf of his client. He called three—but he could have produced twelve—gentlemen, members of the Ashton Club in Great Portland Street, all of whom swore that at three o'clock on the morning of February 6th, that is to say, at the very moment when the cries of 'Murder' roused the inhabitants of Park Square West, and the crime was being committed, Mr. John Ashley was sitting quietly in the club-rooms of the Ashton playing bridge with the three witnesses. He had come in a few minutes before three—as the hall porter of the Club testified—and stayed for about an hour and a half.

"I need not tell you that this undoubted, this fully proved, *alibi* was a positive bombshell in the stronghold of the prosecution. The most accomplished criminal could not possibly be in two places at once, and though the Ashton Club transgresses in many ways against the gambling laws of our very moral country, yet its members belong to the best, most unimpeachable classes of society. Mr. Ashley had been seen and spoken to at the very moment of the crime by at least a dozen gentlemen whose testimony was absolutely above suspicion.

"Mr. John Ashley's conduct throughout this astonishing phase of the inquiry remained perfectly calm and correct. It was no doubt the consciousness of being able to prove his innocence with such absolute conclusion that had steadied his nerves throughout the proceedings.

"His answers to the magistrate were clear and simple, even on the ticklish subject of the revolver.

"'I left the club, sir,' he explained, 'fully determined to speak with Mr. Cohen alone in order to ask him for a delay in the settlement of my debt to him. You will understand that I should not care to do this in the presence of other gentlemen. I went home for a minute or two—not in order to fetch a revolver, as the police assert, for I always carry a revolver about with me in foggy weather—but in order to see if a very important business letter had come for me in my absence.

"'Then I went out again, and met Mr. Aaron Cohen not far from the Harewood Club. I walked the greater part of the way with him, and our conversation was of the most amicable character. We parted at the top of Portland Place, near the gate of the Square, where the policeman saw us. Mr. Cohen then had the intention of cutting across the Square, as being a shorter way to his own house. I thought the Square looked dark and dangerous in the fog, especially as Mr. Cohen was carrying a large sum of money.

"'We had a short discussion on the subject, and finally I persuaded him to take my revolver, as I was going home only through very frequented streets, and moreover carried nothing that was worth stealing. After a little demur Mr. Cohen accepted the loan of my revolver, and that is how it came to be found on the actual scene of the crime; finally I parted from Mr. Cohen a very few minutes after I had heard the church clock striking a quarter before three. I was at the Oxford Street end of Great Portland Street at five minutes to three, and it takes at least ten minutes to walk from where I was to the Ashton Club.'

"This explanation was all the more credible, mind you, because the question of the revolver had never been very satisfactorily explained by the prosecution. A man who has effectually strangled his victim would not discharge two shots of his revolver for, apparently, no other purpose than that of rousing the attention of the nearest passer-by. It was far more likely that it was Mr. Cohen who shot—perhaps wildly into the air, when suddenly attacked from behind. Mr. Ashley's explanation therefore was not only plausible, it was the only possible one.

"You will understand therefore how it was that, after nearly half an hour's examination, the magistrate, the police, and the public were alike pleased to proclaim that the accused left the court without a stain upon his character."

III.

"Yes," interrupted Polly eagerly, since, for once, her acumen had been at least as sharp as his, "but suspicion of that horrible crime only shifted its taint from one friend to another, and, of course, I know—"

"But that's just it," he quietly interrupted, "you don't know—Mr. Walter Hatherell, of course, you mean. So did every one else at once. The friend, weak and willing, committing a crime on behalf of his cowardly, yet more assertive friend who had tempted him to evil. It was a good theory; and was held pretty generally, I fancy, even by the police.

"I say 'even' because they worked really hard in order to build up a case against young Hatherell, but the great difficulty was that of time. At the hour when the policeman had seen the two men outside Park Square together, Walter Hatherell was still sitting in the Harewood Club, which he never left until twenty minutes to two. Had he wished to waylay and rob Aaron Cohen he would not have waited surely till the time when presumably the latter would already have reached home.

"Moreover, twenty minutes was an incredibly short time in which to walk from Hanover Square to Regent's Park without the chance of cutting across the squares, to look for a man, whose whereabouts you could not determine to within twenty yards or so, to have an argument with him, murder him, and ransack his pockets. And then there was the total absence of motive."

"But—" said Polly meditatively, for she remembered now that the Regent's Park murder, as it had been popularly called, was one of those which had remained as impenetrable a mystery as any other crime had ever been in the annals of the police.

The man in the corner cocked his funny birdlike head well on one side and looked at her, highly amused evidently at her perplexity.

"You do not see how that murder was committed?" he asked with a grin.

Polly was bound to admit that she did not.

"If you had happened to have been in Mr. John Ashley's predicament," he persisted, "you do not see how you could conveniently have done away with Mr. Aaron Cohen, pocketed his winnings, and then led the police of your country entirely by the nose, by proving an indisputable *alibi*?"

"I could not arrange conveniently," she retorted, "to be in two different places half a mile apart at one and the same time."

"No! I quite admit that you could not do this unless you also had a friend—"

"A friend? But you say—"

"I say that I admired Mr. John Ashley, for his was the head which planned the whole thing, but he could not have accomplished the fascinating and terrible drama without the help of willing and able hands."

"Even then—" she protested.

"Point number one," he began excitedly, fidgeting with his inevitable piece of string. "John Ashley and his friend Walter Hatherell leave the club together, and together decide on the plan of campaign. Hatherell returns to the club, and Ashley goes to fetch the revolver—the revolver which played such an important part in the drama, but not the part assigned to it by the police. Now try to follow Ashley closely, as he dogs Aaron Cohen's footsteps. Do you believe that he entered into conversation with him? That he walked by his side? That he asked for delay? No! He sneaked behind him and caught him by the throat, as the garroters used to do in the fog. Cohen was apoplectic, and Ashley is young and powerful. Moreover, he meant to kill—"

"But the two men talked together outside the Square gates," protested Polly, "one of whom was Cohen, and the other Ashley."

"Pardon me," he said, jumping up in his seat like a monkey on a stick, "there were not two men talking outside the Square gates. According to the testimony of James Funnell, the constable, two men were leaning arm in arm against the railings and *one* man was talking."

"Then you think that—"

"At the hour when James Funnell heard Holy Trinity clock striking half-past two Aaron Cohen was already dead. Look how simple the whole thing is," he added eagerly, "and how easy after that—easy, but oh, dear me! how wonderfully, how stupendously clever. As soon as James Funnell has passed on, John Ashley, having opened the gate, lifts the body of Aaron Cohen in his arms and carries him across the Square. The Square is deserted, of course, but the way is easy enough, and we must presume that Ashley had been in it before. Anyway, there was no fear of meeting any one.

"In the meantime Hatherell has left the club: as fast as his athletic legs can carry him he rushes along Oxford Street and Portland Place. It had been arranged between the two miscreants that the Square gate should be left on the latch.

"Close on Ashley's heels now, Hatherell too cuts across the Square, and reaches the further gate in good time to give his confederate a hand in disposing the body against the railings. Then, without another instant's delay, Ashley runs back across the gardens, straight to the Ashton Club, throwing away the keys of the dead man, on the very spot where he had made it a point of being seen and heard by a passer-by.

"Hatherell gives his friend six or seven minutes' start, then he begins the altercation which lasts two or three minutes, and finally rouses the neighbourhood with cries of 'Murder' and report of pistol in order to establish that the crime was committed at the hour when its perpetrator has already made out an indisputable *alibi*."

"I don't know what you think of it all, of course," added the funny creature as he fumbled for his coat and his gloves, "but I call the planning of that murder—on the part of novices, mind you—one of the cleverest pieces of strategy I have ever come across. It is one of those cases where there is no possibility whatever now of bringing the crime home to its perpetrator or his abettor. They have not left a single proof behind them; they foresaw everything, and each acted his part with a coolness and courage which, applied to a great and good cause, would have made fine statesmen of them both.

"As it is, I fear, they are just a pair of young blackguards, who have escaped human justice, and have only deserved the full and ungrudging admiration of yours very sincerely."

He had gone. Polly wanted to call him back, but his meagre person was no longer visible through the glass door. There were many things she would have wished to ask of him—what were his proofs, his facts? His were theories, after all, and yet, somehow, she felt that he had solved once again one of the darkest mysteries of great criminal London.

11
The De Genneville Peerage

I.

The man in the corner rubbed his chin thoughtfully, and looked out upon the busy street below.

"I suppose," he said, "there is some truth in the saying that Providence watches over bankrupts, kittens, and lawyers."

"I didn't know there was such a saying," replied Polly, with guarded dignity.

"Isn't there? Perhaps I am misquoting; anyway, there should be. Kittens, it seems, live and thrive through social and domestic upheavals which would annihilate a self-supporting tom-cat, and to-day I read in the morning papers the account of a noble lord's bankruptcy, and in the society ones that of his visit at the house of a Cabinet minister, where he is the most honoured guest. As for lawyers, when Providence had exhausted all other means of securing their welfare, it brought forth the peerage cases."

"I believe, as a matter of fact, that this special dispensation of Providence, as you call it, requires more technical knowledge than any other legal complication that comes before the law courts," she said.

"And also a great deal more money in the client's pocket than any other complication. Now, take the Brockelsby peerage case. Have you any idea how much money was spent over that soap bubble, which only burst after many hundreds, if not thousands, of pounds went in lawyers' and counsels' fees?"

"I suppose a great deal of money was spent on both sides," she replied, "until that sudden, awful issue—"

"Which settled the dispute effectually," he interrupted with a dry chuckle. "Of course, it is very doubtful if any reputable solicitor would have taken up the case. Timothy Beddingfield, the Birmingham lawyer, is a gentleman who—well—has had some misfortunes, shall we say? He is still on the rolls, mind you, but I doubt if any case would have its chances improved by his conducting it. Against that there is just this to be said, that some of these old peerages have such peculiar histories, and own such wonderful archives, that a claim is always worth investigating—you never know what may be the rights of it.

"I believe that, at first, every one laughed over the pretensions of the Hon. Robert Ingram de Genneville to the joint title and part revenues of the old barony of Genneville, but, obviously, he *might* have got his case. It certainly sounded almost like a fairy-tale, this claim based upon the supposed validity of an ancient document over 400 years old. It was *then* that a mediaeval Lord de Genneville, more endowed with muscle than common sense, became during his turbulent existence much embarrassed and hopelessly puzzled through the presentation made to him by his lady of twin-born sons.

"His embarrassment chiefly arose from the fact that my lady's attendants, while ministering to the comfort of the mother, had, in a moment of absent-mindedness, so placed the two infants in their cot that subsequently no one, not even—perhaps least of all—the mother, could tell which was the one who had been the first to make his appearance into this troublesome and puzzling world.

"After many years of cogitation, during which the Lord de Genneville approached nearer to the grave and his sons to man's estate, he gave up trying to solve the riddle as to which of the twins should succeed to his title and revenues; he appealed to his Liege Lord and King—Edward, fourth of that name—and with the latter's august sanction he drew up a certain document, wherein he enacted that both his sons should, after his death, share his titles and goodly revenues, and that the first son born in wedlock of *either* father should subsequently be the sole heir.

"In this document was also added that if in future times should any Lords de Genneville be similarly afflicted with twin sons, who had equal rights to be considered the eldest born, the same rule should apply as to the succession.

"Subsequently a Lord de Genneville was created Earl of Brockelsby by one of the Stuart kings, but for four hundred years after its enactment the extraordinary deed of succession remained a mere tradition, the Countesses of Brockelsby having, seemingly, no predilection for twins. But in 1878 the mistress of Brockelsby Castle presented her lord with twin-born sons.

"Fortunately, in modern times, science is more wide-awake, and attendants more careful. The twin brothers did not get mixed up, and one of them was styled Viscount Tirlemont, and was heir to the earldom, whilst the other, born two hours later, was that fascinating, dashing young Guardsman, well known at Hurlingham, Goodwood, London, and in his own county—the Hon. Robert Ingram de Genneville.

"It certainly was an evil day for this brilliant young scion of the ancient race when he lent an ear to Timothy Beddingfield. This man, and his family before him, had been solicitors to the Earls of Brockelsby for many generations, but Timothy, owing to certain 'irregularities,' had forfeited the confidence of his client, the late earl.

"He was still in practice in Birmingham, however, and, of course, knew the ancient family tradition anent the twin succession. Whether he was prompted by revenge or merely self-advertisement no one knows.

"Certain it is that he did advise the Hon. Robert de Genneville—who apparently had more debts than he conveniently could pay, and more extravagant tastes than he could gratify on a younger son's portion—to lay a claim, on his father's death, to the joint title and a moiety of the revenues of the ancient barony of Genneville, that claim being based upon the validity of the fifteenth-century document.

"You may gather how extensive were the pretensions of the Hon. Robert from the fact that the greater part of Edgbaston is now built upon land belonging to the old barony. Anyway, it was the last straw in an ocean of debt and difficulties, and I have no doubt that Beddingfield had not much trouble in persuading the Hon. Robert to commence litigation at once.

"The young Earl of Brockelsby's attitude, however, remained one of absolute quietude in his nine points of the law. He was in possession both of the title and of the document. It was for the other side to force him to produce the one or to share the other.

"It was at this stage of the proceedings that the Hon. Robert was advised to marry, in order to secure, if possible, the first male heir of the next generation, since the young earl himself was still a bachelor. A suitable *fiancée* was found for him by his friends in the person of Miss Mabel Brandon, the daughter of a rich Birmingham manufacturer, and the marriage was fixed to take place at Birmingham on Thursday, September 15th, 1907.

"On the 13th the Hon. Robert Ingram de Genneville arrived at the Castle Hotel in New Street for his wedding, and on the 14th, at eight o'clock in the morning, he was discovered lying on the floor of his bedroom—murdered.

"The sensation which the awful and unexpected sequel to the Do Genneville peerage case caused in the minds of the friends of both litigants was quite unparalleled. I don't think any crime of modern times created quite so much stir in all classes of society. Birmingham was wild with excitement, and the employés of the Castle Hotel had real difficulty in keeping off the eager and inquisitive crowd who thronged daily to the hall, vainly hoping to gather details of news relating to the terrible tragedy.

"At present there was but little to tell. The shrieks of the chambermaid, who had gone into the Hon. Robert's room with his shaving water at eight o'clock, had attracted some of the waiters. Soon the manager and his secretary came up, and immediately sent for the police.

"It seemed at first sight as if the young man had been the victim of a homicidal maniac, so brutal had been the way in which he had been assassinated. The head and body were battered and bruised by some heavy stick or poker, almost past human shape, as if the murderer had wished to wreak some awful vengeance upon the body of his victim. In fact, it would be impossible to recount the gruesome aspect of that room and of the murdered man's body such as the police and the medical officer took note of that day.

"It was supposed that the murder had been committed the evening before, as the victim was dressed in his evening clothes, and all the lights in the room had been left fully turned on. Robbery, also, must have had a large share in the miscreant's motives, for the drawers and cupboards, the portmanteau and dressing-bag had been ransacked as if in search of valuables. On the floor there lay a pocket-book torn in half and only containing a few letters addressed to the Hon. Robert de Genneville.

"The Earl of Brockelsby, next-of-kin to the deceased, was also telegraphed for. He drove over from Brockelsby Castle, which is about seven miles from Birmingham. He was terribly affected by the awfulness of the tragedy, and offered a liberal reward to stimulate the activity of the police in search of the miscreant.

"The inquest was fixed for the 17th, three days later, and the public was left wondering where the solution lay of the terrible and gruesome murder at the Castle Hotel."

II.

"The central figure in the coroner's court that day was undoubtedly the Earl of Brockelsby in deep black, which contrasted strongly with his florid complexion and fair hair. Sir Marmaduke Ingersoll, his solicitor, was with him, and he had already performed the painful duty of identifying the deceased as his brother. This had been an exceedingly painful duty owing to the terribly mutilated state of the body and face; but the clothes and various trinkets he wore, including a signet ring, had fortunately not tempted the brutal assassin, and it was through them chiefly that Lord Brockelsby was able to swear to the identity of his brother.

"The various employés at the hotel gave evidence as to the discovery of the body, and the medical officer gave his opinion as to the immediate cause of death. Deceased had evidently been struck at the back of the head with a poker or heavy stick, the murderer then venting his blind fury upon the body by battering in the face and bruising it in a way that certainly suggested the work of a maniac.

"Then the Earl of Brockelsby was called, and was requested by the coroner to state when he had last seen his brother alive.

"'The morning before his death,' replied his lordship, 'he came up to Birmingham by an early train, and I drove up from Brockelsby to see him. I got to the hotel at eleven o'clock and stayed with him for about an hour.'

"'And that is the last you saw of the deceased?'

"'That is the last I saw of him,' replied Lord Brockelsby.

"He seemed to hesitate for a moment or two as if in thought whether he should speak or not, and then to suddenly make up his mind to speak, for he added: 'I stayed in town the whole of that day, and only drove back to Brockelsby late in the evening. I had some business to transact, and put up at the Grand, as I usually do, and dined with some friends.'

"'Would you tell us at what time you returned to Brockelsby Castle?'

"'I think it must have been about eleven o'clock. It is a seven-mile drive from here.'

"'I believe,' said the coroner after a slight pause, during which the attention of all the spectators was riveted upon the handsome figure of the young man as he stood in the witness-box, the very personification of a high-bred gentleman, 'I believe that I am right in stating that there was an unfortunate legal dispute between your lordship and your brother?'

"'That is so.'

"The coroner stroked his chin thoughtfully for a moment or two, then he added:

"'In the event of the deceased's claim to the joint title and revenues of De Genneville being held good in the courts of law, there would be a great importance, would there not, attached to his marriage, which was to have taken place on the 15th?'

"'In that event, there certainly would be.'

"'Is the jury to understand, then, that you and the deceased parted on amicable terms after your interview with him in the morning?'

"The Earl of Brockelsby hesitated again for a minute or two, while the crowd and the jury hung breathless on his lips.

"'There was no enmity between us,' he replied at last.

"'From which we may gather that there may have been—shall I say—a slight disagreement at that interview?'

"'My brother had unfortunately been misled by the misrepresentations or perhaps the too optimistic views of his lawyer. He had been dragged into litigation on the strength of an old family document which he had never seen, which, moreover, is antiquated, and, owing to certain wording in it, invalid. I thought that it would be kinder and more considerate if I were to let my brother judge of the document for himself. I knew that when he had seen it he would be convinced of the absolutely futile basis of his claim, and that it would be a terrible disappointment to him. That is the reason why I wished to see him myself about it, rather than to do it through the more formal—perhaps more correct—medium of our respective lawyers. I placed the facts before him with, on my part, a perfectly amicable spirit.'

"The young Earl of Brockelsby had made this somewhat lengthy, perfectly voluntary explanation of the state of affairs in a calm, quiet voice, with much dignity and perfect simplicity, but the coroner did not seem impressed by it, for he asked very drily:

"'Did you part good friends?'

"'On my side absolutely so.'

"'But not on his?' insisted the coroner.

"'I think he felt naturally annoyed that he had been so ill-advised by his solicitors.'

"'And you made no attempt later on in the day to adjust any ill-feeling that may have existed between you and him?' asked the coroner, marking with strange, earnest emphasis every word he uttered.

"'If you mean did I go and see my brother again that day—no, I did not.'

"'And your lordship can give us no further information which might throw some light upon the mystery which surrounds the Hon. Robert de Genneville's death?' still persisted the coroner.

"'I am sorry to say I cannot,' replied the Earl of Brockelsby with firm decision.

"The coroner still looked puzzled and thoughtful. It seemed at first as if he wished to press his point further; every one felt that some deep import had lain behind his examination of the witness, and all were on tenter-hooks as to what the next evidence might bring forth. The Earl of Brockelsby had waited a minute or two, then, at a sign from the coroner, had left the witness-box in order to have a talk with his solicitor.

"At first he paid no attention to the depositions of the cashier and hall porter of the Castle Hotel, but gradually it seemed to strike him that curious statements were being made by these witnesses, and a frown of anxious wonder settled between his brows, whilst his young face lost some of its florid hue.

"Mr. Tremlett, the cashier at the hotel, had been holding the attention of the court. He stated that the Hon. Robert Ingram de Genneville had arrived at the hotel at eight o'clock on the morning of the 13th; he had the room which he usually occupied when he came to the 'Castle,' namely, No. 21, and he went up to it immediately on his arrival, ordering some breakfast to be brought up to him.

"At eleven o'clock the Earl of Brockelsby called to see his brother and remained with him until about twelve. In the afternoon deceased went out, and returned for his dinner at seven o'clock in company with a gentleman whom the cashier knew well by sight, Mr. Timothy Beddingfield, the lawyer, of Paradise Street. The gentlemen had their dinner downstairs, and after that they went up to the Hon. Mr. de Genneville's room for coffee and cigars.

"'I could not say at what time Mr. Beddingfield left,' continued the cashier, 'but I rather fancy I saw him in the hall at about 9.15 P.M. He was wearing an Inverness cape over his dress clothes and a Glengarry cap. It was just at the hour when the visitors who had come down for the night from London were arriving thick and fast; the hall was very full, and there was a large party of Americans monopolising most of our *personnel*, so I could not swear positively whether I did see Mr. Beddingfield or not then, though I am quite sure that it was Mr. Timothy Beddingfield who dined and spent the evening with the Hon. Mr. de Genneville, as I know him quite well by sight. At ten o'clock I am off duty, and the night porter remains alone in the hall.'

"Mr. Tremlett's evidence was corroborated in most respects by a waiter and by the hall porter. They had both seen the deceased come in at seven o'clock in company with a gentleman, and their description of the latter coincided with that of the appearance of Mr. Timothy Beddingfield, whom, however, they did not actually know.

"At this point of the proceedings the foreman of the jury wished to know why Mr. Timothy Beddingfield's evidence had not been obtained, and was informed by the detective-inspector in charge of the case that that gentleman had seemingly left Birmingham, but was expected home shortly. The coroner suggested an adjournment pending Mr. Beddingfield's appearance, but at the earnest request of the detective he consented to hear the evidence of Peter Tyrrell, the night porter at the Castle Hotel, who, if you remember the case at all, succeeded in creating the biggest sensation of any which had been made through this extraordinary and weirdly gruesome case.

"'It was the first time I had been on duty at "The Castle," he said, 'for I used to be night porter at "Bright's," in Wolverhampton, but just after I had come on duty at ten o'clock a gentleman came and asked if he could see the Hon. Robert de Genneville. I said that I thought he was in, but would send up and see. The gentleman said: "It doesn't matter. Don't trouble; I know his room. Twenty-one, isn't it?" And up he went before I could say another word.'

"'Did he give you any name?' asked the coroner.

"'No, sir.'

"'What was he like?'

"'A young gentleman, sir, as far as I can remember, in an Inverness cape and Glengarry cap, but I could not see his face very well as he stood with his back to the light, and the cap shaded his eyes, and he only spoke to me for a minute.'

"'Look all round you,' said the coroner quietly. 'Is there any one in this court at all like the gentleman you speak of?'

"An awed hush fell over the many spectators there present as Peter Tyrrell, the night porter of the Castle Hotel, turned his head towards the body of the court and slowly scanned the many faces there present; for a moment he seemed to hesitate—only for a moment though, then, as if vaguely conscious of the terrible importance his next words might have, he shook his head gravely and said:

"'I wouldn't like to swear.'

"The coroner tried to press him, but with true British stolidity he repeated: 'I wouldn't like to say.'

"'Well, then, what happened?' asked the coroner, who had perforce to abandon his point.

"'The gentleman went upstairs, sir, and about a quarter of an hour later he come down again, and I let him out. He was in a great hurry then, he threw me a half-crown and said: "Good night."'

"'And though you saw him again then, you cannot tell us if you would know him again?'

"Once more the hall porter's eyes wandered as if instinctively to a certain face in the court; once more he hesitated for many seconds which seemed like so many hours, during which a man's honour, a man's life, hung perhaps in the balance.

"Then Peter Tyrrell repeated slowly: 'I wouldn't swear.'

"But coroner and jury alike, aye, and every spectator in that crowded court, had seen that the man's eyes had rested during that one moment of hesitation upon the face of the Earl of Brockelsby."

III.

The man in the corner blinked across at Polly with his funny mild blue eyes.

"No wonder you are puzzled," he continued, "so was everybody in the court that day, every one save myself. I alone could see in my mind's eye that gruesome murder such as it had been committed, with all its details, and, above all, its motive, and such as you will see it presently, when I place it all clearly before you.

"But before you see daylight in this strange case, I must plunge you into further darkness, in the same manner as the coroner and jury were plunged on the following day, the second day of that remarkable inquest. It had to be adjourned, since the appearance of Mr. Timothy Beddingfield had now become of vital importance. The public had come to regard his absence from Birmingham at this critical moment as decidedly remarkable, to say the least of it, and all those who did not know the lawyer by sight wished to see him in his Inverness cape and Glengarry cap such as he had appeared before the several witnesses on the night of the awful murder.

"When the coroner and jury were seated, the first piece of information which the police placed before them was the astounding statement that Mr. Timothy Beddingfield's whereabouts had not been ascertained, though it was confidently expected that he had not gone far and could easily be traced. There was a witness present who, the police thought, might throw some light as to the lawyer's probable destination, for obviously he had left Birmingham directly after his interview with the deceased.

"This witness was Mrs. Higgins, who was Mr. Beddingfield's housekeeper. She stated that her master was in the constant habit—especially latterly—of going up to London on business. He usually left by a late evening train on those occasions, and mostly was only absent thirty-six hours. He kept a portmanteau always ready packed for the purpose, for he often left at a few moments' notice. Mrs. Higgins added that her master stayed at the Great Western Hotel in London, for it was there that she was instructed to wire if anything urgent required his presence back in Birmingham.

"'On the night of the 14th,' she continued, 'at nine o'clock or thereabouts, a messenger came to the door with the master's card, and said that he was instructed to fetch Mr. Beddingfield's portmanteau, and then to meet him at the station in time to catch the 9.35 P.M. up train. I gave him the portmanteau, of course, as he had brought the card, and I had no idea there could be anything wrong; but since then I have heard nothing of my master, and I don't know when he will return.'

"Questioned by the coroner, she added that Mr. Beddingfield had never stayed away quite so long without having his letters forwarded to him. There was a large pile waiting for him now; she had written to the Great Western Hotel, London, asking what she should do about the letters, but had received no reply. She did not know the messenger by sight who had called for the portmanteau. Once or twice before Mr. Beddingfield had sent for his things in that manner when he had been dining out.

"Mr. Beddingfield certainly wore his Inverness cape over his dress clothes when he went out at about six o'clock in the afternoon. He also wore a Glengarry cap.

"The messenger had so far not yet been found, and from this point—namely, the sending for the portmanteau—all traces of Mr. Timothy Beddingfield seem to have been lost. Whether he went up to London by that 9.35 train or not could not be definitely ascertained. The police had questioned at least a dozen porters at the railway, as well as ticket collectors; but no one had any special recollection of a gentleman in an Inverness cape and Glengarry cap, a costume worn by more than one first-class passenger on a cold night in September.

"There was the hitch, you see; it all lay in this. Mr. Timothy Beddingfield, the lawyer, had undoubtedly made himself scarce. He was last seen in company with the deceased, and wearing an Inverness cape and Glengarry cap; two or three witnesses saw him leaving the hotel at about 9.15. Then the messenger calls at the lawyer's house for the portmanteau, after which Mr. Timothy Beddingfield seems to vanish into thin air; but—and that is a great 'but'—the night porter at the 'Castle' seems to have seen some one wearing the momentous Inverness and Glengarry half an hour or so later on, and going up to deceased's room, where he stayed about a quarter of an hour.

"Undoubtedly you will say, as every one said to themselves that day after the night porter and Mrs. Higgins had been heard, that there was a very ugly and very black finger which pointed unpleasantly at Mr. Timothy Beddingfield, especially as that gentleman, for some reason which still required an explanation, was not there to put matters right for himself. But there was just one little thing—a mere trifle, perhaps—which neither the coroner nor the jury dared to overlook, though, strictly speaking, it was not evidence.

"You will remember that when the night porter was asked if he could, among the persons present in court, recognize the Hon. Robert de Genneville's belated visitor, every one had noticed his hesitation, and marked that the man's eyes had rested doubtingly upon the face and figure of the young Earl of Brockelsby.

"Now, if that belated visitor had been Mr. Timothy Beddingfield—tall, lean, dry as dust, with a bird-like beak and clean-shaven chin—no one could for a moment have mistaken his face—even if they only saw it very casually and recollected it but very dimly—with that of young Lord Brockelsby, who was florid and rather short—the only point in common between them was their Saxon hair.

"You see that it was a curious point, don't you?" added the man in the corner, who now had become so excited that his fingers worked like long thin tentacles round and round his bit of string. "It weighed very heavily in favour of Timothy Beddingfield. Added to which you must also remember that, as far as he was concerned, the Hon. Robert de Genneville was to him the goose with the golden eggs.

"The 'De Genneville peerage case' had brought Beddingfield's name in great prominence. With the death of the claimant all hopes of prolonging the litigation came to an end. There was a total lack of motive as far as Beddingfield was concerned."

"Not so with the Earl of Brockelsby," said Polly, "and I've often maintained—"

"What?" he interrupted. "That the Earl of Brockelsby changed clothes with Beddingfield in order more conveniently to murder his own brother? Where and when could the exchange of costume have been effected, considering that the Inverness cape and Glengarry cap were in the hall of the Castle Hotel at 9.15, and at that hour and until ten o'clock Lord Brockelsby was at the Grand

Hotel finishing dinner with some friends? That was subsequently proved, remember, and also that he was back at Brockelsby Castle, which is seven miles from Birmingham, at eleven o'clock sharp. Now, the visit of the individual in the Glengarry occurred some time after 10 P.M."

"Then there was the disappearance of Beddingfield," said the girl musingly. "That certainly points very strongly to him. He was a man in good practice, I believe, and fairly well known."

"And has never been heard of from that day to this," concluded the old scarecrow with a chuckle. "No wonder you are puzzled. The police were quite baffled, and still are, for a matter of that. And yet see how simple it is! Only the police would not look further than these two men—Lord Brockelsby with a strong motive and the night porter's hesitation against him, and Beddingfield without a motive, but with strong circumstantial evidence and his own disappearance as condemnatory signs.

"If only they would look at the case as I did, and think a little about the dead as well as about the living. If they had remembered that peerage case, the Hon. Robert's debts, his last straw which proved a futile claim.

"Only that very day the Earl of Brockelsby had, by quietly showing the original ancient document to his brother, persuaded him how futile were all his hopes. Who knows how many were the debts contracted, the promises made, the money borrowed and obtained on the strength of that claim which was mere romance? Ahead nothing but ruin, enmity with his brother, his marriage probably broken off, a wasted life, in fact.

"Is it small wonder that, though ill-feeling against the Earl of Brockelsby may have been deep, there was hatred, bitter, deadly hatred against the man who with false promises had led him into so hopeless a quagmire? Probably the Hon. Robert owed a great deal of money to Beddingfield, which the latter hoped to recoup at usurious interest, with threats of scandal and what not.

"Think of all that," he added, "and then tell me if you believe that a stronger motive for the murder of such an enemy could well be found."

"But what you suggest is impossible," said Polly, aghast.

"Allow me," he said, "it is more than possible—it is very easy and simple. The two men were alone together in the Hon. Robert de Genneville's room after dinner. You, as representing the public, and the police say that Beddingfield went away and returned half an hour later in order to kill his client. I say that it was the lawyer who was murdered at nine o'clock that evening, and that Robert de Genneville, the ruined man, the hopeless bankrupt, was the assassin."

"Then—"

"Yes, of course, now you remember, for I have put you on the track. The face and the body were so battered and bruised that they were past recognition. Both men were of equal height. The hair, which alone could not be disfigured or obliterated, was in both men similar in colour.

"Then the murderer proceeds to dress his victim in his own clothes. With the utmost care he places his own rings on the fingers of the dead man, his own watch in the pocket; a gruesome task, but an important one, and it is thoroughly well done. Then he himself puts on the clothes of his victim, with finally the Inverness cape and Glengarry, and when the hall is full of visitors he slips out unperceived. He sends the messenger for Beddingfield's portmanteau and starts off by the night express."

"But then his visit at the Castle Hotel at ten o'clock—" she urged. "How dangerous!"

"Dangerous? Yes! but oh, how clever. You see, he was the Earl of Brockelsby's twin brother, and twin brothers are always somewhat alike. He wished to appear dead, murdered by some one, he cared not whom, but what he did care about was to throw clouds of dust in the eyes of the police, and he succeeded with a vengeance. Perhaps—who knows?—he wished to assure himself that he had forgotten nothing in the *mise en scène,* that the body, battered and bruised past all semblance of any human shape save for its clothes, really would appear to every one as that of the Hon. Robert de Genneville, while the latter disappeared for ever from the old world and started life again in the new.

"Then you must always reckon with the practically invariable rule that a murderer always revisits, if only once, the scene of his crime.

"Two years have elapsed since the crime; no trace of Timothy Beddingfield, the lawyer, has ever been found, and I can assure you that it will never be, for his plebeian body lies buried in the aristocratic family vault of the Earl of Brockelsby."

He was gone before Polly could say another word. The faces of Timothy Beddingfield, of the Earl of Brockelsby, of the Hon. Robert de Genneville seemed to dance before her eyes and to mock her for the hopeless bewilderment in which she found herself plunged because of them; then all the faces vanished, or, rather, were merged in one long, thin, bird-like one, with bone-rimmed spectacles on the top of its beak, and a wide, rude grin beneath it, and, still puzzled, still doubtful, the young girl too paid for her scanty luncheon and went her way.

12
The Mysterious Death in Percy Street

I.

Miss Polly Burton had had many an argument with Mr. Richard Frobisher about that old man in the corner, who seemed far more interesting and deucedly more mysterious than any of the crimes over which he philosophised.

Dick thought, moreover, that Miss Polly spent more of her leisure time now in that A.B.C. shop than she had done in his own company before, and told her so, with that delightful air of sheepish sulkiness which the male creature invariably wears when he feels jealous and won't admit it.

Polly liked Dick to be jealous, but she liked that old scarecrow in the A.B.C. shop very much too, and though she made sundry vague promises from time to time to Mr. Richard Frobisher, she nevertheless drifted back instinctively day after day to the tea-shop in Norfolk Street, Strand, and stayed there sipping coffee for as long as the man in the corner chose to talk.

On this particular afternoon she went to the A.B.C. shop with a fixed purpose, that of making him give her his views of Mrs. Owen's mysterious death in Percy Street.

The facts had interested and puzzled her. She had had countless arguments with Mr. Richard Frobisher as to the three great possible solutions of the puzzle— "Accident, Suicide, Murder?"

"Undoubtedly neither accident nor suicide," he said dryly.

Polly was not aware that she had spoken. What an uncanny habit that creature had of reading her thoughts!

"You incline to the idea, then, that Mrs. Owen was murdered. Do you know by whom?"

He laughed, and drew forth the piece of string he always fidgeted with when unravelling some mystery.

"You would like to know who murdered that old woman?" he asked at last.

"I would like to hear your views on the subject," Polly replied.

"I have no views," he said dryly. "No one can know who murdered the woman, since no one ever saw the person who did it. No one can give the faintest description of the mysterious man who alone could have committed that clever deed, and the police are playing a game of blind man's buff."

"But you must have formed some theory of your own," she persisted.

It annoyed her that the funny creature was obstinate about this point, and she tried to nettle his vanity.

"I suppose that as a matter of fact your original remark that 'there are no such things as mysteries' does not apply universally. There is a mystery—that of the death in Percy Street, and you, like the police, are unable to fathom it."

He pulled up his eyebrows and looked at her for a minute or two.

"Confess that that murder was one of the cleverest bits of work accomplished outside Russian diplomacy," he said with a nervous laugh. "I must say that were I the judge, called upon to pronounce sentence of death on the man who conceived that murder, I could not bring myself to do it. I would politely request the gentleman to enter our Foreign Office—we have need of such men. The whole *mise en scène* was truly artistic, worthy of its *milieu*—the Rubens Studios in Percy Street, Tottenham Court Road.

"Have you ever noticed them? They are only studios by name, and are merely a set of rooms in a corner house, with the windows slightly enlarged, and the rents charged accordingly in consideration of that additional five inches of smoky daylight, filtering through dusty windows. On the ground floor there is the order office of some stained glass works, with a workshop in the rear, and on the first floor landing a small room allotted to the caretaker, with gas, coal, and fifteen shillings a week, for which princely income she is deputed to keep tidy and clean the general aspect of the house.

"Mrs. Owen, who was the caretaker there, was a quiet, respectable woman, who eked out her scanty wages by sundry—mostly very meagre—tips doled out to her by impecunious artists in exchange for promiscuous domestic services in and about the respective studios.

"But if Mrs. Owen's earnings were not large, they were very regular, and she had no fastidious tastes. She and her cockatoo lived on her wages; and all the tips added up, and never spent, year after year, went to swell a very comfortable little account at interest in the Birkbeck Bank. This little account had mounted up to a very tidy sum, and the thrifty widow—or old maid—no one ever knew which she was—was generally referred to by the young artists of the Rubens Studios as a 'lady of means.' But this is a digression.

"No one slept on the premises except Mrs. Owen and her cockatoo. The rule was that one by one as the tenants left their rooms in the evening they took their respective keys to the caretaker's room. She would then, in the early morning, tidy and dust the studios and the office downstairs, lay the fire and carry up coals.

"The foreman of the glass works was the first to arrive in the morning. He had a latch-key, and let himself in, after which it was the custom of the house that he should leave the street door open for the benefit of the other tenants and their visitors.

"Usually, when he came at about nine o'clock, he found Mrs. Owen busy about the house doing her work, and he had often a brief chat with her about the weather, but on this particular morning of February 2nd he neither saw nor heard her. However, as the shop had been tidied and the fire laid, he surmised that Mrs. Owen had finished her work earlier than usual, and thought no more about it. One by one the tenants of the studios turned up, and the day sped on without any one's attention being drawn noticeably to the fact that the caretaker had not appeared upon the scene.

"It had been a bitterly cold night, and the day was even worse; a cutting north-easterly gale was blowing, there had been a great deal of snow during the night which lay quite thick on the ground, and at five o'clock in the afternoon, when the last glimmer of the pale winter daylight had disappeared, the confraternity of the brush put palette and easel aside and prepared to go home. The first to leave was Mr. Charles Pitt; he locked up his studio and, as usual, took his key into the caretaker's room.

"He had just opened the door when an icy blast literally struck him in the face; both the windows were wide open, and the snow and sleet were beating thickly into the room, forming already a white carpet upon the floor.

"The room was in semi-obscurity, and at first Mr. Pitt saw nothing, but instinctively realizing that something was wrong, he lit a match, and saw before him the spectacle of that awful and mysterious tragedy which has ever since puzzled both police and public. On the floor, already half covered by the drifting snow, lay the body of Mrs. Owen face downwards, in a nightgown, with feet and ankles bare, and these and her hands were of a deep purple colour; whilst in a corner of the room, huddled up with the cold, the body of the cockatoo lay stark and stiff."

II.

"At first there was only talk of a terrible accident, the result of some inexplicable carelessness which perhaps the evidence at the inquest would help to elucidate.

"Medical assistance came too late; the unfortunate woman was indeed dead, frozen to death, inside her own room. Further examination showed that she had received a severe blow at the back of the head, which must have stunned her and caused her to fall, helpless, beside the open window. Temperature at five degrees below zero had done the rest. Detective Inspector Howell discovered close to the window a wrought-iron gas bracket, the height of which corresponded exactly with the bruise at the back of Mrs. Owen's head.

"Hardly however had a couple of days elapsed when public curiosity was whetted by a few startling headlines, such as the halfpenny evening papers alone know how to concoct.

"'The mysterious death in Percy Street.' 'Is it Suicide or Murder?' 'Thrilling details—Strange developments.' 'Sensational Arrest.'

"What had happened was simply this:

"At the inquest a few certainly very curious facts connected with Mrs. Owen's life had come to light, and this had led to the apprehension of a young man of very respectable parentage on a charge of being concerned in the tragic death of the unfortunate caretaker.

"To begin with, it happened that her life, which in an ordinary way should have been very monotonous and regular, seemed, at any rate latterly, to have been more than usually chequered and excited. Every witness who had known her in the past concurred in the statement that since October last a great change had come over the worthy and honest woman.

"I happen to have a photo of Mrs. Owen as she was before this great change occurred in her quiet and uneventful life, and which led, as far as the poor soul was concerned, to such disastrous results.

"Here she is to the life," added the funny creature, placing the photo before Polly— "as respectable, as stodgy, as uninteresting as it is well possible for a member of your charming sex to be; not a face, you will admit, to lead any youngster to temptation or to induce him to commit a crime.

"Nevertheless one day all the tenants of the Rubens Studios were surprised and shocked to see Mrs. Owen, quiet, respectable Mrs. Owen, sallying forth at six o'clock in the afternoon, attired in an extravagant bonnet and a cloak trimmed with imitation astrakhan which—slightly open in front—displayed a gold locket and chain of astonishing proportions.

"Many were the comments, the hints, the bits of sarcasm levelled at the worthy woman by the frivolous confraternity of the brush.

"The plot thickened when from that day forth a complete change came over the worthy caretaker of the Rubens Studios. While she appeared day after day before the astonished gaze of the tenants and the scandalized looks of the neighbours, attired in new and extravagant dresses, her work was hopelessly neglected, and she was always 'out' when wanted.

"There was, of course, much talk and comment in various parts of the Rubens Studios on the subject of Mrs. Owen's 'dissipations.' The tenants began to put two and two together, and after a very little while the general consensus of opinion became firmly established that the honest caretaker's demoralisation coincided week for week, almost day for day, with young Greenhill's establishment in No. 8 Studio.

"Every one had remarked that he stayed much later in the evening than any one else, and yet no one presumed that he stayed for purposes of work. Suspicions soon rose to certainty when Mrs. Owen and Arthur Greenhill were seen by one of the glass workmen dining together at Gambia's Restaurant in Tottenham Court Road.

"The workman, who was having a cup of tea at the counter, noticed particularly that when the bill was paid the money came out of Mrs. Owen's purse. The dinner had been sumptuous—veal cutlets, a cut from the joint, dessert, coffee and liqueurs. Finally the pair left the restaurant apparently very gay, young Greenhill smoking a choice cigar.

"Irregularities such as these were bound sooner or later to come to the ears and eyes of Mr. Allman, the landlord of the Rubens Studios; and a month after the New Year, without further warning, he gave her a week's notice to quit his house.

"'Mrs. Owen did not seem the least bit upset when I gave her notice,' Mr. Allman declared in his evidence at the inquest; 'on the contrary, she told me that she had ample means, and had only worked latterly for the sake of something to do. She added that she had plenty of friends who would look after her, for she had a nice little pile to leave to any one who would know how "to get the right side of her."'

"Nevertheless, in spite of this cheerful interview, Miss Bedford, the tenant of No. 6 Studio, had stated that when she took her key to the caretaker's room at 6.30 that afternoon she found Mrs. Owen in tears. The caretaker refused to be comforted, nor would she speak of her trouble to Miss Bedford.

"Twenty-four hours later she was found dead.

"The coroner's jury returned an open verdict, and Detective-Inspector Jones was charged by the police to make some inquiries about young Mr. Greenhill, whose intimacy with the unfortunate woman had been universally commented upon.

"The detective, however, pushed his investigations as far as the Birkbeck Bank. There he discovered that after her interview with Mr. Allman, Mrs. Owen had withdrawn what money she had on deposit, some £800, the result of twenty-five years' saving and thrift.

"But the immediate result of Detective-Inspector Jones's labours was that Mr. Arthur Greenhill, lithographer, was brought before the magistrate at Bow Street on the charge of being concerned in the death of Mrs. Owen, caretaker of the Rubens Studios, Percy Street.

"Now that magisterial inquiry is one of the few interesting ones which I had the misfortune to miss," continued the man in the corner, with a nervous shake of the shoulders. "But you know as well as I do how the attitude of the young prisoner impressed the magistrate and police so unfavourably that, with every new witness brought forward, his position became more and more unfortunate.

"Yet he was a good-looking, rather coarsely built young fellow, with one of those awful Cockney accents which literally make one jump. But he looked painfully nervous, stammered at every word spoken, and repeatedly gave answers entirely at random.

"His father acted as lawyer for him, a rough-looking elderly man, who had the appearance of a common country attorney rather than of a London solicitor.

"The police had built up a fairly strong case against the lithographer. Medical evidence revealed nothing new: Mrs. Owen had died from exposure, the blow at the back of the head not being sufficiently serious to cause anything but temporary disablement. When the medical officer had been called in, death had intervened for some time; it was quite impossible to say how long, whether one hour or five or twelve.

"The appearance and state of the room, when the unfortunate woman was found by Mr. Charles Pitt, were again gone over in minute detail. Mrs. Owen's clothes, which she had worn during the day, were folded neatly on a chair. The key of her cupboard was in the pocket of her dress. The door had been slightly ajar, but both the windows were wide open; one of them, which had the sash-line broken, had been fastened up most scientifically with a piece of rope.

"Mrs. Owen had obviously undressed preparatory to going to bed, and the magistrate very naturally soon made the remark how untenable the theory of an accident must be. No one in their five senses would undress with a temperature at below zero, and the windows wide open.

"After these preliminary statements the cashier of the Birkbeck was called and he related the caretaker's visit at the bank.

"'It was then about one o'clock,' he stated. 'Mrs. Owen called and presented a cheque to self for £827, the amount of her balance. She seemed exceedingly happy and cheerful, and talked about needing plenty of cash, as she was going abroad to join her nephew, for whom she would in future keep house. I warned her about being sufficiently careful with so large a sum, and parting from it injudiciously, as women of her class are very apt to do. She laughingly declared that not only was she careful of it in the present, but meant to be so for the far-off future, for she intended to go that very day to a lawyer's office and to make a will.'

"The cashier's evidence was certainly startling in the extreme, since in the widow's room no trace of any kind was found of any money; against that, two of the notes handed over by the bank to Mrs. Owen on that day were cashed by young Greenhill on the very morning of her mysterious death. One was handed in by him to the West End Clothiers Company, in payment for a suit of clothes, and the other he changed at the Post Office in Oxford Street.

"After that all the evidence had of necessity to be gone through again on the subject of young Greenhill's intimacy with Mrs. Owen.

He listened to it all with an air of the most painful nervousness, his cheeks were positively green, his lips seemed dry and parched, for he repeatedly passed his tongue over them, and when Constable E 18 deposed that at 2 A.M. on the morning of February 2nd he had seen the accused and spoken to him at the corner of Percy Street and Tottenham Court Road, young Greenhill all but fainted.

"The contention of the police was that the caretaker had been murdered and robbed during that night before she went to bed, that young Greenhill had done the murder, seeing that he was the only person known to have been intimate with the woman, and that it was, moreover, proved unquestionably that he was in the immediate neighbourhood of the Rubens Studios at an extraordinarily late hour of the night.

"His own account of himself, and of that same night, could certainly not be called very satisfactory. Mrs. Owen was a relative of his late mother's, he declared. He himself was a lithographer by trade, with a good deal of time and leisure on his hands. He certainly had employed some of that time in taking the old woman to various places of amusement. He had on more than one occasion suggested that she should give up menial work, and come and live with him, but, unfortunately, she was a great deal imposed upon by her nephew, a man of the name of Owen, who exploited the good-natured woman in every possible way, and who had on more than one occasion made severe attacks upon her savings at the Birkbeck Bank.

"Severely cross-examined by the prosecuting counsel about this supposed relative of Mrs. Owen, Greenhill admitted that he did not know him—had, in fact, never seen him. He knew that his name was Owen and that was all. His chief occupation consisted in sponging on the kind-hearted old woman, but he only went to see her in the evenings, when he presumably knew that she would be alone, and invariably after all the tenants of the Rubens Studios had left for the day.

"I don't know whether at this point it strikes you at all, as it did both magistrate and counsel, that there was a direct contradiction in this statement and the one made by the cashier of the

Birkbeck on the subject of his last conversation with Mrs. Owen. 'I am going abroad to join my nephew, for whom I am going to keep house,' was what the unfortunate woman had said.

"Now Greenhill, in spite of his nervousness and at times contradictory answers, strictly adhered to his point, that there was a nephew in London, who came frequently to see his aunt.

"Anyway, the sayings of the murdered woman could not be taken as evidence in law. Mr. Greenhill senior put the objection, adding: 'There may have been two nephews,' which the magistrate and the prosecution were bound to admit.

"With regard to the night immediately preceding Mrs. Owen's death, Greenhill stated that he had been with her to the theatre, had seen her home, and had had some supper with her in her room. Before he left her, at 2 A.M., she had of her own accord made him a present of £10, saying: 'I am a sort of aunt to you, Arthur, and if you don't have it, Bill is sure to get it.'

"She had seemed rather worried in the early part of the evening, but later on she cheered up.

"'Did she speak at all about this nephew of hers or about her money affairs? asked the magistrate.

"Again the young man hesitated, but said, 'No! she did not mention either Owen or her money affairs.'

"If I remember rightly," added the man in the corner, "for recollect I was not present, the case was here adjourned. But the magistrate would not grant bail. Greenhill was removed looking more dead than alive—though every one remarked that Mr. Greenhill senior looked determined and not the least worried. In the course of his examination on behalf of his son, of the medical officer and one or two other witnesses, he had very ably tried to confuse them on the subject of the hour at which Mrs. Owen was last known to be alive.

"He made a very great point of the fact that the usual morning's work was done throughout the house when the inmates arrived. Was it conceivable, he argued, that a woman would do that kind of work overnight, especially as she was going to the theatre, and therefore would wish to dress in her smarter clothes? It certainly was a very nice point levelled against the prosecution, who promptly retorted: Just as conceivable as that a woman in those circumstances of life should, having done her work, undress beside an open window at nine o'clock in the morning with the snow beating into the room.

"Now it seems that Mr. Greenhill senior could produce any amount of witnesses who could help to prove a conclusive *alibi* on behalf of his son, if only some time subsequent to that fatal 2 A.M. the murdered woman had been seen alive by some chance passer-by.

"However, he was an able man and an earnest one, and I fancy the magistrate felt some sympathy for his strenuous endeavours on his son's behalf. He granted a week's adjournment, which seemed to satisfy Mr. Greenhill completely.

"In the meanwhile the papers had talked of and almost exhausted the subject of the mystery in Percy Street. There had been, as you no doubt know from personal experience, innumerable arguments on the puzzling alternatives:—

"Accident?

"Suicide?

"Murder?

"A week went by, and then the case against young Greenhill was resumed. Of course the court was crowded. It needed no great penetration to remark at once that the prisoner looked more hopeful, and his father quite elated.

"Again a great deal of minor evidence was taken, and then came the turn of the defence. Mr. Greenhill called Mrs. Hall, confectioner, of Percy Street, opposite the Rubens Studios. She deposed that at 8 o'clock in the morning of February 2nd, while she was tidying her shop window, she saw the caretaker of the Studios opposite, as usual, on her knees, her head and body wrapped in a shawl, cleaning her front steps. Her husband also saw Mrs. Owen, and Mrs. Hall remarked to her husband how thankful she was that her own shop had tiled steps, which did not need scrubbing on so cold a morning.

"Mr. Hall, confectioner, of the same address, corroborated this statement, and Mr. Greenhill, with absolute triumph, produced a third witness, Mrs. Martin, of Percy Street, who from her window on the second floor had, at 7.30 A.M., seen the caretaker shaking mats outside her front door. The description this witness gave of Mrs. Owen's get-up, with the shawl round her head, coincided point by point with that given by Mr. and Mrs. Hall.

"After that Mr. Greenhill's task became an easy one; his son was at home having his breakfast at 8 o'clock that morning—not only himself, but his servants would testify to that.

"The weather had been so bitter that the whole of that day Arthur had not stirred from his own fireside. Mrs. Owen was murdered after 8 A.M. on that day, since she was seen alive by three people at that hour, therefore his son could not have murdered Mrs. Owen. The police must find the criminal elsewhere, or else bow to the opinion originally expressed by the public that Mrs. Owen had met with a terrible untoward accident, or that perhaps she may have wilfully sought her own death in that extraordinary and tragic fashion.

"Before young Greenhill was finally discharged one or two witnesses were again examined, chief among these being the foreman of the glassworks. He had turned up at the Rubens Studios at 9 o'clock, and been in business all day. He averred positively that he did not specially notice any suspicious-looking individual crossing the hall that day. 'But,' he remarked with a smile, 'I don't sit and watch every one who goes up and downstairs. I am too busy for that. The street door is always left open; any one can walk in, up or down, who knows the way.'

"That there was a mystery in connection with Mrs. Owen's death—of that the police have remained perfectly convinced; whether young Greenhill held the key of that mystery or not they have never found out to this day.

"I could enlighten them as to the cause of the young lithographer's anxiety at the magisterial inquiry, but, I assure you, I do not care to do the work of the police for them. Why should I? Greenhill will never suffer from unjust suspicions. He and his father alone—besides myself—know in what a terribly tight corner he all but found himself.

"The young man did not reach home till nearly *five* o'clock that morning. His last train had gone; he had to walk, lost his way, and wandered about Hampstead for hours. Think what his position would have been if the worthy confectioners of Percy Street had not seen Mrs. Owen 'wrapped up in a shawl, on her knees, doing the front steps.'

"Moreover, Mr. Greenhill senior is a solicitor, who has a small office in John Street, Bedford Row. The afternoon before her death Mrs. Owen had been to that office and had there made a will by which she left all her savings to young Arthur Greenhill, lithographer. Had that will been in other than paternal hands, it would have been proved, in the natural course of such things, and one other link would have been added to the chain which nearly dragged Arthur Greenhill to the gallows— 'the link of a very strong motive.'

"Can you wonder that the young man turned livid, until such time as it was proved beyond a doubt that the murdered woman was alive hours after he had reached the safe shelter of his home?

"I saw you smile when I used the word 'murdered,'" continued the man in the corner, growing quite excited now that he was approaching the *dénouement* of his story. "I know that the public, after the magistrate had discharged Arthur Greenhill, were quite satisfied to think that the mystery in Percy Street was a case of accident—or suicide."

"No," replied Polly, "there could be no question of suicide, for two very distinct reasons."

He looked at her with some degree of astonishment. She supposed that he was amazed at her venturing to form an opinion of her own.

"And may I ask what, in your opinion, these reasons are?" he asked very sarcastically.

"To begin with, the question of money," she said— "has any more of it been traced so far?"

"Not another £5 note," he said with a chuckle; "they were all cashed in Paris during the Exhibition, and you have no conception how easy a thing that is to do, at any of the hotels or smaller *agents de change*."

"That nephew was a clever blackguard," she commented.

"You believe, then, in the existence of that nephew?"

"Why should I doubt it? Some one must have existed who was sufficiently familiar with the house to go about in it in the middle of the day without attracting any one's attention."

"In the middle of the day?" he said with a chuckle.

"Any time after 8.30 in the morning."

"So you, too, believe in the 'caretaker, wrapped up in a shawl,' cleaning her front steps?" he queried.

"But—"

"It never struck you, in spite of the training your intercourse with me must have given you, that the person who carefully did all the work in the Rubens Studios, laid the fires and carried up the coals, merely did it in order to gain time; in order that the bitter frost might really and effectually do its work, and Mrs. Owen be not missed until she was truly dead."

"But—" suggested Polly again.

"It never struck you that one of the greatest secrets of successful crime is to lead the police astray with regard to the time when the crime was committed. That was, if you remember, the great point in the Regent's Park murder.

"In this case the 'nephew,' since we admit his existence, would—even if he were ever found, which is doubtful—be able to prove as good an *alibi* as young Greenhill."

"But I don't understand—"

"How the murder was committed?" he said eagerly. "Surely you can see it all for yourself, since you admit the 'nephew'—a scamp, perhaps—who sponges on the good-natured woman. He terrorises and threatens her, so much so that she fancies her money is no longer safe even in the Birkbeck Bank. Women of that class are apt at times to mistrust the Bank of England. Anyway, she withdraws her money. Who knows what she meant to do with it in the immediate future?

"In any case, she wishes to secure it after her death to a young man whom she likes, and who has known how to win her good graces. That afternoon the nephew begs, entreats for more money;

they have a row; the poor woman is in tears, and is only temporarily consoled by a pleasant visit at the theatre.

"At 2 o'clock in the morning young Greenhill parts from her. Two minutes later the nephew knocks at the door. He comes with a plausible tale of having missed his last train, and asks for a 'shake down' somewhere in the house. The good-natured woman suggests a sofa in one of the studios, and then quietly prepares to go to bed. The rest is very simple and elementary. The nephew sneaks into his aunt's room, finds her standing in her nightgown; he demands money with threats of violence; terrified, she staggers, knocks her head against the gas bracket, and falls on the floor stunned, while the nephew seeks for her keys and takes possession of the £800. You will admit that the subsequent *mise en scène*—is worthy of a genius.

"No struggle, not the usual hideous accessories round a crime. Only the open windows, the bitter north-easterly gale, and the heavily falling snow—two silent accomplices, as silent as the dead.

"After that the murderer, with perfect presence of mind, busies himself in the house, doing the work which will ensure that Mrs. Owen shall not be missed, at any rate, for some time. He dusts and tidies; some few hours later he even slips on his aunt's skirt and bodice, wraps his head in a shawl, and boldly allows those neighbours who are astir to see what they believe to be Mrs. Owen. Then he goes back to her room, resumes his normal appearance and quietly leaves the house."

"He may have been seen."

"He undoubtedly *was* seen by two or three people, but no one thought anything of seeing a man leave the house at that hour. It was very cold, the snow was falling thickly, and as he wore a muffler round the lower part of his face, those who saw him would not undertake to know him again."

"That man was never seen nor heard of again?" Polly asked.

"He has disappeared off the face of the earth. The police are searching for him, and perhaps some day they will find him—then society will be rid of one of the most ingenious men of the age."

III.

He had paused, absorbed in meditation. The young girl also was silent. Some memory too vague as yet to take a definite form was persistently haunting her—one thought was hammering away in her brain, and playing havoc with her nerves. That thought was the inexplicable feeling within her that there was something in connection with that hideous crime which she ought to recollect, something which—if she could only remember what it was—would give her the clue to the tragic mystery, and for once ensure her triumph over this self-conceited and sarcastic scarecrow in the corner.

He was watching her through his great bone-rimmed spectacles, and she could see the knuckles of his bony hands, just above the top of the table, fidgeting, fidgeting, fidgeting, till she wondered if there existed another set of fingers in the world which could undo the knots his lean ones made in that tiresome piece of string.

Then suddenly—*á propos* of nothing, Polly *remembered*—the whole thing stood before her, short and clear like a vivid flash of lightning:—Mrs. Owen lying dead in the snow beside her open window; one of them with a broken sash-line, tied up most scientifically with a piece of string. She remembered the talk there had been at the time about this improvised sash-line.

That was after young Greenhill had been discharged, and the question of suicide had been voted an impossibility.

Polly remembered that in the illustrated papers photographs appeared of this wonderfully knotted piece of string, so contrived that the weight of the frame could but tighten the knots, and thus keep the window open. She remembered that people deduced many things from that improvised sash-line, chief among these deductions being that the murderer was a sailor—so wonderful, so complicated, so numerous were the knots which secured that window-frame.

But Polly knew better. In her mind's eye she saw those fingers, rendered doubly nervous by the fearful cerebral excitement, grasping at first mechanically, even thoughtlessly, a bit of twine with which to secure the window; then the ruling habit strongest through all, the girl could see it; the lean and ingenious fingers fidgeting, fidgeting with that piece of string, tying knot after knot, more wonderful, more complicated, than any she had yet witnessed.

"If I were you," she said, without daring to look into that corner where he sat, "I would break myself of the habit of perpetually making knots in a piece of string."

He did not reply, and at last Polly ventured to look up—the corner was empty, and through the glass door beyond the desk, where he had just deposited his few coppers, she saw the tails of his tweed coat, his extraordinary hat, his meagre, shrivelled-up personality, fast disappearing down the street.

Miss Polly Burton (of the *Evening Observer*) was married the other day to Mr. Richard Frobisher (of the *London Mail*). She has never set eyes on the man in the corner from that day to this.

The Case of Miss Elliott

1
The Case of Miss Elliott

I.

The man in the corner was watching me over the top of his great bone-rimmed spectacles.

"Well?" he asked, after a little while.

"Well?" I repeated with some acerbity. I had been wondering for the last ten minutes how many more knots he would manage to make in that same bit of string, before he actually started undoing them again.

"Do I fidget you?" he asked apologetically, whilst his long bony fingers buried themselves, string, knots, and all into the capacious pockets of his magnificent tweed ulster.

"Yes, that is another awful tragedy," he said quietly, after a while. "Lady doctors are having a pretty bad time of it just now."

This was only his usual habit of speaking in response to my thoughts. There was no doubt that at the present moment my mind was filled with that extraordinary mystery which was setting all Scotland Yard by the ears, and had completely thrown into the shade the sad story of Miss Hickman's tragic fate.

The *Daily Telegraph* had printed two columns headed "Murder or Suicide?" on the subject of the mysterious death of Miss Elliott, matron of the Convalescent Home, in Suffolk Avenue—and I must confess that a more profound and bewildering mystery had never been set before our able detective department.

"It has puzzled them this time, and no mistake," said the man in the corner, with one of his most gruesome chuckles, "but I dare say the public is quite satisfied that there is no solution to be found, since the police have found none."

"Can you find one?" I retorted with withering sarcasm.

"Oh, my solution would only be sneered at," he replied. "It is far too simple—and yet how logical! There was Miss Elliott, a good-looking, youngish, lady-like woman, fully qualified in the medical profession and in charge of the Convalescent Home in Suffolk Avenue, which is a private institution largely patronised by the benevolent.

"For some time, already, there had appeared vague comments and rumours in various papers, that the extensive charitable contributions did not all go towards the up-keep of the Home. But, as is usual in institutions of that sort, the public was not allowed to know anything very definite, and contributions continued to flow in, whilst the Honorary Treasurer of the great Convalescent Home kept up his beautiful house in Hamilton Terrace, in a style which would not have shamed a peer of the realm.

"That is how matters stood, when on 2nd November last the morning papers contained the brief announcement that at a quarter past midnight two workmen walking along Blomfield Road, Maida Vale, suddenly came across the body of a young lady, lying on her face, close to the wooden steps of the narrow foot-bridge which at this point crosses the canal.

"This part of Maida Vale, is as you know, very lonely at all times, but at night it is usually quite deserted. Blomfield Road, with its row of small houses and bits of front gardens, faces the canal, and beyond the foot-bridge is continued in a series of small riverside wharves, which is practically unknown ground to the average Londoner. The foot-bridge itself, with steps at right angles and high wooden parapet, would offer excellent shelter at all hours of the night for any nefarious deed.

"It was within its shadows that the men had found the body, and to their credit, be it said, they behaved like good and dutiful citizens—one of them went off in search of the police, whilst the other remained beside the corpse.

"From papers and books found upon her person, it was soon ascertained that the deceased was Miss Elliott, the young matron of the Suffolk Avenue Convalescent Home; and as she was very popular in her profession and had a great many friends, the terrible tragedy caused a sensation, all the more acute as very quickly the rumour gained ground that the unfortunate young woman had taken her own life in a most gruesome and mysterious manner.

"Preliminary medical and police investigation had revealed the fact that Miss Elliott had died through a deep and scientifically-administered gash in the throat, whilst the surgical knife with which the deadly wound was inflicted still lay tightly grasped in her clenched hand."

II.

The man in the corner, ever conscious of any effect he produced upon my excited imagination, had paused for a while, giving me time, as it were, to co-ordinate in my mind the few simple facts he had put before me. I had no wish to make a remark, knowing of old that my one chance of getting the whole of his interesting argument was to offer neither comment nor contradiction.

"When a young, good-looking woman in the heyday of her success in an interesting profession," he began at last, "is alleged to have committed suicide, the outside public immediately want to know the reason why she did such a thing, and a kind of freemasonic, amateur detective work goes on, which generally brings a few important truths to light. Thus, in the case of Miss Elliott, certain facts had begun to leak out, even before the inquest, with its many sensational developments. Rumours concerning the internal administration, or rather maladministration of the Home began to take more definite form.

"That its finances had been in a very shaky condition for some time was known to all those who were interested in its welfare. What was not so universally known was that few hospitals had had more munificent donations and subscriptions showered upon them in recent years, and yet it was openly spoken of by all the nurses that Miss Elliott had on more than one occasion petitioned for actual necessities for the patients—necessities which were denied to her on the plea of necessary economy.

"The Convalescent Home was, as sometimes happens in institutions of this sort, under the control of a committee of benevolent and fashionable people who understood nothing about business, and less still about the management of a hospital. Dr. Kinnaird, President of the institution, was young, eminently successful consultant; he had recently married the daughter of a peer, who had boundless ambitions for herself and her husband.

"Dr. Kinnaird, by adding the prestige of his name to the Home, no doubt felt that he had done enough for its welfare. Against that, Dr. Stapylton, Honorary Secretary and Treasurer of the Home, threw himself heart and soul into the work connected with it, and gave a great deal of his time to it. All subscriptions and donations went, of course, through his hands, the benevolent and fashionable committee being only too willing to shift all their financial responsibilities on to his willing shoulders. He was a very popular man in society—a bachelor with a magnificent house in Hamilton Terrace, where he entertained the more eminent and fashionable clique in his own profession.

"It was the evening papers, however, which contained the most sensational development of this tragic case. It appears that on the Saturday afternoon Mary Dawson, one of the nurses in the Home, was going to the house surgeon's office with a message from the head nurse, when her attention was suddenly arrested in one of the passages by the sound of loud voices proceeding from one of the rooms. She paused to listen for a moment, and at once recognised the voices of Miss Elliott and of Dr. Stapylton, the Honorary Treasurer and Chairman of Committee.

"The subject of conversation was evidently that of the eternal question of finance. Miss Elliott spoke very indignantly, and Nurse Dawson caught the words:

"'Surely you must agree with me that Dr. Kinnaird ought to be informed at once.'

"Dr. Stapylton's voice in reply seems to have been at first bitingly sarcastic, then threatening. Dawson heard nothing more after that, and went on to deliver her message. On her way back she stopped in the passage again, and tried to listen. This time it seemed to her as if she could hear the sound of someone crying bitterly, and Dr. Stapylton's voice speaking very gently.

"'You may be right, Nellie,' he was saying. 'At any rate, wait a few days before telling Kinnaird. You know what he is—he'll make a frightful fuss and—'

"Whereupon Miss Elliott interrupted him.

"'It isn't fair to Dr. Kinnaird to keep him in ignorance any longer. Whoever the thief may be it is your duty or mine to expose him, and if necessary bring him to justice.'

"There was a good deal of discussion at the time, if you remember, as to whether Nurse Dawson had overheard and repeated this speech accurately: whether, in point of fact, Miss Elliott had used the words '*or* mine' or '*and* mine.' You see the neat little point, don't you?" continued the man in the corner. "The little word 'and' would imply that she considered herself at one with Dr. Stapylton in the matter, but 'or' would mean that she was resolved to act alone if he refused to join her in unmasking the thief.

"All these facts, as I remarked before, had leaked out, as such facts have a way of doing. No wonder, therefore, that on the day fixed for the inquest the coroner's court was filled to overflowing, both with the public—ever eager for new sensations—and with the many friends of the deceased lady, among whom young medical students of both sexes and nurses in uniform were most conspicuous.

"I was there early, and therefore had a good seat, from which I could comfortably watch the various actors in the drama about to be performed. People who seemed to be in the know pointed out various personages to one another, and it was a matter of note that, in spite of professional engagements, the members of the staff of the Convalescent Home were present in full force and stayed on almost the whole time. The personages who chiefly arrested my attention were, firstly, Dr. Kinnaird, a good-looking Irishman of about forty, and President of the Institution; also Dr. Earnshaw, a rising young consultant, with boundless belief in himself written all over his pleasant rubicund countenance.

"The expert medical evidence was once again thoroughly gone into. There was absolutely no doubt that Miss Elliott had died from having her throat cut with the surgical knife which was found grasped in her right hand. There were absolutely no signs of a personal struggle in the immediate vicinity of the body, and rigid examination proved that there was no other mark of violence upon the body; there was nothing, therefore, to prove that the poor girl had not committed suicide in a moment of mental aberration or of great personal grief.

"Of course, it was strange that she should have chosen this curious mode of taking her own life. She had access to all kinds of poisons, amongst which her medical knowledge could prompt her to choose the least painful and most efficacious ones. Therefore, to have walked out on a Sunday night to a wretched and unfrequented spot, and there committed suicide in that grim fashion seemed almost the work of a mad woman. And yet the evidence of her family and friends all tended to prove that Miss Elliott was a peculiarly sane, large-minded, and happy individual.

"However, the suicide theory was at this stage of the proceedings taken as being absolutely established, and when Police-Constable Fiske came forward to give his evidence no one in the court was prepared for a statement which suddenly revealed this case to be as mysterious as it was tragic.

"Fiske's story was this: Close upon midnight on that memorable Sunday night he was walking down Blomfield Road along the side of the canal and towards the foot-bridge, when he overtook a lady and gentleman who were walking in the same direction as himself. He turned to look at them, and noticed that the gentleman was in evening dress and wore a high hat, and that the lady was crying.

"Blomfield Road is at best very badly lighted, especially on the side next to the canal, where there are no lamps at all. Fiske, however, was prepared to swear positively that the lady was the deceased. As for the gentleman, he might know him again or he might not.

"Fiske then crossed the foot-bridge, and walked on towards the Harrow Road. As he did so, he heard St. Mary Magdalen's church-clock chime the hour of midnight. It was a quarter of an hour after that that the body of the unfortunate girl was found, and clasping in her hand the knife with which that awful deed had been done. By whom? Was it really by her own self? But if so, why did not that man in evening dress who had last seen her alive come forward and throw some light upon this fast thickening veil of mystery?

"It was Mr. James Elliott, brother of the deceased, however, who first mentioned a name then in open court, which has ever since in the minds of every one been associated with Miss Elliott's tragic fare.

"He was speaking in answer to a question of the coroner's anent his sister's disposition and recent frame of mind.

"'She was always extremely cheerful,' he said, 'but recently had been peculiarly bright and happy. I understood from her that this was because she believed that a man for whom she had a great regard was also very much attached to her, and meant to ask her to be his wife.'

"'And do you know who this man was?' asked the coroner.

"'Oh yes,' replied Mr. Elliott, 'it was Dr. Stapylton.'

"Every one had expected that name, of course, for every one remembered Nurse Dawson's story, yet when it came, there crept over all those present an indescribable feeling that something terrible was impending.

"'Is Dr. Stapylton here?'

"But Dr. Stapylton had sent an excuse. A professional case of the utmost urgency had kept him at a patient's bedside. But Dr. Kinnaird, the President of the institution, came forward.

"Questioned by the coroner, Dr. Kinnaird, however, who evidently had a great regard for his colleague, repudiated any idea that the funds of the institution had ever been tampered with by the Treasurer.

"'The very suggestion of such a thing,' he said, 'was an outrage upon one of the most brilliant men in the profession.'

"He further added that, although he knew that Dr. Stapylton thought very highly of Miss Elliott, he did not think that there was any actual engagement, and most decidedly he (Dr. Kinnaird) had heard nothing of any disagreement between them.

"'Then did Dr. Stapylton never tell you that Miss Elliott had often chafed under the extraordinary economy practised in the richly-endowed Home?' asked the coroner again.

"'No,' replied Dr. Kinnaird.

"'Was not that rather strange reticence?'

"'Certainly not. I am only the Honorary President of the institution—Stapylton has chief control of its finances.'

"'Ah!' remarked the coroner blandly.

"However, it was clearly no business of his at this moment to enter into the financial affairs of the Home. His duty at this point was to try and find out if Dr. Stapylton and the man in evening dress were one and the same person.

"The men who found the body testified to the hour: a quarter past midnight. As Fiske had seen the unfortunate girl alive a little before twelve, she must have been murdered or had committed suicide between midnight and a quarter past. But there was something more to come.

"How strange and dramatic it all was!" continued the man in the corner, with a bland smile, altogether out of keeping with the poignancy of his narrative; "all these people in that crowded court trying to reconstruct the last chapter of that bright young matron's life and then—but I must not anticipate.

"One more witness was to be heard—one whom the police, with a totally unconscious sense of what is dramatic, had reserved for the last. This was Dr. Earnshaw, one of the staff of the Convalescent Home. His evidence was very short, but of deeply momentous import. He explained that he had consulting rooms in Weymouth Street, but resided in Westbourne Square. On Sunday, 1st November, he had been dining out in Maida Vale, and returning home a little before midnight saw a woman standing close by the steps of the foot-bridge in the Blomfield Road.

"'I had been coming down Formosa Street and had not specially taken notice of her, when just as I reached the corner of Blomfield Road, she was joined by a man in evening dress and high hat. Then I crossed the road, and recognised both Miss Elliott and—'

"The young doctor paused, almost as if hesitating before the enormity of what he was about to say, whilst the excitement in court became almost painful.

"'And—?' urged the coroner.

"'And Dr. Stapylton,' said Dr. Earnshaw at last, almost under his breath.

"'You are quite sure?' asked the coroner.

"'Absolutely positive. I spoke to them both, and they spoke to me.'

"'What did you say?'

"'Oh, the usual, "Hello, Stapylton!" to which he replied, "Hello!" I then said "Good-night" to them both, and Miss Elliott also said "Goodnight." I saw her face more clearly then, and thought that she looked very tearful and unhappy, and Stapylton looked ill-tempered. I wondered why they had chosen that unhallowed spot for a midnight walk.'

"'And you say the hour was—?' asked the coroner.

"'Ten minutes to twelve. I looked at my watch as I crossed the foot-bridge, and had heard a quarter to twelve strike five minutes before.'

"Then it was that the coroner adjourned the inquest. Dr. Stapylton's attendance had become absolutely imperative. According to Dr. Earnshaw's testimony, he had been with deceased certainly a quarter of an hour before she met her terrible death. Fiske had seen them together ten minutes later; she was then crying bitterly. There was as yet no actual charge against the fashionable and rich doctor, but already the ghostly bird of suspicion had touched him with its ugly wing."

III.

"As for the next day," continued the man in the corner after a slight pause, "I can assure you that there was not a square foot of standing room in the coroner's court for the adjourned inquest. It was timed for eleven A.M., and at six o'clock on that cold winter's morning the pavement outside the court was already crowded. As for me, I always manage to get a front seat, and I did on that occasion, too. I fancy that I was the first among the general public to note Dr. Stapylton as he entered the room accompanied by his solicitor, and by Dr. Kinnaird, with whom he was chatting very cheerfully and pleasantly.

"Mind you, I am a great admirer of the medical profession, and I think a clever and successful doctor usually has a most delightful air about him—the consciousness of great and good work done with profit to himself—which is quite unique and quite admirable.

"Dr. Stapylton had that air even to a greater extent than his colleague, and from the affectionate way in which Dr. Kinnaird finally shook him by the hand, it was quite clear that the respected chief of the Convalescent Home, at any rate, refused to harbour any suspicion of the integrity of its Treasurer.

"Well, I must not weary you by dwelling on the unimportant details of this momentous inquest. Constable Fiske, who was asked to identify the gentleman in evening dress whom he had seen with the deceased at a few minutes before twelve, failed to recognise Dr. Stapylton very positively: pressed very closely, he finally refused to swear either way. Against that, Dr. Earnshaw repeated, clearly and categorically, looking his colleague straight in the face the while, the damnatory evidence he had given the day before.

"'I saw Dr. Stapylton, I spoke to him, and he spoke to me,' he repeated most emphatically.

"Every one in that court was watching Dr. Stapylton's face, which wore an air of supreme nonchalance, even of contempt, but certainly neither of guilt nor of fear.

"Of course, by that time *I* had fully made up my mind as to where the hitch lay in this extraordinary mystery; but no one else had, and every one held their breath as Dr. Stapylton quietly stepped into the box, and after a few preliminary questions the coroner asked him very abruptly:

"'You were in the company of the deceased a few minutes before she died, Dr. Stapylton?'

"'Pardon me,' replied the latter quietly, 'I last saw Miss Elliott alive on Saturday afternoon, just before I went home from my work.'

"This calm reply, delivered without a tremor, positively made every one gasp. For the moment coroner and jury were alike staggered.

"'But we have two witnesses here who saw you in the company of the deceased within a few minutes of twelve o'clock on the Sunday night!' the coroner managed to gasp out at last.

"'Pardon me,' again interposed the doctor, 'these witnesses were mistaken.'

"'Mistaken!'

"I think every one would have shouted out the word in boundless astonishment had they dared to do so.

"'Dr. Earnshaw was mistaken,' reiterated Dr. Stapylton quietly. 'He neither saw me nor did he speak to me.'

"'You can substantiate that, of course?' queried the coroner.

"'Pardon me,' once more said the doctor, with utmost calm, 'it is surely Dr. Earnshaw who should substantiate *his* statement.'

"'There is Constable Fiske's corroborative evidence for that,' retorted the coroner, somewhat nettled.

"'Hardly, I think. You see, the constable states that he saw a gentleman in evening dress, etc., talking to the deceased at a minute or two before twelve o'clock, and that when he heard the clock of St. Mary Magdalen chime the hour of midnight he was just walking away from the footbridge. Now, just as that very church-clock was chiming that hour, I was stepping into a cab at the corner of Harrow Road, not a hundred yards *in front* of Constable Fiske.'

"'You swear to that?' queried the coroner in amazement.

"'I can easily prove it,' said Dr. Stapylton. 'The cabman who drove me from there to my club is here and can corroborate my statement.'

"And amidst boundless excitement, John Smith, a hansom-cab driver, stated that he was hailed in the Harrow Road by the last witness, who told him to drive to the Royal Clinical Club, in Mardon

Street. Just as he started off, St. Mary Magdalen's Church, close by, struck the hour of midnight.

"At that very moment, if you remember, Constable Fiske had just crossed the foot-bridge, and was walking towards the Harrow Road, and he was quite sure (for he was closely questioned afterwards) that no one overtook him from behind. Now there would be no way of getting from one side of the canal to the other at this point except over that foot-bridge; the nearest bridge is fully two hundred yards further down the Blomfield Road. The girl was alive a minute *before* the constable crossed the foot-bridge, and it would have been absolutely impossible for any one to have murdered a girl, placed the knife in her hand, run a couple of hundred yards to the next bridge and another three hundred to the corner of Harrow Road, all in the space of three minutes.

"This *alibi*, therefore, absolutely cleared Dr. Stapylton from any suspicion of having murdered Miss Elliott. And yet, looking on that man as he sat there, calm, cool and contemptuous, no one could have had the slightest doubt but that he was lying—lying when he said he had not seen Miss Elliott that evening; lying when he denied Dr. Earnshaw's statement; lying when he professed himself ignorant of the poor girl's fate.

"Dr. Earnshaw repeated his statement with the same emphasis, but it was one man's word against another's, and as Dr. Stapylton was so glaringly innocent of the actual murder, there seemed no valid reason at all why he should have denied having seen her that night, and the point was allowed to drop. As for Nurse Dawson's story of his alleged quarrel with Miss Elliott on the Saturday night, Dr. Stapylton again had a simple and logical explanation.

"'People who listen at keyholes,' he said quietly, 'are apt to hear only fragments of conversation, and often mistake ordinary loud voices for quarrels. As a matter of fact, Miss Elliott and I were discussing the dismissal of certain nurses from the Home, whom she deemed incompetent. Nurse Dawson was among that number. She desired their immediate dismissal, and I tried to pacify her. That was the subject of my conversation with the deceased lady. I can swear to every word of it.'"

IV.

The man in the corner had long ceased speaking and was placing quietly before me a number of photographs. One by one I saw the series of faces which had been watched so eagerly in the coroner's court that memorable afternoon by an excited crowd.

"So the fate of poor Miss Elliott has remained wrapt in mystery?" I said thoughtfully at last.

"To every one," rejoined the funny creature, "except to me."

"Ah! What is your theory, then?"

"A simple one, dear lady; so simple that it really amazes me, that no one, not even you, my faithful pupil, ever thought of it."

"It may be so simple that it becomes idiotic," I retorted with lofty disdain.

"Well, that may be. Shall I at any rate try to make it clear?"

"If you like."

"For this I think the best way would be, if you were to follow me through what transpired before the inquest. But first tell me, what do you think of Dr. Earnshaw's statement?"

"Well," I replied, "a good many people thought that it was he who murdered Miss Elliott, and that his story of meeting Dr. Stapylton with her was a he from beginning to end."

"Impossible!" he retorted, making an elaborate knot in his bit of string. "Dr. Earnshaw's friends, with whom he had been dining that night, swore that he was *not* in evening dress, nor wore a high hat. And on that point—the evening dress, and the hat—Constable Fiske was most positive."

"Then Dr. Earnshaw was mistaken, and it was not Dr. Stapylton he met."

"Impossible!" he shrieked, whilst another knot went to join its fellows. "He spoke to Dr. Stapylton, and Dr. Stapylton spoke to him."

"Very well, then," I argued; "why should Dr. Stapylton tell a lie about it? He had such a conclusive *alibi* that there could be no object in his making a false statement about that."

"No object!" shrieked the excited creature. "Why, don't you *see* that he had to tell the lie in order to set police, coroner, and jury by the ears, because he did not wish it to be even remotely hinted at, that the man whom Dr. Earnshaw saw with Miss Elliott, and the man whom Constable Fiske saw with her ten minutes later, were *two different persons?*"

"Two different persons!" I ejaculated.

"Ay! two confederates in this villainy. No one has ever attempted to deny the truth of the shaky finances of the Home; no one has really denied that Miss Elliott suspected certain defalcations and was trying to force the hands of the Honorary Treasurer towards a full enquiry. That the Honorary Treasurer knew where all the money went to was pretty clear all along—his magnificent house in Hamilton Terrace fully testifies to that. That the President of the institution was a party to these defalcations and largely profited by them I for one am equally convinced."

"Dr. Kinnaird?" I ejaculated in amazement.

"Ay, Dr. Kinnaird. Do you mean to tell me that he alone among the entire staff of that Home was ignorant of those defalcations? Impossible! And if he knew of them, and did neither enquire into them nor attempt to stop them, then he *must* have been a party to them. Do you admit that?"

"Yes, I admit that," I replied.

"Very well, then. The rest is quite simple; those two men, unworthy to bear the noble appellation of doctor, must for years have quietly stolen the money subscribed by the benevolent for the Home, and converted it to their own use: then, they suddenly find themselves face to face with immediate discovery in the shape of a young girl determined to unmask the systematic frauds of the past few years. That meant exposure, disgrace, ruin for them both, and they determine to be rid of her.

"Under the pretence of an evening walk, her so-called lover entices her to a lonely and suitable spot; his confederate is close by, hidden in the shadows, ready to give his assistance if the girl struggles and screams. But suddenly Dr. Earnshaw appears. He recognises Stapylton and challenges him. For a moment the villains are nonplussed, then Kinnaird—the cleverer of the two—steps forward, greets the two lovers unconcernedly, and after two minutes' conversation casually reminds Stapylton of an appointment the latter is presumed to have at a club in St. James' Street.

"The latter understands and takes the hint, takes a quick farewell of the girl, leaving her in his friend's charge, then, as fast as he can, goes off, presently takes a cab, leaving his friend to do the deed, whilst the *alibi* he can prove, coupled with Dr. Earnshaw's statement, was sure to bewilder and mislead the police and the public.

'Thus it was that though Dr. Earnshaw saw and recognised Dr. Stapylton, Constable Fiske saw Dr. Kinnaird whom he did *not* recognise, on whom no suspicion had fallen, and whose name had never been coupled with that of Miss Elliott. When Constable Fiske had turned his back, Kinnaird murdered the girl and went off quietly, whilst Dr. Stapylton, on whom all suspicions were bound to fasten sooner or later, was able to prove the most perfect *alibi* ever concocted.

"One day I feel certain that the frauds at the Home will be discovered, and then who knows what else may see the light?

"Think of it all quietly when I am gone, and to-morrow when we meet tell me whether if *I* am wrong what is *your* explanation of this extraordinary mystery."

Before I could reply he had gone, and I was left wondering, gazing at the photographs of two good-looking, highly respectable and respected men, whom an animated scarecrow had just boldly accused of committing one of the most dastardly crimes ever recorded in our annals.

2
The Hocussing of Cigarette

I.

Quite by chance I found myself one morning sitting before a marble-topped table in the A.B.C. shop. I really wondered for the moment what had brought me there, and felt cross with myself for being there at all. Having sampled my tea and roll, I soon buried myself in the capacious folds of my *Daily Telegraph.*

"A glass of milk and a cheese-cake, please," said a well-known voice.

The next moment I was staring into the corner, straight at a pair of mild, watery blue eyes, hidden behind great bone-rimmed spectacles, and at ten long bony fingers, round which a piece of string was provokingly intertwined.

There he was as usual, wearing—for it was chilly—a huge tweed ulster, of a pattern too lofty to be described. Smiling, bland, apologetic, and fidgety, he sat before me as the living embodiment of the reason why I had come to the A.B.C. shop that morning.

"How do you do?" I said, with as much dignity as I could command.

"I see that you are interested in Cigarette," he remarked, pointing to a special column in the *Daily Telegraph.*

"She is quite herself again," I said.

"Yes, but you don't know who tried to poison her and succeeded in making her very ill. You don't know whether the man Palk had anything to do with it, whether he was bribed, or whether it was Mrs. Keeson or the groom Cockram who told a lie, or why—?"

"No," I admitted reluctantly; "I don't know any of these things."

He was fidgeting nervously in the corner, wriggling about like an animated scarecrow. Then suddenly a bland smile illuminated his entire face. His long bony fingers had caught the end of the bit of string, and there he was at it again, just as I had seen him a year ago, worrying and fidgeting, making knot upon knot, and untying them again, whilst his blue eyes peered at me over the top of his gigantic spectacles.

"I would like to know what your theory is about the whole thing," I was compelled to say at last; for the case had interested me deeply, and, after all, I had come to the A.B.C. shop for the sole purpose of discussing the adventures of Cigarette with him.

"Oh, my theories are not worth considering," he said meekly. "The police would not give me five shillings for any one of them. They always prefer a mystery to any logical conclusion, if it is arrived at by an outsider. But you may be more lucky. The owner of Cigarette did offer £100 reward for the elucidation of the mystery. The noble Earl must have backed Cigarette for all he was worth. Malicious tongues go even so far as to say that he is practically a ruined man now, and that the beautiful Lady Agnes is only too glad to find herself the wife of Harold Keeson, the son of the well-known trainer.

"If you ever go to Newmarket," continued the man in the corner after a slight pause, during which he had been absorbed in unravelling one of his most complicated knots, "any one will point out the Keesons' house to you. It is called Manor House, and stands in the midst of beautiful gardens. Mr. Keeson himself is a man of about fifty, and, as a matter of fact, is of very good family, the Keesons having owned property in the Midlands for the past eight hundred years. Of this fact he is, it appears, extremely proud. His father, however, was a notorious spendthrift, who squandered his property, and died in the nick of time, leaving his son absolutely penniless and proud as Lucifer.

"Fate, however, has been kind to George Keeson. His knowledge of horses and of all matters connected with the turf stood him in good stead: hard work and perseverance did the rest. Now, at fifty years of age, he is a very rich man, and practically at the head of a profession, which, if not exactly that of a gentleman, is, at any rate, highly remunerative.

"He owns Manor House, and lived there with his young wife and his only son and heir, Harold.

"It was Mr. Keeson who had trained Cigarette for the Earl of Okehampton, and who, of course, had charge of her during her apprenticeship, before she was destined to win a fortune for her owner, her trainer, and those favoured few who had got wind of her capabilities. For Cigarette was to be kept a dark horse—not an easy matter in these days, when the neighbourhood of every race-course abounds with rascals who eke out a precarious livelihood by various methods, more or less shady, of which the gleaning of early information is perhaps the least disreputable.

"Fortunately for Mr. Keeson, however, he had in the groom, Cockram, a trusted and valued servant, who had been in his employ for over ten years. To say that Cockram took a special pride in Cigarette would be but to put it mildly. He positively loved the mare, and I don't think that any one ever doubted that his interest in her welfare was every bit as keen as that of the Earl of Okehampton or of Mr. Keeson.

"It was to Cockram, therefore, that Mr. Keeson entrusted the care of Cigarette. She was lodged in the private stables adjoining the Manor House, and during the few days immediately preceding the 'Coronation Stakes' the groom practically never left her side, either night or day. He slept in the loose box with her, and ate all his meals in her company; nor was any one allowed to come within measurable distance of the living treasure, save Mr. Keeson or the Earl of Okehampton himself.

"And yet, in spite of all these precautions, in spite of every care that human ingenuity could devise, on the very morning of the race Cigarette was seized with every symptom of poisoning, and although, as you say, she is quite herself again now, she was far too ill to fulfil her engagement, and, if rumour speaks correctly, completed thereby the ruin of the Earl of Okehampton."

II.

The man in the corner looked at me through his bone-rimmed spectacles, and his mild blue eyes gazed pleasantly into mine.

"You may well imagine," he continued, after a while, "what a thunderbolt such a catastrophe means to those whose hopes of a fortune rested upon the fitness of the bay mare. Mr. Keeson lost his temper for an instant, they say—but for one instant only. When he was hastily summoned at six o'clock in the morning to Cigarette's stables, and saw her lying on the straw, rigid and with glassy eyes, he raised his heavy riding-whip over the head of Cockram. Some assert that he actually struck him, and that the groom was too wretched and too dazed to resent either words or blows. After a good deal of hesitation he reluctantly admitted that for the first time since Cigarette had been in his charge he had slept long and heavily.

"'I am such a light sleeper, you know, sir,' he said in a tear-choked voice. 'Usually I could hear every noise the mare made if she stirred at all. But, there—last night I cannot say what happened. I remember that I felt rather drowsy after my supper, and must have dropped off to sleep very quickly. Once during the night I woke up; the mare was all right then.'

"The man paused, and seemed to be searching for something in his mind—the recollection of a dream, perhaps. But the veterinary surgeon, who was present at the time, having also been hastily summoned to the stables, took up the glass which had contained the beer for Cockram's supper. He sniffed it, and then tasted it, and said quietly:

"'No wonder you slept heavily, my man. This beer was drugged: it contained opium.'

"'Drugged!' ejaculated Cockram, who, on hearing this fact, which in every way exonerated him from blame, seemed more hopelessly wretched than he had been before.

"It appears that every night Cockram's supper was brought out to him in the stables by one of the servants from the Manor House. On this particular, night Mrs. Keeson's maid, a young girl named

Alice Image, had brought him a glass of beer and some bread and cheese on a tray at about eleven o'clock.

"Closely questioned by Mr. Keeson, the girl emphatically denied all knowledge of any drug in the beer. She had often taken the supper-tray across to Cockram, who was her sweetheart, she said. It was usually placed ready for her in the hall, and when she had finished attending upon her mistress's night toilet she went over to the stables with it. She had certainly never touched the beer, and the tray had stood in its accustomed place on the hall-table looking just the same as usual. 'As if I'd go and poison my Cockram!' she said in the midst of a deluge of tears.

"All these somewhat scanty facts crept into the evening papers that same day. That an outrage of a peculiarly daring and cunning character had been perpetrated was not for a moment in doubt. So much money had been at stake, so many people would be half-ruined by it, that even the non- racing public at once took the keenest interest in the case. All the papers admitted, of course, that for the moment the affair seemed peculiarly mysterious, yet all commented upon one fact, which they suggested should prove an important clue: this fact was Cockram's strange attitude.

"At first he had been dazed—probably owing to the after-effects of the drug; he had also seemed too wretched even to resent Mr. Keeson's very natural outburst of wrath. But then, when the presence of the drug in his beer was detected, which proved him, at any rate, to have been guiltless in the matter, his answers, according to all accounts, became somewhat confused; and all Mr. Keeson and the 'vet.,' who were present, got out of him after that, was a perpetual ejaculation: 'What's to be done? What's to be done?'

"Two days later the sporting papers were the first to announce, with much glee, that thanks to the untiring energy of the Scotland Yard authorities, daylight seemed at last to have been brought to bear upon the mystery which surrounded the dastardly outrage on the Earl of Okehampton's mare Cigarette, and that an important arrest in connection with it had already been effected.

"It appears that a man named Charles Palk, seemingly of no address, had all along been suspected of having at least a hand in the outrage. He was believed to be a bookmaker's tout, and was a man upon whom the police had long since kept a watchful eye. Palk had been seen loafing around the Manor House for the past week, and had been warned off the grounds once or twice by the grooms.

"It now transpired that on the day preceding the outrage he had hung about the neighbourhood of the Manor House the whole afternoon, trying to get into conversation with the stable-boys, or even with Mr. Keeson's indoor servants. No one, however, would have anything to do with him, as Mr. Keeson's orders in those respects were very strict: he had often threatened any one of his *employés* with instant dismissal if he found him in company with one of these touts.

"Detective Twiss, however, who was in charge of the case, obtained the information that Alice Image, the maid, had been seen on more than one occasion talking to Palk, and that on the very day before the Coronation Stakes she had been seen in his company. Closely questioned by the detective, Alice Image at first denied her intercourse with the tout, but finally was forced to admit that she had held conversation with him once or twice.

"She was fond of putting a bit now and again upon a horse, but Cockram, she added, was such a muff that he never would give her a tip, for he did not approve of betting for young women. Palk had always been very civil and nice-spoken, she further explained. Moreover, he came from Buckinghamshire, her own part of the country, where she was born; anyway, she had never had cause to regret having entrusted a half-sovereign or so of her wages to him.

"All these explanations delivered by Alice Image, with the flow of tears peculiar to her kind, were not considered satisfactory, and the next day she and Charles Palk were both arrested on the charge of being concerned in the poisoning of the Earl of Okehampton's mare Cigarette, with intent to do her grievous bodily harm."

III.

"These sort of cases," continued the man in the corner after a slight pause, during which his nervous fingers toyed incessantly with that eternal bit of string— "these sort of cases always create a great deal of attention amongst the public, the majority of whom in this country have very strong sporting proclivities. It was small wonder, therefore, when Alice Image and Charles Palk were brought before the local magistrates, that the court was crowded to overflowing, both with Pressmen and with the general public.

"I had all along been very much interested in the case, so I went down to Newmarket, and, in spite of the huge crowd, managed to get a good seat, whence I could command a full view of the chief personages concerned in this thrilling sporting drama.

"Firstly, there was the Earl of Okehampton—good-looking, but for an unmistakable air of the broken-down sporting man about his whole person; the trainer, Mr. Keeson—a lean, clean-shaven man, with a fine, proud carriage, and a general air of ancient lineage and the 'Domesday Booke' about him; Mrs. Keeson—a pale, nervous-looking creature, who seemed very much out of place in this sporting set; and, finally, the accused—Alice Image, dissolved in tears, and Charles Palk, over-dressed, defiant, horsey, and unsympathetic.

"There was also Cockram, the groom. My shortsighted eyes had fastened on him the moment I entered the court. A more wretched, miserable, bewildered expression I have never seen on any man's face.

"Both Alice Image and Charles Palk flatly denied the charge. Alice declared, amid a renewed deluge of tears, that she was engaged to be married to Cockram, that she 'no more would have hurt him or the pretty creature he was in charge of, for anything.' How could she? As for Palk—conscious, no doubt, of his own evil reputation—he merely contented himself with shrugging his shoulders and various denials, usually accompanied with emphatic language.

"As neither of the accused attempted to deny that they had been together the day before the outrage, there was no occasion to call witnesses to further prove that fact. Both, however, asserted emphatically that their conversation was entirely confined to the subject of Alice's proposed flutters on the favourite for the next day's race.

"Thus the only really important witness was the groom, Cockram. Once again his attitude as a witness caused a great deal of surprise, and gradually, as he gave his evidence in a peculiarly halting and nervous manner, that surprise was changed into suspicion.

"Questioned by the magistrate, he tried his hardest to exonerate Alice from all blame; and yet when asked whether he had cause to suspect any one else he became more confused than ever, said, 'No,' emphatically first, then, 'Yes,' and finally looked round the court appealingly, like some poor animal at bay. That the man was hiding something, that he was, in point of fact, lying, was apparent to every one. He had drunk the beer, he said, unsuspectingly on that fatal night; he had then dropped off to sleep almost immediately, and never woke until about six A.M., when a glance at the mare at once told him that there was something very wrong.

"However, whether Cockram was lying or not—whether he suspected any one else or was merely trying to shield his sweetheart, there was, in the opinion of the magistrate, quite sufficient evidence to prove that Alice Image, at any rate, had a hand in the hocussing of Cigarette, since it was she who had brought the drugged beer to Cockram. Beyond that there was not sufficient evidence to show either that she was a tool in the hands of Palk, or that they both were merely instruments in the hands of some third person.

"Anyway, the magistrate—it was Major Laverton, a great personal friend of the Earl of Okehampton, and a remarkably clever and acute man—tried his hardest to induce Alice to confess. He questioned the poor girl so closely and so rigorously that gradually she lost what little self-control she had, and every one in the court blamed Major Laverton not a little, for he was gradually getting the poor girl into a state of hysterics.

"As for me, I inwardly commended the learned J.P., for already I had guessed what he was driving at, and was not the least astonished when the dramatic incident occurred which rendered this case so memorable

"Alice Image, namely, now thoroughly unnerved, harassed with the Major's questions, suddenly turned to where Cockram was sitting, and, with hysterical cry, she stretched out both her arms towards him.

"'Joe! my Joe!' she cried; 'you know I didn't do it! Can't you do anything to help me?'

"It was pathetic in the extreme: every one in the court felt deeply moved. As for Cockram, a sudden change came over him. I am accustomed to read the faces of my fellow-men, and in that rough countenance I saw then emerging, in response to the girl's appeal, a quick and firm resolution.

"'Ay, and I will, Alice!' he said, jumping to his feet. 'I have tried to do my duty. If the gentlemen will hear me I will say all I know.'

"Needless to say, 'the gentlemen' were only too ready to hear him. Like a man who, having made up his mind, is now resolved to act upon it, the groom Cockram began his story.

"'I told your worship that, having drunk the, beer that night, I dropped off to sleep very fast and very heavy-like. How long I'd been asleep I couldn't say, when suddenly something seemed not exactly to wake me but to dispel my dreams, so to speak. I opened my eyes, and at first I couldn't see anything, as the gas in the stable was turned on very low; but I put out my hand to feel the mare's fetlocks, just byway of telling her that I was there all right enough, and looking after her—bless her! At that moment, your worship, I noticed that the stable-door was open, and that some one—I couldn't see who it was—was goin' out of it. "Who goes there?" says I, for I still felt very sleepy and dull, when, to my astonishment, who should reply to me but—'

"The man paused, and once more over his rough, honest face came the old look of perplexity and misery.

"'But—?' queried the magistrate, whose nerves were obviously as much on tension as those of every one else in that court.

"'Speak, Joe—won't you?' appealed Alice Image pathetically.

"'But the mistress—Mrs. Keeson, sir,' came from the groom in an almost inaudible whisper. 'You know, ma'am,' he added, while the gathering tears choked his voice, 'I wouldn't 'ave spoke. But she's my sweetheart, ma'am; and I couldn't bear that the shame should rest on her.'

"There was a moment's deadly silence in that crowded court. Every one's eyes wandered towards the pale face of Mrs. Keeson, which, however, though almost livid in colour, expressed nothing but the most boundless astonishment. As for Mr. Keeson, surprise, incredulity, then furious wrath at the slander, could be seen chasing one another upon his handsome face.

"'What lie is this?' burst involuntarily from his lips, as his fingers closed more tightly upon the heavy riding-whip which he was holding.

"'Silence, please!' said the Major with authority. 'Now, Cockram, go on. You say Mrs. Keeson spoke to you. What did she say?'

"'She seemed rather upset, sir,' continued Cockram, still looking with humble apology across at his mistress, 'for she only stammered something about: "Oh, it's nothing, Cockram. I only wanted to speak to my son—er—to Mr. Harold—I—"'

"'Harold?' thundered Mr. Keeson, who was fast losing his temper.

"'I must ask you, Mr. Keeson, to be silent,' said the Major. 'Go on, Cockram.'

"And Cockram continued his narrative:

"'"Mr. Harold, ma'am?" I said. "What should 'e be doing 'ere in the stables at this time of night?" "Oh, nothing," says she to me, "I thought I saw him come in here. I must have been mistaken. Never mind, Cockram; it's all right. Good-night."

"'I said good-night, too, and then fell to wondering what Mr. 'Arold could have wanted prowling round the stables at this hour of the night. Just then the clock of St. Saviour's struck four o'clock, and while I was still wondering I fell asleep again, and never awoke until six, when the mare was as sick as she could be. And that's the whole truth, gentlemen; and I would never have spoke—for Mr. and Mrs. Keeson have always been good to me, and I'd have done anything to save them the disgrace—but Alice is goin' to be my wife, and I couldn't bear any shame to rest upon 'er.'

"When Cockram had finished speaking you might have heard a pin drop as Major Laverton asked Mrs. Keeson to step into the witness-box. She looked fragile and pale, but otherwise quite self-possessed as she quietly kissed the book and said in a very firm tone of voice:

"'I can only say in reply to the extraordinary story which this man has just told that the drug in the beer must have given him peculiarly vivid dreams. At the hour he names I was in bed fast asleep, as my husband can testify; and the whole of Cockram's narrative is a fabrication from beginning to end. I may add that I am more than willing to forgive him. No doubt his brain was clouded by the opiate; and now he is beside himself owing to Alice Image's predicament. As for my son Harold, he was absent from home that night; he was spending it with some bachelor friends at the "Stag and Mantle" hotel in Newmarket.'

"'Yes! By the way,' said the magistrate, 'where is Mr. Harold Keeson? I have no doubt that he will be able to give a very good account of himself on that memorable night.'

"'My son is abroad, your worship,' said Mrs. Keeson, while a shade of a still more livid hue passed over her face.

"'Abroad, is he?' said the magistrate cheerfully. 'Well, that settles the point satisfactorily for him, doesn't it? When did he go?'

"'Last Thursday, your worship,' replied Mrs. Keeson.

"Then there was silence again in the court, for that last Thursday was the day of the 'Coronation Stakes'—the day immediately following the memorable night on which the mare Cigarette had been poisoned by an unknown hand."

IV.

"I doubt whether in all the annals of criminal procedure there ever occurred a more dramatic moment than that when so strange a ray of daylight was shed on the mysterious outrage on Cigarette. The magistrate, having dismissed Mrs. Keeson, hardly dared to look across at the trainer, who was a personal friend of his, and who had just received such a cruel blow through this terrible charge against his only son—for at that moment I doubt if there were two people in that court who did not think that Mrs. Keeson had just sworn a false oath, and that both she and her son had been in the stables that night—for what purpose only they and their own conscience could tell.

"Alice Image and Charles Palk were both discharged; and it is greatly to the credit of Cockram that in the midst of his joy in seeing his sweetheart safe he still remained very gloomy and upset. As for Mr. Keeson, he must have suffered terribly at all this mud cast at his only son. He had been wounded in what he worshipped more than anything else in the world—his family honour. What was the use of money and the old estates if such a stain rested upon his name?

"As for Mrs. Keeson, public sympathy was very much overshadowed with contempt for her stupidity. Had she only held her tongue when Cockram challenged her, suspicion would never have fastened upon Harold. The fact that she had lied in the witness-box in order to try and remedy her blunder was also very severely commented upon. The young man had gone abroad on that memorable Thursday accompanied by two of his bachelor friends. They had gone on a fishing expedition to Norway, and were not expected home for three weeks. As they meant to move from place to place they had left no address: letters and telegrams were therefore useless.

"During those three weeks pending Harold Keeson's return certain facts leaked out which did not tend to improve his case. It appears that he had long been in love with Lady Agnes Stourcliffe, the daughter of the Earl of Okehampton. Some people asserted that the young people were actually—though secretly—engaged. The Earl, however, seems all along to have objected to the marriage of his daughter with the son of a trainer, and on more than one occasion had remarked that he had not sunk quite so low yet as to allow so preposterous a *mésalliance*. Mr. Keeson, whose family pride was at least equal to that of the Earl, had naturally very much resented this attitude, and had often begged his son to give up his pretensions, since they were manifestly so unwelcome.

"Harold Keeson, however, was deeply in love; and Lady Agnes stuck to him with womanly constancy and devotion. Unfortunately a climax was reached some days before the disastrous events at Newmarket. The Earl of Okehampton suddenly took up a very firm stand on the subject of Harold Keeson's courtship of his daughter.

Some hot words were exchanged between the two men, ending in an open breach, the Earl positively forbidding the young man ever to enter his house again.

"Harold was terribly unhappy at this turn of events. Pride forbade him to take an unfair advantage of a young girl's devotion, and, acting on the advice of his parents, he started for his tour in Norway, ostensibly in order to try and forget the fair Lady Agnes. This unhappy love affair, ending in an open and bitter quarrel between himself and the owner of Cigarette, did—as I said before—the young man's case no good. At the instance of the Earl of Okehampton, who determined to prosecute him, he was arrested on landing at Harwich.

"Well," continued the man in the corner, "the next events must be still fresh in your mind. When Harold Keeson appeared in the dock, charged with such meanness as to wreak his private grievance upon a dumb animal, public sympathy at once veered round in his favour. He looked so handsome, so frank and honest, that at once one felt convinced that *his* hand, at any rate, could never have done such a dastardy thing.

"Mr. Keeson, who was a rich man, moreover had enlisted the services of Sr. Arthur Inglewood, who had, in the short time at his disposal, collected all the most important evidence on behalf of his client.

"The two young men who had been travelling in Norway with Harold Keeson had been present with him on the memorable night at a bachelor party given by a mutual friend at the 'Stag and Mantle.' Both testified that the party had played bridge until the small hours of the morning, that between two rubbers—the rooms being very hot—they had all strolled out to smoke a cigar in the streets. Just as they were about to re-enter the hotel two church clocks—one of which was St. Saviour's—chimed out the hour—four o'clock.

"Four o'clock was the hour when Cockram said that he had spoken to Mrs. Keeson. Harold had not left the party at the 'Stag and Mantle' since ten o'clock, which was an hour before Alice Image took the drugged beer to the groom. The whole edifice of the prosecution thus crumbled together like a house of cards, and Harold Keeson was discharged, without the slightest suspicion clinging to him.

"Six months later he married Lady Agnes Stourcliffe. The Earl, now a completely ruined man, offered no further opposition to the union of his daughter with a man who, at any rate, could keep her in comfort and luxury; for though both Mr. Keeson and his son lost heavily through Cigarette's illness, yet the trainer was sufficiently rich to offer his son and his bride a very beautiful home."

The man in the corner called to the waitress, and paid for his glass of milk and cheese-cake, whilst I remained absorbed in thought, gazing at the *Daily Telegraph*, which, in its "London Day by Day." had this very morning announced that Mr. and Lady Agnes Keeson had returned to town from "The Rookery," Newmarket.

V.

"But who poisoned Cigarette?" I asked after a while; "and why?"

"Ah, who did, I wonder?" he replied with exasperating mildness.

"Surely you have a theory," I suggested.

"Ah, but my theories are not worth considering. The police would take no notice of them."

"Why did Mrs. Keeson go to the stables that night? Did she go?" I asked.

"Cockram swears she did."

"She swears she didn't. If she did why should she have asked for her son? Surely she did not wish to incriminate her son in order to save herself?"

"No," he replied; "women don't save themselves usually at the expense of their children, and women don't usually 'hocus' a horse. It is not a female crime at all—is it?"

The aggravating creature was getting terribly sarcastic; and I began to fear that he was not going to speak, after all. He was looking dejectedly all around him. I had one or two parcels by me. I undid a piece of string from one of them, and handed it to him with the most perfectly indifferent air I could command.

"I wonder if it was Cockram who told a lie?" I then said unconcernedly.

But already he had seized on that bit of string, and nervously now, his long fingers began fashioning a series of complicated knots.

"Let us take things from the beginning," he said at last. "The beginning of the mystery was the contradictory statements made by the groom Cockram and Mrs. Keeson respectively. Let us take, first of all, the question of the groom. The matter is simple enough either he saw Mrs. Keeson or he did not. If he did not see her then he must have told a lie, either unintentionally or by design—unintentionally if he was mistaken; but this could not very well be since he asserted that Mrs. Keeson spoke to him, and even mentioned her son, Mr. Harold Keeson. Therefore, if Cockram did not see Mrs. Keeson he told a lie by design for some purpose of his own. You follow me?"

"Yes," I replied; "I have thought all that out for myself already."

"Very well. Now, could there be some even remotely plausible motive why Cockram should have told that deliberate lie?"

"To save his sweetheart, Alice Image," I said.

"But you forget that his sweetheart was not accused at first, and that, from the very beginning, Cockram's manner, when questioned on the subject of the events of that night, was strange and contradictory in the extreme."

"He may have known from the first that Alice Image was guilty," I argued.

"In that case he would have merely asserted that he had seen and heard nothing during the night, or, if he wished to lie about it, he would have said that it was Palk, the tout, who sneaked into the stables, rather than incriminate his mistress, who had been good and kind to him for years."

"He may have wished to be revenged on Mrs. Keeson for some reason which has not yet transpired."

"How? By making a statement which, if untrue, could be so easily disproved by Mr. Keeson himself, who, as a matter of fact, could easily assert that his wife did not leave her bedroom that night, or by incriminating Mr. Harold Keeson, who could prove an *alibi*? Not much of a revenge there, you must admit. No, no; the more you reflect seriously upon these possibilities the deeper will become your conviction that Cockram did not lie either accidentally or on purpose; that he did see Mrs. Keeson at that hour at the stable-door; that she did speak to him; and that it was she who told the lie in open court."

"But," I asked, feeling more bewildered than before, "why should Mrs. Keeson have gone to the stables and asked for her son when she must have known that he was not there, but that her enquiry would make it, to say the least, extremely unpleasant for him?"

"Why?" he shrieked excitedly, jumping up like a veritable jack-in-the-box. "Ah, if you would only learn to reflect you might in time become a fairly able journalist. Why did Mrs. Keeson momentarily incriminate her son?—for it was only a momentary incrimination. Think, think! A woman does not incriminate her child to save herself; but she might do it to save some one else—some one who was dearer to her than that child."

"Nonsense!" I protested.

"Nonsense, is it?" he replied. "You have only to think of the characters of the chief personages who figured in the drama—of the trainer Keeson, with his hasty temper and his inordinate family pride. Was it likely when the half-ruined Earl of Okehampton talked of *mésalliance*, and forbade the marriage of his daughter with his trainer's son that the latter would not resent that insult with terrible bitterness? and, resenting it, not think of some means of being even with the noble Earl? Can you not imagine the proud man boiling with indignation on hearing his son's tale of how Lord Okehampton had forbidden him the house? Can you not hear him saying to himself:

"'Well, by — the trainer's son *shall* marry the Earl's daughter!'

"And the scheme—simple and effectual—whereby the ruin of the arrogant nobleman would be made so complete that he would be only too willing to allow his daughter to marry any one who would give her a good home and him a helping hand?"

"But," I objected, "why should Mr. Keeson take the trouble to drug the groom and sneak out to the stables at dead of night when he had access to the mare at all hours of the day?"

"Why?" shrieked the animated scarecrow. "Why? Because Keeson was just one of those clever criminals, with a sufficiency of brains to throw police and public alike off the scent. Cockram, remember, spent every moment of the day and night with the mare. Therefore, if he had been in full possession of his senses and could positively swear that no one had had access to Cigarette but his master and himself, suspicion was bound to fasten, sooner or later, on Keeson. But Keeson was a bit of a genius in the criminal line. Seemingly he could have had no motive for drugging the groom, yet he added that last artistic touch to his clever crime, and thus threw a final bucketful of sand in the eyes of the police."

"Even then," I argued, "Cockram might just have woke up—might just have caught Keeson in the act."

"Exactly. And that is, no doubt, what Mrs. Keeson feared.

"She was a brave woman, if ever there was one. Can you not picture her knowing her husband's violent temper, his indomitable pride, and guessing that he would find some means of being revenged on the Earl of Okehampton? Can you not imagine her watching her husband and gradually guessing, realising what he had in his mind when, in the middle of the night, she saw him steal out of bed and out of the house? Can you not see her following him stealthily—afraid of him, perhaps—not daring to interfere—terrified above all things of the consequences of his crime, of the risks of Cockram waking up, of the exposure, the disgrace?

"Then the final tableau:—Keeson having accomplished his purpose, goes back towards the house, and she—perhaps with a vague hope that she might yet save the mare by taking away the poison which Keeson had prepared—in her turn goes to the stables. But this time the groom is half-awake, and challenges her. Then her instinct—that unerring instinct which always prompts a really good woman when the loved one is in danger—suggests to Mrs. Keeson the clever subterfuge of pretending that she had seen her son entering the stables.

"She asks for him, *knowing well that she could do him no harm,* since he could so easily prove an *alibi*, but thereby throwing a veritable cloud of dust in the eyes of the keenest enquirer, and casting over the hocussing of Cigarette so thick a mantle of mystery that suspicion, groping blindly round, could never fasten tightly on any one.

"Think of it all," he added as, gathering up his hat and umbrella, he prepared to go, "and remember at the same time that it was Mr. Keeson alone who could disprove that his wife never left her room that night, that he did not do this, that he guessed what she had done and why she had done it, and I think that you will admit that not one link is missing in the chain of evidence which I have had the privilege of laying before you."

Before I could reply he had gone, and I saw his strange scarecrow-like figure disappearing through the glass door. Then I had a good think on the subject of the hocussing of Cigarette, and I was reluctantly bound to admit that once again the man in the corner had found the only possible solution to the mystery.

3
The Tragedy of Dartmoor Terrace

I.

"It is not by any means the Law and Police Courts that form the only interesting reading in the daily papers," said the man in the corner airily, as he munched his eternal bit of cheese-cake and sipped his glass of milk, like a frowsy old torn cat.

"You don't agree with me," he added, for I had offered no comment to his obvious remark.

"No?" I answered. "I suppose you were thinking—"

"Of the tragic death of Mrs. Yule, for instance," he replied eagerly. "Beyond the inquest, and its very unsatisfactory verdict, very few circumstances connected with that interesting case ever got into the papers at all."

"I forget what the verdict actually was," I said, eager, too, on my side to hear him talk about that mysterious tragedy, which, as a matter of fact, had puzzled a good many people.

"Oh, it was as vague and as wordy as the English language would allow. The jury found that 'Mrs. Yule had died through falling downstairs, in consequence of a fainting attack, but how she came to fall is not clearly shown.'

"What had happened was this: Mrs. Yule was a rich and eccentric old lady, who lived very quietly in a small house in Kensington; No. 9 Dartmoor Terrace is, I believe, the correct address.

"She had no expensive tastes, for she lived, as I said before, very simply and quietly in a small Kensington house, with two female servants—a cook and a housemaid—and a young fellow whom she had adopted as her son.

"The story of this adoption is, of course, the pivot round which all the circumstances of the mysterious tragedy revolved. Mrs. Yule, namely, had an only son, William, to whom she was passionately attached; but, like many a fond mother, she had the desire of mapping out that son's future entirely according to her own ideas. William Yule, on the other hand, had his own views with regard to his own happiness, and one fine day went so far as to marry the girl of his choice, and that in direct opposition to his mother's wishes.

"Mrs. Yule's chagrin and horror at what she called her son's base ingratitude knew no bounds; at first it was even thought that she would never get over it.

"'He has gone in direct opposition to my fondest wishes, and chosen a wife whom I could never accept as a daughter; he shall have none of the property which has enriched me, and which I know he covets.'

"At first her friends imagined that she meant to leave all her money to charitable institutions but oh dear me, no Mrs. Yule was one of those women who never did anything that other people expected her to. Within three years of her son's marriage she had filled up the place which he had vacated, both in her house and in her heart. She had adopted a son, preferring, as she said, that her money should benefit an individual rather than an institution.

"Her choice had fallen upon the only son of a poor man—an ex-soldier—who used to come twice a week to Dartmoor Terrace to tidy up the small garden at the back: he was very respectable and very honest—was born in the same part of England as Mrs. Yule, and had an only son whose name happened to be William; he rejoiced in the surname of Bloggs.

"'It suits me in every way,' explained Mrs. Yule to old Mr. Statham, her friend and solicitor. 'You see, I am used to the name of William, and the boy is nice-looking and has done very well at the Board School. Moreover, old Bloggs will die within a year or two, and William will be left without any encumbrances.'

"Herein Mrs. Yule's prophecy proved to be correct. Old Bloggs did die very soon, and his son was duly adopted by the rich and eccentric old lady, sent to a good school, and finally given a berth in the Union Bank.

"I saw young Bloggs—it is not a euphonious name, is it?—at that memorable inquest later on. He was very young and unassuming, and used to keep very much out of the way pf Mrs. Yule's friends, who, mind you, strongly disapproved of his presence in the rich old widow's house, to the detriment of the only legitimate son and heir.

"What happened within the intimate and close circle of 9 Dartmoor Terrace during the next three years of course nobody can tell. Certain it is that by the time young Bloggs was nearing his twenty-first birthday, he had become the very apple of his adopted mother's eye.

"During those three years Mr. Statham and other old friends had worked hard in the interests of William Yule. Every one felt that the latter was being very badly treated indeed. He had studied painting in his younger days, and now had set up a small studio in Hampstead, and was making perhaps a couple of hundred or so a year, and that, with much difficulty, whilst the gardener's son had supplanted him in his mother's affections, and, worse still, in his mother's purse.

"The old lady was more obdurate than ever. In deference to the strong feelings of her friends she had agreed to see her son occasionally, and William Yule would call upon his mother from time to time—in the middle of the day when Bloggs was out of the way at the Bank—stay to tea, and part from her in frigid, though otherwise amicable, terms.

"'I have no ill-feeling against my son,' the old lady would say, 'but when he married against my wishes, he became a stranger to me—that is all—a stranger, however, whose pleasant acquaintanceship I am pleased to keep up.'

"That the old lady meant to carry her eccentricities in this respect to the bitter end, became all the more evident when she sent for her old friend and lawyer, Mr. Statham, and explained to him that she wished to make over to young Bloggs the whole of her property by deed of gift, during her lifetime—on condition that on his twenty-first birthday he legally took up the name of Yule.

"Mr. Statham subsequently made public, as you know, the whole of this interview which he had with Mrs. Yule.

"'I tried to dissuade her, of course,' he said, 'for I thought it so terribly unfair on William Yule and his children. Moreover, I had always hoped that when Mrs. Yule grew older and more feeble she would surely relent towards her only son. But she was terribly obstinate.'

"'It is because I may become weak in my dotage,' she said, 'that I want to make the whole thing absolutely final—I don't want to relent. I wish that William should suffer, where I think he will suffer most, for he was always over-fond of money. If I make a will in favour of Bloggs, who knows I might repent it, and alter it at the eleventh hour? One is apt to become maudlin when one is dying, and has people weeping all round one. No!—I want the whole thing to be absolutely irrevocable; and I shall present the deed of gift to young Bloggs on his twenty-first birthday. I can always make it a condition that he keeps me in moderate comfort to the end of my days. He is too big a fool to be really ungrateful, and after all I don't think I should very much mind ending my life in the workhouse.'

"'What could I do?' added Mr. Statham. 'If I had refused to draw up that iniquitous deed of gift, she only would have employed some other lawyer to do it for her. As it is, I secured an annuity of £500 a year for the old lady, in consideration of a gift worth some £30,000 made over absolutely to Mr. William Bloggs.'

"The deed was drawn up," continued the man in the corner, "there is no doubt of that. Mr. Statham saw to it. The old lady even insisted on having two more legal opinions upon it, lest there should be the slightest flaw that might render the deed invalid. Moreover, she caused herself to be examined by two specialists in order that they might testify that she was absolutely sound in mind, and in full possession of all her faculties.

"When the deed was all that the law could wish, Mr. Statham handed it over to Mrs. Yule, who wished to keep it by her until 3rd April—young Bloggs' twenty-first birthday—on which day she meant to surprise him with it.

"Mr. Statham handed over the deed to Mrs. Yule on 14th February, and on 28th March—that is to say, six days before Bloggs' majority—the old lady was found dead at the foot of the stairs in Dartmoor Terrace, whilst her desk was found to have been broken open, and the deed of gift had disappeared."

II.

"From the very first the public took a great interest a the sad death of Mrs. Yule. The old lady's eccentricities were pretty well known throughout all her neighbourhood, at any rate. Then, she had a large circle of friends, who all took sides, either for the disowned son or for the old lady's rigid and staunch principles of filial obedience.

"Directly, therefore, that the papers mentioned the sudden death of Mrs. Yule, tongues began to wag, and, whilst some asserted 'Accident,' others had already begun to whisper 'Murder.'

"For the moment nothing definite was known. Mr. Bloggs had sent for Mr. Statham, and the most persevering and most inquisitive persons of both sexes could glean no information from the cautious old lawyer.

"The inquest was to be held on the following day, and perforce curiosity had to be bridled until then. But you may imagine how that coroner's court at Kensington was packed on that day. I, of course, was at my usual place—well to the front, for I was already keenly interested in the tragedy, and knew that a palpitating mystery lurked behind the old lady's death.

"Annie, the housemaid at Dartmoor Terrace, was the first, and I may say the only really important, witness during the interesting inquest. The story she told amounted to this Mrs. Yule, it appears, was very religious, and, in spite of her advancing years and decided weakness of the heart, Was in the habit of going to early morning service every day of her life at six o'clock. She would get up before any one else in the house, and winter or summer, rain, snow, or fine, she would walk round to St Matthias' Church, coming home at about a quarter to seven, just when her servants were getting up.

"On this sad morning (28th March) Annie explained that she got up as usual and went downstairs (the servants slept at the top of the house) at seven o'clock. She noticed nothing wrong; her mistress's bedroom-door was open as usual, Annie merely remarking to herself that the mistress was later than usual from church that morning. Then suddenly, in the hall at the foot of the stairs, she caught sight of Mrs. Yule lying head downwards, her head on the mat, motionless.

"'I ran downstairs as quickly as I could,' continued Annie, 'and I suppose I must 'ave screamed, for cook came out of 'er room upstairs, and Mr. Bloggs, too, shouted down to know what was the matter. At first we only thought Mrs. Yule was unconscious-like. Me and Mr. Bloggs carried 'er to 'er room, and then Mr. Bloggs ran for the doctor.'

"The rest of Annie's story," continued the man in the corner, "was drowned in a deluge of tears. As for the doctor, he could add but little to what the public had already known and guessed. Mrs. Yule undoubtedly suffered from a weak heart, although she had never been known to faint. In this instance, however, she undoubtedly must have turned giddy, as she was about to go downstairs, and fallen headlong. She was of course very much injured, the doctor explained, but she actually died of heart failure, brought on by the shock of the fall. She must have been on her way to church, for her prayer-book was found on the floor close by her, also a candle—which she must have carried, as it was a dark morning—had rolled along and extinguished itself as it rolled. From these facts, therefore, it was gathered that the poor old lady came by this tragic death at about six o'clock, the hour at which she regularly started out for morning service. Both the servants and also Mr. Bloggs slept at the top of the house, and it is a known fact that sleep in most cases is always heaviest in the early morning hours; there was, therefore, nothing strange in the fact that no one heard either the fall or a scream, if Mrs. Yule uttered one, which is doubtful.

"So far, you see," continued the man in the corner, after a slight pause, "there did not appear to be anything very out of the way or mysterious about Mrs. Yule's tragic death. But the public had expected interesting developments, and I must say their expectations were more than fully realised.

"Jane, the cook, was the first witness to give the public an inkling of the sensations to come.

"She deposed that on Thursday, the 27th, she was alone in the kitchen in the evening after dinner, as it was the housemaid's evening out, when, at about nine o'clock, there was a ring at the bell.

"'I went to answer the door,' said Jane, 'and there was a lady, all dressed in black, as far as I Could see—as the 'all gas always did burn very badly—still, I think she was dressed dark, and she 'ad on a big 'at and a veil with spots. She says to me: "Mrs. Yule lives 'ere?" I says, "She do, 'm," though I don't think she was quite the lady, so I don't know why I said 'm, but—'

"'Yes, yes!' here interrupted the coroner somewhat impatiently, 'it doesn't matter what you said. Tell us what happened.'

"'Yes, sir,' continued Jane, quite undisturbed, as I was saying, I asked the lady her name, and she says: "Tell Mrs. Yule I would wish to speak with 'er," then as she saw me 'esitating, for I didn't like leaving 'er all alone in the 'all, she said, "Tell Mrs. Yule that Mrs. William Yule wishes to speak with 'er."

"Jane paused to take breath, for she talked fast and volubly, and all eyes were turned to a corner of the room, where William Yule, dressed in the careless fashion affected by artists, sat watching and listening eagerly to everything that was going on. At the mention of his wife's name he shrugged his shoulders, and I thought for the moment that he would jump up and say something; but he evidently thought better of it, and remained as before, silent and quietly watching.

"'You showed the lady upstairs?' asked the coroner, after an instant's most dramatic pause.

"'Yes, sir,' replied Jane; 'but I went to ask the mistress first. Mrs. Yule was sitting in the drawing-room, reading. She says to me, "Show the lady up at once; and, Jane," she says, "ask Mr. Bloggs to kindly come to the drawing-room." I showed the lady up, and I told Mr. Bloggs, 'o was smoking in the library, and 'e went to the drawing-room.

"'When Annie come in,' continued Jane with increased volubility, 'I told 'er 'oo 'ad come, and she and me was very astonished, because we 'ad often seen Mr. William Yule come to see 'is mother, but we 'ad never seen 'is wife. "Did you see what she was like, cook?" says Annie to me. "No," I says, "the 'all gas was burnin' that badly, and she 'ad a veil on." Then Annie ups and says, "I must go up, cook," she says, "for my things is all wet. I never did see such rain in all my life. I tell you my boots and petticoats is all soaked through." Then up she runs, and I thought then that per'aps she meant to see if she couldn't 'ear anything that was goin' on upstairs. Presently she come down—'

"But at this point Jane's flow of eloquence received an unexpected check. The coroner preferred to hear from Annie herself whatever the latter may have overheard, and Jane, very wrathful and indignant, had to stand aside, while Annie, who was then recalled, completed the story.

"'I don't know what made me stop on the landing,' she explained timidly, 'and I'm sure I didn't mean to listen. I was going upstairs to change my things, and put on my cap and apron, in case the mistress wanted anything.

"'Then, I don't think I ever 'eard Mrs. Yule's voice so loud and angry.'

"'You stopped to listen?' asked the coroner.

"'I couldn't 'elp it, sir. Mrs. Yule was shouting at the top of 'er voice. "Out of my 'ouse," she says; "I never wish to see you or your precious husband inside my doors again."'

"'You are quite sure that you heard those very words?' asked the coroner earnestly.

"'I'll take my Bible oath on every one of them, sir,' said Annie emphatically. 'Then I could 'ear some one crying and moaning: "Oh!

what 'ave I done? Oh! what 'ave I done?" I didn't like to stand on the landing then, for fear some one should come out, so I ran upstairs, and put on my cap and apron, for I was all in a tremble, what with what I'd 'eard, and the storm outside, which was coming down terrible.

"'When I went down again, I 'ardly durst stand on the landing, but the door of the drawing-room was ajar, and I 'eard Mr. Bloggs say: "Surely you will not turn a human being, much less a woman, out on a night like this?" And the mistress said, still speaking very angry "Very well, you may sleep here; but remember, I don't wish to see your face again. I go to church at six and come home again at seven; mind you are out of the house before then. There are plenty of trains after seven o'clock."'

"After that," continued the man in the corner, "Mrs. Yule rang for the housemaid and gave orders that the spare room should be got ready, and that the visitor should have some tea and toast brought to her in the morning as soon as Annie was up.

"But Annie was rather late on that eventful morning of the 28th. She did not go downstairs till seven o'clock. When she did, she found her mistress lying dead at the foot of the stairs. It was not until after the doctor had been and gone that both the servants suddenly recollected the guest in the spare room. Annie knocked at her door, and, receiving no answer, she walked in; the bed had not been slept in, and the spare room was empty.

"'There, now!' was the housemaid's decisive comment, 'me and cook did 'ear someone cross the 'all, and the front door bang about an hour after every one else was in bed.'

"Presumably, therefore, Mrs. William Yule had braved the elements and left the house at about midnight, leaving no trace behind her, save, perhaps, the broken lock of the desk that had held the deed of gift in favour of young Bloggs."

III.

"Some say there's a Providence that watches over us," said the man in the corner, when he had looked at me keenly, and assured himself that I was really interested in his narrative, "others use the less poetic and more direct formula, that 'the devil takes care of his own.' The impression of the general public during this interesting coroner's inquest was that the devil was taking special care of his own—('his own' being in this instance represented by Mrs. William Yule, who, by the way, was not present).

"What the Evil One had done for her was this: He caused the hall gas to burn so badly on that eventful Thursday night, 27th March, that Jane, the cook, had not been able to see Mrs. William Yule at all distinctly. He, moreover, decreed that when Annie went into the drawing-room later on to take her mistress's orders with regard to the spare room, Mrs. William was apparently dissolved in tears, for she only presented the back of her head to the inquisitive glances of the young housemaid.

"After that the two servants went to bed, and heard some one cross the hall and leave the house about an hour or so later; but neither of them could swear positively that they would recognise the mysterious visitor if they set eyes on her again.

"Throughout all these proceedings, however, you may be sure that Mr. William Yule did not remain a passive spectator. In fact, I, who watched him, could see quite clearly that he had the greatest possible difficulty in controlling himself. Mind you, I knew by then exactly where the hitch lay, and I could, and will presently, tell you exactly all that occurred on Thursday evening, 27th March, at No. 9 Dartmoor Terrace, just as if I had spent that memorable night there myself; and I can assure you that it gave me great pleasure to watch the faces of the two men most interested in the verdict of this coroner's jury.

"Every one's sympathy had by now entirely veered round to young Bloggs, who for years had been brought up to expect a fortune, and had then, at the last moment, been defrauded of it, through what looked already much like a crime. The deed of gift had, of course, not been what the lawyers call 'completed.' It had rested in Mrs. Yule's desk, and had never been 'delivered' by the donor to the donee, or even to another person on his behalf.

"Young Bloggs, therefore, saw himself suddenly destined to live his life as penniless as he had been when he was still the old gardener's son.

"No doubt the public felt that what lurked mostly in his mind was a desire for revenge, and I think every one forgave him when he gave his evidence with a distinct tone of animosity against the woman who had apparently succeeded in robbing him of a fortune.

"He had only met Mrs. William Yule once before, he explained, but he was ready to swear that it was she who called that night. As for the original motive of the quarrel between the two ladies, young Bloggs was inclined to think that it was mostly on the question of money.

"'Mrs. William,' continued the young man, 'made certain peremptory demands on Mrs. Yule, which the old lady bitterly resented.'

"But here there was an awful and sudden interruption. William Yule, now quite beside himself with rage, had with one bound reached the witness-box, and struck young Bloggs a violent blow in the face.

"'Liar and cheat! ' he roared, 'take that!'

And he prepared to deal the young man another even more vigorous blow, when he was overpowered and seized by the constables. Young Bloggs had become positively livid; his face looked grey and ashen, except there, where his powerful assailant's fist had left a deep purple mark.

"'You have done your wife's cause no good,' remarked the coroner drily, as William Yule, sullen and defiant, was forcibly dragged back to his place. 'I shall adjourn the inquest until Monday, and will expect Mrs. Yule to be present and explain exactly what happened after her quarrel with the deceased, and why she left the house so suddenly and mysteriously that night.'

"William Yule tried an explanation even then. His wife had never left the studio in Sheriff Road, West Hampstead, the whole of that Thursday evening. It was a fearfully stormy night, and she never went outside the door. But the Yules kept no servant at the cheap little rooms; a charwoman used to come in every morning only for an hour or two, to do the rough work; there was no one, therefore, except the husband himself to prove Mrs. William Yule's *alibi*.

"At the adjourned inquest, on the Monday, Mrs. William Yule duly appeared; she was a young, delicate-looking woman, with a patient and suffering face, that had not an atom of determination or vice in it.

"Her evidence was very simple; she merely swore solemnly that she had spent the whole evening indoors, she had never been to 9 Dartmoor Terrace in her life, and, as a matter of fact, would never have dared to call on her irreconciliable mother-in-law. Neither she nor her husband were specially in want of money either.

"'My husband had just sold a picture at the Water Colour Institute,' she explained, 'we were not hard up; and certainly I should never have attempted to make the slightest demand on Mrs. Yule.'

"There the matter had to rest with regard to the theft of the document, for that was no business of the coroner's or of the jury. According to medical evidence the old lady's death had been due to a very natural and possible accident—a sudden feeling of giddiness—and the verdict had to be in accordance with this.

"There was no real proof against Mrs. William Yule—only one man's word, that of young Bloggs; and it would no doubt always have been felt that his evidence might not be wholly unbiased. He was therefore well advised not to prosecute. The world was quite content to believe that the Yules had planned and executed the theft, but he never would have got a conviction against Mrs. William Yule just on his own evidence."

IV.

"Then William Yule and his wife were left in full possession of their fortune? " I asked eagerly.

"Yes, they were," he replied; "but they had to go and travel abroad for a while, feeling was so high against them. The deed, of course, not having been 'delivered,' could not be upheld in a court of law; that was the opinion of several eminent counsel whom Mr. Statham, with a lofty sense of justice, consulted on behalf of young Bloggs."

"And young Bloggs was left penniless?"

"No," said the man in the corner, as, with a weird and satisfied smile, he pulled a piece of string out of his pocket; "the friends of the late Mrs. Yule subscribed the sum of £1,000 for him, for they all thought he had been so terribly badly treated, and Mr. Statham has taken him in his office as articled pupil. No! no! young Bloggs has not done so badly either—"

"What seems strange to me," I remarked, "is that, for all she knew, Mrs. William Yule might have committed only a silly and purposeless theft. If Mrs. Yule had not died suddenly and accidentally the next morning, she would, no doubt, have executed a fresh deed of gift, and all would have been *in statu quo*."

"Exactly," he replied drily, whilst his fingers fidgeted nervously with his bit of string.

"Of course," I suggested, for I felt that the funny creature wanted to be drawn out; "she may have reckoned on the old lady's weak heart, and the shock to her generally, but it was, after all, very problematical."

"Very," he said, "and surely you are not still under the impression that Mrs. Yule's death was purely the result of an accident?"

"What else could it be?" I urged.

"The result of a slight push from the top of the stairs," he remarked placidly, whilst a complicated knot went to join a row of its fellows.

"But Mrs. William Yule had left the house before midnight—or, at any rate, some one had. Do you think she had an accomplice?

"I think," he said excitedly, "that the mysterious visitor who left the house that night had an instigator whose name was William Bloggs."

"I don't understand," I gasped in amazement.

"Point No. 1," he shrieked, while the row of knots followed each other in rapid succession. "Young Bloggs swore a lie when he swore that it was Mrs. William Yule who called at Dartmoor Terrace that night."

"What makes you say that? " I retorted.

"One very simple fact," he replied, "so simple that it was, of course, overlooked. Do you remember that one of the things which Annie overheard was old Mrs. Yule's irate words, 'Very well, you may sleep here; but, remember, I do not wish to see your face again. You can leave my house before I return from church; you can get plenty of trains after seven o'clock.' Now what do you make of that?" he added triumphantly.

"Nothing in particular," I rejoined; "it was an awfully wet night, and—"

"And High Street Kensington Station within two minutes' walk of Dartmoor Terrace, with plenty of trains to West Hampstead, and Sheriff Road within two minutes of this latter station," he shrieked, getting more and more excited, "and the hour only about ten o'clock, when there are plenty of trains from one part of London to another? Old Mrs. Yule, with her irascible temper and obstinate ways, would have said: 'There's the station, not two minutes' walk; get out of my house, and don't ever let me see your face again.' Wouldn't she, now?"

"It certainly seems more likely."

"Of course it does. She only allowed the woman to stay because the woman had either a very long way to go to get a train, or perhaps had missed her last train—a connection on a branch line presumably—and could not possibly get home at all that night."

"Yes, that sounds logical," I admitted.

"Point No. 2," he shrieked. "Young Bloggs having told a lie, had some object in telling it. That was my starting-point; from there I worked steadily until I had reconstructed the events of that Thursday night—nay, more, until I knew something more about young Bloggs' immediate future, in order that I might then imagine his past.

"And this is what I found.

"After the tragic death of Mrs. Yule, young Bloggs went abroad at the expense of some kind friends, and came home with a wife, whom he is supposed to have met and married in Switzerland. From that point everything became clear to me. Young Bloggs had told a lie when he swore that it was Mrs. William Yule who called that night—it was certainly *not* Mrs. William Yule; therefore it was somebody who either represented herself as such, or who believed herself to be Mrs. William Yule.

"The first supposition," continued the funny creature, "I soon dismissed as impossible; young Bloggs knew Mrs. William Yule by sight—and since he had lied, he had done so deliberately. Therefore to my mind, the lady who called herself Mrs. William Yule did so because she believed that she had a right to that name; that she had married a man, who, for purposes of his own, had chosen to call himself by that name. From this point to that of guessing who that man was was simple enough."

"Do you mean young Bloggs himself?" I asked in amazement.

"And whom else?" he replied. "Isn't that sort of thing done every day? Bloggs was a hideous name, and Yule was eventually to be his own. With William Yule's example before him, he must have known that it would be dangerous to broach the marriage question at all before the old lady, and probably only meant to wait for a favourable opportunity of doing so. But after a while the young wife would naturally become troubled and anxious, and, like most women under the same circumstances, would become jealous and inquisitive as well.

"She soon found out where he lived, and no doubt called there, thinking that old Mrs. Yule was her husband's own fond mother.

"You can picture the rest. Mrs. Yule, furious at having been deceived, herself destroys the deed of gift which she meant to present to her adopted son, and from that hour young Bloggs sees himself penniless.

"The false Mrs. Yule left the house, and young Bloggs waited for his opportunity on the dark landing of a small London house. One push and the deed was done. With her weak heart, Mrs. Yule was sure to die of the shock, if not of the fall.

"Before that, already the desk had been broken open and every appearance of a theft given to it. After the tragedy, then, young Bloggs retired quietly to his room. The whole thing looked so like an accident that, even had the servants heard the fall at once, there would still have been time enough for the young villain to sneak into his room, and then to reappear at his door, as if he, too, had been just awakened by the noise.

"The result turned out just as he expected. The William Yules have been and still are suspected of the theft; and young Bloggs is a hero of romance with whom every one is in sympathy."

4
Who Stole The Black Diamonds?

I.

"Do you know who that is?" said the man in the corner, as he pushed a small packet of photos across the table.

The picture on the top represented an entrancingly beautiful woman, with bare arms and neck, and a profusion of pearl and diamond ornaments about her head and throat.

"Surely this is the Queen of—?"

"Hush!" he broke in abruptly, with mock dismay; "you must mention no names."

"Why not?" I asked, laughing, for he looked so droll in his distress.

"Look closely at the photo," he replied, "and at the necklace and tiara that the lady is wearing." Yes," I said. "Well?

"Do you mean to say you don't recognise them?"

I looked at the picture more closely, and then there suddenly came back to my mind that mysterious story of the Black Diamonds, which had not only bewildered the police of Europe, but also some of its diplomats.

"Ah! I see you do recognise the jewels!" said the funny creature, after a while. "No wonder! for their design is unique, and photographs of that necklace and tiara were circulated practically throughout all the world.

"Of course I am not going to mention names, for you know very well who the royal heroes of this mysterious adventure were. For the purposes of my narrative, suppose I call them the King and Queen of 'Bohemia.'

"The value of the stones was said to be fabulous, and it was only natural when the King of 'Bohemia' found himself somewhat in want of money—a want which has made itself felt before now with even the most powerful European monarchs—that he should decide to sell the precious trinkets, worth a small kingdom in themselves. In order to be in closer touch with the most likely customers, their Majesties of 'Bohemia' came over to England during the season of 1902—a season memorable alike for its deep sorrow and its great joy.

"After the sad postponement of the Coronation festivities, they rented Eton Chase, a beautiful mansion just outside Chislehurst, for the summer months. There they entertained right royally, for the Queen was very gracious and the King a real sportsman—there also the rumour first got about that His Majesty had decided to sell the world-famous *parure* of Black Diamonds.

"Needless to say, they were not long in the market: quite a host of American millionaires had already coveted them for their wives, and brisk and sensational offers were made to His Majesty's business man both by letter and telegram.

"At last, however, Mr. Wilson, the multimillionaire, was understood to have made an offer, for the necklace and tiara, of £500,000, which had been accepted.

"But a very few days later, that is to say, on the Sunday and Monday, 6th and 7th July, there appeared in the papers the short, but deeply sensational announcement that a burglary had occurred at Eton Chase, Chislehurst, the mansion inhabited by Their Majesties the King and Queen of 'Bohemia,' and that among the objects stolen was the famous *parure* of Black Diamonds, for which a bid of half a million sterling had just been made and accepted.

"The burglary had been one of the most daring and most mysterious ones ever brought under the notice of the police authorities. The mansion was full of guests at the time, among whom were many diplomatic notabilites, and also Mr. and Mrs. Wilson, the future owners of the gems; there was also a very large staff of servants. The burglary must have occurred between the hours of 10 and 11.30 P.M., though the precise moment could not be ascertained.

"The house itself stands in the midst of a large garden, and has deep French windows opening out upon a terrace at the back. There are ornamental iron balconies to the windows of the upper floors, and it was to one of these, situated immediately above the dining-room, that a rope-ladder was found to be attached.

"The burglar must have chosen a moment when the guests were dispersed in the smoking, billiard, and drawing rooms; the servants were having their own meal, and the dining-room was deserted. He must have slung his rope-ladder, and entered Her Majesty's own bedroom by the window which—as the night was very warm—had been left open. The jewels were locked up in a small iron box, which stood upon the dressing-table, and the burglar took the box bodily away with him, and then, no doubt, returned the way he came.

"The wonderful point in this daring attempt was the fact that most of the windows on the ground floor were slightly open that night, that the rooms themselves were filled with guests, and that the dining-room was not empty for more than a few minutes at a time, as the servants were still busy clearing away after dinner.

"At nine o'clock some of the younger guests had strolled out on to the terrace, and the last of these returned to the drawing-room at ten o'clock; at half-past eleven one of the servants caught sight of the rope-ladder in front of one of the dining-room windows, and the alarm was given.

"All traces of the burglar, however, and of his princely booty had completely disappeared."

II.

"Not only did this daring burglary cause a great deal of excitement," continued the man in the corner, "but it also roused a good deal of sympathy in the public mind for the King and Queen of 'Bohemia,' who thus found their hope of raising half a million sterling suddenly dashed to the ground. The loss to them would, of course, be irreparable.

"Matters were, however, practically at a standstill, all enquiries from enterprising journalists only eliciting the vague information that the police 'held a clue.' We all know what that means. Then all at once a wonderful rumour got about.

"Goodness only knows how these rumours originate—sometimes solely in the imagination of the man in the street. In this instance, certainly, that worthy gentleman had a very sensational theory. It was, namely, rumoured all over London that the clue which the police held pointed to no less a person than Mr. Wilson himself.

"What had happened was this: Minute enquiries on the part of the most able detectives of Scotland Yard had brought to light the fact that the burglary at Eton Chase must have occurred precisely between ten minutes and a quarter past eleven; at every other moment of the entire evening somebody or other had observed either the terrace or the dining-room windows.

"I told you that until ten o'clock some of Their Majesties' guests were walking up and down the terrace; between ten and half-past servants were clearing away in the dining-room, and here it was positively ascertained beyond any doubt that no burglar could have slung a rope-ladder and climbed up it immediately outside those windows, for one or other of the six servants engaged in clearing away the dinner must of necessity have caught sight of him.

"At half-past ten John Lucas, the head gardener, was walking through the gardens with a dog at his heels, and did not get back to the lodge until just upon eleven. He certainly did not go as far as the terrace, and as that side of the house was in shadow he could not say positively whether the ladder was there or not, but he certainly did assert most emphatically that there was no burglar about the *grounds* then, for the dog was a good watchdog and would have barked if any stranger was about. Lucas took the dog in with him and gave him a bit of supper, and only fastened him to his kennel outside at a quarter-past eleven.

"Surmising, therefore, that at half-past ten, when John Lucas started on his round, the deed was not yet done, that quarter of an hour would give the burglar the only possible opportunity of entering the premises *from the outside*, without being barked at by the dog. Now, during most of that same quarter of an hour, His Majesty the King of 'Bohemia' himself had retired into a small library with his private secretary, in order to glance through certain despatches which had arrived earlier in the evening.

"The window of this library was immediately next to the one outside which the ladder was found, and both the secretary and His Majesty himself think that they would have seen something or heard a noise if the rope-ladder had been slung while they were in the room. They both, however, returned to the drawing-room at ten minutes past eleven.

"And here," continued the man in the corner, rubbing his long, bony fingers together, "arose the neatest little complication I have ever come across in a case of this kind. His Majesty had, it appears, privately made up his mind to accept Mr. Wilson's bid, but the transaction had not yet been completed. Mr. Wilson and his wife came down to stay at Eton Chase on 29th June, and directly they arrived many of those present noticed that Mr. Wilson was obviously repenting of his bargain. This impression had deepened day by day, Mrs. Wilson herself often throwing out covert hints about 'fictitious value' and 'fancy prices for merely notorious trinkets.' In fact, it became very obvious that the Wilsons were really seeking a loophole for evading the conclusion of the bargain.

"On the memorable evening of 5th July Mrs. Wilson had been forced to retire to her room early in the evening, owing, she said, to a bad headache; her room was in the west wing of the Chase, and opened out on the same corridor as the apartments of Her Majesty the Queen. At half-past eleven Mrs. Wilson rang for her maid—Mary Pritchard, who, on entering her mistress's room, met Mr. Wilson just coming out of it, and the girl heard him say: 'Oh, don't worry! I'll have the whole reset when we get back.'

"The detectives, on the other hand, had obtained information that two or three days previously Mr. Wilson had sustained a very severe loss on the 'Change, and that he had subsequently remarked to two or three business friends that the Black Diamonds had become a luxury which he had no right to afford.

"Be this as it may, certain it is that within a week of the notorious burglary the rumour was current in every club in London that James S. Wilson, the reputed American millionaire, having found himself unable to complete the purchase of the Black Diamonds, had found this other very much less legitimate means of gaining possession of the gems.

"You must admit that the case looked black enough against him—all circumstantial, of course, for there was absolutely nothing to prove that he had the jewels in his possession; in fact no trace of them whatever had been found, but the public argued that Mr. Wilson would lie low with them for a while, and then have them reset when he returned to America.

"Of course, ugly rumours of that description don't become general about a man without his getting some inkling of them. Mr. Wilson very soon found his position in London absolutely intolerable: his friends ignored him at the club, ladies ceased to call upon his wife, and one fine day he was openly cut by Lord Barnsdale, a M.F.H., in the hunting field.

"Then Mr. Wilson thought it high time to take action. He placed the whole matter in the hands of an able, if not very scrupulous, solicitor, who promised within a given time to find him a defendant with plenty of means, against whom he could bring a sensational libel suit, with thundering damages.

"The solicitor was as good as his word. He bribed some of the waiters at the Canton, and so laid his snares that within six months, Lord and Lady Barnsdale had been overheard to say in public what everybody now thought in private, namely, that Mr. James S. Wilson, finding himself unable to purchase the celebrated Black Diamonds, had thought it more profitable to steal them.

"Two days later Mr. James S. Wilson entered an action in the High Courts for slander against Lord and Lady Barnsdale, claiming damages to the tune of £50,000."

III.

"Still the mystery of the lost jewels was no nearer to its solution. Their Majesties the King and Queen of 'Bohemia,' had left

England soon after the disastrous event which deprived them of what amounted to a small fortune.

"It was expected that the sensational slander case would come on in the autumn, or rather more than sixteen months after the mysterious disappearance of the Black Diamonds.

"This last season was not a very brilliant one, if you remember; the wet weather, I believe, had quite a good deal to do with the fact; nevertheless London, that great world centre, was, as usual, full of distinguished visitors, among whom Mrs. Vanderdellen, who arrived the second week in July, was perhaps the most interesting.

"Her enormous wealth spread a positive halo round her, it being generally asserted that she was the richest woman in the world. Add to this that she was young, strikingly handsome, and a widow, and you will easily understand what a *furore* her appearance during this London season caused in all high social circles.

"Though she was still in slight mourning for her husband, she was asked everywhere, went everywhere, and was courted and admired by everybody, including some of the highest in the land; her dresses and jewellery were the talk of the ladies' papers, her style and charm the gossip of all the clubs. And no doubt that, although the July evening Court promised to be very brilliant, every one thought that it would be doubly so, since Mrs. Vanderdellen had been honoured with an invitation, and would presumably be present.

"I like to picture to myself that scene at Buckingham Palace," continued the man in the corner, as his fingers toyed lovingly with a beautiful and brand-new bit of string. "Of course, I was not present actually, but I can see it all before me: the lights, the crowds, the pretty women, the glistening diamonds; then, in the midst of the chatter, a sudden silence fell as 'Mrs. Vanderdellen' was announced.

"All women turned to look at the beautiful American as she entered, because her dress—on this her first appearance at the English Court—was sure to be a vision of style and beauty. But for once nobody noticed the dress from Felix, nobody even gave a glance at the exquisitely lovely face of the wearer. Every one's eyes had fastened on one thing only, and every one's lips framed but one exclamation, and that an 'Oh!' half of amazement and half of awe.

"For round her neck and upon her head Mrs. Vanderdellen was wearing a gorgeously magnificent *parure* composed of black diamonds."

IV.

"I don't know how the case of Wilson v. Barnsdale was settled, for it never came into court. There were many people in London who owed the Wilsons an apology, and it is to be hoped that these were tendered in full.

"As for Mrs. Vanderdellen, she seemed quite unaware why her appearance at Their Majesties' Court had caused quite so much sensation. No one, of course, broached the subject of the diamonds to her, and she no doubt attributed those significant 'Oh's' to her own dazzling beauty.

"The next day, however, Detective Marsh, of Scotland Yard, had a very difficult task before him. He had to go and ask a beautiful, rich, and refined woman how she happened to be in possession of stolen jewellery.

"Luckily for Marsh, however, he had to deal with a woman who was also charming, and who met his polite enquiry with an equally pleasant reply:

"'My husband gave me the Black Diamonds,' she said, 'a year ago, on his return from Europe. I had them set in Vienna last spring, and wore them for the first time last night. Will you please tell me the reason of this strange enquiry?'

"'Your husband?' echoed Marsh, ignoring her question, 'Mr. Vanderdellen?'

"'Oh yes,' she replied sweetly, 'I dare say you have never heard of him. His name is very well known in America, where they call him the "Petrol King." One of his hobbies was the collection of gems, which he was very fond of seeing me wear, and he gave me some magnificent jewels. The Black Diamonds certainly are very handsome. May I now request you to tell me,' she repeated, with a certain assumption of hauteur, 'the reason of all these enquiries?'

'The reason is simple enough, madam,' replied the detective abruptly. 'Those diamonds were the property of Her Majesty the Queen of "Bohemia," and were stolen from Their Majesties' residence, Eton Chase, Chislehurst, on the 5th of July last year.'

"'Stolen!' she repeated, aghast and obviously incredulous.

"'Yes, stolen,' said old Marsh. 'I don't wish to distress you unnecessarily, Madam, but you will see how imperative it is that you should place me in immediate communication with Mr. Vanderdellen, as an explanation from him has become necessary.'

"'Unfortunately, that is impossible,' said Mrs. Vanderdellen, who seemed under the spell of a strong emotion.

"'Impossible?'

"'Mr. Vanderdellen has been dead just over a year. He died three days after his return to New York, and the Black Diamonds were the last present he ever made me.'

"There was a pause after that. Marsh—experienced detective though he was—was literally at his wits' ends what to do. He said afterwards that Mrs. Vanderdellen, though very young and frivolous outwardly, seemed at the same time an exceedingly shrewd, far-seeing business woman. To begin with, she absolutely refused to have the matter hushed up, and to return the jewels until their rightful ownership had been properly proved.

"'It would be tantamount,' she said, 'to admitting that my husband had come by them unlawfully.'

"At the same time she offered the princely reward of £10,000 to any one who found the true solution of the mystery: for, mind you, the late Mr. Vanderdellen sailed from Havre for New York on July the 8th, 1902, that is to say, three clear days after the theft of the diamonds from Eton Chase, and he presented his wife with the loose gems immediately on his arrival in New York. Three days after that he died.

"It was difficult to suppose that Mr. Vanderdellen purchased those diamonds not knowing that they must have been stolen, since directly after the burglary the English police telegraphed to all their

Continental colleagues, and within four-and-twenty hours a description of the stolen jewels was circulated throughout Europe.

"It was, to say the least of it, very strange that an experienced business man and shrewd collector like Mr. Vanderdellen should have purchased such priceless gems without making some enquiries as to their history, more especially as they must have been offered to him in a more or less 'hole-in-the-corner' way.

"Still, Mrs. Vanderdellen stuck to her guns, and refused to give up the jewels pending certain enquiries she wished to make. She declared that she wished to be sued for the diamonds in open court, charged with wilfully detaining stolen goods if necessary, for the more publicity was given to the whole affair the better she would like it, so firmly did she believe in her husband's innocence.

"The matter was indeed brought to the High Courts, and the sensational action brought against Mrs. Vanderdellen by the representative of His Majesty the King of 'Bohemia' for the recovery of the Black Diamonds is, no doubt, still fresh in your memory.

"No one was allowed to know what witnesses Mrs. Vanderdellen would bring forward in her defence. She had engaged the services of Sir Arthur Inglewood, and of some of the most eminent counsel at the Bar. The court was packed with the most fashionable crowd ever seen inside the Law Courts; and both days that the action lasted Mrs. Vanderdellen appeared in exquisite gowns and ideal hats.

"The evidence for the Royal plaintiff was simple enough. It all went to prove that the very day after the burglary not a jeweller, pawnbroker, or diamond merchant throughout the whole of Europe could have failed to know that a unique *parure* of black diamonds had been stolen, and would probably be offered for sale. The Black Diamonds in themselves, and out of their setting, were absolutely unique, and if the late Mr. Vanderdellen purchased them in Paris from some private individual, he must at least have very strongly suspected that they were stolen.

"Throughout the whole of that first day Mrs. Vanderdellen sat in court, absolutely calm and placid. She listened to the evidence, made little notes, and chatted with two or three American friends—elderly men—who were with her.

"Then came the turn of the defence.

"Everybody had expected something sensational, and listened more eagerly than ever as the name of Mr. Albert V. B. Sedley was called. He was a tail, elderly man, the regular angular type of the American, with his nasal twang and reposeful manner.

"His story was brief and simple. He was a great friend of the late Mr. Vanderdellen, and had gone on a European tour with him in the early spring of 1902. They were together in Vienna in the month of March, staying at the Hotel Imperial, when one day Vanderdellen came to his room with a remarkable story.

"'He told me,' continued Mr. Albert V. B. Sedley, 'that he had just purchased some very beautiful diamonds, which he meant to present to his wife on his return to New York. He would not tell me where he bought them, nor would he show them to me, but he spoke about the beauty and rarity of the stones, which were that rarest of all things, beautiful black diamonds.

"'As the whole story sounded to me a little bit queer and mysterious, I gave him a word of caution, but he was quite confident as to the integrity of the vendor of the jewels, since the latter had made a somewhat curious bargain. Vanderdellen was to have the diamonds in his keeping for three months without paying any money, merely giving a formal receipt for them; then, if after three months he was quite satisfied with his bargain, and there had been no suspicion or rumour of any kind that the diamonds were stolen, then only was the money, £500,000, to be paid.

"'Vanderdellen thought this very fair and above-board, and so it sounded to me. The only thing I didn't like about it all was that the vendor had given what I thought was a false name and no address; the money was to be paid over to him in French notes when the three months had expired, at an hotel in Paris where Vanderdellen would be staying at the time, and where he would call for it.

"'I heard nothing more about the mysterious diamonds and their still more mysterious vendor,' continued Mr. Sedley, amidst intense excitement, 'for Vanderdellen and I soon parted company after that, he going one way and I another. But at the beginning of July I met him in Paris, and on the 4th I dined with him at the Elysee Palace Hotel, where he was staying.

"'Mr. Cornelius R. Shee was there too, and Vanderdellen related to him during dinner the history of his mysterious purchase of the Black Diamonds, adding that the vendor had called upon him that very day as arranged, and that he (Vanderdellen) had had no hesitation in handing him over the agreed price of £500,000, which he thought a very low one. Both Mr. Shee and I agreed that the whole thing must have been clear and aboveboard, for jewels of such fabulous value could not have been stolen since last spring without the hue and cry being in every paper in Europe.

"'It is my opinion, therefore,' said Mr. Albert V. B. Sedley, at the conclusion of this remarkable evidence, 'that Mr. Vanderdellen bought those diamonds in perfect good faith. He would never have wittingly subjected his wife to the indignity of being seen in public with stolen jewels round her neck. If after 5th July he did happen to hear that a *parure* of black diamonds had been stolen in England at the date, he could not possibly think that there could be the slightest connection between these and those he had purchased more than three months ago.'

"And, amidst indescribable excitement, Mr. Albert V. B. Sedley stepped back into his place.

"That he had spoken the truth from beginning to end no one could doubt for a single moment. His own social position, wealth, and important commercial reputation placed him above any suspicion of committing perjury, even for the sake of a dead friend. Moreover, the story told by Vanderdellen at the dinner in Paris was corroborated by Mr. Cornelius R. Shee in every point.

"But there! a dead man's words are *not* evidence in a court of law. Unfortunately, Mr. Vanderdellen had not shown the diamonds to his friends at the time. He had certainly drawn enormous sums of money from his bank about the end of June and beginning of July, amounting in all to just over a million sterling; and there was nothing to prove which special day he had paid away a sum of £500,000, whether *before* or *after* the burglary at Eton Chase.

"He had made extensive purchases in Paris of pictures, furniture, and other works of art, all of priceless value, for the decoration of his new palace in Fifth Avenue, and no diary of private expenditure was produced in court. Mrs. Vanderdellen herself had said that after her husband's death, as all his affairs were in perfect order, she had destroyed his personal and private diaries.

"Thus the counsel for the plaintiff was able to demolish the whole edifice of the defence bit by bit, for it rested on but very ephemeral foundations: a story related by a dead man.

"Judgment was entered for the plaintiff, although every one's sympathy, including that of judge and of jury, was entirely for the defendant, who had so nobly determined to vindicate her husband's reputation.

"But Mrs. Vanderdellen proved to the last that she was no ordinary every-day woman. She had kept one final sensation up her sleeve. Two days after she had legally been made to give up the Black Diamonds, she offered to purchase them back for £500,000. Her bid was accepted, and during last autumn, on the occasion of the last Royal visit to London and the consequent grand society functions, no one was more admired, more *fêted* and envied, than beautiful Mrs. Vanderdellen as she entered a drawing-room exquisitely gowned, and adorned with the *parure*, of which an Empress might have been proud."

The man in the corner had paused, and was idly tapping his fingers on the marble-topped table of the A.B.C. shop.

"It was a curious story, wasn't it?" said the funny creature after a while. "More like a romance than a reality."

"It is absolutely bewildering," I said.

"What is your theory? " he asked.

"What about?" I retorted.

"Well, there are so many points, aren't there, of which only one is quite clear, namely, that the *parure* of Black Diamonds disappeared from Eton Chase, Chislehurst, on 5th July 1902, and that the next time they were seen they were on the neck and head of Mrs. Vanderdellen, the widow of one of the richest men of modern times, whilst the story of how her husband came by them was, to all intents and purposes, legally disbelieved."

"Then," I argued, "the only logical conclusion to arrive at in all this is that the Black Diamonds, owned by His Majesty the King of 'Bohemia,' were not unique, and that Mr. Vanderdellen bought some duplicate ones."

"If you knew anything about diamonds," he said irritably, "you would also know that your statement is an absurdity. There are no such things as 'duplicate' diamonds."

"Then what *is* the only logical conclusion to arrive at?" I retorted, for he had given up playing with the photos and was twisting and twining that bit of string as if his brain was contained inside it and he feared it might escape.

"Well, to me," he said, "the only logical conclusion of the affair is that the Black Diamonds which Mrs. Vanderdellen wore were the only and original ones belonging to the Crown of 'Bohemia.'

"Then you think that a man in Mr. Vanderdellen's position would have been fool enough to buy gems worth £500,000 at the very moment when there was a hue and cry for them all over Europe?"

"No, I don't," he replied quietly.

"But then—" I began.

"No?" he repeated once again, as his long fingers completed knot number one in that eternal piece of string. "The Black Diamonds which Mrs. Vanderdellen wore were bought by her husband in all good faith from the mysterious vendor in Vienna in March 1902."

"Impossible!" I retorted. "Her Majesty the Queen of 'Bohemia' wore them regularly during the months of May and June, and they were stolen from Eton Chase on July the 5th."

"Her Majesty the Queen of 'Bohemia' wore *a parure* of Black Diamonds during those months, and those certainly were stolen on July the 5th," he said excitedly; "but what was there to prove that *those* were the genuine stones?"

"Why!—" I ejaculated.

"Point No. 2," he said, jumping about like a monkey on a stick; "although Mr. Wilson was acknowledged to be innocent of the theft of the diamonds, isn't it strange that no one has ever been proved guilty of it?"

"But I don't understand—"

"Yet it is simple as daylight. I maintain that His Majesty the King of 'Bohemia' being short, very short, of money, decided to sell the celebrated Black Diamonds; to avoid all risks the stones were taken out of their settings, and a trusted and secret emissary is then deputed to find a possible purchaser; his choice falls on the multi-millionaire Vanderdellen, who is travelling in Europe, is a noted collector of rare jewellery, and has a beautiful young wife—three attributes, you see, which make him a very likely purchaser.

"The emissary then seeks him out, and offers him the diamonds for sale. Mr. Vanderdellen at first hesitates, wondering how such valuable gems had come in the vendor's possession, but the bargain suggested by the latter—the three months during which the gems are to be held on trust by the purchaser—seems so fair and above-board, that Mr. Vanderdellen's objections fall to the ground; he accepts the bargain, and three months later completes the purchase."

"But I don't understand," I repeated again, more bewildered than before. "You say the King of 'Bohemia' sold the loose gems originally to Mr. Vanderdellen; then, what about the *parure* worn by the Queen and offered for sale to Mr. and Mrs. Wilson? What about the theft at Eton Chase?"

"Point No. 3," he shrieked excitedly, as another series of complicated knots went to join its fellows. "I told you that the King of 'Bohemia' was *very* short of money, every one knows *that*. He sells the Black Diamonds to Mr. Vanderdellen, but before he does it, he causes duplicates of them to be made, but this time in exquisite, beautiful, perfect Parisian imitation, and has these mounted into the original settings by some trusted man who, you may be sure, was well paid to hold his tongue. Then it is given out that the *parure* is for sale; a purchaser is found, and a few days later the false diamonds are stolen."

"By whom?"

"By the King of 'Bohemia's' valued and trusted friend, who has helped in the little piece of villainy throughout; it is he who drops a rope-ladder through Her Majesty's bedroom window on to the terrace below, and then hands the imitation *parure* to his Royal master, who sees to its complete destruction and disappearance. Then there is a hue and cry for the *real* stones, and after a year or so they are found on the person of a lady, who is legally forced to give them up. And thus His Majesty the King of 'Bohemia' got one solid million for the Black Diamonds, instead of half that sum, for if Mrs. Vanderdellen had not purchased the jewels, some one else would have done so."

And he was gone, leaving me to gaze at the pictures of three lovely women, and wondering if indeed it was the Royal lady herself who could best solve the mystery of who stole the Black Diamonds.

5
The Murder of Miss Pebmarsh

I.

"You must admit," said the man in the corner to me one day, as I folded up and put aside my *Daily Telegraph*, which I had been reading with great care, "that it would be difficult to find a more interesting plot, or more thrilling situations, than occurred during the case of Miss Pamela Pebmarsh. As for downright cold-blooded villainy, commend me to some of the actors in that real drama.

"The facts were simple enough: Miss Lucy Ann Pebmarsh was an old maid who lived with her young niece Pamela and an elderly servant in one of the small, newly-built houses not far from the railway station at Boreham Wood. The fact that she kept a servant at all, and that the little house always looked very spick and span, was taken by the neighbours to mean that Miss Pebmarsh was a lady of means; but she kept very much to herself, seldom went to church, and never attended any of the mothers' meetings, parochial teas, and other social gatherings for which that popular neighbourhood has long been famous.

"Very little, therefore, was known of the Pebmarsh household, save that the old lady had seen better days, that she had taken her niece to live with her recently, and that the latter had had a somewhat chequered career before she had found her present haven of refuge; some more venturesome gossips went so far as to hint—but only just above a whisper—that Miss Pamela Pebmarsh had been on the stage.

"Certain it is that that young lady seemed to chafe very much under the restraint imposed upon her by her aunt, who seldom allowed her out of her sight, and evidently kept her very short of money, for, in spite of Miss Pamela's obvious love of fine clothes, she had latterly been constrained to wear the plainest of frocks and most unbecoming of hats.

"All very commonplace and uninteresting, you see, until that memorable Wednesday in October, after which the little house in Boreham Wood became a nine-days' wonder throughout newspaper-reading England.

"On that day Miss Pebmarsh's servant, Jemima Gadd, went over to Luton to see a sick sister; she was not expected back until the next morning. On that same afternoon Miss Pamela—strangely enough—seems also to have elected to go up to town, leaving her aunt all alone in the house and not returning home until the late train, which reaches Boreham Wood a few minutes before one.

"It was about five minutes past one that the neighbours in the quiet little street were roused from their slumbers by most frantic and agonised shrieks. The next moment Miss Pamela was seen to rush out of her aunt's house and then to hammer violently at the door of one of her neighbours, still uttering piercing shrieks. You may imagine what a commotion such a scene at midnight would cause in a place like Boreham Wood. Heads were thrust out of the windows; one or two neighbours in hastily-donned miscellaneous attire came running out; and very soon the news spread round like wildfire that Miss Pamela on coming home had found her aunt lying dead in the sitting-room.

"Mr. Miller, the local greengrocer, was the first to pluck up sufficient courage to effect an entrance into the house. Miss Pamela dared not follow him; she had become quite hysterical, and was shrieking at the top of her voice that her aunt had been murdered. The sight that greeted Mr. Miller and those who had been venturesome enough to follow him, was certainly calculated to unhinge any young girl's mind.

"In the small bow-window of the sitting-room stood a writing-table, with drawers open and papers scattered all over and around it; in a chair in front of it, half-sitting and half-lying across the table, face downwards, and with arms outstretched, was the dead body of Miss Pebmarsh. There was sufficient indications to show to the most casual observer that, undoubtedly, the unfortunate lady had been murdered.

"One of the neighbours, who possessed a bicycle, had in the meantime had the good sense to ride over to the police station. Very soon two constables were on the spot; they quickly cleared the room of gossiping neighbours, and then endeavoured to obtain from Miss Pamela some lucid information as to the terrible event.

"At first she seemed quite unable to answer coherently the many questions which were being put to her; however, with infinite patience and wonderful kindness, Sergeant Evans at last managed to obtain from her the following statement.

"'I had had an invitation to go to the theatre this evening; it was an old invitation, and my aunt had said long ago that I might accept it. When Jemima Gadd wanted to go to Luton, I didn't see why I should give up the theatre and offend my friend, just because of her. My aunt and I had some words about it, but I went.... I came back by the last train, and walked straight home from the station. I had taken the latch-key with me, and went straight into the sitting-room; the lamp was alight, and—and—'

"The rest was chaos in the poor girl's mind; she was only conscious of having seen something awful and terrible, and of having rushed out screaming for help. Sergeant Evans asked her no further questions then; a kind neighbour had offered to take charge of Pamela for the night, and took her away with her, the constable remaining in charge of the body and the house until the arrival of higher authorities."

II.

"Although, as you may well suppose," continued the man in the corner, after a pause, "the excitement was intense at Boreham Wood, it had not as yet reached the general newspaper-reading public. As the tragic event had occurred at one o'clock in the morning, the papers the following day only contained a brief announcement that an old lady had been found murdered at Boreham Wood under somewhat mysterious circumstances. Later on, the evening editions added that the police were extremely reticent, but that it was generally understood that they held an important clue.

"The following day had been fixed for the inquest, and I went down myself in the morning, for somehow I felt that this case was going to be an interesting one. A murder which at first seems absolutely purposeless always, in my experience, reveals, sooner or later, an interesting trait in human nature.

"As soon as I arrived at Boreham Wood, I found that the murder of Miss Pebmarsh and the forthcoming inquest seemed to be the sole subjects of gossip and conversation. After I had been in the place half an hour the news began to spread like wildfire that the murderer had been arrested. Five minutes later the name of the murderer was on everybody's lips.

"It was that of the murdered woman's niece, Miss Pamela Pebmarsh.

"'Oh, oh!' I said to myself, 'my instincts have not deceived me: this case is indeed going to be interesting.'

"It was about two o'clock in the afternoon when I at last managed to find my way to the little police station, where the inquest was to be held. There was scarcely standing-room, I can tell you, and I had some difficulty in getting a front place from which I could see the principal actors in this village drama.

"Pamela Pebmarsh was there in the custody of two constables—she, a young girl scarcely five-and-twenty, stood there accused of having murdered, in a peculiarly brutal way, an old lady of seventy, her relative who had befriended her and given her a home."

The man in the corner paused for a moment, and from the capacious pocket of his magnificent ulster he drew two or three small photos, which he placed before me.

"This is Miss Pamela Pebmarsh," he said, pointing to one of these; "tall and good-looking, in spite of the shabby bit of mourning with which she had contrived to deck herself. Of course, this photo does not give you an idea of what she looked like that day at the inquest. Her face then was almost ashen in colour; her large eyes were staring before her with a look of horror and of fear; and her hands were twitching incessantly, with spasmodic and painful nervousness.

"It was pretty clear that public feeling went dead against her from the very first. A murmur of disapproval greeted her appearance, to which she seemed to reply with a look of defiance. I could hear many uncharitable remarks spoken all round me; Boreham Wood found it evidently hard to forgive Miss Pamela her good looks and her unavowed past.

"The medical evidence was brief and simple. Miss Pebmarsh had been stabbed in the back with some sharp instrument, the blade of which had pierced the left lung. She had evidently been sitting in the chair in front of her writing-table when the murderer had caught her unawares. Death had ensued within the next few seconds.

"The medical officer was very closely questioned upon this point by the coroner; it was evident that the latter had something very serious in his mind, to which the doctor's replies would give confirmation.

"'In your opinion,' he asked, 'would it have been possible for Miss Pebmarsh to do anything after she was stabbed? Could she have moved, for instance?'

"'Slightly, perhaps,' replied the doctor; 'but she did not attempt to rise from her chair.'

"'No; but could she have tried to reach the hand-bell, for instance, which was on the table, or—the pen and ink—and written a word or two?'

"'Well, yes,' said the doctor thoughtfully; 'she might have done that, if pen and ink, or the hand-bell, were *very* close to her hand. I doubt, though, if she could have written anything very clearly, but still it is impossible to say quite definitely—anyhow, it could only have been a matter of a few seconds.'

"Delightfully vague, you see," continued the man in the corner, "as these learned gentlemen's evidence usually is.

"Sergeant Evans then repeated the story which Pamela Pebmarsh had originally told him, and from which she had never departed in any detail. She had gone to the theatre, leaving her aunt all alone in the house; she had arrived home at one o'clock by the late Wednesday-night train, and had gone straight into the sitting-room, where she had found her aunt dead before her writing-table.

"That she travelled up to London in the afternoon was easily proved; the station-master and the porters had seen her go. Unfortunately for her *alibi*, however, those late 'theatre' trains on that line are always very crowded; the night had been dark and foggy, and no one at or near the station could swear positively to having seen her arrive home again by the train she named.

"There was one thing more; although the importance of it had been firmly impressed upon Pamela Pebmarsh, she absolutely refused to name the friends with whom she had been to the theatre that night, and who, presumably, might have helped her to prove at what hour she left London for home.

"Whilst all this was going on, I was watching Pamela's face intently. That the girl was frightened—nay more, terrified—there could be no doubt; the twitching of her hands, her eyes dilated with terror, spoke of some awful secret which she dare not reveal, but which she felt was being gradually brought to light. Was that secret the secret of a crime—a crime so horrible, so gruesome, that surely so young a girl would be incapable of committing?

"So far, however, what struck every one mostly during this inquest was the seeming purposelessness of this cruel murder. The old lady, as far as could be ascertained, had no money to leave, so why should Pamela Pebmarsh have deliberately murdered the aunt who provided her, at any rate, with the comforts of a home? But the police, assisted by one of the most able detectives on the staff, had not effected so sensational an arrest without due cause; they had a formidable array of witnesses to prove their case up to the hilt. One of these was Jemima Gadd, the late Miss Pebmarsh's servant.

"She came forward attired in deep black, and wearing a monumental crape bonnet crowned with a quantity of glistening black beads. With her face the colour of yellow wax, and her thin lips pinched tightly together, she stood as the very personification of Puritanism and uncharitableness.

"She did not look once towards Pamela, who gazed at her like some wretched bird caught in a net, which sees the meshes tightening round it more and more.

"Replying to the coroner, Jemima Gadd explained that on the Wednesday morning she had had a letter from her sister at Luton, asking her to come over and see her some day.

"'As there was plenty of cold meat in the 'ouse,' she said, 'I asked the mistress if she could spare me until the next day, and she said yes, she could. Miss Pamela and she could manage quite well.'

"'She said nothing about her niece going out, too, on the same day?' asked the coroner.

"'No,' replied Jemima acidly, 'she did not, And later on, at breakfast, Miss Pebmarsh said to Miss Pamela before me: "Pamela," she says, "Jemima is going to Luton, and won't be back until to-morrow. You and I will be alone in the 'ouse until then."'

"'And what did the accused say?'

"'She says, "All right, aunt."'

"'Nothing more?'

"'No, nothing more.'

"'There was no question, then, of the accused going out also, and leaving Miss Pebmarsh all alone in the house?'

"'None at all,' said Jemima emphatically. 'If there 'ad been I'd 'ave 'eard of it. I needn't 'ave gone that day. Any day would 'ave done for me.'

"She closed her thin lips with a snap, and darted a vicious look at Pamela. There was obviously some old animosity lurking beneath that gigantic crape monument on the top of Jemima's wax-coloured head.

"'You know nothing, then, about any disagreement between the deceased and the accused on the subject of her going to the theatre that day?' asked the coroner, after a while.

"'No, not about *that*,' said Jemima curtly, 'but there was plenty of disagreements between those two, I can tell you.'

"'Ah? what about?'

"'Money, mostly. Miss Pamela was over-fond of fine clothes, but Miss Pebmarsh, who was giving 'er a 'ome and 'er daily bread, 'adn't much money to spare for fallalery. Miss Pebmarsh 'ad a small pension from a lady of the haristocracy, but it wasn't much—a pound a week it was. Miss Pebmarsh might 'ave 'ad a lot more if she'd wanted to.'

"'Oh?' queried the coroner, 'how was that?'

"'Well, you see, that fine lady 'ad not always been as good as she ought to be. She'd been Miss Pamela's friend when they were both on the stage together, and pretty goings on, I can tell you, those two were up to, and—'

"'That'll do,' interrupted the coroner sternly. 'Confine yourself, please, to telling the jury about the pension Miss Pebmarsh had from a lady.'

"'I was speaking about that,' said Jemima, with another snap of her thin lips. 'Miss Pebmarsh knew a thing or two about this fine lady, and she 'ad some letters which she often told me that fine lady would not care for 'er 'usband or 'er fine friends to read. Miss Pamela got to know about these letters, and she worried 'er poor aunt to death, for she wanted to get those letters and sell them to the fine lady for 'undreds of pounds. I 'ave 'eard 'er ask for those letters times and again, but Miss Pebmarsh wouldn't give them to 'er, and they was locked up in the writing-table drawer, and Miss Pamela wanted those letters, for she wanted to get 'undreds of pounds from the fine lady, and my poor mistress was murdered for those letters—and she was murdered by that wicked girl 'oo eat 'er bread and 'oo would 'ave starved but for 'er. And so I tell you, and I don't care 'oo 'ears me say it.'

"No one had attempted to interrupt Jemima Gadd as she delivered herself of this extraordinary tale, which so suddenly threw an unexpected and lurid light upon the mystery of poor Miss Pebmarsh's death.

"That the tale was a true one, no one doubted for a single instant. One look at the face of the accused was sufficient to prove it beyond question. Pamela Pebmarsh had become absolutely livid;

she tottered almost as if she would fall, and the constable had to support her until a chair was brought forward for her.

"As for Jemima Gadd, she remained absolutely impassive. Having given her evidence, she stepped aside automatically like a yellow waxen image, which had been wound up and had now run down. There was silence for a while. Pamela Pebmarsh, more dead than alive, was sipping a glass of brandy and water, which alone prevented her from falling in a dead faint.

"Detective Inspector Robinson now stepped forward. All the spectators there could read on his face the consciousness that his evidence would be of the most supreme import.

"'I was telegraphed for from the Yard,' he said, in reply to the coroner, 'and came down here by the first train on the Thursday morning. Beyond the short medical examination the body had not been touched: as the constables know, we don't like things interfered with in cases of this kind. When I went up to look at deceased, the first thing I saw was a piece of paper just under her right hand Sergeant Evans had seen it before, and pointed it out to me. Deceased had a pen in her hand, and the ink-bottle was close by. This is the paper I found, sir.'

"And amidst a deadly silence, during which nothing could be heard but the scarcely-perceptible rustle of the paper, the inspector handed a small note across to the coroner. The latter glanced at it for a moment, and his face became very grave and solemn as he turned towards the jury.

"'Gentlemen of the jury,' he said, 'these are the contents of the paper which the inspector found under the hand of the deceased.'

"He paused once more before he began to read, whilst we all in that crowded court held our breath to listen

"'*I am dying. My murderess is my niece, Pam—*'

"'That is all, gentlemen,' added the coroner, as he folded up the note. 'Death overtook the unfortunate woman in the very act of writing down the name of her murderess.'

"Then there was a wild and agonised shriek of horror. Pamela Pebmarsh, with hair dishevelled and eyes in which the light of madness had begun to gleam, threw up her hands, and without a word, and without a groan, fell down senseless upon the floor."

III.

"Yes," said the man in the corner with a chuckle, "there was enough evidence there to hang twenty people, let alone that one fool of a girl who had run her neck so madly into a noose. I don't suppose that any one left the court that day with the slightest doubt in their minds as to what the verdict would be; for the coroner had adjourned the inquest, much to the annoyance of the jury, who had fully made up their minds and had their verdict pat on the tips of their tongues: 'Wilful murder against Pamela Pebmarsh.'

"But this was a case which to the last kept up its reputation for surprises. By the next morning rumour had got about that 'the lady of the aristocracy' referred to by Jemima Gadd, and who was supposed to have paid a regular pension to Miss Pebmarsh, was none other than Lady de Chavasse.

"When the name was first mentioned, every one—especially the fair sex—shrugged their shoulders, and said: 'Of course what else *could* one expect?'

"As a matter of fact, Lady de Chavasse, *née* Birdie Fay, was one of the most fashionable women in society; she was at the head of a dozen benevolent institutions, was a generous patron of hospitals, and her house was one of the most exclusive ones in London. True, she had been on the stage in her younger days, and when Sir Percival de Chavasse married her, his own relations looked somewhat askance at the showy, handsome girl who had so daringly entered the ancient county family.

"Sir Percival himself was an extraordinarily proud man—proud of his lineage, of his social status, of the honour of his name. His very pride had forced his relations, had forced society, to accept his beautiful young wife, and to Lady de Chavasse's credit be it said, not one breath of scandal as to her past life had ever become public gossip. No one could assert that they *knew* anything derogatory to Birdie Fay before she became the proud baronet's wife. As a matter of fact, all society asserted that Sir Percival would never have married her and introduced her to his own family circle if there had been any gossip about her.

"Now suddenly the name of Lady de Chavasse was on everybody's tongue. People at first spoke it under their breath, for every one felt great sympathy with her. She was so rich, and entertained so lavishly. She was very charming, too; most fascinating in her ways; deferential to her austere mother-in-law; not a little afraid of her proud husband; very careful lest by word or look she betrayed her early connection with the stage before him.

"On the following day, however, we had further surprises in store for us. Pamela Pebmarsh, advised by a shrewd and clear-headed solicitor, had at last made up her mind to view her danger a little more coolly, and to speak rather more of the truth than she had done hitherto.

"Still looking very haggard, but perhaps a little less scared, she now made a statement which, when it was fully substantiated, as she stated it could be, would go far towards clearing her of the terrible imputation against her. Her story was this: On the memorable day in question, she did go up to town, intending to go to the theatre. At the station she purchased an evening paper, which she began to read. This paper in its fashionable columns contained an announcement which arrested her attention; this was that Sir Percival and Lady de Chavasse had returned to their flat in town at 51 Marsden Mansions, Belgravia, from 'The Chase,' Melton Mowbray.

"'De Chavasse,' continued Pamela, 'was the name of the lady who paid my aunt the small pension on which she lived. I knew her years ago, when she was on the stage, and I suddenly thought I would like to go and see her, just to have a chat over old times. Instead of going to the theatre I went and had some dinner at Slater's, in Piccadilly, and then I thought I would take my chance, and go and see if Lady de Chavasse was at home. I got to 51 Marsden Mansions about eight o'clock, and was fortunate enough to see Lady de Chavasse at once. She kept me talking some considerable time; so much so, in fact, that I missed the 11-train from St. Pancras. I only left Marsden Mansions at a quarter to eleven, and had to wait at St. Pancras until twenty minutes past midnight.'

"This was all reasonable and clear enough, and, as her legal adviser had subpoenaed Lady de Chavasse as a witness, Pamela Pebmarsh seemed to have found an excellent way out of her terrible difficulties, the only question being whether Lady de Chavasse's testimony alone would, in view of her being Pamela's friend, be sufficient to weigh against the terribly overwhelming evidence of Miss Pebmarsh's dying accusation.

"But Lady de Chavasse settled this doubtful point in the way least expected by any one. Exquisitely dressed, golden-haired, and brilliant-complexioned, she looked strangely out of place in this fusty little village court, amidst the local dames in their plain gowns and antiquated bonnets. She was, moreover, extremely self-possessed, and only cast a short, very haughty, look at the unfortunate girl whose life probably hung upon that fashionable woman's word.

"'Yes,' she said sweetly, in reply to the coroner, she was the wife of Sir Percival de Chavasse, and resided at 51 Marsden Mansions, Belgravia.

"'The accused, I understand, has been known to you for some time?' continued the coroner.

"'Pardon me,' rejoined Lady de Chavasse, speaking in a beautifully modulated voice, 'I did know this young—hem—person, years ago, when I was on the stage, but, of course, I had not seen her for years.'

"'She called on you on Wednesday last at about nine o'clock?'

"'Yes, she did, for the purpose of levying blackmail upon me.'

"There was no mistaking the look of profound aversion and contempt which the fashionable lady now threw upon the poor girl before her,

"'She had some preposterous story about some letters which she alleged would be compromising to my reputation,' continued Lady de Chavasse quietly. 'These she had the kindness to offer me for sale for a few hundred pounds. At first her impudence staggered me, as, of course, I had no knowledge of any such letters.

She threatened to take them to my husband, however, and I then—rather foolishly, perhaps—suggested that she should bring them to me first. I forget how the conversation went on, but she left me with the understanding that she would get the letters from her aunt, Miss Pebmarsh, who, by the way, had been my governess when I was a child, and to whom I paid a small pension in consideration of her having been left absolutely without means.'

"And Lady de Chavasse, conscious of her own disinterested benevolence, pressed a highly-scented bit of cambric to her delicate nose.

"'Then the accused did spend the evening with you on that Wednesday?' asked the coroner, while a great sigh of relief seemed to come from poor Pamela's breast.

"'Pardon me," said Lady de Chavasse, 'she spent a little time with me. She came about nine o'clock.'

"'Yes. And when did she leave?'

"'I really couldn't tell you—about ten o'clock, I think.'

"'You are not sure?' persisted the coroner. 'Think, Lady de Chavasse,' he added earnestly, 'try to think—the life of a fellow-creature may, perhaps, depend upon your memory.'

"'I am indeed sorry,' she replied in the same musical voice. 'I could not swear without being positive, could I? And I am not quite positive.'

"'But your servants?'

"'They were at the back of the flat—the girl let herself out.'

"'But your husband?'

"'Oh! when he saw me engaged with the girl, he went out to his club, and was not yet home when she left.'

"'Birdie! Birdie! won't you try and remember?' here came in an agonised cry from the unfortunate girl, who thus saw her last hope vanish before her eyes.

"But Lady de Chavasse only lifted a little higher a pair of very prettily-arched eyebrows, and having finished her evidence she stepped on one side and presently left the court, leaving behind her a faint aroma of violet sachet powder, and taking away with her, perhaps, the last hope of an innocent fellow-creature."

IV.

"But Pamela Pebmarsh?" I asked after a while, for he had paused and was gazing attentively at the photograph of a very beautiful and exquisitely-gowned woman.

"Ah yes, Pamela Pebmarsh," he said with a smile. "There was yet another act in that palpitating drama of her life—one act—the *dénouement* as unexpected as it was thrilling. Salvation came where it was least expected—from Jemima Gadd, who seemed to have made up her mind that Pamela had killed her aunt, and yet who was the first to prove her innocence.

"She had been shown the few words which the murdered woman was alleged to have written after she had been stabbed. Jemima, not a very good scholar, found it difficult to decipher the words herself.

"'Ah, well, poor dear,' she said after a while, with a deep sigh, ''er 'andwriting was always peculiar, seein' as 'ow she wrote always with 'er left 'and.'

"'*Her left hand!!!*' gasped the coroner, while public and jury alike, hardly liking to credit their ears, hung upon the woman's thin lips, amazed, aghast, puzzled.

"'Why, yes!' said Jemima placidly. 'Didn't you know she 'ad a bad accident to 'er right 'and when she was a child, and never could 'old anything in it? 'Er fingers were like paralysed; the ink-pot was always on the left of 'er writing-table. Oh! she couldn't write with 'er right 'and at all.'

"Then a strange revulsion of feeling came over every one there.

"Stabbed in the back, with her lung pierced through and through, how could she have done, dying, what she never did in life?

"Impossible!

"The murderer, whoever it was, had placed pen and paper to her hand, and had written on it the cruel words which were intended to delude justice and to send an innocent fellow-creature—a young girl not five-and-twenty—to an unjust and ignominious death. But, fortunately for that innocent girl, the cowardly miscreant had ignored the fact that Miss Pebmarsh's right hand had been paralysed for years.

"The inquest was adjourned for a week," continued the man in the corner, "which enabled Pamela's solicitor to obtain further evidence of her innocence. Fortunately for her, he was enabled to find two witnesses who had seen her in an omnibus going towards St. Pancras at about 11.15 P.M., and a passenger on the 12.25 train, who had travelled down with her as far as Hendon. Thus, when the inquest was resumed, Pamela Pebmarsh left the court without a stain upon her character.

"But the murder of Miss Pebmarsh has remained a mystery to this day—as has also the secret history of the compromising letters. Did they exist or not? is a question the interested spectators at that memorable inquest have often asked themselves. Certain is it that failing Pamela Pebmarsh, who might have wanted them for purposes of blackmail, no one else could be interested in them except Lady de Chavasse."

"Lady de Chavasse!" I ejaculated in surprise. "Surely you are not going to pretend that that elegant lady went down to Boreham Wood in the middle of the night in order to murder Miss Pebmarsh, and then to lay the crime at another woman's door?"

"I only pretend what's logic," replied the man in the corner with inimitable conceit; "and in Pamela Pebmarsh's own statement, she was with Lady de Chavasse at 51 Marsden Mansions until eleven o'clock, and there is no train from St. Pancras to Boreham Wood between eleven and twenty-five minutes past midnight. Pamela's *alibi* becomes that of Lady de Chavasse, and is quite conclusive. Besides, that elegant lady was not one to do that sort of work for herself."

"What do you mean?" I asked.

"Do you mean to say you never thought of the real solution of this mystery?" he retorted sarcastically.

"I confess—" I began a little irritably.

"Confess that I have not yet taught you to think logically, and to look at the beginning of things."

"What do you call the beginning of this case, then?

"Why! the compromising letters, of course."

"But—" I argued.

"Wait a minute!" he shrieked excitedly, whilst with frantic haste he began fidgeting, fidgeting again at that eternal bit of string. "These did exist, otherwise why did Lady de Chavasse parley with Pamela Pebmarsh? Why did she not order her out of the house then and there, if she had nothing to fear from her?"

"I admit that," I said.

"Very well; then, as she was too fine, too delicate to commit the villainous murder of which she afterwards accused poor Miss Pamela, who was there sufficiently interested in those letters to try and gain possession of them for her?"

"Who, indeed?" I queried, still puzzled, still not understanding.

"Ay! who but her husband?" shrieked the funny creature, as with a sharp snap he broke his beloved string in two.

"Her husband!" I gasped.

"Why not? He had plenty of time, plenty of pluck. In a flat it is easy enough to overhear conversations that take place in the next room—he was in the house at the time, remember, for Lady de Chavasse said herself that he went out afterwards. No doubt he overheard everything—the compromising letters, and Pamela's attempt at levying blackmail. What the effect of such a discovery must have been upon the proud man I leave you to imagine—his wife's social position ruined, a stain upon his ancient name, his relations pointing the finger of scorn at his folly.

"Can't you picture him, hearing the two women's talk in the next room, and then resolving at all costs to possess himself of those compromising letters? He had just time to catch the 10 train to Boreham Wood.

"Mind you, I don't suppose that he went down there with any evil intent. Most likely he only meant to buy those letters from Miss Pebmarsh. What happened, however, nobody can say but the murderer himself.

"Who knows? But the deed done, imagine the horror of a refined, aristocratic man, face to face with such a crime as that.

"Was it this terror, or merely rage at the girl who had been the original cause of all this, that prompted him to commit the final villainy of writing out a false accusation and placing it under the dead woman's hand? Who can tell?

"Then, the deed done, and the *mise-en-scène* complete, he is able to catch the last train—11.23 —back to town. A man travelling alone would pass practically unperceived.

"Pamela's innocence was proved, and the murder of Miss Pebmarsh has remained a mystery, but if you will reflect on my conclusions, you will admit that no one else—*no one else*—could have committed that murder, for no one else had a greater interest in the destruction of those letters."

6
The Lisson Grove Mystery

I.

The man in the corner ordered another glass of milk, and timidly asked for a second cheese-cake at the same time.

"I am going down to the Marylebone Police Court, to see those people brought up before the 'beak,'" he remarked.

"What people?" I queried.

"What people!" he exclaimed, in the greatest excitement. "You don't mean to say that you have not studied the Lisson Grove Mystery?

I had to confess that my knowledge on that subject was of the most superficial character.

"One of the most interesting cases that has cropped up in recent years," he said, with an indescribable look of reproach.

"Perhaps. I did not study it in the papers because I preferred to hear you tell me all about it," I said.

"Oh, if that's it," he replied, as he settled himself down in his corner like a great bird after the rain, "then you showed more sense than lady journalists usually possess. I can, of course, give you a far clearer account than the newspapers have done; as for the police—well! I never saw such a muddle as they are making of this case."

"I daresay it is a peculiarly difficult one," I retorted, for I am ever a champion of that hardworking department.

"H'm!" he said, "so, so—it is a tragedy in a prologue and three acts. I am going down this afternoon to see the curtain fall for the third time on what, if I mistake not, will prove a good burlesque; but it all began dramatically enough. It was last Saturday, 21st November, that two boys, playing in the little spinney just outside Wembley Park Station, came across three large parcels done up in American cloth.

"With the curiosity natural to their age, they at once proceeded to undo these parcels, and what they found so upset the little beggars that they ran howling through the spinney and the polo ground, straight as a dart to Wembley Park Station. Half-frantic with excitement, they told their tale to one of the porters off duty, who walked back to the spinney with them. The three parcels, in point of fact, contained the remains of a dismembered human body. The porter sent one of the boys for the local police, and the remains were duly conveyed to the mortuary, where they were kept for identification.

"Three days later—that is to say, on Tuesday, 24th November—Miss Amelia Dyke, residing at Lisson Grove Crescent, returned from Edinburgh, where she had spent three or four days with a friend. She drove up from St. Pancras in a cab, and carried her small box up herself to the door of the flat, at which she knocked loudly and repeatedly—so loudly and so persistently, in fact, that the inhabitants of the neighbouring flats came out on to their respective landings to see what the noise was about.

"Miss Amelia Dyke was getting anxious. Her father, she said, must be seriously ill, or else why did he not come and open the door to her? Her anxiety, however, reached its culminating point when Mr. and Mrs. Pitt, who reside in the flat immediately beneath that occupied by the Dykes, came forward with the alarming statement that, as a matter of fact, they had themselves been wondering if anything were wrong with old Mr. Dyke, as they had not heard any sound overhead for the last few days.

"Miss Amelia, now absolutely terrified, begged one of the neighbours to fetch either the police or a locksmith, or both. Mr. Pitt ran out at once, both police and locksmith were brought upon the scene, the door was forcibly opened, and amidst indescribable excitement Constable Turner, followed by Miss Dyke, who was faint and trembling with apprehension, effected an entrance into the flat.

"Everything in it was tidy and neat to a degree, all the fires were laid, the beds made, the floors were clean and washed, the brasses polished, only a slight, very slight layer of dust lay over everything, dust that could not have accumulated for more than a few days. The flat consisted of four rooms and a bathroom; in not one of them was there the faintest trace of old Mr. Dyke.

"In order fully to comprehend the consternation which all the neighbours felt at this discovery," continued the man in the corner, "you must understand that old Mr. Dyke was a helpless cripple; he had been a mining engineer in his young days, and a terrible blasting accident deprived him, at the age of forty, of both legs. They had been amputated just above the knee, and the unfortunate man—then a widower with one little girl—had spent the remainder of his life on crutches. He had a small—a very small—pension, which, as soon as his daughter Amelia was grown up, had enabled him to live in comparative comfort in the small flat in Lisson Grove Crescent.

"His misfortune, however, had left him terribly sensitive; he never could bear the looks of compassion thrown upon him, whenever he ventured out on his crutches, and even the kindliest sympathy was positive torture to him. Gradually, therefore, as he got on in life, he took to staying more and more at home, and after a while gave up going out altogether. By the time he was sixty-five years old and Miss Amelia a fine young woman of seven-and-twenty, old Dyke had not been outside the door of his flat for at least five years.

"And yet, when Constable Turner aided by the locksmith entered the flat on that memorable 24th November, there was not a trace anywhere of the old man.

"Miss Amelia was in the last stages of despair, and at first she seemed far too upset and hysterical to give the police any coherent and definite information. At last, however, from amid the chaos of tears and of ejaculations, Constable Turner gathered the following facts.

"Miss Amelia had some great friends in Edinburgh whom she had long wished to visit, her father's crippled condition making this extremely difficult. A fortnight ago, however, in response to a very urgent invitation, she at last decided to accept it, but in order to leave her father altogether comfortable, she advertised in the local paper for a respectable woman who would come to the flat every day and see to all the work, cook his dinner, make the bed, and so on.

"She had several applications in reply to this advertisement, and ultimately selected a very worthy-looking elderly person, who, for seven shillings a week, undertook to come daily from seven in the morning until about six in the afternoon, to see to all Mr. Dyke's comforts.

"Miss Amelia was very favourably impressed with this person's respectable and motherly appearance, and she left for Edinburgh by the 5.15 A.M. train on the morning of Thursday, 19th November, feeling confident that her father would be well looked after. She certainly had not heard from the old man while she was away, but she had not expected to hear unless, indeed, something had been wrong.

"Miss Amelia was quite sure that something dreadful had happened to her father, as he could not possibly have walked downstairs and out of the house alone; certainly his crutches were nowhere to be found, but this only helped to deepen the mystery of the old man's disappearance.

"The constable, having got thus far with his notes, thought it best to refer the whole matter at this stage to higher authority. He got from Miss Amelia the name and address of the charwoman, and then went back to the station.

"There, the very first news that greeted him was that the medical officer of the district had just sent round to the various police stations his report on the human remains found in Wembley Park the previous Saturday. They had proved to be the dismembered body of an old man between sixty and seventy years of age, the immediate cause of whose death had undoubtedly been a violent blow on the back of the head with a heavy instrument, which had shattered the cranium. Expert examination further revealed the fact that deceased had had in early life both legs removed by a surgical operation just above the knee.

"That was the end of the prologue in the Lisson Grove tragedy," continued the man in the corner, after a slight and dramatic pause, "as far as the public was concerned. When the curtain was subsequently raised upon the first act, the situation had been considerably changed.

"The remains had been positively identified as those of old Mr. Dyke, and a charge of wilful murder had been brought against Alfred Wyatt, of no occupation, residing in Warlock Road, Lisson Grove, and against Amelia Dyke for complicity in the crime. They are the two people whom I am going to see this afternoon brought before the 'beak' at the Marylebone Police Court."

II.

"Two very important bits of evidence, I must tell you, had come to light, on the first day of the inquest and had decided the police to make this double arrest.

"In the first place, according to one or two of the neighbours, who happened to know something of the Dyke household, Miss Amelia had kept company for some time with a young man named Alfred Wyatt; he was an electrical engineer, resided in the neighbourhood, and was some years younger than Miss Dyke. As he was known not to be very steady, it was generally supposed that the old man did not altogether approve of his daughter's engagement.

"Mrs. Pitt, residing in the flat immediately below the one occupied by the Dykes, had stated, moreover, that on Wednesday the 18th, at about midday, she heard very loud and angry voices proceeding from above, Miss Amelia's shrill tones being specially audible. Shortly afterwards she saw Wyatt go out of the house; but the quarrel continued for some little time without him, for the neighbours could still hear Miss Amelia's high-pitched voice, speaking very excitedly and volubly.

"'An hour later,' further explained Mrs. Pitt, 'I met Miss Dyke on the stairs; she seemed very flushed and looked as if she had been crying. I suppose she saw that I noticed this, for she stopped and said to me:

"'"All this fuss, you know, Mrs. Pitt, because Alfred asked me to go for a drive with him this afternoon, but I am going all the same."'

"'Later in the afternoon—it must have been quite half-past four, for it was getting dark—young Wyatt drove up in a motor-car, and presently I heard Miss Dyke's voice on the stairs saying very pleasantly and cheerfully: "All right, daddy, we shan't be long." Then Mr. Dyke must have said something which I didn't hear, for she added, "Oh, that's all right; I am well wrapped up, and we have plenty of rugs."'

"Mrs. Pitt then went to her window and saw Wyatt and Amelia Dyke start off in a motor. She concluded that the old man had been mollified, for both Amelia and Wyatt waved their hands affectionately up towards the window. They returned from their drive about six o'clock; Wyatt saw Amelia to the door, and then went off again. The next day Miss Dyke went to Scotland.

"As you see," continued the man in the corner, "Alfred Wyatt had become a very important personality in this case; he was Amelia's sweetheart, and it was strange—to say the least of it—that she had never as yet even mentioned his name. Therefore, when she was recalled in order to give further evidence, you may be sure that she was pretty sharply questioned on the subject of Alfred Wyatt.

"In her evidence before the coroner, she adhered fairly closely to her original statement

"'I did not mention Mr. Wyatt's name,' she explained, 'because I did not think it was of any importance; if he knew anything about my dear father's mysterious fate he would have come forward at once, of course, and helped me to find out who the cowardly murderer was who could attack a poor, crippled old man. Mr. Wyatt was devoted to my father, and it is perfectly ridiculous to say that daddy objected to my engagement; on the contrary, he gave us his full consent, and we were going to be married directly after the New Year, and continue to live with father in the flat.'

"'But,' questioned the coroner, who had not by any means departed from his severity, 'what about this quarrel which the last witness overheard on the subject of your going out driving with Mr. Wyatt?'

"'Oh, that was nothing,' replied Miss Dyke very quietly. 'Daddy only objected because he thought that it was rather too late to start at four o'clock, and that I should be cold. When he saw that we had plenty of rugs he was quite pleased for me to go.'

"'Isn't it rather astonishing, then', asked the coroner, 'seeing that Mr. Wyatt was on such good terms with your father, that he did not go to see him while you were away?'

"'Not at all,' she replied unconcernedly; 'Alfred went down to Edinburgh on the Thursday evening. He couldn't travel with me in the morning, for he had some business to see to in town that day; but he joined me at my friends' house on the Friday morning, having travelled all night.'

"'Ah! ' remarked the coroner drily, 'then he had not seen your father since you left.'

"'Oh yes,' said Miss Amelia; 'he called round to see dad during the day, and found him looking well and cheerful.'

"Miss Amelia Dyke, as she gave this evidence, seemed absolutely unconscious of saying anything that might in any way incriminate her lover. She is a handsome, though somewhat coarse-looking, woman, nearer thirty I should say, than she would care to own. I was present at the inquest, mind you, for that case had too many mysteries about it from the first for it to have eluded my observation, and I watched her closely throughout. Her voice struck me as fine and rich, with—in this instance also—a shade of coarseness in it; certainly, it was very far from being high-pitched, as Mrs. Pitt had described it.

"When she had finished her evidence she went back to her seat, looking neither flustered nor uncomfortable, although many looks of contempt and even of suspicion were darted at her from every corner of the crowded court.

"Nor did she lose her composure in the slightest degree when Mr. Parlett, clerk to Messrs. Snow and Patterson, solicitors, of Bedford Row, in his turn came forward and gave evidence; only while the little man spoke her full red lips curled and parted with a look of complete contempt.

"Mr. Parlett's story was indeed a remarkable one, inasmuch as it suddenly seemed to tear asunder the veil of mystery which so far had surrounded the murder of old Dyke by supplying it with a motive—a strong motive, too: the eternal greed of gain.

"In June last, namely, it appears that Messrs. Snow and Patterson received intimation from a firm of Melbourne solicitors that a man of the name of Dyke had died there recently, leaving a legacy of £4,000 to his only brother, James Arthur Dyke, a mining engineer, who in 1890 was residing at Lisson Grove Crescent. The Melbourne solicitors in their communication asked for Messrs. Snow and Patterson's kind assistance in helping them to find the legatee.

"The search was easy enough, since James Arthur Dyke, mining engineer, had never ceased to reside at Lisson Grove Crescent. Armed, therefore, with full instructions from their Melbourne correspondent, Messrs. Snow and Patterson communicated with Dyke, and after a little preliminary correspondence, the sum of £4,000 in Bank of Australia notes and various securities were handed over by Mr. Parlett to the old cripple.

"The money and securities were—so Mr. Parlett understood—subsequently deposited by Mr. Dyke at the Portland Road Branch of the London and South-Western Bank; as the old man apparently died intestate, the whole of the £4,000 would naturally devolve upon his only daughter and natural legatee.

"Mind you, all through the proceedings the public had instinctively felt that money was somewhere at the bottom of this gruesome and mysterious crime. There is not much object in murdering an old cripple except for purposes of gain, but now Mr. Parlett's evidence had indeed furnished a damning motive for the appalling murder.

"What more likely than that Alfred Wyatt, wanting to finger that £4,000, had done away with the old man? And if Amelia Dyke did not turn away from him in horror, after such a cowardly crime, then she must have known of it and had perhaps connived in it.

"As for Nicholson, the charwoman, her evidence had certainly done more to puzzle everybody all round than any other detail in this strange and mysterious crime.

"She deposed that on Friday, 13th November, in answer to an advertisement in the Marylebone Star she had called on Miss Dyke at Lisson Grove, when it was arranged that she should do a week's work at the flat, beginning Thursday, the 19th, from seven in the morning until six in the afternoon. She was to keep the place clean, get Mr. Dyke—who, she understood, was an invalid—all his meals, and make herself generally useful to him.

"Accordingly, Nicholson turned up on the Thursday morning. She let herself into the flat, as Miss Dyke had entrusted the latch-key to her, and went on with the work. Mr. Dyke was in bed, and she got him all his meals that day. She thought she was giving him satisfaction, and was very astonished when, at six o'clock, having cleared away his tea, he told her that he would not require her again. He gave her no explanation, asked her for the latch-key, and gave her her full week's money—seven shillings in full. Nicholson then put on her bonnet, and went away.

"Now," continued the man in the corner, leaning excitedly forward, and marking each sentence he uttered with an exquisitely complicated knot in his bit of string, "an hour later, another neighbour, Mrs. Marsh, who lived on the same floor as the Dykes, on starting to go out, met Alfred Wyatt on the landing. He took off his hat to her, and then knocked at the door of the Dykes' flat.

"When she came home at eight o'clock, she again passed him on the stairs; he was then going out. She stopped to ask him how Mr. Dyke was, and Wyatt replied: 'Oh, fairly well, but he misses his daughter, you know.'

"Mrs. Marsh, now closely questioned, said that she thought Wyatt was carrying a large parcel under his arm, but she could not distinguish the shape of the parcel as the angle of the stairs, where she met him, was very dark. She stated, though, that he was running down the stairs very fast.

"It was on all that evidence that the police felt justified in arresting Alfred Wyatt for the murder of James Arthur Dyke, and Amelia Dyke for connivance in the crime. And now this very morning, those two young people have been brought before the magistrate, and at this moment evidence—circumstantial, mind you, but positively damning—is being heaped upon them by the prosecution. The police did their work quickly. The very evening after the first day of the inquest, the warrant was out for their arrest."

He looked at a huge silver watch which he always carried in his waistcoat pocket.

"I don't want to miss the defence," he said, "for I know that it will be sensational. But I did not want to hear the police and medical evidence all over again. You'll excuse me, won't you? I shall be back here for five o'clock tea. I know you will be glad to hear all about it."

III.

When I returned to the A.B.C. shop for my tea at five minutes past five, there he sat in his accustomed corner, with a cup of tea before him, another placed opposite to him, presumably for me, and a long piece of string between his bony fingers.

"What will you have with your tea?" he asked politely, the moment I was seated.

"A roll and butter and the end of the story," I replied.

"Oh, the story has no end," he said with a chuckle; "at least, not for the public. As for me, why, I never met a more simple 'mystery.' Perhaps that is why the police were so completely at sea."

"Well, and what happened?" I queried, with some impatience.

"Why, the usual thing," he said, as he once more began to fidget nervously with his bit of string. "The prisoners had pleaded not guilty, and the evidence for the prosecution was gone into in full. Mr. Parlett repeated his story of the £4,000 legacy, and all the neighbours had some story or other to tell about Alfred Wyatt, who, according to them, was altogether a most undesirable young man.

"I heard the fag end of Mrs. Marsh's evidence. When I reached the court she was repeating the story she had already told to the police.

"Some one else in the house had also heard Wyatt running helter-skelter downstairs at eight o'clock on the Thursday evening; this was a point, though a small one, in favour of the accused. A man cannot run downstairs when he is carrying the whole weight of a dead body, and the theory of the prosecution was that Wyatt had murdered old Dyke on that Thursday evening, got into his motorcar somewhere, scorched down to Wembley with the dismembered body of his victim, deposited it in the spinney where it was subsequently found, and finally had driven back to town, stabled his motor-car, and reached King's Cross in time for the 11.30 night express to Edinburgh. He would have time for all that, remember, for he would have three hours and a half to do it in.

"Besides which the prosecution had unearthed one more witness, who was able to add another tiny link to the already damning chain of evidence built up against the accused.

"Wilfred Poad, namely, manager of a large cycle and motor-car depot in Euston Road, stated that on Thursday afternoon, 19th November, at about half-past six o'clock, Alfred Wyatt, with whom he had had some business dealings before, had hired a small car from him, with the understanding that he need not bring it back until after 11 p.m. This was agreed to, Poad keeping the place open until just before eleven, when Wyatt drove up in the car, paid for the hire of it, and then walked away from the shop in the direction of the Great Northern terminus.

"That was pretty strong against the male prisoner, wasn't it? For, mind you, Wyatt had given no satisfactory account whatever of his time between 8 p.m., when Mrs. Marsh had met him going out of Lisson Grove Crescent, and 11 p.m., when he brought back the car to the Euston Road shop. 'He had been driving about aimlessly,' so he said. Now, one doesn't go out motoring for hours on a cold, drizzly night in November for no purpose whatever.

"As for the female prisoner, the charge against her was merely one of complicity.

"This closed the case for the prosecution," continued the funny creature, with one of his inimitable chuckles, "leaving but one tiny point obscure, and that was, the murdered man's strange conduct in dismissing the woman Nicholson.

"Yes, the case was strong enough, and yet there stood both prisoners in the dock, with that sublime air of indifference and contempt which only complete innocence or hardened guilt could give.

"Then when the prosecution had had their say, Alfred Wyatt chose to enter the witness-box and make a statement in his own defence. Quietly, and as if he were making the most casual observation he said:

"'I am not guilty of the murder of Mr. Dyke, and in proof of this I solemnly assert that on Thursday, 19th November, the day I am supposed to have committed the crime, the old man was still alive at half-past ten o'clock in the evening.'

"He paused a moment, like a born actor, watching the effect he had produced. I tell you, it was astounding.

"'I have three separate and independent witnesses here,' continued Wyatt, with the same deliberate calm, 'who heard and saw Mr. Dyke as late as half-past ten that night. Now, I understand that the dismembered body of the old man was found close to Wembley Park. How could I, between half-past ten and eleven o'clock, have killed Dyke, cut him up, cleaned and put the flat all tidy, carried the body to the car, driven on to Wembley, hidden the corpse in the spinney, and be back in Euston Road, all in the space of half an hour? I am absolutely innocent of this crime, and, fortunately, it is easy for me now to prove my innocence.'

"Alfred Wyatt had made no idle boast. Mrs. Marsh had seen him running downstairs at 8 P.M. An hour after that, the Pitts in the flat beneath heard the old man moving about overhead.

"'Just as usual,' observed Mrs. Pitt. 'He always went to bed about nine, and we could always hear him most distinctly.'

"John Pitt, the husband, corroborated this statement; the old man's movements were quite unmistakable because of his crutches.

"Henry Ogden, on the other hand, who lived in the house facing the block of flats, saw the light in Dyke's window that evening, and the old man's silhouette upon the blind from time to time. The light was put out at half-past ten. This statement again was corroborated by Mrs. Ogden, who also had noticed the silhouette and the light being extinguished at half-past ten.

"But this was not all; both Mr. and Mrs. Ogden had seen old Dyke at his window, sitting in his accustomed armchair, between half-past eight and nine o'clock. He was gesticulating, and apparently talking to some one else in the room whom they could not see.

"Alfred Wyatt, therefore, was quite right when he said that he would have no difficulty in proving his innocence. The man whom he was supposed to have murdered was, according to the testimony, alive at six o'clock; according to Mr. and Mrs. Ogden he was alive and sitting in his window until nine; again, he was heard to move about until ten o'clock by both the Pitts, and at half-past ten only was the light put out in his flat. Obviously, therefore, as his dead body was found twelve miles away, Wyatt, who was out of the Crescent at eight, and in Euston Road at eleven, could not have done the deed.

"He was discharged, of course, the magistrate adding a very severe remark on the subject of 'carelessly collected evidence.' As for Miss Amelia, she sailed out of the court like a queen after her coronation, for with Wyatt's discharge the case against her naturally collapsed. As for me, I walked out too, with an elated feeling at the thought that the intelligence of the British race had not yet sunk so low as our friends on the Continent would have us believe."

IV.

"But then, who murdered the old man?" I asked, for I confess the matter was puzzling me in an irritating kind of a way.

"Ah! who indeed?" he rejoined sarcastically, while an artistic knot went to join its fellows along that never-ending bit of string.

"I wish you'd tell me what's in your mind," I said, feeling peculiarly irritated with him just at that moment.

"What's in my mind?" he replied, with a shrug of his thin shoulders. "Oh, only a certain degree of admiration!"

"Admiration at what?"

"At a pair of exceedingly clever criminals."

"Then you do think that Wyatt murdered Dyke?"

"I don't think—I am sure."

"But when did they do it?"

"Ah, that's more to the point. Personally, I should say between them on Wednesday morning, 18th November."

"The day they went for that motor-car ride?" I gasped.

"And carried away the old man's remains beneath a multiplicity of rugs," he added.

"But he was *alive* long after that!" I urged. "The woman Nicholson—"

"The woman Nicholson saw and spoke to a man in bed, whom she *supposed* was old Mr. Dyke. Among the many questions put to her by those clever detectives, no one thought, of course, of asking her to describe the old man. But even if she had done so, Wyatt was far too great an artist in crime not to have contrived a make-up which, described by a witness who had never before seen Dyke, would easily pass as a description of the old man himself."

"Impossible!" I said, struck in spite of myself by the simplicity of his logic.

"Impossible, you say?" he shrieked excitedly.

"Why, I call that crime a masterpiece from beginning to end; a display of ingenuity which, fortunately, the criminal classes seldom possess, or where would society be? Here was a crime committed, where everything was most beautifully stage-managed, nothing left unforeseen. Shall I reconstruct it for you?"

"Do!" I said, handing across the table to him a brand-new, beautiful bit of string, on which his talon-like fingers fastened as upon a prey.

"Very well," he said, marking each point with a scientific knot. "Here, it is, scene by scene. There was Alfred Wyatt and Amelia Dyke—a pair of blackguards, eager to obtain that £4,000 which only the old man's death could secure for them. They decide upon killing him, and: Scene 1.—Miss Amelia makes *her* arrangements.

She advertises for a charwoman, and engages one, who is to be a very useful witness presently.

"Scene 2.—The murder, brutal, horrible, on the person of an old cripple, whilst his own daughter stands by, and the dismembering of the body.

"Scene 3.—The ride in the motor-car—after dark, remember, and with plenty of rugs, beneath which the gruesome burden is concealed. The scene is accompanied by the comedy of Miss Dyke speaking to her father, and waving her hand affectionately at him from below. I tell you, that woman must have had some nerve!

"Then, Scene 4.—The arrival at Wembley, and the hiding of the remains.

"Scene 5.—Amelia goes to Edinburgh by the 5.15 A.M. train, and thus secures her own *alibi*. After that, the comedy begins in earnest. The impersonation of the dead man by Wyatt during the whole of that memorable Thursday. Mind you, that was not very difficult; it only needed the brain to invent, and the nerve to carry it through. The charwoman had never seen old Dyke before; she only knew that he was an invalid. What more natural than that she should accept as her new master the man who lay in bed all day, and only spoke a few words to her? A very slight make-up of hair and beard would complete the illusion.

"Then, at six o'clock, the woman gone, Wyatt steals out of the house, bespeaks the motor-car, leaves it in the street in a convenient spot, and is back in time to be seen by Mrs. Marsh at seven.

"The rest is simplicity itself. The silhouette at the window was easy enough to arrange; the sound of a man walking on crutches is easily imitated with a couple of umbrellas—the actual crutches were, no doubt, burned directly after the murder. Lastly, the putting out of the light at half-past ten was the crowning stroke of genius.

"One little thing might have upset the whole wonderful plan, but that one thing only; and that was if the body had been found *before* the great comedy scene of Thursday had been fully played. But that spinney near Wembley was well chosen. People don't go wandering under trees and in woods on cold November days, and the remains were not found until the Saturday.

"Ah, it was cleverly stage-managed, and no mistake. I couldn't have done it better myself. Won't you have another cup of tea? No? Don't look so upset. The world does not contain many such clever criminals as Alfred Wyatt and Amelia Dyke."

7
The Tremarn Case

I.

"Well, it certainly is most amazing!" I said that day, when I had finished reading about it all in the *Daily Telegraph*.

"Yet the most natural thing in the world," retorted the man in the corner, as soon as he had ordered his lunch. "Crime invariably begets crime. No sooner is a murder, theft, or fraud committed in a novel or striking way, than this method is aped—probably within the next few days—by some other less imaginative scoundrel.

"Take this case, for instance," he continued, as he slowly began sipping his glass of milk, "which seems to amaze you so much. It was less than a year ago, was it not? that in Paris a man was found dead in a cab, stabbed in a most peculiar way—right through the neck, from ear to ear— with, presumably, a long, sharp instrument of the type of an Italian stiletto.

"No one in England took much count of the crime, beyond a contemptuous shrug of the shoulders at the want of safety of the Paris streets, and the incapacity of the French detectives, who not only never discovered the murderer, who had managed to slip out of the cab unperceived, but who did not even succeed in establishing the identity of the victim.

"But this case," he added, pointing once more to my daily paper, "strikes nearer home. Less than a year has passed, and last week, in the very midst of our much vaunted London streets, a crime of a similar nature has been committed. I do not know if your paper gives full details, but this is what happened: Last

Monday evening two gentlemen, both in evening dress and wearing opera hats, hailed a hansom in Shaftesbury Avenue. It was about a quarter past eleven, and the night, if you remember, was a typical November one—dark, drizzly, and foggy. The various theatres in the immediate neighbourhood were disgorging a continuous stream of people after the evening performance.

"The cabman did not take special notice of his fares. They jumped in very quickly, and one of them, through the little trap above, gave him an address in Cromwell Road. He drove there as quickly as the fog would permit him, and pulled up at the number given. One of the gentlemen then handed him up a very liberal fare—again through the little trap—and told him to drive his friend on to Westminster Chambers, Victoria Street.

"Cabby noticed that the 'swell,' when he got out of the hansom, stopped for a moment to say a few words to his friend, who had remained inside; then he crossed over the road and walked quickly in the direction of the Natural History Museum.

"When the cabman pulled up at Westminster Chambers, he waited for the second fare to get out; the latter seemingly making no movement that way, cabby looked down at him through the trap.

"'I thought 'e was asleep,' he explained to the police later on. ''E was leaning back in 'is corner, and 'is 'ead was turned towards the window. I gets down and calls to 'im, but 'e don't move. Then I gets on to the step and give 'im a shake. . . . There!—I'll say no more. . . . We was near a lamp-post, the mare took a step forward, and the light fell full on the gent's face. 'E was dead and no mistake. I saw the wound just underneath 'is ear, and "Murder!" I says to myself at once.'

"Cabby lost no time in whistling for the nearest point-policeman, then he called the night porter of the Westminster Chambers. The latter looked at the murdered man, and declared that he knew nothing of him; certainly he was not a tenant of the Chambers.

"By the time a couple of policemen arrived upon the scene, quite a crowd had gathered around the cab, in spite of the lateness of the hour and the darkness of the night. The matter was such an important one that one of the constables thought it best at once to jump into the hansom beside the murdered man and to order the cabman to drive to the nearest police station.

"There the cause of death was soon ascertained; the victim of this daring outrage had been stabbed through the neck from ear to ear with a long, sharp, instrument, in shape like an antique stiletto, which, I may tell you, was subsequently found under the cushions of the hansom. The murderer must have watched his opportunity, when his victim's head was turned away from him, and then dealt the blow, just below the left ear, with amazing swiftness and precision.

"Of course the papers were full of it the next day; this was such a lovely opportunity for driving home a moral lesson, of how one crime engenders another, and how—but for that murder in Paris a year ago—we should not now have to deplore a crime committed in the very centre of fashionable London, the detection of which seems likely to completely baffle the police.

"Plenty more in that strain, of course, from which the reading public quickly jumped to the conclusion that the police held absolutely no clue as to the identity of the daring and mysterious miscreant.

"A most usual and natural thing had happened; cabby could only give a very vague description of his other 'fare,' of the 'swell' who had got out at Cromwell Road, and been lost to sight after having committed so dastardly and so daring a crime.

"This was scarcely to be wondered at, for the night had been very foggy, and the murderer had been careful to pull his opera hat well over his face, thus hiding the whole of his forehead and eyes; moreover, he had always taken the additional precaution of only communicating with the cabman through the little trap-door.

"All cabby had seen of him was a clean-shaven chin. As to the murdered man, it was not until about noon, when the early editions of the evening papers came out with a fuller account of the crime and a description of the victim, that his identity was at last established.

"Then the news spread like wildfire, and the evening papers came out with some of the most sensational headlines it had ever been their good fortune to print. The man who had been so mysteriously murdered in the cab was none other than Mr. Philip Le Cheminant, the nephew and heir-presumptive of the Earl of Tremarn."

II.

"In order fully to realise the interest created by this extraordinary news, you must be acquainted with the various details of that remarkable case, popularly known as the 'Tremarn Peerage Case,'" continued the man in the corner, as he placidly munched his cheese-cake. "I do not know if you followed it in its earlier stages, when its many details—which read like a romance—were first made public."

I looked so interested and so eager that he did not wait for my reply.

"I must try and put it all clearly before you," he said; "I was interested in it all from the beginning, and from the numerous wild stories afloat I have sifted only what was undeniably true. Some points of the case are still in dispute, and will, perhaps, now for ever remain a mystery. But I must take you back some five-and-twenty years. The Hon. Arthur Le Cheminant, second son of the late Earl of Tremarn, was then travelling round the world for health and pleasure.

"In the course of his wanderings he touched at Martinique, one of the French West Indian islands, which was devastated by volcanic eruptions about two years ago. There he met and fell in love with a beautiful half-caste girl named Lucie Legrand, who had French blood in her veins, and was a Christian, but who, otherwise, was only partially civilised, and not at all educated.

"How it all came about it is difficult to conjecture, but one thing is absolutely certain, and that is that the Hon. Arthur Le Cheminant, the son of one of our English peers, married this half-caste girl at the parish church of St. Pierre, in Martinique, according to the forms prescribed by French laws, both parties being of the same religion.

"I suppose now no one will ever know whether that marriage was absolutely and undisputably a legal one—but, in view of subsequent events, we must presume that it was. The Hon. Arthur, however, in any case, behaved like a young scoundrel. He only spent a very little time with his wife, quickly tired of her, and within two years of his marriage callously abandoned her and his child, then a boy about a year old.

"He lodged a sum of £2,000 in the local bank in the name of Mme. Le Cheminant, the interest of which was to be paid to her regularly for the maintenance of herself and child, then he calmly sailed for England, with the intention never to return. This intention fate itself helped him to carry out, for he died very shortly afterwards, taking the secret of his incongruous marriage with him to his grave.

"Mme. Le Cheminant, as she was called out there, seems to have accepted her own fate with perfect equanimity. She had never known anything about her husband's social position in his own country, and he had left her what, in Martinique amongst the coloured population, was considered a very fair competence for herself and child.

"The grandson of an English earl was taught to read and write by the worthy *curê* of St. Pierre, and during the whole of her life, Lucie never once tried to find out who her husband was, and what had become of him.

"But here the dramatic scene comes in this strange story," continued the man in the corner, with growing excitement; "two years ago St. Pierre, if you remember, was completely destroyed by volcanic eruptions. Nearly the entire population perished, and every house and building was in ruins. Among those who fell a victim to the awful catastrophe was Mme. Le Cheminant, otherwise the Hon. Mrs. Arthur Le Cheminant, whilst amongst those who managed to escape and ultimately found refuge in the English colony of St. Vincent, was her son, Philip.

"Well, you can easily guess what happened, can't you? In that English-speaking colony the name of Le Cheminant was, of course, well known, and Philip had not been in St. Vincent many weeks, before he learned that his father was none other than a younger brother of the present Earl of Tremarn, and that he himself—seeing that the present peer was over fifty and still unmarried—was heir-presumptive to the title and estates.

"You know the rest. Within two or three months of the memorable St. Pierre catastrophe Philip Le Cheminant had written to his uncle, Lord Tremarn, demanding his rights. Then he took passage on board a French liner and crossed over to Havre *en route* for Paris and London.

"He and his mother—both brought up as French subjects—had, mind you, all the respect which French people have for their papers of identification; and when the house in which they had lived for twenty years was tumbling about the young man's ears, when his mother had already perished in the flames, he made a final and successful effort to rescue the papers which proved him to be a French citizen, the son of Lucie Legrand by her lawful marriage with Arthur Le Cheminant at the church of the Immaculate Conception of St. Pierre.

"What happened immediately afterwards it is difficult to conjecture. Certain it is, however, that over here the newspapers soon were full of vague allusions about the newly-found heir to the Earldom of Tremarn, and within a few weeks the whole of the story of the secret marriage at St. Pierre was in everybody's mouth.

"It created an immense sensation; the Hon. Arthur Le Cheminant had lived a few years in England after his return from abroad, and no one, not even his brother, seemed to have had the slightest inkling of his marriage.

"The late Lord Tremarn, you must remember, had three sons, the eldest of whom is the present peer, the second was the romantic Arthur, and the third, the Hon. Reginald, who also died some years ago, leaving four sons, the eldest of whom, Harold, was just twenty-three, and had always been styled heir-presumptive to the Earldom.

"Lord Tremarn had brought up these four nephews of his, who had lost both father and mother, just as if they had been his own children, and his affection for them, and notably for the eldest boy, was a very beautiful trait in his otherwise unattractive character.

"The news of the existence and claim of this unknown nephew must have come upon Lord Tremarn as a thunderbolt. His attitude, however, was one of uncompromising incredulity. He refused to believe the story of the marriage, called the whole tale a tissue of falsehoods, and denounced the claimant as a bare-faced and impudent impostor.

"Two or three months more went by; the public were eagerly awaiting the arrival of this semi-exotic claimant to an English peerage, and sensations, surpassing those of the Tichborne case, were looked forward to with palpitating interest.

"But in the romances of real life, it is always the unexpected that happens. The claimant did arrive in London about a year ago. He was alone, friendless, and moneyless, since the £2,000 lay buried somewhere beneath the ruins of the St. Pierre bank. However, he called upon a well- known London solicitor, who advanced him some money and took charge of all the papers relating to his claim.

"Philip Le Cheminant then seems to have made up his mind to make a personal appeal to his uncle, trusting apparently in the old adage that 'blood is thicker than water.'

"As was only to be expected, Lord Tremarn flatly refused to see the claimant, whom he was still denouncing as an impostor. It was by stealth, and by bribing the servants at the Grosvenor Square mansion, that the young man at last obtained an interview with his uncle.

"Last New Year's Day he gave James Tovey, Lord Tremarn's butler, a five-pound note, to introduce him, surreptitiously, into his master's study. There uncle and nephew at last met face to face.

"What happened at that interview nobody knows; was the cry of blood and of justice so convincing that Lord Tremarn dare not resist it? Perhaps.

"Anyway, from that moment the new heir-presumptive was installed within his rights. After a single interview with Philip Le Cheminant's solicitor, Lord Tremarn openly acknowledged the claimant to be his brother Arthur's only son, and therefore his own nephew and heir.

"Nay, more, every one noticed that the proud, bad-tempered old man was as wax in the hands of this newly-found nephew. He seemed even to have withdrawn his affection from the four other young nephews, whom hitherto he had brought up as his own children, and bestowed it all upon his brother Arthur's son—some people said in compensation for all the wrong that had been done to the boy in the past.

"But the scandal around his dead brother's name had wounded the old man's pride very deeply, and from this he never recovered. He shut himself away from all his friends, living alone with his newly-found nephew in his gloomy house in Grosvenor Square. The other boys, the eldest of whom, Harold, was just twenty-three, decided very soon to leave a house where they were no longer welcome. They had a small private fortune of their own from their father and mother; the youngest boy was still at college, two others had made a start in their respective professions.

"Harold had been brought up as an idle young man about town, and on him the sudden change of fortune fell most heavily. He was undecided what to do in the future, but, in the meanwhile, partly from a spirit of independence, and partly from a desire to keep a home for his younger brothers he took and furnished a small flat, which, it is interesting to note, is just off Exhibition Road, not far from the Natural History Museum in Kensington.

"This was less than a year ago. Ten months later the newly-found heir to the peerage of Tremarn was found murdered in a hansom cab, and Harold Le Cheminant is once more the future Earl."

III.

"The papers, as you know, talked of nothing else but the mysterious murder in the hansom cab. Every one's sympathy went out at once to Lord Tremarn, who, on hearing the terrible news, had completely broken down, and was now lying on a bed of sickness, from which they say he may never recover.

"From the first there had been many rumours of the terrible enmity which existed between Harold Le Cheminant and the man who had so easily captured Lord Tremarn's heart, as well as the foremost place in the Grosvenor Square household.

"The servants in the great and gloomy mansion told the detectives in charge of the case many stories of terrible rows which occurred at first between the cousins. And now every one's eyes were already turned with suspicion on the one man who could most benefit by the death of Philip Le Cheminant.

"However careful and reticent the police may be, details in connection with so interesting a case have a wonderful way of leaking out. Already one other most important fact had found its way into the papers. It appears that in their endeavours to reconstruct the last day spent by the murdered man the detectives had come upon most important evidence.

"It was Thomas Sawyer, hall-porter of the Junior Grosvenor Club, who first told the following interesting story. He stated that deceased was a member of the club, and had dined there on the evening preceding his death.

"'Mr. Le Cheminant was just coming downstairs after his dinner,' explained Thomas Sawyer to the detectives, 'when a stranger comes into the hall of the club; Mr. Le Cheminant saw him as soon as I did, and appeared very astonished. "What do you want?" he says rather sharply. "A word with you," replies the stranger. Mr. Le Cheminant seemed to hesitate for a moment. He lights a cigar, whilst the stranger stands there glaring at him with a look in his eye I certainly didn't like.

"'Mind you,' added Thomas Sawyer, 'the stranger was a gentleman in evening dress, and all that. Presently Mr. Le Cheminant says to him: "This way, then," and takes him along into one of the club rooms. Half an hour later the stranger comes out again. He looked flushed and excited. Soon after Mr. Le Cheminant comes out too; but he was quite calm and smoking a cigar. He asks for a cab, and tells the driver to take him to the Lyric Theatre.'

"This was all that the hall-porter had to say, but his evidence was corroborated by one of the waiters of the club who saw Mr. Le

Cheminant and the stranger subsequently enter the dining-room, which was quite deserted at the time.

"'They 'adn't been in the room a minute,' said the waiter, 'when I 'eard loud voices, as if they was quarrelling frightful. I couldn't 'ear what they said, though I tried, but they was shouting so, and drowning each other's voices. Presently there's a ring at my bell, and I goes into the room. Mr. Le Cheminant was sitting beside one of the tables, quietly lighting a cigar. "Show this—er—gentleman out of the club," 'e says to me. The stranger looked as if 'e would strike 'im. "You'll pay for this," 'e says, then 'e picks up 'is 'at, and dashes out of the club helter-skelter. "One is always pestered by these beggars," says Mr. Le Cheminant to me, as 'e stalks out of the room.'

"Later on it was arranged that both Thomas Sawyer and the waiter should catch sight of Harold Le Cheminant, as he went out of his house in Exhibition Road. Neither of them had the slightest hesitation in recognising in him the stranger who had called at the club that night.

"Now that they held this definite clue, the detectives continued their work with a will. They made enquiries at the Lyric Theatre, but there they only obtained very vague testimony; one point, however, was of great value, the commissionaire outside one of the neighbouring theatres stated that, some time after the performance had begun, he noticed a gentleman in evening dress walking rapidly past him.

"He seemed strangely excited, for as he went by he muttered quite audibly to himself: 'I can stand it no longer, it must be he or I.' Then he disappeared in the fog, walking away towards Shaftesbury Avenue. Unfortunately the commissionaire, just like the cabman, was not prepared to swear to the identity of this man, whom he had only seen momentarily through the fog.

"But add to all this testimony the very strong motive there was for the crime, and you will not wonder that, within twenty-four hours of the murder, the strongest suspicions had already fastened on Harold Le Cheminant, and it was generally understood that, even before the inquest, the police already had in readiness a warrant for his arrest on the capital charge."

IV.

"It would be difficult, I think, for any one who was not present at that memorable inquest to have the least idea of the sensation which its varied and dramatic incidents caused among the crowd of spectators there.

"At first the proceedings were of the usual kind. The medical officer gave his testimony as to the cause of death; this was, of course, not in dispute. The stiletto was produced; it was of an antique and foreign pattern, probably of Eastern or else Spanish origin. In England, it could only have been purchased at some *bric-à-brac* shop.

"Then it was the turn of the servants at Grosvenor Square, of the cabman, and of the commissionaire. Lord Tremarn's evidence, which he had sworn to on his sick-bed, was also read. It added nothing to the known facts of the case, for he had last seen his favourite nephew alive in the course of the afternoon preceding the latter's tragic end.

"After that the *employês* of the Junior Grosvenor Club re-told their story, and they were the first to strike the note of sensation which was afterwards raised to its highest possible pitch.

"Both of them, namely, were asked each in their turn to look round the court and see if they could recognise the stranger who had called at the club that memorable evening. Without the slightest hesitation, both the hall-porter and the waiter pointed to Harold Le Cheminant, who sat with his solicitor in the body of the court.

"But already an inkling of what was to come had gradually spread through that crowded court—instinctively every one felt that behind the apparent simplicity of this tragic case there lurked another mystery, more strange even than that murder in the hansom cab.

"Evidence was being taken as to the previous history of the deceased, his first appearance in London, his relationship with his uncle, and subsequently his enmity with his cousin Harold. At this point a man was brought forward as a witness, who it was understood had communicated with the police at the very last moment, offering to make a statement which he thought would throw considerable light upon the mysterious affair.

"He was a man of about fifty years of age, who looked like a very seedy, superannuated clerk of some insurance office.

"He gave his name as Charles Collins, and said that he resided in Caxton Road, Clapham.

"In a perfectly level tone of voice, he then explained that some three years ago, his son William, who had always been idle and good for nothing, had suddenly disappeared from home.

"'We heard nothing of him for over two years,' continued Charles Collins, in that same cheerless and even voice which spoke of a monotonous existence of ceaseless, patient grind, 'but some few weeks ago my daughter went up to the West End to see about an engagement—she plays dance music at parties sometimes—when, in Regent Street, she came face to face with her brother William. He was no longer wretched, as we all are,' added the old man pathetically, 'he was dressed like a swell, and when his sister spoke to him, he pretended not to know her. But she's a sharp girl, and guessed at once that there was something strange there which William wished to hide. She followed him from a distance, and never lost sight of him that day, until she saw him about six o'clock in the evening go into one of the fine houses in Grosvenor Square. Then she came home and told her mother and me all about it.'

"I can assure you," continued the man in the corner, "that you might have heard a pin drop in that crowded court whilst the old man spoke. That he was stating the truth no one doubted for a moment. The very fact that he was brought forward as a witness showed that his story had been proved, at any rate, to the satisfaction of the police.

"The Collins's seem to have been very simple, good-natured people. It never struck any of them to interfere with William, who appeared, in their own words, to have 'bettered himself.' They concluded that he had obtained some sort of position in a rich family, and was now ashamed of his poor relations at Clapham.

"Then one morning they read in the papers the story of the mysterious murder in the hansom cab, together with a description of the victim, who had not yet been identified. 'William,' they said with one accord. Michael Collins, one of the younger sons, went up to London to view the murdered man at the mortuary. There was no doubt whatever that it was William, and yet all the papers persisted in saying that the deceased was the heir to some grand peerage.

"'So I wrote to the police,' concluded Charles Collins, 'and my wife and children were all allowed to view the body, and we are all prepared to swear that it is that of my son, William Collins, who was no more heir to a peerage than your worship.'

"And mopping his forehead with a large coloured handkerchief, the old man stepped down from the box.

"Well, you may imagine what this bombshell was in the midst of that coroner's court. Every one looked at his neighbour, wondering if this was real life, or some romantic play being acted upon a stage. Amidst indescribable excitement, various other members of the Collins family corroborated the old man's testimony, as did also one or two friends from Clapham. All those who had been allowed to view the body of the murdered man pronounced it without hesitation to be that of William Collins, who had disappeared from home three years ago.

"You see, it was like a repetition of the Tichborne case, only with this strange difference: This claimant was dead, but all his papers were in perfect order, the certificate of marriage between Lucie Legrand and Arthur Le Cheminant at Martinique, as well as the birth and baptismal certificate of Philip Le Cheminant, their son. Yet there were all those simple, honest folk swearing that the deceased had been born in Clapham, and the mother, surely, could not have been mistaken.

"That is where the difference with the other noteworthy case came in, for in this instance, as far as the general public is concerned, the actual identity of the murdered man will always remain a matter of doubt—Philip Le Cheminant or William Collins took that part of his secret, at any rate, with him to his grave."

V.

"But the murder?" I asked eagerly, for the man in the corner had paused, intent upon the manufacture of innumerable knots in a long piece of string.

"Ah, yes, the murder, of course," he replied, with a chuckle, "the second mystery in this extraordinary case. Well, of course, whatever the identity of the deceased really was, there was no doubt in the minds of the police that Harold Le Cheminant had murdered him. To him, at any rate, the Collins family were unknown; he only knew the man who had supplanted him in his uncle's affections, and snatched a rich inheritance away from him. The charge brought against him at the Westminster Court was also one of the greatest sensations of this truly remarkable case.

"It looked, indeed, as if the unfortunate young man had committed a crime which was as appalling as it was useless. Instead of murdering the impostor—if impostor he was—how much more simple it would have been to have tried to unmask him. But, strange to say, this he never seems to have done, at any rate, as far as the public knew.

"But here again mystery stepped in. When brought before the magistrate, Harold Le Cheminant was able to refute the terrible charge brought against him by the simple means of a complete *alibi*. After the stormy episode at the Junior Grosvenor Club, he had gone to his own club in Pall Mall, and fortunately for him, did not leave it until twenty minutes past eleven, some few minutes *after* the two men in evening dress got into the hansom in Shaftesbury Avenue.

"But for this lucky fact, for which he had one or two witnesses, it might have fared ill with him, for feeling unduly excited, he walked all the way home afterwards; and had he left his club earlier, he might have found it difficult to account for his time. As it was, he was of course discharged.

"But one more strange fact came out during the course of the magisterial investigation, and that was that Harold Le Cheminant, on the very day preceding the murder, had booked a passage for St. Vincent. He admitted in court that he meant to conduct certain investigations there, with regard to the identity of the supposed heir to the Tremarn peerage.

"And thus the curtain came down on the last act of that extraordinary drama, leaving two great mysteries unsolved: the real identity of the murdered man, and that of the man who killed him. Some people still persist in thinking it was Harold Le Cheminant. Well, we may easily dismiss *that* supposition. Harold had decided to investigate the matter for himself; he was on his way to St. Vincent.

"Surely common sense would assert that, having gone so far, he would assure himself first whether the man was an impostor or not, before he resorted to crime, in order to rid himself of him. Moreover, the witnesses who saw him leave his own club at twenty minutes past eleven were quite independent and very emphatic.

"Another theory is that the Collins' gang tried to blackmail Philip Le Cheminant—or William Collins, whichever we like to call him—and that it was one of them who murdered him out of spite, when he refused to submit to the blackmailing process.

"Against that theory, however, there are two unanswerable arguments—firstly, the weapon used, which certainly was not one that would commend itself to the average British middle-class man on murder intent—a razor or knife would be more in his line; secondly, there is no doubt whatever that the murderer wore evening dress and an opera hat, a costume not likely to have been worn by any member of the Collins' family, or their friends. We may, therefore, dismiss that theory also with equal certainty."

And he surveyed placidly the row of fine knots in his bit of string.

"But then, according to you, who was the man in evening dress, and who but Harold Le Cheminant had any interest in getting rid of the claimant?" I asked at last.

"'Who, indeed?" he replied with a chuckle, "who but the man who was as wax in the hands of that impostor?"

"Whom do you mean?" I gasped.

"Let us take things from the beginning," he said with ever-growing excitement, "and take the one thing which is absolutely beyond dispute, and that is the authenticity of the *papers*—the marriage certificate of Lucie Legrand, etc.—as against the authenticity of the *man*. Let us admit that the real Philip Le Cheminant was a refugee at St. Vincent, that he found out about his parentage, and determined to go to England. He writes to his uncle, then sails for Europe, lands at Havre, and arrives in Paris."

"Why Paris?" I asked.

"Because you, like the police and like the public, have persistently shut your eyes to an event which, to my mind, has bearing upon the whole of this mysterious case, and that is the original murder committed in Paris a year ago, also in a cab, also with a stiletto—which that time was *not* found—in fact, in the self-same manner as this murder a week ago."

"Well, that crime was never brought home to its perpetrator any more than this one will be. But my contention is, that the man who committed that murder a year ago, repeated this crime last week—that the man who was murdered in Paris was the real Philip Le Cheminant, whilst the man who was murdered in London was some friend to whom he had confided his story, and probably his papers, and who then hit upon the bold plan of assuming the personality of the Martinique creole, heir to an English peerage."

"But what in the world makes you imagine such a preposterous thing?" I gasped.

"One tiny unanswerable fact," he replied quietly. "William Collins, the impostor, when he came to London, called upon a solicitor, and deposited with him the valuable papers; *after that* he obtained his interview with Lord Tremarn. Then mark what happens. Without any question, immediately after that interview, and, therefore, without even having seen the papers of identification, Lord Tremarn accepts the claimant as his newly-found nephew.

"And why?

"Only because that claimant has a tremendous hold over the Earl, which makes the old man as wax in his hands, and it is only logical to conclude that that hold was none other than that Lord Tremarn had met his real nephew in Paris, and had killed him, sooner than to see him supplant his beloved heir, Harold.

"I followed up the subsequent history of that Paris crime, and found that the Paris police had never established the identity of the murdered man. Being a stranger, and moneyless, he had apparently lodged in one of those innumerable ill-famed little hotels that abound in Paris, the proprietors of which have very good cause to shun the police, and therefore would not even venture so far as to go and identify the body when it lay in the Morgue.

"But William Collins knew who the murdered man was; no doubt he lodged at the same hotel, and could lay his hands on the all-important papers. I imagine that the two young men originally met in St. Vincent, or perhaps on board ship. He assumed the personality of the deceased, crossed over to England, and confronted Lord Tremarn with the threat to bring the murder home to him if he ventured to dispute his claim.

"Think of it all, and you will see that I am right. When Lord Tremarn first heard from his brother Arthur's son, he went to Paris in order to assure himself of the validity of his claim. Seeing that there was no doubt of that, he assumed a friendly attitude towards the young man, and one evening took him out for a drive in a cab and murdered him on the way.

"Then came Nemesis in the shape of William Collins, whom he dared not denounce, lest his crime be brought home to him. How could he come forward and say: 'I know that this man is an impostor, as I happened to have murdered my nephew myself'?

"No; he preferred to temporise, and bide his time until, perhaps, chance would give him his opportunity. It took a year in coming. The yoke had become too heavy. 'It must be he or I!' he said to himself that very night. Apparently he was on the best of terms with his tormentor, but in his heart of hearts he had always meant to be even with him at the last.

"Everything favoured him; the foggy night, even the dispute between Harold and the impostor at the club. Can you not picture him meeting William Collins outside the theatre, hearing from him the story of the quarrel, and then saying, 'Come with me to Harold's; I'll soon make the young jackanapes apologise to you'?

"Mind you, a year had passed by since the original crime. William Collins, no doubt, never thought he had anything to fear from the old man. He got into the cab with him, and thus this remarkable story has closed, and Harold Le Cheminant is once more heir to the Earldom of Tremarn.

"Think it all over, and bear in mind that Lord Tremarn never made the slightest attempt to prove the rights or wrongs of the impostor's claim. On this base your own conclusions, and then see if they do not inevitably lead you to admit mine as the only possible solution of this double mystery."

He was gone, leaving me bewildered and amazed staring at my *Daily Telegraph*, where, side by side with a long recapitulation of the mysterious claimant to the Earldom, there was the following brief announcement:

"We regret to say that the condition of Lord Tremarn is decidedly worse to-day, and that but little hope is entertained of his recovery. Mr. Harold Le Cheminant has been his uncle's constant and devoted companion during the noble Earl's illness."

8
The Fate of the *Artemis*

I.

"Well, I'm—!" was my inelegant mental comment upon the news in that morning's paper.

"So are most people," rejoined the man in the corner, with that eerie way he had of reading my thoughts. "The *Artemis* has come home, having safely delivered her dangerous cargo, and Captain Jutland's explanations only serve to deepen the mystery."

"Then you admit there is one in this case?" I said.

"Only to the public. Not to me. But I do admit that the puzzle is a hard one. Do you remember the earlier details of the case? It was towards the end of 1903. Negotiations between Russia and Japan were just reaching a point of uncomfortable tension, and the man in the street guessed that war in the Far East was imminent.

"Messrs. Mills and Co. had just completed an order for a number of their celebrated quick-firing guns for the Russian Government, and these—according to the terms of the contract—were to be delivered at Port Arthur on or about 1st February 1904. Effectively, then, on 1st December last, the *Artemis*, under the command of Captain Jutland, sailed from Goole, with her valuable cargo on board, and with orders to proceed along as fast as possible, in view of the probable outbreak of hostilities.

"Less than two hours after she had started, Messrs. Mills received intimation from the highest official quarters, that in all probability before the *Artemis* could reach Port Arthur, and in view of coming eventualities, the submarine mines would have been laid at the entrance to the harbour. A secret plan of the port was therefore sent to the firm for Captain Jutland's use, showing the only way through which he could possibly hope to navigate the *Artemis* safely into the harbour, and without which she would inevitably come in contact with one of those terrible engines of wholesale destruction, which have since worked such awful havoc in this war.

"But *there* was the trouble. This official intimation, together with the plan, reached Messrs. Mills just two hours too late; it is a way peculiar to many official intimations. Fortunately, however, the *Artemis* was to touch at Portsmouth on private business of the firm's, and, therefore, it only meant finding a trustworthy messenger to meet Captain Jutland there, and to hand him over that all-important plan.

"Of course, there was no time to be lost, but, above all, some one of extreme trustworthiness must be found for so important a mission. You must remember that the great European Power in question is beset by many foes in the shape of her own disaffected children, who desire her downfall even more keenly than does her Asiatic opponent. Also, in times like these, when every method is fair which gives one adversary an advantage over the other, we must remember that our plucky little allies of the Far East are past masters in that art which is politely known as secret intelligence.

"All this, you see, made it an absolute necessity to keep the mission to Captain Jutland a profound secret. I need not impress upon you the fact, I think, that it is not expedient for the plans of an important harbour to fall under prying eyes.

"Finally, the choice fell on Captain Markham, R.N.R., lately of the mercantile marine, and at the time in the employ of our own Secret Intelligence Department, to which he has rendered frequent and valuable services. This choice was determined also mainly through the fact that Captain Markham's wife had relatives living in Portsmouth, and that, therefore, his journey thither could easily be supposed to have an unofficial and quite ordinary character—especially if he took his wife with him, which he did.

"Captain and Mrs. Markham left Waterloo for Portsmouth at ten minutes past twelve on Wednesday, 2nd December, the secret plan lying safely concealed at the bottom of Mrs. Markham's jewel-case.

"As the *Artemis* would not touch at Portsmouth until the following morning, Captain Markham thought it best not to spend the night at an hotel, but to go into rooms; his choice fell on a place, highly recommended by his wife's relations, and which was situated in a quiet street on the Southsea side of the town. There he and his wife stayed the night, pending the arrival of the *Artemis*.

"But at twelve o'clock on the following morning the police were hastily called in by Mrs. Bowden, the landlady of 49 Gastle Street, where the Markhams had been staying. Captain Markham had been found lying half-insensible, gagged and bound, on the floor of the sitting-room, his hands and feet tightly pinioned, and a woollen comforter wound closely round his mouth and neck; whilst Mrs. Markham's jewel-case, containing valuable jewellery and the secret plans of Port Arthur, had disappeared."

II.

"Mind you," continued the man in the corner, after he had assured himself of my undivided attention, "all these details were unknown to the public at first. I have merely co-ordinated them, and told them to you in the actual sequence in which they occurred, so that you may be able to understand the subsequent events.

"At the time—that is to say, on 3rd December 1903—the evening papers only contained an account of what was then called 'the mysterious outrage at Gastle Street, Portsmouth.' A private gentleman was presumably assaulted and robbed in broad daylight, and inside a highly respectable house in a busy part of the city.

"Mrs. Bowden, the landlady, was, as you may imagine, most excited and indignant. Her house and herself had been grossly insulted by this abominable outrage, and she did her level best to throw what light she could on this mysterious occurrence.

"The story she told the police was indeed extraordinary, and as she repeated it to all her friends, and subsequently to one or two journalists, it roused public excitement to its highest pitch.

"'What she related at great length to the detective in charge of the case, was briefly this:

"Captain and Mrs. Markham, it appears, arrived at 49 Gastle Street, on Wednesday afternoon, 2nd December, and Mrs. Bowden accommodated them with a sitting-room and bedroom, both on the ground floor. In the evening Mrs. Markham went out to dine with her brother, a Mr. Paulton, who is a well-known Portsmouth resident, but Captain Markham stayed in and had dinner alone in his sitting-room.

"According to Mrs. Bowden's version of the story, at about nine o'clock a stranger called to see Captain Markham. This stranger was obviously a foreigner, for he spoke broken English. Unfortunately, the hall at 49 Gastle Street was very dark, and, moreover, the foreigner was attired in a magnificent fur coat, the collar of which hid the lower part of his face. All Mrs. Bowden could see of him was that he was very tall, and wore gold-rimmed spectacles.

"'He was so very peremptory in his manner,' continued Mrs. Bowden, 'that I had to show him in at once. The Captain seemed surprised to see him—in fact, he looked decidedly annoyed, I might say; but just as I was closing the door I heard the stranger laugh, and say quite pleasantly: "You gave me the slip, my friend, but you see I have found you out all right."'

"Mrs. Bowden, after the manner of her class, seems to have made vigorous efforts to hear what went on in the sitting-room after that," continued the man in the corner, "but she was not successful. Later on, however, the Captain rang and ordered whiskies and sodas. Both gentlemen were then sitting by the fire, looking quite friendly.

"'I took a look round the room,' explained the worthy landlady, 'and took particular notice that the jewel-case was on the table, with the lid open. Captain Markham, as soon as he saw me, closed it very quickly.'

"The stranger seems to have gone away again at about half-past ten, and subsequently Mrs. Markham came home, accompanied by her brother, Mr. Paulton. The next morning she went out at a quarter-past eleven o'clock, and about half an hour later the mysterious stranger called again.

"This time he pushed his way straight into the sitting-room; but the very next moment he uttered a cry of intense horror and astonishment, and rushed back into the hall, gesticulating wildly, and shrieking: 'A robbery!—a murder!—I go for the police!' And before Mrs. Bowden could stop him or even could realise what had occurred, he had dashed out of the house.

"'I called to Meggie,' continued Mrs. Bowden, 'I was so frightened, I didn't dare go into the parlour alone. But she was more frightened than I was, and we stood trembling in the hall waiting for the police. At last I began to have my suspicions, and I got Meggie to run out into the street and see if she could bring in a policeman.'

"When the police at last arrived upon the scene, they pushed open the sitting-room door, and there found Captain Markham in a most helpless condition, his hands tied behind his back and himself half-choked by the scarf over his mouth. As soon as he recovered his breath, he explained that he had no idea who his assailant was; he was standing with his back to the door, when he was suddenly dealt a blow on the head from behind, and he remembered nothing more.

"In the meantime Mrs. Markham had come home, and of course was horrified beyond measure at the outrage which had been committed. She declared that her jewel-case was in the sitting-room when she went out in the morning—a fact confirmed by Captain Markham himself.

"But here, at once, the police were seriously puzzled. Mrs. Bowden, of course, told her story of the foreigner—a story which was corroborated by her daughter, Meggie. Captain Markham, pressed by the police, and by his wife, admitted that a friend had visited him the evening before.

"'He is an old friend I met years ago abroad, who happened to be in Portsmouth yesterday, and quite accidentally caught sight of me as I drove up to this door, and naturally came in to see me,' was the Captain's somewhat lame explanation.

"Nothing more was to be got out of him that day; he was still feeling very bewildered, he said, and certainly he looked very ill. Mrs. Markham then put the whole matter in the hands of the police.

"Captain Markham had given a description of 'the old friend he had met years ago abroad.' This description vaguely coincided with that given by Mrs. Bowden of the mysterious foreigner. But the Captain's replies to the cross-questionings of the detectives in charge of the case were always singularly reticent and lame. 'I had lost sight of him for nearly twenty years,' he explained, 'and do not know what his present abode and occupation might be. When I knew him years ago, he was a man of independent means, without a fixed abode, and a great traveller. I believe that he is a German by nationality, but I don't think that I ever knew this as a fact. His name was Johann Schmidt."

"I may as well tell you here, at once, that the mysterious foreigner managed to make good his escape. He was traced as far as the South-Western Railway Station, where he was seen to rush through the barrier, just in time to catch the express up to town. At Waterloo he was lost sight of in the crowd.

"The police were keenly on the alert; no trace of the missing jewels had as yet been found. Then it was that, gradually, the story of the secret plan of Port Arthur reached the ears of the general public. Who first told it and to whom, it is difficult to conjecture, but you know what a way things of that sort have of leaking out.

"The secret of Captain Markham's mission had of necessity been known to several people, and a secret shared by many soon ceases to be one at all; anyway, within a week of the so-called 'Portsmouth outrage,' it began to be loudly whispered that the robbery of Mrs. Markham's jewels was only a mask that covered the deliberate theft of the plans of Port Arthur.

"And then the inevitable happened. Already Captain Markham's strange attitude had been severely commented upon, and now the public, backed by the crowd of amateur detectives who read penny novelettes and form conclusions of their own, had made up its mind that Captain Markham was a party to the theft—that he was either the tool or the accomplice of the mysterious foreigner, and that, in fact, he had been either bribed or terrorised into giving up the plan of Port Arthur to an enemy of the Russian Government. The crime was all the more heinous as by this act of treachery a British ship, manned by a British crew, had been sent to certain destruction.

"What rendered the whole case doubly mysterious was that Messrs. Mills and Co. seemed to take the matter with complete indifference. They refused to be interviewed, or to give any information about the *Artemis* at all, and seemed callously willing to await events.

"The public was furious; the newspapers stormed; every one felt that the *Artemis* should be stopped at any cost at her next port of call, and not allowed to continue her perilous journey.

"And yet the days went by; the public read with horror at Lloyds' that the *Artemis* had called at Malta, at Port Said, at Aden, and was now well on her way to the Far East. Feeling ran so high throughout England, that, if the mysterious stranger had been discovered by the police, no protection from them would have saved him from being lynched.

"As for Captain Markham, public opinion reserved its final judgment. A cloud hung over him, of that there was no doubt; many said openly that he had sold the secret plans of Port Arthur, either to the Japanese or to the Nihilists, either through fear or intimidation, if not through greed.

"Then the inevitable climax came: A certain Mr. Carleton constituted himself the spokesman of the general public; he met Captain Markham one day at one of the clubs in London. There were hot words between them. Mr. Carleton did not mince matters; he openly accused Captain Markham of that which public opinion had already whispered, and finally, completely losing his temper, he struck the Captain in the face, calling him every opprobrious name he could think of.

"But for the timely interference of friends, there would have been murder committed then and there; as it was, Captain Markham was induced by his own friends to bring a criminal charge of slander and of assault against Mr. Carleton, as the only means of making the whole story public, and possibly vindicating his character."

III.

"A criminal action for slander and assault is always an interesting one," continued the man in the corner, after a while, "as it always argues an unusual amount of personal animosity on the part of the plaintiff.

"In this case, of course, public interest was roused to its highest pitch. Practically, though Captain Markham was the prosecutor, he would stand before his fellow-citizens after this action either as an innocent man, or as one of the most dastardly scoundrels this nation has ever known.

"The case for the Captain was briefly stated by his counsel. For the defence Sir Arthur Inglewood, on behalf of Mr. Carleton, pleaded justification. With wonderful eloquence Sir Arthur related the whole story of the secret plan of Port Arthur confided to the honour of Captain Markham, and which involved the safety of the British ship and the lives of a whole British crew.

"The first witnesses called for the defence were Mrs. Bowden and her daughter, Meggie. Both related the story I have already told you. When they came to the point of having seen the jewel-case *open* on the table during that interview between Captain Markham and the mysterious stranger, there was a regular murmur of indignation throughout the whole crowd, so much so, that the judge threatened to clear the court, for Sir Arthur argued this to be a proof that Captain Markham had been a willing accomplice in the theft of the secret plans, and had merely played the comedy of being assaulted, bound, and gagged.

"But there was more to come.

"It appears that on the morning of 2nd December—that is to say, before going to Portsmouth—Captain Markham, directly after breakfast, and while his wife was up in her own room, received a message, which seemed greatly to disturb him. It was Jane Mason, the parlour-maid at the Markhams' town house, who told the story.

"A letter bearing no stamp had been dropped into the letter-box; she had taken it to her master, who, on reading it, became greatly agitated; he tore up the letter, stuffed it into his pocket, and presently took up his hat and rushed out of the house.

"'When the master was gone,' continued Jane, 'I found a scrap of paper, which had fallen out of his pocket.'

"This scrap of paper Jane Mason had carefully put away. She was a shrewd girl, and scented some mystery. It was now produced in court, and the few fragmentary words were read out by Sir Arthur Inglewood, amidst boundless excitement:

"'....if you lend a hand .... Port Arthur safely ....hold my tongue.....'

"And at the end there were four letters in large capitals, 'STOW.'

"In view of all the evidence taken, there was momentous significance to be attached to those few words, of which only the last four letters seemed mysterious, but these probably were part of the confederate's signature, who had—no one doubted it now—some hold upon Captain Markham, and had by a process of blackmail induced him to send the *Artemis* to her doom.

"After that, according to a statement made by the head clerk of Messrs. Mills and Co., Captain Markham came round to the office, begging that some one else should be sent to meet Captain Jutland at Portsmouth. 'This,' explained the head clerk, who had been subpoenaed for the defence, 'was quite impossible at this eleventh hour, and in the absence of the heads of the firm, I had, on Mr. Mills' behalf, to hold Captain Markham to his promise.'

"This closed the case for the defence, and, in view of the lateness of the hour, counsels' speeches were reserved for the following day. There was not a doubt in anybody's mind that Captain Markham was guilty, and but for the presence of a large body of police, I assure you he would have been torn to pieces by the crowd."

The man in the corner paused in his narrative and blinked at me over his bone-rimmed spectacles, like some lean and frowzy tom-cat eager for a fight.

"Well?" I said eagerly.

"Well, surely you remember what happened the following day?" he replied, with a dry chuckle.

"Personally, I don't think that there ever was quite so much sensation in any English court of law.

"It was crowded, of course, when counsel for the plaintiff rose to speak. He made, however, only a short statement, briefly and to the point; but this statement caused every one to look at his neighbour, wondering if he were awake or dreaming.

"Counsel began by saying that Messrs. Mills and Co., in view of the obvious conspiracy that had existed against the *Artemis*, had decided, in conjunction with Captain Markham himself, to say nothing about the safety of the ship until she was in port; but now counsel had much pleasure in informing the court and public that the *Artemis* had safely arrived at Port Arthur, had landed her guns, and was on her way home again by now. A cablegram via St. Petersburg had been received by Messrs. Mills and Co. from Captain Jutland that very morning.

"That cablegram was read by counsel in court, and was received with loud and prolonged cheering which could not be suppressed.

"With heroic fortitude—explained counsel—Captain Markham had borne the gross suspicions against his integrity, only hoping that news of the safety of the *Artemis* would reach England in time to allow him to vindicate his character. But until Captain Jutland was safe in port, he had sworn to hold his tongue, and to bear insult and violence, sooner than once more jeopardise the safety of the British ship by openly avowing that she carried the plans of the important port with her.

"Well, you know the rest. The parties, at the suggestion of the judge, arranged the case amicably, and, Captain Markham being fully satisfied, Mr. Carleton was nominally ordered to come up for trial when called upon.

"Captain Markham was the hero of the hour; but presently, after the first excitement had subsided, sensible people began to ponder. Every one, of course, appreciated the fact that Messrs. Mills and Co., prompted by the highest authorities, had insisted on not jeopardising the safety of the *Artemis* by shouting on the housetops that she was carrying the plans of Port Arthur on board. Hostilities in the Far East were on the point of breaking out, and I need not insist, I think, on the obvious fact that silence in such matters and at such a time was absolutely imperative.

"But what sensible people wanted to know was, what part had Captain Markham played in all this?

"In the evening of that memorable 2nd December, he was sitting amicably by the fire with the mysterious stranger, who was evidently blackmailing him, and with the jewel-case, which contained the plans of Port Arthur, open between them. What, then, had caused Captain Markham to change his attitude? What dispelled the fear of the stranger? Was he really assaulted? Was the jewel-case really stolen?

"Captain Jutland, of the *Artemis*, has explained that he was only on shore for one hour at Portsmouth on the memorable morning of 3rd December, namely, between 10.30 and 11.30 A.M. On landing at the Hard from his gig, he was met by a gentleman whom he did not know, and who, without a word of comment, handed him some papers, which proved to be plans of Port Arthur.

"Now, at that very hour Captain Markham was lying helpless in his bedroom, and the question now is, who abstracted the plans from the jewel-case, and then mysteriously handed them to Captain Jutland? Why was it not done openly? Why?—why? and, above all, by whom?—"

IV.

"Indeed, why?" I retorted, for he had paused, and was peering at me through his bone-rimmed spectacles. "You must have a theory," I added, as I quietly handed him a beautiful bit of string across the table.

"Of course, I have a theory," he replied placidly; "nay, more, the only explanation of those mysterious events. But for this I must refer you to the scrap of paper found by Jane Mason, and containing the four fragmentary sentences which have puzzled every one, and which Captain Markham always refused to explain.

"Do you remember," he went on, as he began feverishly to construct knot upon knot on that piece of string, "the wreck of the *Ridstow* some twenty years ago? She was a pleasure boat belonging to Mr. Eyres, the great millionaire financier, and was supposed to have been wrecked in the South Seas, with nearly all hands. Five of her crew, however, were picked up by H.M.S. *Pomona*, on a bit of rocky island to which they had managed to swim.

"I looked up the files of the newspapers relating to the rescue of these five shipwrecked mariners, who told a most pitiable tale of the loss of the yacht and their subsequent escape to, and sufferings on, the island. Fire had broken out in the hull of the *Ridstow*, and all her crew were drowned, with the exception of three sailors, a Russian friend, or rather secretary, of Mr. Eyres, and a young petty officer named Markham.

"You see, the letters STOW had given me the clue. Clearly Markham, on receiving the message in the morning of 2nd December, was frightened, and when we analyse the fragments of that message and try to reconstruct the missing fragments, do we not get something like this:

"'*If you lend a hand* in allowing the *Artemis* to reach *Port Arthur safely*, and to land her cargo there, I will no longer *hold my tongue* about the events which occurred on board the *Ridstow*.'

"Clearly the mysterious stranger had a great hold over Captain Markham, for every scrap of evidence, if you think it over, points to his having been *frightened*. Did he not beg the clerk to find some one else to meet Captain Jutland in Portsmouth? He did not wish *to lend a hand* in allowing the *Artemis* to reach *Port Arthur safely*.

"We must, therefore, take it that on board the *Ridstow* some such tragedy was enacted as, alas! is not of unfrequent occurrence. The tragedy of a mutiny, a wholesale murder, the robbery of the rich financier, the burning of the yacht. Markham, then barely twenty, was no doubt an unwilling, perhaps passive, accomplice; one can trace the hand of a cunning, daring Russian in the whole of this mysterious tragedy.

"Since then, Markham, through twenty years' faithful service of his country, had tried to redeem the passive crime of his early years. But then came the crisis: The cunning leader of that bygone tragedy no doubt kept a strong hand over his weaker accomplices.

"What happened to the other three we do not know, but we have seen how terrified Markham is of him, how he dare not resist him, and when the mysterious Russian—some Nihilist, no doubt, at war with his own Government—wishes to deal his country a terrible blow by possessing himself of the plan of her most important harbour, so that he might sell it to her enemies, Markham dare not say him nay.

"But mark what happens. Captain Markham terrorised, confronted with a past crime, threatened with exposure, is as wax in the hands of his unscrupulous tormentor. But beside him there is the saving presence of his wife."

"His wife?" I gasped.

"Yes, the woman! Did you think this was a crime without the inevitable woman? I sought her, and found her in Captain Markham's wife. To save her husband both from falling a victim to his implacable accomplice, and from committing another even more heinous crime, she suggests the comedy which was so cleverly enacted in the morning of 3rd December.

"When the landlady and her daughter saw the jewel-case open on the table the evening before, Markham was playing the first act of the comedy invented by his wife. She had the plan safely in her own keeping by then. He pretended to agree to the Russian's demands, but showed him that he had not then the plan in his possession, promising, however, to deliver it up on the morrow.

"Then in the morning, Mrs. Markham helps to gag and strap her husband down; he pretends to he unconscious, and she goes out, carrying the jewel-case. Her brother, Mr. Paulton, of course, helps them both; without him it would have been more difficult; as it is, he takes charge of the jewel-case, abstracts the plan and papers, and finally meets Captain Jutland at the Hard, and hands him over the plan of Port Arthur.

"Thus through the wits of a clever and devoted woman, not only are the *Artemis* and her British crew saved, but Captain Markham is effectually rid of the blackmailer, who otherwise would have poisoned his life, and probably out of revenge at being foiled, have ruined his victim altogether.

"To my mind, that was the neatest thing in the whole plan. The general public believed that Captain Markham (who obviously at the instigation of his wife had confided in Messrs. Mills and Co.) held his tongue as to the safety of the *Artemis* merely out of heroism, in order not to run her into any further danger. Now, I maintain that this was the master-stroke of that clever woman's plan.

"By holding his tongue, by letting the public fear for the safety of the British crew and British ship, public feeling was stirred to such a pitch of excitement that the Russian now would never *dare* show himself. Not only—by denouncing Captain Markham now—would he never be even listened to for a moment, but, if he came forward at all, if he even showed himself, he would stand before the British public self-convicted as the man who had tried through the criminal process of blackmail to terrorise an Englishman into sending a British ship and thirty British sailors to certain annihilation.

"No; I think we may take it for granted that the Russian will not dare to show his face in England again."

And the funny creature was gone before I could say another word.

9
The Disappearance of Count Collini

I.

He was very argumentative that morning; whatever I said he invariably contradicted flatly and at once, and we both had finally succeeded in losing our temper.

The man in the corner was riding one of his favourite hobby-horses.

"It is *impossible* for any person to completely disappear in a civilised country," he said emphatically, "provided that person has either friends or enemies of means and substance, who are interested in finding his or her whereabouts."

"Impossible is a sweeping word," I rejoined.

"None too big for the argument," he concluded, as he surveyed with evident pride and pleasure a gigantic and complicated knot, which his bony fingers had just fashioned.

"I think that, nevertheless, you should not use it," I said placidly. "It is not *impossible*, though it may be very difficult to disappear without leaving the slightest clue or trace behind you."

"Prove it," he said, with a snap of his thin lips.

"I can, quite easily."

"Now I know what is going on in your mind," said the uncanny creature; "you are thinking of that case last autumn."

"Well, I was," I admitted. "And you cannot deny that Count Collini has disappeared as effectually as if the sea had swallowed him up—many people think it did."

"Many idiots, you mean," he rejoined drily. "Yes, I knew you would quote that case. It certainly was a curious one; all the more so, perhaps, as there was no inquest, no sensational police-court proceedings, nothing dramatic, in fact, save that strange and wonderful disappearance.

"I don't know if you call to mind the whole plot of that weird drama. There was Thomas Checkfield, a retired biscuit-baker of Reading, who died leaving a comfortable fortune, mostly invested in freehold property, and amounting to about £80,000, to his only child, Alice.

"At the time of her father's death Alice Checkfield was just eighteen, and at school in Switzerland, where she had spent most of her life. Old Checkfield had been a widower ever since the birth of his daughter, and seems to have led a very lonely and eccentric life, leaving the girl at school abroad for years, only going very occasionally to see her, and seemingly having but little affection for her.

"The girl herself had not been home in England since she was eight years old, and even when old Checkfield was dying he would not allow the girl to be apprised of his impending death, and to be brought home to a house of loneliness and mourning.

"'What's the good of upsetting a young girl, not eighteen,' he said to his friend, Mr. Turnour, 'by letting her see all the sad paraphernalia of death? She hasn't seen much of her old father anyway, and will soon get over her loss, with young company round her, to help her bear up.'

"But though Thomas Checkfield cared little enough for his daughter, when he died he left his entire fortune to her, amounting altogether to £80,000; and he appointed his friend, Reginald Turnour, to be her trustee and guardian until her marriage or until she should attain her majority.

"It was generally understood that the words 'until her marriage' were put in because it had all along been arranged that Alice should marry Hubert Turnour, Reginald's younger brother.

"Hubert was old Checkfield's godson, and if the old man had any affection for anybody, it certainly was for Hubert. The latter had been a great deal in his godfather's house, when he and Alice were both small children, and had called each other 'hubby' and 'wifey' in play, when they were still in the nursery. Later on, whenever, old Checkfield went abroad to see his daughter, he always took Hubert with him, and a boy-and-girl flirtation sprang up between the two young people; a flirtation which had old Checkfield's complete approval, and no doubt he looked upon their marriage as a *fait accompli*, merely desiring the elder Mr. Turnour to administer the girl's fortune until then.

"Hubert Turnour, at the time of the subsequent tragedy, was a good-looking young fellow, and by profession what is vaguely known as a 'commission agent.' He lived in London, where he had an office in a huge block of buildings close to Cannon Street Station.

"There is no doubt that at the time of old Checkfield's death, Alice looked upon herself as the young man's *fiancée*. When the girl reached her nineteenth year, it was at last decided that she should leave school and come to England. The question as to what should be done with her until her majority, or until she married Hubert, was a great puzzle to Mr. Turnour. He was a bachelor, who lived in comfortable furnished rooms in Reading, and he did not at all relish the idea of starting housekeeping for the sake of his young ward, whom he had not seen since she was out of the nursery, and whom he looked upon as an intolerable nuisance.

"Fortunately for him this vexed question was most satisfactorily and unexpectedly settled by Alice herself. She wrote to her guardian, from Geneva, that a Mrs. Brackenbury, the mother of her dearest school-fellow, had asked her to come and live with them, at any rate for a time, as this would be a more becoming arrangement than that of a young girl sharing a bachelor's establishment.

"Mr. Turnour seems to have hesitated for some time: he was a conscientious sort of man, who took his duties of guardianship very seriously. What ultimately decided him, however, was that his brother Hubert added the weight of his eloquent letters of appeal to those of Alice herself. Hubert naturally was delighted at the idea of having his rich *fiancée* under his eye in London, and after a good deal of correspondence, Mr. Turnour finally gave his consent, and Alice Checkfield duly arrived from Switzerland in order to make a prolonged stay in Mrs. Brackenbury's house."

II.

"All seems to have gone on happily and smoothly for a time in Mrs. Brackenbury's pretty house in Kensington," continued the man in the corner. "Hubert Turnour was a constant visitor there, and the two young people seem to have had all the freedom of an engaged couple.

"Alice Checkfield was in no sense of the word an attractive girl; she was not good-looking, and no effort on Mrs. Brackenbury's part could succeed in making her look stylish. Still, Hubert Turnour seemed quite satisfied, and the girl herself ready enough at first to continue the boy-and-girl flirtation as of old.

"Soon, however, as time went on, things began to change. Now that Alice had become mistress of a comfortable fortune there were plenty of people ready to persuade her that a 'commission agent,' with but vague business prospects, was not half-good enough for her, and that her £80,000 entitled her to more ambitious matrimonial hopes. Needless to say that in these counsels Mrs. Brackenbury was very much to the fore.

"She lived in Kensington, and had social ambitions, foremost among which was to see her daughter's bosom friend married to, at least, a baronet, if not a peer.

"A young girl's head is quickly turned. Within six months of her stay in London, Alice was giving Hubert Turnour the cold shoulder, and the young man had soon realised that she was trying to get out of her engagement.

"Scarcely had Alice reached her twentieth birthday, than she gave her erstwhile *fiancée* his formal *congé*.

"At first Hubert seems to have taken his discomfiture very much to heart. £80,000 were not likely to come his way again in a hurry. According to Mrs. Brackenbury's servants, there were one or two violent scenes between him and Alice, until finally Mrs. Brackenbury herself was forced to ask the young man to discontinue his visits.

"It was soon after that that Alice Checkfield first met Count Collini at one of the brilliant subscription dances given by the Italian colony in London, the winter before last. Mrs. Brackenbury was charmed with him, Alice Checkfield was enchanted! The Count, having danced with Alice half the evening, was allowed to pay his respects at the house in Kensington.

"He seemed to be extremely well off, for he was staying at the Carlton, and, after one or two calls on Mrs. Brackenbury, he began taking the ladies to theatres and concerts, always presenting them with the choicest and most expensive flowers, and paying them various other equally costly attentions.

"Mrs. and Miss Brackenbury welcomed the Count with open arms (figuratively speaking). Alice was shy, but apparently over head and ears in love at first sight.

"At first Mrs. Brackenbury did her best to keep this new acquaintanceship a secret from Hubert Turnour. I suppose that the old matchmaker feared another unpleasant scene. But the inevitable soon happened. Hubert, contrite, perhaps still hopeful, called at the house one day, when the Count was there, and, according to the story subsequently told by Miss Brackenbury herself, there was a violent scene between him and Alice. As soon as the fascinating foreigner had gone, Hubert reproached his *fiancée* for her fickleness in no measured language, and there was a good deal of evidence to prove that he then and there swore to be even with the man who had supplanted him in her affections. There was nothing to do then but for Mrs. Brackenbury to 'burn her boats.' She peremptorily ordered Hubert out of her house, and admitted that Count Collini was a suitor, favoured by herself, for the hand of Alice Checkfield.

"You see, I am bound to give you all these details of the situation," continued the man in the corner, with his bland smile, "so that you may better form a judgment as to the subsequent fate of Count Collini. From the description which Mrs. Brackenbury herself subsequently gave to the police, the Count was then in the prime of life; of a dark olive complexion, dark eyes, extremely black hair and moustache. He had a very slight limp, owing to an accident he had had in early youth, which made his walk and general carriage unusual and distinctly noticeable. His was certainly not a personality that could pass unperceived in a crowd.

"Hubert Turnour, furious and heartsick, wrote letter after letter to his brother, to ask him to interfere on his behalf; this Mr. Turnour did, to the best of his ability, but he had to deal with an ambitious matchmaker and with a girl in love, and it is small wonder that he signally failed. Alice Checkfield by now had become deeply enamoured of her Count, his gallantries flattered her vanity, his title and the accounts he gave of his riches and his estates in Italy fascinated her, and she declared that she would marry him, either with or without her guardian's consent, either at once, or as soon as she had attained her majority, and was mistress of herself and of her fortune.

"Mr. Turnour did all he could to prevent this absurd marriage. Being a sensible, middle-class Britisher, he had no respect for foreign titles, and little belief in foreign wealth. He wrote the most urgent letters to Alice, warning her against a man whom he firmly believed to be an impostor: finally, he flatly refused to give his consent to the marriage.

"Thus a few months went by. The Count had been away in Italy all through the winter and spring, and returned to London for the season, apparently more enamoured with the Reading biscuit-baker's daughter than ever. Alice Checkfield was then within nine months of her twenty-first birthday, and determined to marry the Count. She openly defied her guardian.

"'Nothing,' she wrote to him, 'would ever induce me to marry Hubert.'

"I suppose it was this which finally induced Mr. Turnour to give up all opposition to the marriage. Seeing that his brother's chances were absolutely *nil*, and that Alice was within nine months of her majority, he no doubt thought all further argument useless, and with great reluctance finally gave his consent.

"The marriage, owing to the difference of religion, was to be performed before a registrar, and was finally fixed to take place on 22nd October 1903, which was just a week after Alice's twenty-first birthday.

"Of course the question of Alice's fortune immediately cropped up: she desired her money in cash, as her husband was taking her over to live in Italy, where she desired to make all further investments. She, therefore, asked Mr. Turnour to dispose of her freehold property for her. There again Mr. Turnour hesitated, and argued, but once he had given his consent to the marriage, all opposition was useless, more especially as Mrs. Brackenbury's solicitors had drawn up a very satisfactory marriage settlement, which the Count himself had suggested, by which Alice was to retain sole use and control of her own private fortune.

"The marriage was then duly performed before a registrar on that 22nd of October, and Alice Checkfield could henceforth style herself Countess Collini. The young couple were to start for Italy almost directly, but meant to spend a day or two at Dover quietly together. There were, however, one or two tiresome legal formalities to go through. Mr. Turnour had, by Alice's desire, handed over the sum of £80,000 in notes to her solicitor, Mr. R. W. Stanford. Mr. Stanford had gone down to Reading two days before the marriage, had received the money from Mr. Turnour, and then called upon the new Countess, and formally handed her over her fortune in Bank of England notes.

"Then it was necessary, in view of immediate and future arrangements, to change the English money into foreign, which the Count and his young wife did themselves that afternoon.

"At 5 o'clock P.M. they started for Dover, accompanied by Mrs. Brackenbury, who desired to see the last of her young friend, prior to the latter's departure for abroad. The Count had engaged a magnificent suite of rooms at the Lord Warden Hotel, and thither the party proceeded.

"So far, you see," added the man in the corner, "the story is of the utmost simplicity. You might even call it commonplace. A foreign Count, an ambitious matchmaker, and a credulous girl; these form the ingredients of many a domestic drama, that culminates at the police courts. But at this point this particular drama becomes more complicated, and, if you remember, ends in one of the strangest mysteries that has ever baffled the detective forces on both sides of the Channel."

III.

The man in the corner paused in his narrative. I could see that he was coming to the palpitating part of the story, for his fingers fidgeted incessantly with that bit of string.

"Hubert Turnour, as you may imagine," he continued after a while, "did not take his final discomfiture very quietly. He was a very violent-tempered young man, and it was certainly enough to make any one cross. According to Mrs. Brackenbury's servants he used most threatening language in reference to Count Collini; and on one occasion was with difficulty prevented from personally assaulting the Count in the hall of Mrs. Brackenbury's pretty Kensington house.

"Count Collini finally had to threaten Hubert Turnour with the police court: this seemed to have calmed the young man's nerves somewhat, for he kept quite quiet after that, ceased to call on Mrs. Brackenbury, and subsequently sent the future Countess a wedding present.

"When the Count and Countess Collini, accompanied by Mrs. Brackenbury, arrived at the Lord Warden, Alice found a letter awaiting her there. It was from Hubert Turnour. In it he begged her forgiveness for all the annoyance he had caused her, hoped that she would always look upon him as a friend, and finally expressed a strong desire to see her once more before her departure for abroad, saying that he would be in Dover either this same day or the next, and would give himself the pleasure of calling upon her and her husband.

"Effectively at about eight o'clock, when the wedding party was just sitting down to dinner, Hubert Turnour was announced. Every one was most cordial to him, agreeing to let bygones be bygones: the Count, especially, was most genial and pleasant towards his former rival, and insisted upon his staying and dining with them.

"Later on in the evening, Hubert Turnour took an affectionate leave of the ladies, Count Collini offering to walk back with him to the Grand Hotel, where he was staying. The two men went out together, and—well! you know the rest! for that was the last the young Countess Collini ever saw of her husband. He disappeared as effectively, as completely, as if the sea had swallowed him up.

"'And so it had,' say the public," continued the man in the corner, after a slight pause, "that delicious, short-sighted, irresponsible public is wondering, to this day, why Hubert Turnour was not hung for the murder of that Count Collini."

"Well! and why wasn't he?" I retorted.

"For the very simple reason," he replied, "that in this country you cannot hang a man for murder unless there is proof positive that a murder has been committed. Now, there was absolutely no proof that the Count was murdered at all. What happened was this: The Countess Collini and Mrs. Brackenbury became anxious as time went on and the Count did not return. One o'clock, then two in the morning, and their anxiety became positive alarm. At last, as Alice was verging on hysterics, Mrs. Brackenbury, in spite of the lateness of the hour, went round to the police station.

"It was, of course, too late to do anything in the middle of the night; the constable on duty tried to reassure the unfortunate lady, and promised to send word round to the Lord Warden at the earliest possible opportunity in the morning.

"Mrs. Brackenbury went back with a heavy heart. No doubt Mr. Turnour's sensible letters from Reading recurred to her mind. She had already ascertained from the distracted bride that the Count had taken the strange precaution to keep in his own pocket-book the £80,000 now converted into French and Italian banknotes, and Mrs. Brackenbury feared not so much that he had met with some accident, but that he had absconded with the whole of his girl-wife's fortune.

"The next morning brought but scanty news. No one answering to the Count's description had met with an accident during the night, or been conveyed to a hospital, and no one answering his description had crossed over to Calais or Ostend by the night boats. Moreover, Hubert Turnour, who presumably had last been in Count Collini's company, had left Dover for town by the boat-train at 1.50 A.M.

"Then the search began in earnest after the missing man, and primarily Hubert Turnour was subjected to the closest and most searching cross-examination, by one of the most able men on our detective staff, Inspector Macpherson.

"Hubert Turnour's story was briefly this: He had strolled about on the parade with Count Collini for awhile. It was a very blustery night, the wind blowing a regular gale, and the sea was rolling gigantic waves, which looked magnificent, as there was brilliant moonlight. 'Soon after ten o'clock,' he continued, 'the Count and I went back to the Grand Hotel, and we had whiskies and sodas up in my room, and a bit of a chat until past eleven o'clock. Then he said good-night and went off.'

"'You saw him down to the hall, of course?' asked the detective.

"'No, I did not,' replied Hubert Turnour. 'I had a few letters to write, and meant to catch the 1.50 A.M. back to town.'

"'How long were you in Dover altogether?' asked Macpherson carelessly.

"'Only a few hours. I came down in the afternoon.'

"'Strange, is it not, that you should have taken a room with a private sitting-room, at an expensive hotel, just for those few hours?'

"'Not at all. I originally meant to stay longer. And my expenses are nobody's business, I take it,' replied Hubert Turnour, with some show of temper. 'Anyway,' he added impatiently, after a while, 'if you choose to disbelieve me, you can make inquiries at the hotel, and ascertain if I have told the truth.'

"Undoubtedly he had spoken the truth; at any rate, to that extent. Inquiries at the Grand Hotel went to prove that he had arrived there in the early part of the afternoon, had engaged a couple of rooms, and then gone out. Soon after ten o'clock in the evening he came in, accompanied by a gentleman, whose description, as given by three witnesses, *employés* of the hotel, who saw him corresponded exactly with that of the Count.

"Together the two gentlemen went up to Mr. Hubert Turnour's rooms, and at half-past ten they ordered whisky to be taken up to them. But at this point all trace of Count Collini had completely vanished. The passengers arriving by the 10.49 boat train, and who had elected to spend the night in Dover, owing to the gale, had crowded up and filled the hall.

"No one saw Count Collini leave the Grand Hotel. But Mr. Hubert Turnour came down into the hall at about half-past eleven. He said he would be leaving by the 1.50 A.M. boat-train for town, but would walk round to the station as he only had a small bag with him. He paid his account, then waited in the coffee-room until it was time to go.

"And there the matter has remained. Mrs. Brackenbury has spent half her own fortune in trying to trace the missing man. She has remained perfectly convinced that he slipped across the Channel, taking Alice Checkfield's money with him. But, as you know, at all ports of call on the South Coast, detectives are perpetually on the watch. The Count was a man of peculiar appearance, and there is no doubt that no one answering to his description crossed over to France or Belgium that night. By the following morning the detectives on both sides of the Channel were on the alert. There is no disguise that would have held good. If the Count had tried to cross over, he would have been spotted either on board or on landing; and we may take it as an absolute and positive certainty that he did not cross the Channel.

"He remained in England, but in that case, where is he? You would be the first to admit that, with the whole of our detective staff at his heels, it seems incredible that a man of the Count's singular appearance could hide himself so completely as to baffle detection. Moreover, the question at once arises, that if he did not cross over to France or Belgium, what in the world did he do with the money? What was the use of disappearing and living the life of a hunted beast hiding for his life, with £80,000 worth of foreign money, which was practically useless to him?

"Now, I told you, from the first," concluded the man in the corner, with a dry chuckle, "that this strange episode contained no sensational incident, nor dramatic inquest or criminal procedure. Merely the complete, total disappearance, one may almost call it extinction, of a striking-looking man, in the midst of our vaunted civilisation, and in spite of the untiring energy and constant watch of a whole staff of able men."

IV.

"Very well, then," I retorted in triumph, "that proves that Hubert Turnour murdered Count Collini out of revenge, not for greed of money, and probably threw the body of his victim, together with the foreign banknotes, into the sea."

"But where? When? How?" he asked, smiling good-humouredly at me over his great bone- rimmed spectacles.

"Ah! that I don't know."

"No, I thought not," he rejoined placidly.

"You had, I think, forgotten one incident, namely, that Hubert Turnour, accompanied by the Count, was in the former's room at the Grand Hotel drinking whisky at half-past ten o'clock. You must admit that, even though the hall of the hotel was very crowded later on, a man would nevertheless find it somewhat difficult to convey the body of his murdered enemy through a whole concourse of people."

"He did not murder the Count in the hotel," I argued. "The two men walked out again, when the hall was crowded, and they passed unnoticed. Hubert Turnour led the Count to a lonely part of the cliffs, then threw him into the sea."

"The nearest point at which the cliffs might be called 'lonely' for purposes of a murder, is at least twenty minutes' walk from the Grand Hotel," he said, with a smile, "always supposing that the Count walked quickly and willingly to such a lonely spot at eleven o'clock at night, and with a man who had already, more than once, threatened his life. Mr. Hubert Turnour, remember, was seen in the hall of the hotel at half-past eleven, after which hour he only left the hotel to go to the station after 1 o'clock A.M.

"The hall was crowded by the passengers from the boat-train a little after eleven. There was no time between that and half-past to lead even a willing enemy to the slaughter, throw him into the sea, and come back again, all in the space of five-and-twenty minutes."

"Then what is your explanation of that extraordinary disappearance?" I retorted, beginning to feel very cross about it all.

"A simple one," he rejoined quietly, as he once more began to fidget with his bit of string. "A very simple one indeed; namely, that Count Collini, at the present moment, is living comfortably in England, calmly awaiting a favourable opportunity of changing his foreign money back into English notes."

"But you say yourself that that is impossible, as the most able detectives in England are on the watch for him."

"They are on the watch for a certain Count Collini," he said drily, "who might disguise himself, perhaps, but whose hidden identity would sooner or later be discovered by one of these intelligent human bloodhounds."

"Yes? Well?" I asked.

"Well, that Count Collini never existed. It was *his* personality that was the disguise. Now it is thrown off. The Count is not dead, he is not hiding, he has merely ceased to exist. There is no fear that he will ever come to life again. Mr. Turnour senior will see to that."

"Mr. Turnour!" I ejaculated.

"Why, yes," he rejoined excitedly; "do you mean to tell me you never saw through it all? The money lying in his hands; his brother about to wed the rich heiress; then Mrs. Brackenbury's matrimonial ambitions, Alice Checkfield's coldness to Hubert Turnour, the golden prize slipping away right out of the family for ever. Then the scheme was evolved by those two scoundrels, who deserve to be called geniuses in their criminal way. It could not be managed, except by collaboration, but as it was, the scheme was perfect in conception, and easy of execution.

"Remember that disguise *previous* to a crime is always fairly safe from detection, for then it has no suspicion to contend against, it merely deceives those who have no cause to be otherwise *but* deceived. Mrs. Brackenbury lived in London, Reginald Turnour in Reading; they did not know each other personally, nor did they know each other's friends, of course; whilst Alice Checkfield had not seen her guardian since she was quite a child.

"Then the disguise was so perfect. I went down to Reading, some little time ago, and Reginald Turnour was pointed out to me: he is a Scotchman, with very light, sandy hair. That face clean-shaved, made swarthy, the hair, eyebrows, and lashes dyed a jet black, would render him absolutely unrecognisable. Add to this the fact that a foreign accent completely changes the voice, and that the slight limp was a master-stroke of genius to hide the general carriage.

"Then the winter came round; it was, perhaps, important that Mr. Turnour should not be absent too long from Reading, for fear of exciting suspicion there; and the scoundrel played his part with marvellous skill. Can't you see him yourself leaving the Carlton Hotel, ostensibly going abroad, driving to Charing Cross, but only booking to Cannon Street?

"Then getting out at that crowded station and slipping round to his brother's office in one of those huge blocks of buildings where there is perpetual coming and going, and where any individual would easily pass unperceived?

"There, with the aid of a little soap and water, Mr. Turnour resumed his Scotch appearance, went on to Reading, and spent winter and spring there, only returning to London to make a formal proposal, as Count Collini, for Alice Checkfield's hand. Hubert Turnour's office was undoubtedly the place where he changed his identity, from that of the British middle-class man, to the interesting personality of the Italian nobleman.

"He had, of course, to repeat the journey to Reading a day or two before his wedding, in order to hand over his ward's fortune to Mrs. Brackenbury's solicitor. Then there were the supposed rows between Hubert Turnour and his rival; the letters of warning from the guardian, for which Hubert no doubt journeyed down to Reading, in order to post them there: all this was dust thrown into the eyes of two credulous ladies.

"After that came the wedding, the meeting with Hubert Turnour, who, you see, was obliged to take a room in one of the big hotels, wherein, with more soap and water, the Italian Count could finally disappear. When the hall of the hotel was crowded, the sandy-haired Scotchman slipped out of it quite quietly: he was not remarkable, and no one specially noticed him. Since then the hue and cry has been after a dark Italian, who limps, and speaks broken English; and it has never struck any one that such a person never existed.

"Mr. Turnour is fairly safe by now; and we may take it for granted that he will not seek the acquaintanceship of the Brackenburys, whilst Alice Checkfield is no longer his ward. He will wait a year or two longer perhaps, then he and Hubert will begin quietly to re-convert their foreign money into English notes—they will take frequent little trips abroad, and gradually change the money at the various *bureaux de change*, on the Continent.

"Think of it all, it is so simple—not even dramatic, only the work of a genius from first to last, worthy of a better cause, perhaps, but undoubtedly worthy of success."

He was gone, leaving me quite bewildered. Yet his disappearance had always puzzled me, and now I felt that that animated scarecrow had found the true explanation of it after all.

10
The Ayrsham Mystery

I.

"I have never had a great opinion of our detective force here in England," said the man in the corner, in his funny, gentle, apologetic manner, "but the way that department mismanaged the affair at Ayrsham simply passes comprehension."

"Indeed?" I said, with all the quiet dignity I could command. "It is a pity they did not consult you in the matter, isn't it?"

"It is a pity," he retorted with aggravating meekness, "that they do not use a little common sense. The case resembles that of Columbus' egg, and is every bit as simple.

"It was one evening last October, wasn't it? that two labourers walking home from Ayrsham village, turned down a lane, which, it appears, is a short cut to the block of cottages some distance off, where they lodged.

"The night was very dark, and there was a nasty drizzle in the air. In the picturesque vernacular of the two labourers, 'You couldn't see your 'and before your eyes.' Suddenly they stumbled over the body of a man lying right across the path.

"'At first we thought 'e was drunk,' explained one of them subsequently, 'but when we took a look at 'im, we soon saw there was something very wrong. Me and my mate turned 'im over, and "foul play" we both says at once. Then we see that it was Old Man Newton. Poor chap, 'e was dead, and no mistake.'

"Old Man Newton, as he was universally called by his large circle of acquaintances, was very well known throughout the entire neighbourhood, most particularly at every inn and public bar for some miles round.

"He also kept a local sweet-stuff shop at Ayrsham. No wonder that the men were horrified at finding him in such a terrible condition; even in their uneducated minds there could be no doubt that the old man had been murdered, for his skull had been literally shattered by a fearful blow, dealt him from behind by some powerful assailant.

"Whilst the labourers were cogitating as to what they had better do next, they heard footsteps also turning into the lane, and the next moment Samuel Holder, a well-known inhabitant of Ayrsham, arrived upon the scene.

"'Hello! is that you, Mat Newton?' shouted Samuel, as he came near.

"'Ay! 'tis Old Man Newton, right enough,' replied one of the labourers, 'but 'e won't answer you no more.'

"Samuel Holder seemed absolutely horrified when he saw the body of Old Man Newton; he uttered various ejaculations, which the two labourers, however, did not take special notice of at the time.

"Then the three men held a brief consultation together, with the result that one of them ran back to Ayrsham village to fetch the local police, whilst the two others remained in the lane to guard the body.

"The mystery—for it seemed one from the first—created a great deal of sensation in Ayrsham and all round the neighbourhood, and much sympathy was felt for, and shown to, Mary Newton, the murdered man's only child, a young girl about two-or-three-and-twenty, who, moreover, was in ill-health.

"True, Old Man Newton was not a satisfactory protector for a young girl. He was very much addicted to drink; he neglected the little bit of local business he had; and, moreover, had recently shamefully ill-treated his daughter, the neighbours testifying to the many and loud quarrels that occurred in the small back parlour behind the sweet-stuff shop.

"A case of murder—the moment an element of mystery hovers around it—immediately excites the attention of the newspaper-reading public, who is always seeking for new sensations.

"Very soon the history of Old Man Newton and of his daughter found its way into the London and provincial dailies, and the Ayrsham murder became a topic of all-absorbing interest.

"It appears that Old Man Newton was at one time a highly respectable local tradesman, always in a very small way, as there is not much business doing at Ayrsham. It is a poor and straggling village, although its railway station is an important junction on the Midland system.

"There is some very good shooting in the neighbourhood, and about four or five years ago some of it, together with 'The Limes,' a pretty house just outside the village, was rented for the autumn by Mr. Ledbury and his brother.

"You know the firm of Ledbury and Co., do you not—the great small-arms manufacturers? The elder Mr. Ledbury was the recipient of birthday honours last year, and is the present Lord Walterton. His younger brother, Mervin, was in those days, and is still, a handsome young fellow in the Hussars.

"At the time—I mean about five years ago—Mary Newton was the local beauty of Ayrsham; she did a little dressmaking in her odd moments, but it appears that she spent most of her time in flirting. She was nominally engaged to be married to Samuel Holder, a young carpenter, but there was a good deal of scandal talked about her, for she was thought to be very fast; village gossip coupled her name with that of several young men in the neighbourhood, who were known to have paid the village beauty marked attention, and among these admirers of Mary Newton during the autumn of which I am speaking, young Mr. Mervin Ledbury figured conspicuously.

"Be that as it may, certain it is that Mary Newton had a very bad reputation among the scandal mongers of Ayrsham, and though everybody was shocked, no one was astonished when one fine day in the winter following she suddenly left her father and her home, and went no one knew whither. She left, it appears, a very pathetic letter behind, begging for her father's forgiveness, and that of Samuel Holder, whom she was jilting, but she was going to marry a gentleman above them all in station, and was going to be a real lady; then only would she return home.

"A very usual village tragedy, as you see. Four years went by, and Mary Newton did not return home. As time went by and with it no news of his daughter, Old Man Newton took her disappearance very much to heart. He began to neglect his business, and then his house, which became dirty and ill-kept by an occasional charwoman who would do a bit of promiscuous tidying for him from time to time. He was ill-tempered, sullen, and morose, and very soon became hopelessly addicted to drink.

"Then suddenly, as unexpectedly as she had gone, Mary Newton returned to her home one fine day, after an absence of four years. What had become of her in the interim no one in the village ever knew; she was generally supposed to have earned a living by dressmaking, until her failing health had driven her well-nigh to starvation, and then back to the home and her father she had so heedlessly left.

"Needless to say that all talk of her 'marriage with a gentleman above her in station' was entirely at an end. As for Old Man Newton, he seems, after his daughter's return, to have become more sullen and morose than ever, and the neighbours now busied themselves with talk of the fearful rows which frequently occurred in the back parlour of the little sweet-stuff shop.

"Father and daughter seemed to be leading a veritable cat-and-dog life together. Old Man Newton was hardly ever sober, and at the village inns he threw out weird and strange hints about 'breach of promise actions with £5,000 damages, which his daughter should get, if only he knew where to lay hands upon the scoundrel.'

"He also made vague and wholly useless enquiries about young Mervin Ledbury, but in a sleepy, out-of-the-way village like Ayrsham, no one knows anything about what goes on beyond a narrow five-mile radius at most. 'The Limes' and the shooting were let to different tenants year after year, and neither Lord Walterton nor Mr. Mervin Ledbury had ever rented them again."

II.

"That was the past history of old Newton," continued the man in the corner, after a brief pause; "that is to say, of the man who on a dark night last October was found murdered in a lonely lane, not far from Ayrsham. The public, as you may well imagine, took a very keen interest in the case from the outset; the story of Mark Newton, of the threatened breach of promise, of the £5,000 damages, roused masses of conjecture to which no one as yet dared to give definite shape.

"One name, however, had already been whispered significantly, that of Mr. Mervin Ledbury, the young Hussar, one of Mary Newton's admirers at the very time she left home in order, as she said, to be married to some one above her in station.

"Many thinking people, too, wanted to know what Samuel Holder, Mary's jilted *fiancée*, was doing close to the scene of the murder that night, and how he came to make the remark: 'Hello! is that you, Mat Newton?' when the old man lived nearly half a mile away, and really had no cause for being in that particular lane, at that hour of the night in the drizzling rain.

"The inquest, which, for want of other accommodation, was held at the local police station, was, as you imagine, very largely attended.

"I had read a brief statement of the case in the London papers, and had hurried down to Ayrsham Junction as I scented a mystery, and knew I should enjoy myself.

"When I got there, the room was already packed, and the medical evidence was being gone through.

"Old Man Newton, it appears, had been knocked on the head by a heavily-leaded cane, which was found in the ditch close to the murdered man's body.

"The cane was produced in court; it was as stout as an old-fashioned club, and of terrific weight. The man who wielded it must have been very powerful, for he had only dealt one blow, but that blow had cracked the old man's skull. The cane was undoubtedly of foreign make, for it had a solid silver ferrule at one end, which was not English hall-marked.

"In the opinion of the medical expert, death was the result of the blow, and must have been almost instantaneous.

"The labourers who first came across the body of the murdered man then repeated their story; they had nothing new to add, and their evidence was of no importance. But after that there was some stir in the court. Samuel Holder had been called and sworn to tell the whole truth, and nothing but the truth.

"He was a youngish, heavily-built man of about five-and-thirty, with a nervous, not altogether prepossessing, expression of face. Pressed by the coroner, he gave us a few details of Old Man Newton's earlier history, such as I have already told you.

"'Old Mat,' he explained, with some hesitation, 'was for ever wanting to find out who the gentleman was who had promised marriage to Mary four years ago. But Mary was that obstinate, and wouldn't tell him, and this exasperated the old man terribly, so that they had many rows on the subject.'

"'I suppose,' said the coroner tentatively, 'that you never knew who that gentleman was?'

"Samuel Holder seemed to hesitate for a moment. His manner became even more nervous than before; he shifted his position from one foot to the other; finally he said:

"'I don't know as I ought to say, but—'

"'I am quite sure that you must tell us everything you know which might throw light upon this extraordinary and terrible murder,' retorted the coroner sternly.

"'Well,' replied Samuel Holder, whilst great beads of perspiration stood out upon his forehead, 'Mary never would give up the letters she had had from him, and she would not hear anything about a breach of promise case and £5,000 damages; but old Mat 'e often says to me, says 'e, "It's young Mr. Ledbury," 'e says, "she's told me that once. I got it out of 'er, and if I only knew where to find 'im—"'

"'You are quite sure of this?' asked the coroner, for Holder had paused, and seemed quite horrified at the enormity of what he had said.

"'Yes—yes—your worship—your honour—' stammered Holder. ''E's told me 'twas young Mr. Ledbury times out of count, and—'

"But Samuel Holder here completely broke down; he seemed unable to speak, his lips twitched convulsively, and the coroner, fearing that the man would faint, had him conveyed into the next room to recover himself, whilst another witness was brought forward.

"This was Michael Pitkin, landlord of the Fernhead Arms, at Ayrsham, who had been on very intimate terms with old Newton during the four years which elapsed after Mary's disappearance. He had a very curious story to tell, which aroused public excitement to its highest pitch.

"It appears that to him also the old man had often confided the fact that it was Mr. Ledbury who had promised to marry Mary, and then had shamefully left her stranded and moneyless in London.

"'But of course,' added the jovial and pleasant-looking landlord of the Fernhead Arms, 'the likes of us down here didn't know what became of Mr. Ledbury after he left "The Limes," until one day I reads in the local paper that Sir John Fernhead's daughter is going to be married to Captain Mervin Ledbury. Of course, your honour and me, and all of us know Sir John, our squire, down at Fernhead Towers, and I says to old Mat: "It strikes me," I says, "that you've got your man." Sure enough it was the same Mr. Ledbury who rented "The Limes" years ago, who was engaged to the young lady up at The Towers, and last week there was grand doings there—lords and ladies and lots of quality staying there, and also the Captain.'

"'Well?' asked the coroner eagerly, whilst every one held their breath, wondering what was to come.

"'Well,' continued Michael Pitkin, 'Old Man Newton went down to The Towers one day. 'E was determined to see young Mr. Ledbury, and went. What 'appened I don't know, for old Mat wouldn't tell me, but 'e came back mighty furious from 'is visit, and swore 'e would ruin the young man and make no end of a scandal, and he would bring the law agin' 'im and get £5,000 damages.'

"This story, embellished, of course, by many details, was the gist of what the worthy landlord of the Fernhead Arms had to say, but you may imagine how every one's excitement and curiosity was aroused; in the meanwhile Samuel Holder was getting over his nervousness, and was more ready to give a clear account of what happened on the fatal night itself.

"'It was about nine o'clock,' he explained, in answer to the coroner, 'and I was hurrying back to Ayrsham, through the fields; it was dark and raining, and I was about to strike across the hedge into the lane when I heard voices—a woman's, then a man's. Of course, I could see nothing, and the man spoke in a whisper, but I had recognised Mary's voice quite plainly. She kept on saying:

"'Tisn't my fault" she says, "it's father's, 'e 'as made up 'is mind. I held out as long as I could, but 'e worried me, and now 'e's got your letters, and it's too late."

"Samuel Holder again paused a moment, then continued:

"'They talked together for a long time: Mary seemed very upset and the man very angry. Presently 'e says to 'er: "Well, tell your father to come out here and speak to me for a moment. I'll see what I can do." Mary seemed to 'esitate for a time, then she went away, and the man waited there in the drizzling rain, with me the other side of the 'edge watchin' 'im. I waited for a long time, for I wanted to know what was goin' to 'appen; then time went on. I thought perhaps that old Mat was at the Fernhead Arms, and that Mary couldn't find 'im, so I went back to Ayrsham by the fields, 'oping to find the old man. The stranger didn't budge. 'E seemed inclined to wait—so I left 'im there—and—and—that's all. I went to the Fernhead Arms, saw old Mat wasn't there—then I went back to the lane—and—Old Man Newton was dead, and the stranger was gone.'

"There was a moment or two of dead silence in the court when Samuel Holder had given his evidence, then the coroner asked quietly:

"'You do not know who the stranger was?'

"'Well, I couldn't be sure, your honour,' replied Samuel nervously, 'it was pitch-dark. I wouldn't like to swear a fellow-creature's life and character away.'

"'No, no, quite so,' rejoined the coroner; 'but do you happen to know what time it was when all this occurred?

"'Oh yes, your honour,' said Samuel decisively, 'as I walked away from the Fernhead Arms I 'eard Ayrsham church clock strike ten o'clock.'

"'Ah that's always something,' said the coroner, with a sigh of satisfaction. 'Call Mary Newton. please.'

III.

"You may imagine," continued the man in the corner, after a slight pause, "with what palpitating interest we all watched the pathetic little figure, clad in deep black, who now stepped forward to give evidence.

"It was difficult to imagine that Mary Newton could ever have been pretty; trouble had obviously wrought havoc with her good looks. She was now a wizened little thing, with dark rings under her eyes, and a pale, anaemic complexion. She stood perfectly listlessly before the coroner, waiting to be questioned, but otherwise not seeming to take the slightest interest in the proceedings. In an even, toneless voice she told her name, age, and status, then waited for further questions.

"'Your father went out a little before ten o'clock on Tuesday night last, did he not?' asked the coroner very kindly.

"'Yes, sir, he did,' replied Mary quietly.

"'You had brought him a message from a gentleman whom you had met in the lane, and who wished to speak with your father?'

"'No, sir,' replied Mary, in the same even and toneless voice; 'I brought no message to father, and he went out on his own.'

"'But the gentleman you met in the lane?' insisted the coroner with some impatience.

"'I didn't meet any one in the lane, sir. I never went out of the house that Tuesday night, it rained so.'

"'But the last witness, Samuel Holder, heard you talking in the lane at nine o'clock.'

"'Samuel Holder was mistaken,' she replied imperturbably; 'I wasn't out of the house the whole of that night.'

"It would be useless for me," continued the man in the corner, "to attempt to convey to you the intense feeling of excitement which pervaded that crowded court, as that wizened little figure stood there for over half an hour, quietly and obstinately parrying the most rigid cross- examination.

"That she was lying—lying to shield the very man who perhaps had murdered her father—no one doubted for a single instant. Yet there she stood, sullen, apathetic, and defiant, flatly denying Samuel Holder's story from end to end, strictly adhering and swearing to her first statement, that her father went out 'on his own,' that she did not know where he was going to, and that she herself had never left the house that fatal Tuesday night.

"It did not seem to occur to her that by these statements she was hopelessly incriminating Samuel Holder, whom she was thus openly accusing of deliberate lies; on the contrary, many noticed a distinct touch of bitter animosity in the young girl against her former sweetheart, which was singularly emphasised when the coroner asked her whether she approved of the idea of a breach of promise action being brought against Mr. Ledbury.

"'No,' she said; 'all that talk about damages and breach of promise was between father and Sam Holder, because Sam had told father that he wouldn't mind marrying me if I had £5,000 of my own.'

"It would be impossible to render the tone of hatred and contempt with which the young girl uttered these words. One seemed to live through the whole tragedy of the past few months—the girl, pestered by the greed of her father, yet refusing obstinately to aid in causing a scandal, perhaps disgrace, to the man whom she had once loved and trusted.

"As nothing more could be got out of her, and as circumstances now seemed to demand it, the coroner adjourned the inquest. The police, as you may well imagine, wanted to make certain enquiries. Mind you, Mary Newton flatly refused to mention Mr. Ledbury's name; she was questioned and cross-questioned, yet her answer uniformly was:

"'I don't know what you're talking about. The person I was going to marry four years ago has gone out of my life—I have never seen him since. I saw no one on that Tuesday night.'

"Against that, when she was asked to swear that it was *not* Mr.—now Captain—Ledbury who had promised her marriage she flatly refused to do so.

"Of course, there was not a soul there who had not made up his or her mind that Captain Ledbury had met Mary Newton in the lane, and had heard from her that all his love-letters to her were now in her father's hands, and that the old man meant to use these in order to extort money from him.

"Fearing the exposure and disgrace of so sensational a breach of promise action, and not having the money with which to meet Mat Newton's preposterous demands, he probably lost control over himself, and in a moment of impulse and mad rage had silenced the old man for ever.

"I assure you that at the adjourned inquest everybody expected to see Captain Ledbury in the custody of two constables. The police in the interim had been extremely reticent, and no fresh details of the extraordinary case had found its way into the papers, but fresh details of a sensational character were fully expected, and I can assure you the public were not disappointed.

"It is no use my telling you all the proceedings of that second most memorable day; I will try and confine myself to the most important points of this interesting mystery.

"I must tell you that the story told by the landlord of the Fernhead Arms was fully corroborated by several witnesses, all of whom testified to the fact that the old man came back from his visit to Fernhead Towers in a terrible fury, swearing to bring disgrace upon the scoundrel who had ruined his daughter.

"What occurred during that visit was explained by Edward Sanders, the butler at The Towers. According to the testimony of this witness, there was a large house-party staying with Sir John Fernhead to celebrate the engagement of his daughter; the party naturally included Captain Mervin Ledbury, his brother, Lord Walterton, with the latter's newly-married young wife, also many neighbours and friends.

"At about six o'clock on Monday evening, it appears, a disreputable-looking old man, who Edward Sanders did not know, but who gave the name of Newton, rang at the front door bell of The Towers and demanded to see Mr. Ledbury. Sanders naturally refused to admit him, but the old man was so persistent, and used such strange language, that the butler, after much hesitation, decided to apprise Captain Ledbury of his extraordinary visitor.

"Captain Ledbury, on hearing that Old Man Newton wished to speak to him, much to Sanders' astonishment, came downstairs and elected to interview his extraordinary visitor in the dining-room, which was then deserted. Sanders showed the old man in, and waited in the hall. Very soon, however, he heard loud and angry voices, and the next moment Captain Ledbury threw open the dining-room door, and said:

"'This man is mad or drunk; show him out, Sanders.'

"And without another word the Captain walked upstairs, leaving Sanders the pleasant task of 'showing the old man out.' That this was done very speedily and pretty roughly we may infer from Old Man Newton's subsequent fury, and the threats he uttered even while he was being 'shown out.'

"Now you see, do you not?" continued the man in the corner, "that this evidence seemed to add another link to the chain which was incriminating young Mr. Ledbury in this terrible charge of murdering Old Man Newton.

"The young man himself was now with his regiment stationed at York. It appears that the house-party at Fernhead Towers was breaking up on the very day of Old Man Newton's strange visit thither. Lord and Lady Walterton left for town on the Tuesday morning, and Captain Ledbury went up to York on that very same fatal night.

"You must know that the small local station of Fernhead is quite close to The Towers. Captain Ledbury took the late local train there for Ayrsham Junction after dinner that night, arriving at the latter place at 9.15, with the intention of picking up the Midland express to the north at 10.15 P.M. later on.

"The police had ascertained that Captain Ledbury had got out of the local train at Ayrsham Junction at 9.15, and aimlessly strolled out of the station. Against that, it was definitely proved by several witnesses that the young man did catch the Midland express at 10.15 P.M., and travelled up north by it.

"Now, there was the hitch, do you see?" added the funny creature excitedly. "Samuel Holder overheard a conversation in the fatal lane between Mary Newton and the stranger, whom everybody by now believed to be Captain Ledbury. Good! That was between 9 P.M. and 10 P.M., and, as it happened, the young man does seem to have unaccountably strolled about in the neighbourhood whilst waiting for his train; but remember that when Sam Holder left the stranger waiting in the lane, and went back towards Ayrsham in order to try and find Old Man Newton, he distinctly heard Ayrsham church clock striking ten.

"Now, the lane where the murder occurred is two and a half miles from Ayrsham Junction station, therefore it could not have been Captain Ledbury who was there lying in wait for the old man, as he could not possibly have had his interview with old Mat, quarrelled with him and murdered him, and then caught his train two and a half miles further on, all in the space of fifteen minutes.

"Thus, even before the final verdict of 'wilful murder against some person or persons unknown,' the case against Captain Mervin Ledbury had completely fallen to the ground. He must also have succeeded in convincing Sir John Fernhead of his innocence, as I see by the papers that Miss Fernhead has since become Mrs. Ledbury.

"But the result has been that the Ayrsham tragedy has remained an impenetrable mystery.

"'Who killed Old Man Newton? and why?' is a question which many people, including our clever criminal investigation department, have asked themselves many a time.

"It was not a case of vulgar assault and robbery, as the old man was not worth robbing, and the few coppers he possessed were found intact in his waistcoat pocket.

"Many people assert that Samuel Holder quarrelled with the old man and murdered him, but there are three reasons why that theory is bound to fall to the ground. Firstly, the total absence of any motive. Samuel Holder could have no possible object in killing the old man, but still, we'll waive that; people do quarrel—especially if they are confederates, as these two undoubtedly were—and quarrels do sometimes end fatally. Secondly, the weapon which caused the old man's death—a heavily-leaded cane of foreign make, with solid silver ferrule.

"Now, I ask you, where in the world could a village carpenter pick up an instrument of that sort? Moreover no one ever saw such a thing in Sam Holder's hands or in his house. When he walked to the Fernhead Arms in order to try and find the old man, he had nothing of the sort in his hand, and in spite of the most strenuous efforts on the part of the police, the history of that cane was never traced.

"Then, there is a third reason why obviously Sam Holder was not guilty of the murder, though that reason is a moral one; I am referring to Mary Newton's attitude at the inquest. She lied, of that there could not be a shadow of doubt; she was determined to shield her former lover, and incriminated Sam Holder only because she wished to save another man.

"Obviously, old Newton went out on that dark, wet night in order to meet some one in the lane; that some one could not have been Sam Holder, whom he met anywhere and everywhere, and every day in his own house.

"There! you see that Sam Holder was obviously innocent, that Captain Ledbury could not have committed the murder, that surely Mary Newton did not kill her own father, and that in such a case, common sense should have come to the rescue, and not have left this case, what it now is, a tragic and impenetrable mystery."

IV.

"But," I said at last, for indeed I was deeply mystified, "what does common sense argue?—the case seems to me absolutely hopeless."

He surveyed his beloved bit of string for a moment, and his mild blue eyes blinked at me over his hone-rimmed spectacles.

"Common sense," he said at last, with his most apologetic manner, "tells me that Ayrsham village is a remote little place, where a daily paper is unknown, and where no one reads the fashionable intelligence or knows anything about birthday honours."

"What *do* you mean?" I gasped in amazement.

"Simply this, that no one at Ayrsham village, certainly not Mary Newton herself, had realised that one of the Mr. Ledburys, whom all had known at 'The Limes' four years ago, had since become Lord Walterton.

"Lord Walterton!" I ejaculated, wholly incredulously.

"Why, yes!" he replied quietly. "Do you mean to say you never thought of that? that it never occurred to you that Mary Newton may have admitted to her father that Mr. Ledbury had been the man who had so wickedly wronged her, but that she, in her remote little village, had also no idea that the Mr. Ledbury she meant was recently made, and is now styled, Lord Walterton?

"Old Man Newton, who knew of the gossip which had coupled his daughter's name, years ago, with the younger Mr. Ledbury, naturally took it for granted that she was referring to him. Moreover, we may take it from the girl's subsequent attitude that she did all she could to shield the man whom she had once loved; women, you know, have that sort of little way with them.

"Old Newton, fully convinced that young Ledbury was the man he wanted, went up to The Towers and had the stormy interview, which no doubt greatly puzzled the young Hussar. He undoubtedly spoke of it to his brother, Lord Walterton, who, newly married and of high social position, would necessarily dread a scandal as much as anybody.

"Lord Walterton went up to town with his young wife the following morning. Ayrsham is only forty minutes from London. He came down in the evening, met Mary in the lane, asked to see her father, and killed him in a moment of passion, when he found that the old man's demands were preposterously unreasonable. Moreover, Englishmen in all grades of society have an innate horror of being bullied or blackmailed; the murder probably was not premeditated, but the outcome of rage at being browbeaten by the old man.

"You see, the police did not use their common sense over so simple a matter. They naturally made no enquiries as to Lord

Walterton's movements, who seemingly had absolutely nothing to do with the case. If they had, I feel convinced that they would have found that his lordship would have had some difficulty in satisfying everybody as to his whereabouts on that particular Tuesday night.

"Think of it, it is so simple—the only possible solution of that strange and unaccountable mystery."

11

The Affair at The Novelty Theatre

I.

"Talking of mysteries," said the man in the corner, rather irrelevantly, for he had not opened his mouth since he sat down and ordered his lunch, "talking of mysteries, it is always a puzzle to me how few thefts are committed in the dressing-rooms of fashionable actresses during a performance."

"There have been one or two," I suggested, but nothing of any value was stolen."

"Yet you remember that affair at the Novelty Theatre a year or two ago, don't you?" he added. "It created a great deal of sensation at the time. You see, Miss Phyllis Morgan was, and still is, a very fashionable and popular actress, and her pearls are quite amongst the wonders of the world. She herself valued them at £10,000, and several experts who remember the pearls quite concur with that valuation.

"During the period of her short tenancy of the Novelty Theatre last season, she entrusted those beautiful pearls to Mr. Kidd, the well-known Bond Street jeweller, to be re-strung. There were seven rows of perfectly matched pearls, held together by a small diamond clasp of 'art-nouveau' design.

"Kidd and Co. are, as you know, a very eminent and old-established firm of jewellers. Mr. Thomas Kidd, its present sole representative, was some time president of the London Chamber of Commerce and a man whose integrity has always been held to be above suspicion. His clerks, salesmen, and book-keeper had all been in his employ for years, and most of the work was executed on the premises.

"In the case of Miss Phyllis Morgan's valuable pearls, they were re-strung and re-set in the back shop by Mr. Kidd's most valued and most trusted workman, a man named James Rumford, who is justly considered to be one of the cleverest craftsmen here in England.

"When the pearls were ready, Mr. Kidd himself took them down to the theatre, and delivered them into Miss Morgan's own hands.

"It appears that the worthy jeweller was extremely fond of the theatre but, like so many persons in affluent circumstances, he was also very fond of getting a free seat when he could.

"All along he had made up his mind to take the pearls down to the Novelty Theatre one night, and to see Miss Morgan for a moment before the performance; she would then, he hoped, place a stall at his disposal.

"His previsions were correct. Miss Morgan received the pearls, and Mr. Kidd was on that celebrated night accommodated with a seat in the stalls.

"I don't know if you remember all the circumstances connected with that case, but, to make my point clear, I must remind you of one or two of the most salient details.

"In the drama in which Miss Phyllis Morgan was acting at the time, there is a brilliant masked ball scene which is the crux of the whole play; it occurs in the second act, and Miss Phyllis Morgan, as the hapless heroine dressed in the shabbiest of clothes, appears in the midst of a gay and giddy throng; she apostrophises all and sundry there, including the villain, and has a magnificent scene which always brings down the house, and nightly adds to her histrionic laurels.

"For this scene a large number of supers are engaged, and in order to further swell the crowd, practically all the available stage hands have to 'walk on' dressed in various coloured dominoes, and all wearing masks.

"You have, of course, heard the name of Mr. Howard Dennis in connection with this extraordinary mystery. He is what is usually called 'a young man about town,' and was one of Miss Phyllis Morgan's most favoured admirers. As a matter of fact, he was generally understood to be the popular actress's *fiancée*, and as such, had of course the *entrée* of the Novelty Theatre.

"Like many another idle young man about town, Mr. Howard Dennis was stage-mad, and one of his greatest delights was to don nightly a mask and a blue domino, and to 'walk on' in the second act, not so much in order to gratify his love for the stage, as to watch Miss Phyllis Morgan in her great scene and to be present, close by her, when she received her usual salvo of enthusiastic applause from a delighted public.

"On this eventful night—it was on 20th July last—the second act was in full swing; the supers, the stage hands, and all the principals were on the scene, the back of the stage was practically deserted. The beautiful pearls, fresh from the hands of Mr. Kidd, were in Miss Morgan's dressing-room, as she meant to wear them in the last act.

"Of course, since that memorable affair, many people have talked of the foolhardiness of leaving such valuable jewellery in the sole charge of a young girl—Miss Morgan's dresser—who acted with unpardonable folly and carelessness, but you must remember that this part of the theatre is only accessible through the stage door, where sits enthroned that uncorruptible dragon, the stage door-keeper.

"No one can get at it from the front, and the dressing-rooms for the supers and lesser members of the company are on the opposite side of the stage to that reserved for Miss Morgan and one or two of the principals.

"It was just a quarter to ten, and the curtain was about to be rung down, when George Finch, the stage door-keeper, rushed excitedly into the wings; he was terribly upset, and was wildly clutching his coat, beneath which he evidently held something concealed.

"In response to the rapidly-whispered queries of the one or two stage hands that stood about, Finch only shook his head excitedly. He seemed scarcely able to control his impatience, during the close of the act, and the subsequent prolonged applause.

"When at last Miss Morgan, flushed with her triumph, came off the stage, Finch made a sudden rush for her.

"'Oh, Madam!' he gasped excitedly, 'it might have been such an awful misfortune! The rascal! I nearly got him, though! but he escaped— fortunately it is safe—I have got it—!

"It was some time before Miss Morgan understood what in the world the otherwise sober stage door-keeper was driving at. Every one who heard him certainly thought that he had been drinking. But the next moment from under his coat he pulled out, with another ejaculation of excitement, the magnificent pearl necklace which Miss Morgan had thought safely put away in her dressing-room.

"'What in the world does all this mean?' asked Mr. Howard Dennis, who, as usual, was escorting his *fiancée*. 'Finch, what are you doing with Madam's necklace?'

"Miss Phyllis Morgan herself was too bewildered to question Finch; she gazed at him, then at her necklace, in speechless astonishment.

"'Well, you see, Madam, it was this way,' Finch managed to explain at last, as with awestruck reverence he finally deposited the precious necklace in the actress's hands. 'As you know, Madam, it is a very hot night. I had seen every one into the theatre and counted in the supers; there was nothing much for me to do, and I got rather tired and very thirsty. I seed a man loafing close to the door, and I ask him to fetch me a pint of beer from round the corner, and I give him some coppers; I had noticed him loafing round before, and it was so hot I didn't think I was doin' no harm.'

"'No, no,' said Miss Morgan impatiently. 'Well!'

"'Well,' continued Finch, 'the man, he brought me the beer, and I had some of it—and—and—afterwards, I don't quite know how it happened—it was the heat, perhaps—but—I was sitting in my box, and I suppose I must have dropped asleep. I just remember hearing the ring-up for the second act, and the call-boy calling you, Madam, then there's a sort of a blank in my mind. All of a sudden I seemed to wake with the feeling that there was something wrong somehow. In a moment I jumped up, and I tell you I was wide awake then, and I saw a man sneaking down the passage, past my box, towards the door. I challenged him, and he tried to dart past me, but I was too quick for him, and got him by the tails of his coat, for I saw at once that he was carrying something, and I had recognised the loafer who brought me the beer. I shouted for help, but there's never anybody about in this back street, and the loafer, he struggled like old Harry, and sure enough he managed to get free from me and away before I could stop him, but in his fright the rascal dropped his booty, for which Heaven be praised! and it was your pearls, Madam. Oh, my! but I did have a tussle,' concluded the worthy door-keeper, mopping his forehead, 'and I do hope, Madam, the scoundrel didn't take nothing else.'

"That was the story," continued the man in the corner, "which George Finch had to tell, and which he subsequently repeated without the slightest deviation. Miss Phyllis Morgan, with the light-heartedness peculiar to ladies of her profession, took the matter very quietly; all she said at the time was that she had nothing else of value in her dressing-room, but that Miss Knight—the dresser—deserved a scolding for leaving the room unprotected.

"'All's well that ends well,' she said gaily, as she finally went into her dressing-room, carrying the pearls in her hand.

"It appears that the moment she opened the door, she found Miss Knight sitting in the room, in a deluge of tears. The girl had overheard George Finch telling his story, and was terribly upset at her own carelessness.

"In answer to Miss Morgan's questions, she admitted that she had gone into the wings, and lingered there to watch the great actress's beautiful performance. She thought no one could possibly get to the dressing-room, as nearly all hands were on the stage at the time, and of course George Finch was guarding the door.

"However, as there really had been no harm done, beyond a wholesome fright to everybody concerned, Miss Morgan readily forgave the girl and proceeded with her change of attire for the next act. Incidentally she noticed a bunch of roses, which were placed on her dressing-table, and asked Knight who had put them there.

"'Mr. Dennis brought them,' replied the girl.

"Miss Morgan looked pleased, blushed, and dismissing the whole matter from her mind, she proceeded with her toilette for the next act, in which, the hapless heroine having come into her own again, she was able to wear her beautiful pearls around her neck.

"George Finch, however, took some time to recover himself; his indignation was only equalled by his volubility. When his excitement had somewhat subsided, he took the precaution of saving the few drops of beer which had remained at the bottom of the mug, brought to him by the loafer. This was subsequently shown to a chemist in the neighbourhood, who, without a moment's hesitation, pronounced the beer to contain an appreciable quantity of chloral."

II.

"The whole matter, as you may imagine, did not affect Miss Morgan's spirits that night," continued the man in the corner, after a slight pause.

"'All's well that ends well,' she had said gaily, since almost by a miracle, her pearls were once more safely round her neck.

"But the next day brought the rude awakening. Something had indeed happened which made the affair at the Novelty Theatre, what it has ever since remained, a curious and unexplainable mystery.

"The following morning Miss Phyllis Morgan decided that it was foolhardy to leave valuable property about in her dressing-room, when, for stage purposes, imitation jewellery did just as well. She therefore determined to place her pearls in the bank until the termination of her London season.

"The moment, however, that, in broad daylight, she once more handled the necklace, she instinctively felt that there was something wrong with it. She examined it eagerly and closely, and, hardly daring to face her sudden terrible suspicions, she rushed round to the nearest jeweller, and begged him to examine the pearls.

"The examination did not take many moments: the jeweller at once pronounced the pearls to be false. There could be no doubt about it; the necklace was a perfect imitation of the original, even the clasp was an exact copy. Half-hysterical with rage and anxiety, Miss Morgan at once drove to Bond Street, and asked to see Mr. Kidd.

"Well, you may easily imagine the stormy interview that took place. Miss Phyllis Morgan, in no measured language, boldly accused Mr. Thomas Kidd, late president of the London Chamber of Commerce, of having substituted false pearls for her own priceless ones.

"The worthy jeweller, at first completely taken by surprise, examined the necklace, and was horrified to see that Miss Morgan's statements were, alas too true. Mr. Kidd was indeed in a terribly awkward position.

"The evening before, after business hours, he had taken the necklace home with him. Before starting for the theatre, he had examined it to see that it was quite in order. He had then, with his own hands, and in the presence of his wife, placed it in its case, and driven straight to the Novelty, where he finally gave it over to Miss Morgan herself.

"To all this he swore most positively; moreover, all his *employés* and workmen could swear that they had last seen the necklace just after closing time at the shop, when Mr. Kidd walked off towards Piccadilly, with the precious article in the inner pocket of his coat.

"One point certainly was curious, and undoubtedly helped to deepen the mystery which to this day clings to the affair at the Novelty Theatre.

"When Mr. Kidd handed the packet containing the necklace to Miss Morgan, she was too busy to open it at once. She only spoke to Mr. Kidd through her dressing-room door, and never opened the packet till nearly an hour later, after she was dressed ready for the second act; the packet at that time had been untouched, and was wrapped up just as she had had it from Mr. Kidd's own hands. She undid the packet, and handled the pearls; certainly, by the artificial light she could see nothing wrong with the necklace.

"Poor Mr. Kidd was nearly distracted with the horror of his position. Thirty years of an honest reputation suddenly tarnished with this awful suspicion—for he realised at once that Miss Morgan refused to believe his statements; in fact, she openly said that she would—unless immediate compensation was made to her—place the matter at once in the hands of the police.

"From the stormy interview in Bond Street, the irate actress drove at once to Scotland Yard; but the old-established firm of Kidd and Co. was not destined to remain under any cloud that threatened its integrity.

"Mr. Kidd at once called upon his solicitor, with the result that an offer was made to. Miss Morgan, whereby the jeweller would deposit the full value of the original necklace, *i.e.* £10,000, in the hands of Messrs. Bentley and Co., bankers, that sum to be held by them for a whole year, at the end of which time, if the perpetrator of the fraud had not been discovered, the money was to be handed over to Miss Morgan in its entirety.

"Nothing could have been more fair, more equitable, or more just, but at the same time nothing could have been more mysterious.

"As Mr. Kidd swore that he had placed the real pearls in Miss Morgan's hands, and was ready to back his oath by the sum of £10,000, no more suspicion could possibly attach to him. When the announcement of his generous offer appeared in the papers, the entire public approved and exonerated him, and then turned to wonder who the perpetrator of the daring fraud had been.

"How came a valueless necklace in exact imitation of the original one to be in Miss Morgan's dressing-room? Where were the real pearls? Clearly the loafer who had drugged the stage door-keeper, and sneaked into the theatre to steal a necklace, was not aware that he was risking several years' hard labour for the sake of a worthless trifle. He had been one of the many dupes of this extraordinary adventure.

"Macpherson, one of the most able men on the detective staff, had, indeed, his work cut out. The police were extremely reticent, but, in spite of this, one or two facts gradually found their way into the papers, and aroused public interest and curiosity to its highest pitch.

"What had transpired was this:

"Clara Knight, the dresser, had been very rigorously cross-questioned, and, from her many statements, the following seemed quite positive.

"After the curtain had rung up for the second act, and Miss Morgan had left her dressing-room, Knight had waited about for some time, and had even, it appears, handled and admired the necklace. Then, unfortunately, she was seized with the burning desire of seeing the famous scene from the wings. She thought that the place was quite safe, and that George Finch was as usual at his post.

"'I was going along the short passage that leads to the wings,' she exclaimed to the detectives, 'when I became aware of some one moving some distance behind me. I turned and saw a blue domino about to enter Miss Morgan's dressing-room.

"'I thought nothing of that,' continued the girl, 'as we all know that Mr. Dennis is engaged to Miss Morgan. He is very fond of "walking on" in the ball-room scene, and he always wears a blue domino when he does; so I was not at all alarmed. He had his mask on as usual, and he was carrying a bunch of roses. When he saw me at the other end of the passage, he waved his hand to me and pointed to the flowers. I nodded to him, and then he went into the room.'

"These statements, as you may imagine, created a great deal of sensation; so much so, in fact, that Mr. Kidd, with his £10,000 and his reputation in mind, moved heaven and earth to bring about the prosecution of Mr. Dennis for theft and fraud.

"The papers were full of it, for Mr. Howard Dennis was well known in fashionable London society. His answer to these curious statements was looked forward to eagerly; when it came it satisfied no one and puzzled everybody.

"'Miss Knight was mistaken,' he said most emphatically, 'I did not bring any roses for Miss Morgan that night. It was not I that she saw in a blue domino by the door, as I was on the stage before the curtain was rung up for the second act, and never left it until the close.'

"This part of Howard Dennis' statement was a little difficult to substantiate. No one on the stage could swear positively whether he was 'on' early in the act or not, although, mind you, Macpherson had ascertained that in the whole crowd of supers on the stage, he was the only one who wore a blue domino.

"Mr. Kidd was very active in the matter, but Miss Morgan flatly refused to believe in her *fiancée's* guilt. The worthy jeweller maintained that Mr. Howard Dennis was the only person who knew the celebrated pearls and their quaint clasp well enough to have a facsimile made of them, and that when Miss Knight saw him enter the dressing-room, he actually substituted the false necklace for the real one; while the loafer who drugged George Finch's beer was—as every one supposed—only a dupe.

"Things had reached a very acute and painful stage, when one more detail found its way into the papers, which, whilst entirely clearing Mr. Howard Dennis' character, has helped to make the whole affair a hopeless mystery.

"Whilst questioning George Finch, Macpherson had ascertained that the stage door-keeper had seen Mr. Dennis enter the theatre some time before the beginning of the celebrated second act. He stopped to speak to George Finch for a moment or two, and the latter could swear positively that Mr. Dennis was not carrying any roses then.

"On the other hand a flower-girl, who was selling roses in the neighbourhood of the Novelty Theatre late that memorable night, remembers selling some roses to a shabbily-dressed man, who looked like a labourer out of work. When Mr. Dennis was pointed out to her she swore positively that it was not he.

"'The man looked like a labourer,' she explained. 'I took particular note of him, as I remember thinking that he didn't look much as if he could afford to buy roses.'

"Now you see," concluded the man in the corner excitedly, "where the hitch lies. There is absolutely no doubt, judging from the evidence of George Finch and of the flower-girl, that the loafer had provided himself with the roses, and had somehow or other managed to get hold of a blue domino, for the purpose of committing the theft. His giving drugged beer to Finch, moreover, proved his guilt beyond a doubt.

"But here the mystery becomes hopeless," he added with a chuckle, "for the loafer dropped the booty which he had stolen—that booty was the false necklace, and it has remained an impenetrable mystery to this day as to who made the substitution and when.

"A whole year has elapsed since then, but the real necklace has never been traced or found; so Mr. Kidd has paid, with absolute quixotic chivalry, the sum of £10,000 to Miss Morgan, and thus he has completely cleared the firm of Kidd and Co. of any suspicion as to its integrity."

III.

"But then, what in the world is the explanation of it all?" I asked bewildered, as the funny creature paused in his narrative and seemed absorbed in the contemplation of a beautiful knot he had just completed in his bit of string.

"The explanation is so simple," he replied, "for it is obvious, is it not? that only four people could possibly have committed the fraud."

"Who are they?" I asked.

"Well," he said, whilst his bony fingers began to fidget with that eternal piece of string, "there is, of course, old Mr. Kidd; but as the worthy jeweller has paid £10,000 to prove that he did not steal the real necklace and substitute a false one in its stead, we must assume that he was guiltless. Then, secondly, there is Mr. Howard Dennis."

"Well, yes," I said, "what about him?"

"There were several points in his favour," he rejoined, marking each point with a fresh and most complicated knot; "it was not he who bought the roses, therefore it was not he who, clad in a blue domino, entered Miss Morgan's dressing-room directly after Knight left it.

"And mark the force of this point," he added excitedly.

"Just before the curtain rang up for the second act, Miss Morgan had been in her room, and had then undone the packet, which, in her own words, was just as she had received it from Mr. Kidd's hands.

"After that Miss Knight remained in charge, and a mere ten seconds after she left the room she saw the blue domino carrying the roses at the door.

"The flower-girl's story and that of George Finch have proved that the blue domino could not have been Mr. Dennis, but it was the loafer who eventually stole the false necklace.

"If you bear all this in mind you will realise that there was no time in those ten seconds for Mr. Dennis to have made the substitution before the theft was committed. It stands to reason that he could not have done it afterwards.

"Then, again, many people suspected Miss Knight, the dresser; but this supposition we may easily dismiss. An uneducated, stupid girl, not three-and-twenty, could not possibly have planned so clever a substitution. An imitation necklace of that particular calibre and made to order would cost far more money than a poor theatrical dresser could ever afford; let alone the risks of ordering such an ornament to be made.

"No," said the funny creature, with comic emphasis, "there is but one theory possible, which is my own."

"And that is?" I asked eagerly.

"The workman, Rumford, of course," he responded triumphantly. "Why! it jumps to the eyes, as our French friends would tell us. Who other than he, could have the opportunity of making an exact copy of the necklace which had been entrusted to his firm?

"Being in the trade he could easily obtain the false stones without exciting any undue suspicion; being a skilled craftsman, he could easily make the clasp, and string the pearls in exact imitation of the original; he could do this secretly in his own home and without the slightest risk.

"Then the plan, though extremely simple, was very cleverly thought out. Disguised as the loafer—"

"The loafer!" I exclaimed.

"Why, yes! the loafer," he replied quietly, "disguised as the loafer, he hung round the stage door of the Novelty after business hours, until he had collected the bits of gossip and information he wanted; thus he learnt that Mr. Howard Dennis was Miss Morgan's accredited *fiancée*; that he, like everybody else who was available, 'walked on' in the second act; and that during that time the back of the stage was practically deserted.

"No doubt he knew all along that Mr. Kidd meant to take the pearls down to the theatre himself that night, and it was quite easy to ascertain that Miss Morgan—as the hapless heroine—wore no jewellery in the second act, and that Mr. Howard Dennis invariably wore a blue domino.

"Some people might incline to the belief that Miss Knight was a paid accomplice, that she left the dressing-room unprotected on purpose, and that her story of the blue domino and the roses was prearranged between herself and Rumford, but that is not my opinion.

"I think that the scoundrel was far too clever to need any accomplice, and too shrewd to put himself thereby at the mercy of a girl like Knight.

"Rumford, I find, is a married man: this to me explains the blue domino, which the police were never able to trace to any business place, where it might have been bought or hired. Like the necklace itself, it was 'home-made.'

"Having got his properties and his plans ready, Rumford then set to work. You must remember that a stage door-keeper is never above accepting a glass of beer from a friendly acquaintance; and, no doubt, if George Finch had not asked the loafer to bring him a glass, the latter would have offered him one. To drug the beer was simple enough; then Rumford went to buy the roses, and, I should say, met his wife somewhere round the corner, who handed him the blue domino and the mask; all this was done in order to completely puzzle the police subsequently, and also in order to throw suspicion, if possible, upon young Dennis.

"As soon as the drug took effect upon George Finch, Rumford slipped into the theatre. To slip a mask and domino on and off is, as you know, a matter of a few seconds. Probably his intention had been—if he found Knight in the room—to knock her down if she attempted to raise an alarm; but here fortune favoured him. Knight saw him from a distance, and mistook him easily for Mr. Dennis.

"After the theft of the real necklace, Rumford sneaked out of the theatre. And here you see how clever was the scoundrel's plan: if he had merely substituted one necklace for another there would have been no doubt whatever that the loafer—whoever he was—was the culprit—the drugged beer would have been quite sufficient proof for that. The hue and cry would have been after the loafer, and, who knows? there might have been someone or something which might have identified that loafer with himself.

"He must have bought the shabby clothes somewhere; he certainly bought the roses from a flower-girl; anyhow, there were a hundred and one little risks and contingencies which might have brought the theft home to him.

"But mark what happens: he steals the real necklace, and keeps the false one in his hand, intending to drop it sooner or later, and thus sent the police entirely on the wrong scent. As the loafer, he was supposed to have stolen the false necklace, then dropped it whilst struggling with George Finch. The result is that no one has troubled about the loafer; no one thought that he had anything to do with the substitution, which was the main point at issue, and no very great effort has ever been made to find that mysterious loafer.

"It never occurred to any one that the fraud and the theft were committed by one and the same person, and that that person could be none other than James Rumford."

12
The Tragedy of Barnsdale Manor

I.

"We have heard so much about the evils of Bridge," said the man in the corner that afternoon, "but I doubt whether that fashionable game has ever been responsible for a more terrible tragedy than the one at Barnsdale Manor."

"You think, then," I asked, for I saw he was waiting to be drawn out, "you think that the high play at Bridge did have something to do with that awful murder?"

"Most people think that much, I fancy," he replied, "although no one has arrived any nearer to the solution of the mystery which surrounds the tragic death of Mme. Quesnard at Barnsdale Manor on the 23rd September last.

"On that fateful occasion, you must remember that the house party at the Manor included a number of sporting and fashionable friends of Lord and Lady Barnsdale, among whom Sir Gilbert Culworth was the only one whose name was actually mentioned during the hearing of this extraordinary case.

"It seems to have been a very gay house party indeed. In the day-time Lord Barnsdale took some of his guests to shoot and fish, whilst a few devotees remained at home in order to indulge their passion for the modern craze of Bridge. It was generally understood that Lord Barnsdale did not altogether approve of quite so much gambling. He was not by any means well off; and although he was very much in love with his beautiful wife, he could ill afford to pay her losses at cards.

"This was the reason, no doubt, that Bridge at Barnsdale Manor was only indulged in whilst the host himself was out shooting or fishing; in the evenings there was music or billiards, but never any cards.

"One of the most interesting personalities in the Barnsdale *ménage* was undoubtedly Madame Nathalie Quesnard, a sister of Lord Barnsdale's mother, who, if you remember, was a Mademoiselle de la Trémouille. This Mme. Quesnard was extremely wealthy, the widow of a French West Indian planter, who had made millions in Martinique.

"She was very fond of her nephew, to whom, as she had no children or other relatives of her own, she intended to leave the bulk of her vast fortune. Pending her death, which was not likely to occur for some time, as she was not more than fifty, she took up her abode at Barnsdale Manor, together with her companion and amanuensis, a poor girl named Alice Holt.

"Mme. Quesnard was seemingly an amiable old lady, the only unpleasant trait in her character being her intense dislike of her nephew's beautiful and fashionable young wife. The old Frenchwoman, who, with all her wealth, had the unbounded and innate thriftiness peculiar to her nation, looked with perfect horror on Lady Barnsdale's extravagances, and above all on her fondness for gambling; and subsequently several of the servants at the Manor testified to the amount of mischief the old lady strove to make between her nephew and his young wife.

"Mme. Quesnard's dislike for Lady Barnsdale seems, moreover, to have been shared by her dependent and companion, the girl Alice Holt. Between them, these two ladies seem to have cordially hated the brilliant and much-admired mistress of Barnsdale Manor.

"Such were the chief inmates of the Manor last September, at the time the tragedy occurred. On that memorable night Alice Holt, who occupied a bedroom immediately above that of Mme. Quesnard, was awakened in the middle of the night by a persistent noise, which undoubtedly came from her mistress's room. The walls and floorings at the old Manor are very thick, and the sound was a very confused one, although the girl was quite sure that she could hear Mme. Quesnard's shrill voice raised as if in anger.

"She tried to listen for a time, and presently she heard a sound as if some piece of furniture had been knocked over, then nothing more. Somehow the sudden silence seemed to have frightened the girl more than the noise had done. Trembling with nervousness she waited for some few minutes, then, unable to bear the suspense any longer, she got out of bed, slipped on her shoes and dressing-gown, and determined to run downstairs to see if anything were amiss.

"To her horror she found on trying her door that it had been locked on the outside. Quite convinced now that something must indeed be very wrong, she started screaming and banging against the door, determined to arouse the household, which she, of course, quickly succeeded in doing.

"The first to emerge from his room was Lord Barnsdale. He at once realised that the shrieks proceeded from Alice Holt's room. He ran upstairs helter-skelter, and as the key had been left in the door, he soon released the unfortunate girl, who by now was quite hysterical with anxiety for her mistress.

"Altogether, I take it, some six or seven minutes must have elapsed from the time when Alice Holt was first alarmed by the sudden silence following the noise in Mme. Quesnard's room until she was released by Lord Barnsdale.

"As quickly and as coherently as she could, she blurted forth all her fears about her mistress. I can imagine how picturesque the old Manor House must have looked then, with everybody, ladies and gentlemen, and servants, crowding into the hall, arrayed in various *néglig*é attire, asking hurried questions, getting in each other's way, and all only dimly to be seen by the light of candles, carried by some of the more sensible ones in this motley crowd.

"However, in the meanwhile, Lord Barnsdale had managed to understand Alice Holt. He ran downstairs again and knocked at his aunt's door; he received no reply—he tried the handle, but the door was locked from the inside.

"Genuinely frightened now, he forced open the door, and then recoiled in horror.

"The window was wide open, and a brilliant moonlight streamed into the room, weirdly illumining Mme. Quesnard's inanimate body, which lay full length upon the ground. Hastily begging the ladies not to follow him, Lord Barnsdale quickly went forward and bent over his aunt's body.

"There was no doubt that she was dead. An ugly wound at the back of her head, some red marks round her throat, all testified to the fact that the poor old lady had been assaulted and murdered. Lord Barnsdale at once sent for the nearest doctor, whilst he and Miss Holt lifted the unfortunate lady back to bed.

"The messenger who had gone for the doctor was at the same time instructed to deliver a note, hastily scribbled by Lord Barnsdale, at the local police station.

"That a hideous crime had been committed, with burglary for its object, no one could be in doubt for a moment. Lord Barnsdale and two or three of his guests had already thrown a glance into the next room, a little boudoir, which Mme. Quesnard used as a sitting-room. There the heavy oak bureau bore silent testimony to the motive of this dastardly outrage. Mme. Quesnard, with the unfortunate and foolhardy habit peculiar to all French people, kept a very large quantity of loose and ready money by her. That habit, mind you, is the chief reason why burglary is so rife and so profitable all over France.

"In this case the old lady's national characteristic was evidently the chief cause of her tragic fate; the drawer of the bureau had been forced open, and no one could doubt for a moment that a large sum of money had been abstracted from it.

"The burglar had then obviously made good his escape through the window, which he could do quite easily, as Mme. Quesnard's apartments were on the ground floor. She suffered from shortness of breath, it appears, and had a horror of stairs; she was, moreover, not the least bit nervous, and her windows were usually barred and shuttered.

"One very curious fact, however, at once struck all those present, even before the arrival of the detectives, and that was, that the old lady was partially dressed when she was found lying on the ground. She had slipped on an elaborate dressing-gown, had smoothed her hair, and put on her slippers. In fact, it was evident that she had in some measure prepared herself for the reception of the burglar.

"Throughout these hasty and amateurish observations conducted by Lord Barnsdale and two of his male guests, Alice Holt had remained seated beside her late employer's bedside sobbing bitterly. In spite of Lord Barnsdale's entreaties she refused to move; and wildly waved aside any attempt at consolation offered to her by one or two of the older female servants who were present.

"It was only when everybody at last made up their minds to return to their rooms, that some one mentioned Lady Barnsdale's name. She had been taken ill and faint the evening before, and had not been well all night. Jane Barlow, her maid, expressed the hope that her ladyship was none the worse for this awful commotion, and must be wondering what it all meant.

"At this, suddenly, Alice Holt jumped up, like a madwoman.

"'What it all means?' she shrieked, whilst every one looked at her in speechless horror. 'It means that that woman has murdered my mistress, and robbed her. I know it—I know it—I know it!'

"And once more sinking beside the bed, she covered her dead mistress's hand with kisses, and sobbed and wailed as if her heart would break."

II.

"You may well imagine the awful commotion the girl's wild outburst had created in the old Manor House. Lady Barnsdale had been taken ill the previous evening, and, of course, no one had breathed a word of it to her, but equally, of course, it was freely talked about at Barnsdale Manor, in the neighbourhood, and even so far as in the London clubs.

"Lord and Lady Barnsdale were very well known in London society, and Lord Barnsdale's adoration for his beautiful wife was quite notorious.

"Alice Holt, after her frantic outburst, had not breathed another word. Silent and sullen she went up to her room, packed her things, and left the house, where, of course, it became impossible that she should stay another day. She refused Lord Barnsdale's generous offer of money and help, and only stayed long enough to see the detectives and reply to the questions they thought fit to put to her.

"The whole neighbourhood was in a fever of excitement; many gossips would have it that the evidence against Lady Barnsdale was conclusive, and that a warrant for her arrest had already been applied for.

"What had transpired was this:

"It appears that the day preceding the tragedy, Bridge was, as usual, being played for, I believe, guinea-points. Lord Barnsdale was out shooting all day, and though the guests at the Manor were very loyal to their hostess, and refused to make any positive statements, there seems to be no doubt that Lady Barnsdale lost a very large sum of money to Sir Gilbert Culworth.

"Be that as it may, nothing further could be gleaned by enterprising reporters fresh from town; the police were more than usually reticent, and every one eagerly awaited the opening of the inquest, when sensational developments were expected in this mysterious case.

"It was held on September the 25th, in the servants' hall of Barnsdale Manor, and you may be sure that the large room was crowded to its utmost capacity. Lord Barnsdale was, of course, present, so was Sir Gilbert Culworth, but it was understood that Lady Barnsdale was still suffering from nervous prostration, and was unable to be present.

"When I arrived there, and gradually made my way to the front rank, the doctor who had been originally summoned to the murdered lady's bedside was giving his evidence.

"He gave it as his opinion that the fractured skull from which Mme. Quesnard died was caused through her hitting the back of her head against the corner of the marble-topped washstand, in the immediate proximity of which she lay outstretched, when Lord

Barnsdale first forced open the door. The stains on the marble had confirmed him in that opinion. Mme. Quesnard, he thought, must have fallen, owing to an onslaught made upon her by the burglar; the marks round the old lady's throat testified to this, although these were not the cause of death.

"After this there was a good deal of police evidence with regard to the subsequent movements of the unknown miscreant. He had undoubtedly broken open the drawer of the bureau in the adjoining boudoir, the door of communication between this and Mme. Quesnard's bedroom being always kept open, and it was presumed that he had made a considerable haul both in gold and notes. He had then locked the bedroom door on the inside and made good his escape through the window.

"Immediately beneath this window, the flower-bed, muddy with the recent rain, bore the imprint of having been hastily trampled upon; but all actual footmarks had been carefully obliterated. Beyond this, all round the house the garden-paths are asphalted, and the burglar had evidently taken the precaution to keep to these asphalted paths, or else to cross the garden by the lawns.

"You must understand," continued the man in the corner, after a slight pause, "that throughout all this preliminary evidence, everything went to prove that the crime had been committed by an inmate of the house or at any rate by some one well acquainted with its usages and its *ménage*. Alice Holt, whose room was immediately above that of Mme. Quesnard, and who was, therefore, most likely to hear the noise of the conflict and to run to her mistress's assistance, had been first of all locked up in her room. It had, therefore, become quite evident that the miscreant had commenced operations from inside the house, and had entered Mme. Quesnard's room by the door, and not by the window, as had been at first supposed.

"But," added the funny creature excitedly, "if the old lady had, according to evidence, locked her door that night, it became more and more clear, as the case progressed, that she must of her own accord have admitted the person who subsequently caused her tragic death. This was, of course, confirmed by the fact that she was partially dressed when she was subsequently found dead.

"Strangely enough, with the exception of Alice Holt, no one else had heard any noise during the night. But, as I remarked before, the walls of these old houses are very thick, and no one else slept on the ground floor.

"Another fact which in the early part of the inquest went to prove that the outrage was committed by some one familiar with the house, was that Ben, the watch-dog, had not raised any alarm. His kennel was quite close to Mme. Quesnard's windows, and he had not even barked.

"I doubt if the law would take official cognisance of the dumb testimony of a dog; nevertheless, Ben's evidence was in this case quite worthy of consideration.

"You may imagine how gradually, as these facts were unfolded, excitement grew to fever pitch, and when at last Alice Holt was called, every one literally held their breath, eagerly waiting to hear what was coming.

"She is a tall, handsome-looking girl, with fine eyes and a rich voice. Dressed in deep black she certainly looked an imposing figure as she stood there, repeating the story of how she was awakened in the night by the sound of her mistress' angry voice, of the noise and sudden silence, and also of her terror, when she found that she had been locked up in her room.

"But obviously the girl had more to tell, and was only waiting for the coroner's direct question.

"'Will you tell the jury the reason why you made such an extraordinary and unwarrantable accusation against Lady Barnsdale?' he asked her at last, amid breathless silence in the crowded room.

"Every one instinctively looked across the room to where Lord Barnsdale sat between his friend Sir Gilbert Culworth and his lawyer, Sir Arthur Inglewood, who had evidently come down from London in order to watch the case on his client's behalf. Alice Holt, too, looked across at Lord Barnsdale for a moment. He seemed attentive and interested, but otherwise quite calm and impassive.

"I, who watched the girl, saw a look of pity cross her face as she gazed at him, and I think, when we bear in mind that the distinguished English gentleman and the poor paid companion had known each other years ago, when they were girl and boy together in old Mme. Quesnard's French home, we may make a pretty shrewd guess why Alice Holt hated the beautiful Lady Barnsdale.

"'It was about six o'clock in the afternoon,' she began at last, in the same quiet tone of voice. 'I was sitting sewing in Madame's boudoir, when Lady Barnsdale came into the bedroom. She did not see me, I know, for she began at once talking volubly to Madame about a serious loss she had just sustained at Bridge; several hundred pounds, she said.'

"'Well?' queried the coroner, for the girl had paused, almost as if she regretted what she had already said. She certainly threw an appealing look at Lord Barnsdale, who, however, seemed to take no notice of her.

"'Well,' she continued with sudden resolution, 'Madame was very angry at this; she declared that Lady Barnsdale deserved a severe lesson; her extravagances were a positive scandal. "Not a penny will I give you to pay your gambling debts," said Madame; "and, moreover, I shall make it my business to inform my nephew of your goings-on whilst he is absent."

"'Lady Barnsdale was in a wild state of excitement. She begged and implored Madame to say nothing to Lord Barnsdale about it, and did her very best to try to induce her to help her out of her difficulties, just this once more. But Madame was obdurate. Thereupon Lady Barnsdale turned on her like a fury, called her every opprobrious name under the sun, and finally flounced out of the room, banging the door behind her.

"'Madame was very much upset after this,' continued Alice Holt, 'and I was not a bit astonished when directly after dinner she rang for me, and asked to be put to bed. It was then nine o'clock.

"'That is the last I saw of poor Madame alive.

"'She was very excited then, and told me that she was quite frightened of Lady Barnsdale—a gambler, she said, was as likely as not to become a thief, if opportunity arose. I offered to sleep on the sofa in the next room, for the old lady seemed quite nervous, a thing I have never known her to be. But she was too proud to own to nervousness, and she dismissed me finally, saying that she would lock her door, for once: a thing she scarcely ever did.'

"It was a curious story, to say the least of it, which Alice Holt thus told to an excited public. Cross-examined by the coroner, she never departed from a single point of it, her calm and presence of mind being only equalled throughout this trying ordeal by that of Lord Barnsdale, who sat seemingly unmoved whilst these terrible insinuations were made against his wife.

"But there was more to come. Sir Gilbert Culworth had been called; in the interests of justice, and in accordance with his duty as a citizen, he was forced to stand up and, all unwillingly, to add another tiny link to the chain of evidence that implicated his friend's wife in this most terrible crime.

"Right loyally he tried to shield her in every possible way, but cross-questioned by the coroner, harassed nearly out of his senses, he was forced to admit two facts—namely, that Lady Barnsdale had lost nearly £800 at Bridge the day before the murder, and that she had paid her debt to himself in full, on the following morning, in gold and notes.

"He had been forced, much against his will, to show the notes to the police; unfortunately for the justice of the case, however, the numbers of these could not be directly traceable as having been in Mme. Quesnard's possession at the time of her death. No diaries or books of accounts of any kind were found. Like most French people, she arranged all her money affairs herself, receiving her vast dividends in foreign money, and converting this into English notes and gold, as occasion demanded, at the nearest money-changer's that happened to be handy.

"She had, like a great many foreigners, a holy horror of banks. She would have mistrusted the Bank of England itself; as for solicitors, she held them in perfect abhorrence. She only went once to one in her life, and that was in order to make a will leaving everything she possessed unconditionally to her beloved nephew, Lord Barnsdale.

"But in spite of this difficulty about the notes, you see for yourself, do you not? how terribly strong was the circumstantial evidence against Lady Barnsdale. Her losses at cards, her appeal to Mme. Quesnard, the latter's refusal to help her, and finally the payment in full of the debt to Sir Gilbert Culworth on the following morning.

"There was only one thing that spoke for her, and that was the very horror of the crime itself. It was practically impossible to conceive that a woman of Lady Barnsdale's refinement and education should have sprung upon an elderly woman, like some navvy's wife by the docks, and then that she should have had the presence of mind to jump out of the window, to obliterate her footmarks in the flower-bed, and, in fact, to have given the crime the look of a clever burglary.

"Still, we all know that money difficulties will debase the noblest of us, that greed will madden the sanest and most refined. When the inquest was adjourned, I can assure you that no one had any doubt whatever that within twenty-four hours Lady Barnsdale would be arrested on the capital charge."

III.

"But the detectives in charge of the case had reckoned without Sir Arthur Inglewood, the great lawyer, who was watching the proceedings in behalf of his aristocratic clients," said the man in the corner, when he had assured himself of my undivided attention.

"The adjourned inquest brought with it, I assure you, its full quota of sensation. Again Lord Barnsdale was present, calm, haughty, and impassive, whilst Lady Barnsdale was still too ill to attend. But she had made a statement upon oath, in which, whilst flatly denying that her interview with the deceased at 6 P.M. had been of an acrimonious character as alleged by Alice Holt, she swore most positively that all through the night she had been ill, and had not left her room after 11.30 P.M.

"The first witness called after this affidavit had been read was Jane Barlow, Lady Barnsdale's maid.

"The girl deposed that on that memorable evening preceding the murder, she went up to her mistress's room at about 11.30 in order to get everything ready for the night. As a rule, of course, there was nobody about in the bedroom at that hour, but on this occasion when Jane Barlow entered the room, which she did without knocking, she saw her mistress sitting by her desk.

"'Her ladyship looked up when I came in,' continued Jane Barlow, 'and seemed very cross with me for not knocking at the door. I apologised, then began to get the room tidy; as I did so I could see that my lady was busy counting a lot of money. There were lots of sovereigns and banknotes. My lady put some together in an envelope and addressed it, then she got up from her desk and went to lock up the remainder of the money in her jewel safe.'

"'And this was at what time?' asked the coroner.

"'At about half-past eleven, I think, sir,' repeated the girl.

"'Well,' said the coroner, 'did you notice anything else?'

"'Yes,' replied Jane, 'whilst my lady was at her safe, I saw the envelope in which she had put the money lying on the desk. I couldn't help looking at it, for I knew it was ever so full of banknotes, and I saw that my lady had addressed it to Sir Gilbert Culworth.'

"At this point Sir Arthur Inglewood jumped to his feet and handed something over to the coroner; it was evidently an envelope which had been torn open. The coroner looked at it very intently, then suddenly asked Jane Barlow if she had happened to notice anything about the envelope which was lying on her ladyship's desk that evening.

"'Oh yes, sir!' she replied unhesitatingly, 'I noticed my lady had made a splotch, right on top of the C in Sir Gilbert Culworth's name.'

"'This, then, is the envelope,' was the coroner's quiet comment, as he handed the paper across to the girl.

"'Yes, there's the splotch,' she replied. 'I'd know it anywhere.'

"So you see," continued the man in the corner, with a chuckle, "that the chain of circumstantial evidence against Lady Barnsdale was getting somewhat entangled. It was indeed fortunate for her that Sir Gilbert Culworth had not destroyed the envelope in which she had handed him over the money on the following day.

"Alice Holt, as you know, heard the conflict and raised the alarm much later in the night, when everybody was already in bed, whilst long before that Lady Barnsdale was apparently in possession of the money with which she could pay back her debt.

"Thus the motive for the crime, so far as she was concerned, was entirely done away with. Directly after the episode witnessed by Jane Barlow, Lady Barnsdale had a sort of nervous collapse, and went to bed feeling very ill. Lord Barnsdale was terribly concerned about her; he and the maid remained alternately by her bedside for an hour or two; finally Lord Barnsdale went to sleep in his dressing-room, whilst Jane also finally retired to rest.

"Ill as Lady Barnsdale undoubtedly was then, it was absolutely preposterous to conceive that she could after that have planned and carried out so monstrous a crime, without any motive whatever. To have locked Alice bit's door, then gone downstairs, forced her way into the old lady's room, struggled with her, to have jumped out of the window, and run back into the house by the garden, might have been the work of a determined woman, driven mad by the desire for money, but became absolutely out of the question in the case of a woman suffering from nervous collapse, and having apparently no motive for the crime.

"Of course Sir Arthur Inglewood made the most of the fact that no mud was found on any shoes or dress belonging to Lady Barnsdale. The flower-bed was very soft with the heavy rain of the day before, and Lady Barnsdale could not possibly have jumped even from a ground-floor window and trampled on the flower-bed, without staining her skirts.

"Then there was another point which the clever lawyer brought to the coroner's notice. As Alice Holt had stated in her sworn evidence that Mme. Quesnard had owned to being frightened of Lady Barnsdale that night, was it likely that she would *of her own accord* have opened the door to her in the middle of the night, without at least calling for assistance?

"Thus the matter has remained a strange and unaccountable puzzle. It has always been called the 'Barnsdale Mystery' for that very reason. Every one, somehow, has always felt that Lady Barnsdale did have something to do with that terrible tragedy. Her husband has taken her abroad, and they have let Barnsdale Manor; it almost seems as if the ghost of the old Frenchwoman had driven them forth from their own country.

"As for Alice bit, she maintains to this day that Lady Barnsdale was the culprit, and I understand that she has not yet given up all hope of collecting a sufficiency of evidence to have the beautiful and fashionable woman of society arraigned for this hideous murder."

IV.

"Will she succeed, do you think?" I asked at last.

"Succeed? Of course she won't," he retorted excitedly. "Lady Barnsdale never committed that murder; no woman, except, perhaps, an East-end factory hand, could have done it at all."

"But then—" I urged.

"Why, then," he replied, with a chuckle, "the only logical conclusion is that the robbery and the murder were not committed by the same person, nor at the same hour of the night; moreover, I contend that there was no premeditated murder, but that the old lady died from the result of a pure accident."

"But how?" I gasped.

"This is my version of the story," he said excitedly, as his long bony fingers started fidgeting, fidgeting with that eternal bit of string. "Lady Barnsdale, pressed for money, made an appeal to Mme. Quesnard, which the latter refused, as we know. Then there was an acrimonious dispute between the two ladies, after which came the dinner-hour, then Madame, feeling ill and upset, went up to bed at nine o'clock.

"Now my contention is that undoubtedly the robbery had been committed before that, between the dispute and Madame's bedtime."

"By whom?"

"By Lady Barnsdale, of course, who, as the mistress of the house, could come and go from room to room without exciting any comment; who, moreover, at 6 P.M. was hard pressed for money, and who but a few hours later was handling a mass of gold and banknotes.

"But the strain of committing even an ordinary theft is very great upon a refined woman's organisation. Lady Barnsdale has a nervous breakdown. Well! what is the most likely thing to happen? Why! that she should confess everything to her husband, who worships her, and no doubt express her repentance at what she had done.

"Then imagine Lord Barnsdale's horror! The old lady had not discovered the theft before going to bed. That was only natural, since she was feeling unwell, and was not likely to sit up at night counting her money; the lock of the bureau drawer having been tampered with would perhaps not attract her attention at night.

"But in the morning, the very first thing, she would discover everything, at once suspect the worst, and who knows? make a scandal, talk of it before Alice Holt, Lady Barnsdale's arch enemy, and all before restitution could be made.

"No, no, that restitution must be made at once; not a minute must be lost, since any moment might bring forth discovery, and perhaps an awful catastrophe.

"I take it that Mme. Quesnard and her nephew were on very intimate terms. He hoped to arouse no one by going to his aunt's room, but in order to make quite sure that Alice Holt, hearing a noise in her mistress's room, should not surreptitiously come down, and perhaps play eavesdropper at the momentous interview, he turned the key of the girl's door as he went past, and locked her in.

"Then he knocked at his aunt's door (gently, of course, for old people are light sleepers), and called her by name. Mme. Quesnard, recognising her nephew's voice, slipped on her dressing-gown, smoothed her hair, and let him in.

"Exactly what took place at the interview it is, of course, impossible for any human being to say. Here even I can but conjecture," he added, with inimitable conceit, "but we can easily imagine that, having heard Lord Barnsdale's confession of his wife's folly, the old lady, who as a Frenchwoman was of quick temper and unbridled tongue, would indulge in not very elegant rhetoric on the subject of the woman she had always disliked.

"Lord Barnsdale would, of course, defend his wife, and the old lady, with feminine obstinacy, would continue the attack. Then some insulting epithet, a word only, perhaps, roused the devoted husband's towering indignation—the meekest man on earth becomes a mad bull when he really loves, and the woman he loves is insulted.

"I maintain that the old lady's death was really due to a pure accident; that Lord Barnsdale gripped her by the throat, in a moment of mad anger, at some hideous insult hurled at his wife; of that I am as convinced as if I had witnessed the whole scene. Then the old lady fell, hit her head against the marble, and Lord Barnsdale realized that he was alone at night in his aunt's room, and that he had killed her.

"What would any one do under the circumstances?" he added excitedly. "Why, of course, collect his senses and try to save himself from what might prove to be consequences of the most awful kind. This Lord Barnsdale thought he could best do by giving the accident, which looked so like murder, the appearance of a burglary.

"The lock of the desk in the next room had already been forced open; he now locked the door on the inside, threw open the shutter and the window, jumped out as any burglar would have done; and, being careful to obliterate his own footmarks, he crept back into the house, and thence into his own room, without alarming the watchdog, who naturally knew his own master. He was, of course, just in time before Alice Holt succeeded in rousing the household with her screams.

"And thus you see," he added, "there are no such things as mysteries. The police call them so, so do the public, but every crime has its perpetrator, and every puzzle its solution. My experience is that the simplest solution is invariably the right one."

The Glasgow Mystery

The Glasgow Mystery

I

"It has often been declared," remarked the man in the corner, "that a murder—a successful murder, I mean—can never be committed single-handed in a busy city, and that on the other hand, once a murder *is* committed by more than one person, one of the accomplices is sure to betray the other, and that is the reason why comparatively so few crimes remain undetected. Now I must say I quite agree with this latter theory."

It was some few weeks after my first introduction to the man in the corner and the inevitable bit of string he always played with when unravelling his mysteries, and some time before he recounted to me his grim version of the tragedy in Percy-street, which I have already retold in the *Royal.*

Now I had made it a hard and fast rule whenever he made an assertion of that kind to disagree with it. This invariably irritated him; he became comically excited, produced his bit of string, and started off at rattling speed, after a few rude remarks directed at lady journalists in general and myself in particular, on one of his madly bewildering, true cock-and-bull stories.

"What about the Glasgow murder, then?" I remarked sceptically.

"Ah, the Glasgow murder," he repeated "Yes, what about the Glasgow murder? I see you are one of those people who, like the police, believe that Yardley was an accomplice to that murder, and you still continue to hope, as they do, that sooner or later he, and the other man, Upton, will meet, divide the spoils, and throw themselves into the expectant arms of the Glasgow police."

"Do you mean to tell me that you don't think Yardley had anything to do with that murder?"

"What does it matter whit a humble amateur like myself thinks of that or any other case? Pshaw!" he added, breaking his bit of string between his bony fingers in his comical excitement. "Why, think a moment how simple is the whole thing! There was Mrs. Carmichael, the widow of a medical officer, young, good-looking, and fairly well-off, who for the sake of company, more than for actual profit-making, rents one of the fine houses in Woodbine Crescent with a view to taking in 'paying guests.' Her house is beautifully furnished—I told you she was fairly well-off. She has no difficulty in getting boarders.

"The house is soon full. At the time of which I am speaking she had ten or eleven 'guests'—mostly men out at business all day, also a married couple, an officer's widow with her daughter, and two journalists. At first she kept four female servants; then one day there was a complaint among the gentlemen boarders that their boots were insufficiently polished and their clothes very sketchily brushed. Chief among these complainants was Mr. Yardley, a voting man who wrote verses for magazines, called himself a poet, and, in consequence, indulged in sundry eccentric habits which furnished food for gossip both in the kitchen and in the drawing-room over the coffee-cups.

"As I said before, it was he who was loudest in his complaint on the subject of his boots; it was he, again, who, when Mrs. Carmichael expressed herself willing to do anything to please her boarders, recommended her a quiet, respectable man named Upton to come in for a couple of hours daily, clean boots, knives, windows, and what-nots, and make himself 'generally useful'—I believe that is the technical expression. Upton, it appears, had been known to Mr. Yardley for some time, had often run errands and delivered messages for him, and had even been intrusted with valuable poetical MSS. to be left at various editorial offices.

"It was in July of last year, was it not, that Glasgow—honest, stodgy, busy Glasgow—was thrilled to its very marrow by the recital in its evening papers of one of the most ghastly and most dastardly crimes?

"At two o'clock that afternoon, namely, Mrs. Carmichael, of Woodbine Crescent, was found murdered in her room. Her safe had been opened, and all its contents—which were presumed to include a good deal of jewellery and money—had vanished. The evening papers had also added that the murderer was known to the police, and that no doubt was entertained as to his speedy arrest.

"It appears that in the household at Woodbine Crescent it was the duty of Mary, one of the maids, to take up a cup of tea to Mrs. Carmichael every morning at seven o'clock. The girl was not supposed to go into the room, but merely to knock at the door, wait for a response from her mistress, and then leave the tray outside on the mat.

"Usually Mrs. Carmichael took the tray in immediately, and was down to breakfast with her boarders at half-past eight. But on that eventful morning Mary seems to have been in a hurry. She could not positively state afterwards whether she had heard her mistress's answer to her knock or not; against that, she was quite sure that she had taken up the tray at seven o'clock precisely.

"When everybody went down to breakfast a couple of hours or so later, it was noticed that Mrs. Carmichael had not taken in her tea-tray as usual. A few anxious comments were made as to the genial hostess being unwell, and then the matter was dropped. The servants did not seem to have been really anxious about their mistress during the morning. Mary, who had been in the house two years, said that once before Mrs. Carmichael had stayed in bed with a bad headache until one o'clock.

"However, when the lunch hour came and went, Mrs. Tyrrell, one of the older lady boarders, became alarmed. She went up to her hostess's door and knocked at it loudly and repeatedly, but received no reply. The door, mind you, was locked or bolted, presumably, of course, from the inside. After consultation with her fellow boarders, Mrs. Tyrrell at last, feeling that something must he very wrong, took it upon herself to call in the police. Constable Rae came in; he too knocked and called, shook the door, and finally burst it open.

"It is not for me," continued the man in the corner, "to give you a description of that room as it appeared before the horrified eyes of the constable, the servants, and lady boarders; that lies more in your province than in mine.

"Suffice it to say that the unfortunate lady lay in her bed with her throat cut.

"No key or bolt was found on the inside of the door; the murderer, therefore, having accomplished his ghastly deed, must have locked his victim in, and probably taken the key away with him. Hardly had the terrible discovery been made than Emma the cook, half hysterical with fear and horror, rushed up to Constable Rae, and, clutching him wildly by the arm, whispered under her breath, 'Upton, Upton; he did it, I know ... My poor mistress; he cut her throat with that fowl carver this morning. I saw it in his hand ... It is him, constable!'

"'Where is he?' asked the constable peremptorily. 'See that no one leaves the house. Who has seen this man?'

"But neither the constable, nor anyone else for that matter, was much surprised to find that on searching the house throughout, the man Upton had disappeared."

II.

"At first, of course, the case seemed simplicity itself. No doubt existed, either in the public mind or that of the police, as to Upton being the author of the grim and horrible tragedy. The only difficulty, so far, was the fact that Upton had managed not only to get away on the day of the murder, but also had contrived to evade the rigorous search instituted throughout the city after him by the police—a search, I assure you, in which many an amateur detective readily joined.

"The inquest had been put off for a day or two in the hope that Upton might be found before it occurred. However, three days had now elapsed, and it could not be put off any longer. Little did the public expect the sensational developments which the case suddenly began to assume.

"The medical evidence revealed nothing new. On the contrary, it added its usual quota of vague indefiniteness which so often helps to puzzle the police. The medical officer had been called in by Constable Rae, directly after his discovery of the murder. That was about two o'clock in the afternoon, a good many hours about two o'clock Death had occurred before that time, stated Dr. Dawlish—possibly nine or ten hours; but it might also have been eleven or twelve hours previously.

"Then Emma the cook was called. Her evidence was, of course, most important, as she had noticed and talked to the man Upton the very morning of the crime. He came as usual to his work, about a quarter to seven, but the cook immediately noticed that he seemed very strange and excited.

"'What do you mean by strange?' asked the coroner.

"'Well, it was strange of him, sir, to start first thing in the morning cleaning knives when we had as many knives as we wanted clean for breakfast.'

"'Yes? He started cleaning knives, and then what did he do?'

"'Oh, he turned and turned that there knife machine so as I told him he would be turning all the edges. Then he suddenly took up the fowl carver and said to me; "This fowl carver is awful blunt—where's the steel?" I says to him: "In the sideboard, of course, in the dining-room," and he goes off with the fowl carver in his hand, and that is the last I ever saw of that carver and of Upton himself.'

"'Have you known Upton long?' asked the coroner.

"'No, sir, he had only been in the house two days. Mr. Yardley gave him a character, and the mistress took him on, to clean boots and knives. His hours were half-past six to ten, but he used to turn up about a quarter to seven. He seemed obliging and willing, but not much up to his work, and didn't say much. But I hadn't seen him so funny except that morning when the poor missus was murdered.'

"'Is this the carver you speak of?' asked the coroner, directing a constable to show one he held in his hand to the witness.

"With renewed hysterical weeping Emma identified the carver as the one she had last seen in Upton's hand. It appears that Detective McMurdoch had found the knife, together with the key of Mrs. Carmichael's bedroom door, under the hall mat. Sensational, wasn't it?" laughed the man in the corner; "quite in the style of the penny novelette—sensational, but not very mysterious.

"Then Mrs. Tyrrell had to be examined, as it was she who had first been alarmed about Mrs. Carmichael, and who had taken it upon herself to call in the police. Whether through spite or merely accidentally Mrs. Tyrrell insisted in her evidence on the fact that it was Mr. Yardley who was indirectly responsible for the awful tragedy, since it was he who had introduced the man Upton into the house.

"The coroner felt more interested. He thought he would like to put a few questions to Mr. Yardley. Now Mr. Yardley when called up did not certainly look prepossessing; and from the first most persons present were prejudiced against him. He was, as I think I said before, that *rara avis*, a successful poet: he wrote dainty scraps for magazines and weekly journals.

"In appearance he was a short, sallow, thin man, with no body and long limbs, and carried his head so much to one side as to almost appear deformed. Here is a snapshot I got of him some time subsequently. He is no beauty, is he?

"Still his manner, his small shapely hands, and quiet voice undoubtedly proclaimed him a gentleman.

"It was very well known throughout the household that Mr. Yardley was very eccentric; being a poet he would enjoy the privilege with impunity. It appears that his most eccentric habit was to get up at unearthly hours in the morning—four o'clock sometimes—and wander about the streets of Glasgow.

"'I have written my best pieces,' he stated in response to the coroner's astonished remark upon this strange custom of his, 'leaning against a lamp post in Sauchiehall Street at five o'clock in the morning. I spend my afternoons in the various public libraries, reading. I have only boarded and lodged in this house for two or three months, but, as the servants will tell you, I leave it long before they are up in the morning. I am never in to breakfast or luncheon, but always in to dinner. I go to bed early, naturally, as I require several hours sleep.'

"Mr. Yardley was then very closely questioned as to his knowledge of the man Upton.

"'I first met the man,' replied Mr. Yardley, 'about a year ago. He was loafing in Buchanan Street, outside the *Herald* office, and spoke to me, telling me a most pitiable tale—namely, that he was an ex-compositor, had had to give up his work owing to failing eyesight, that he had striven for weeks and months to get some other kind of employment, spending in the meanwhile the hard-earned savings of many years' toil; that he had come to his last shilling two days ago, and had been reduced to begging, not for money, but for some kind of job—anything to earn a few honest coins.

"'Well, I somehow liked the look of the man; moreover, as I just happened to want to send a message to the other end of the city, I sent Upton. Since then I have seen him almost every day. He takes my manuscripts for me to the editorial offices, and runs various errands. I have recommended him to one or two of my friends, and they have always found him honest and sober. He has eked out a very meagre livelihood in this way, and when Mrs. Carmichael thought of having a man in the house to do odd jobs, I thought I should be doing a kind act by recommending Upton to her. Little did I dream then what terrible consequences such a kind act would bring in its trail. I can only account for the man's awful crime by thinking that perhaps his mind had become suddenly unhinged.'

"All this scorned plain and straightforward enough. Mr. Yardley spoke quietly, without the slightest nervousness or agitation. The coroner and jury both pressed him with questions on the subject of Upton, but his attitude remained equally self-possessed throughout. Perhaps he felt, after a somewhat severe cross-examination on the part of the coroner, who prided himself on his talent in that direction, that a certain amount of doubt might lurk in the minds of the jury and consequently the public. Be that as it may, he certainly begged that two or three of the servants might be recalled in order to enable them to state definitely that he was out of the house, as usual, when they came downstairs that morning.

"One of the housemaids, recalled, fully corroborated that statement. Mr. Yardley's room, she said, was on the ground floor, next to the dining-room. She went into it soon after half-past six, turned down the bed, and began tidying it up generally.

"There was only one other witness of any importance to examine. One other boarder—Mr. James Lucas, a young journalist, employed on the editorial staff of the *Glasgow Banner*.

"The reason why he had been called specially was because he was well known to be one of the privileged guests of the house, and had been more intimate with the deceased than any of her other boarders. This privilege, it appears, chiefly consisted in being admitted to coffee, and possibly whiskey and soda after dinner, in Mrs. Carmichael's special private sitting-room. Moreover, there was a generally accepted theory among the other boarders that Mr. James Lucas entertained certain secret hopes with regard to his amiable hostess, and that, but for the fact that he was several years her junior, she might have encouraged these hopes.

"Now, Mr. James Lucas was the exact opposite of Mr. Yardley, the poet; tall, fair, athletic, his appearance would certainly prepossess everyone in his favour. He seemed very much upset, and recounted with much, evidently genuine, feeling, his last interview with the unfortunate lady—the evening before the murder.

"'I spent about an hour with Mrs. Carmichael in her sitting-room,' he concluded, and parted from her about ten o'clock. I then went to my club, where I stayed pretty late, until closing time, in fact. After that I went for a stroll, and it was a quarter past two by my watch when I came in. I let myself in with my latch-key.

"'It was pitch dark in the outer hall, and I was groping for my candle, when I heard the sound of a door opening and shutting on one of the floors above, and directly after someone coming down the stairs. As you have seen yourself, the outer hall is divided from the inner one by a glass door, which on this occasion stood open. In the inner hall there was a faint glimmer of light, which worked its way down from a skylight on one of the landings, and by this glimmer I saw Mr. Yardley descending the stairs, cross the hall, and go into his room. He did not see me, and I did not speak.'

"An extraordinary, almost breathless, hush had descended over all those assembled there. The coroner sat with his chin buried in his hand, his eyes resting searchingly on the witness who had just spoken. The jury had not uttered a sound. At last the coroner queried:

"'Is the jury to understand, Mr. Lucas, that you can swear positively that at a quarter-past two in the morning, or thereabouts, you saw Mr. Yardley come down the stairs from one of the floors above and go into his own room, which is on the ground floor?'

"'Positively.'

"That was enough. Mr. Lucas was dismissed and Mr. Yardley was recalled. As he once more stood before the coroner, his curious one-sided stoop, his sallowness, and length of limb seemed even more marked than before. Perhaps he was a shade or two paler, but certainly neither his hands nor his voice trembled in the slightest degree.

"Questioned by the coroner, he replied quietly:

"'Mr. Lucas was obviously mistaken. At the hour he names I was in bed and asleep.'

"There had been excitement and breathless interest when Mr. James Lucas had made his statement, but that excitement and breathlessness was as nothing compared with the absolutely dumbfounded awe which fell over everyone there, as the sallow, half-deformed, little poet, gave the former witness so completely, so emphatically the lie.

"The coroner himself hardly knew how to keep up his professional dignity as he almost gasped the query:

"'Then is the jury to understand that you can swear positively that at a quarter-past two o'clock on that particular morning you were in bed and asleep?'

"'Positively.'

"It seemed as if Mr. Yardley had repeated purposely the other man's emphatic and laconic assertion. Certainly his voice was as steady, his eye as clear, his manner as calm as that of Mr. Lucas. The coroner and jury were silent, and Mr. Yardley turned to where young Lucas had retired in a further corner of the room. The eyes of the two met, almost like the swords of two duellists before the great attack; neither flinched. One or the other was telling a lie. A terrible lie since it might entail loss of honour, or life perhaps to the other, yet *neither* flinched. One was telling a lie, remember, and in everyone's mind there arose at once the great all absorbing queries 'Which?' and 'Wherefore!'"

III.

I had been so absorbed in listening to the thrilling narrative of that highly dramatic inquest that I really had not noticed until then that the man in the corner was recounting it as if he had been present at it himself.

"That is because I heard it all from an eye-witness," he suddenly replied with that eerie knack he seemed to possess of reading my thoughts, "but it must have been very dramatic, and, above all, terribly puzzling. You see there were two men swearing against one another, both in good positions, both educated men; it was impossible for any jury to take either evidence as absolutely convincing, and it could not be proved that either of them lied. Mr. Lucas might have done so from misapprehension. There was just a possibility that he had had more whiskey at his club than was good for him. Mr. Yardley, on the other hand, if he lied, lied because he had something to hide, something to hide in that case which might have been terrible.

"Of course Dr. Dawlish was recalled, and with wonderful learning and wonderful precision he repeated his vague medical statements:

"'When I examined the body with my colleague, Dr. Swanton, death had evidently supervened several hours ago. Personally, I believe that it must have occurred certainly more like twelve hours ago than seven.'

"More than that he could not say. After all, medical science has its limits.

"Then Emma, the cook, was again called. There was an important point which, oddly enough, had been overlooked up to this moment. The question, namely, of the doormat under which the knife (which, by the way, was blood-stained) and also the key of Mrs. Carmichael's bedroom door was found. Emma, however, could make a very clear and very definite statement on that point. She had cleaned the hall and shaken the mat at half-past six that morning. At that hour the housemaid was making Mr. Yardley's bed; he had left the house already. There certainly was neither key nor knife under the mat then.

"The balance of evidence, which perhaps for one brief moment had inclined oh, ever so slightly, against Mr. Yardley, returned to its original heavy weight against the man Upton. Of course there was practically nothing to implicate Mr. Yardley seriously. The coroner made a résumé of the case before his jury worthy of a judge in the High Courts.

"He recapitulated all the evidence. It was very strong, undeniable, damning against Upton, and the jury could arrive but at one conclusion with regard to him. Then there was the medical evidence. That certainly favoured Upton a very little, if at all. Remember that both the medical gentlemen refused to make a positive statement as to the time; their evidence could not, therefore, be said to weigh either for or against anyone.

"There was then the strange and unaccountably conflicting evidence between two gentlemen of the house—Mr. Lucas and Mr. Yardley. That was a matter which for the present must rest between either of these gentlemen and their conscience. There was also the fact that the man Upton—the evident actual murderer—had been introduced into the house by Mr. Yardley. The jury knew best themselves if this fact should or should not weigh with them in their decision.

"That was the sum total of the evidence. The jury held but a very brief consultation. Their foreman pronounced their verdict of 'Wilful murder against Upton.' Not a word about Mr. Yardley.

What could they have said? There was really no evidence against him—not enough, certainly, to taint his name for ever with so hideous a blight.

"In a case like that, remember, the jury are fully aware that the police would never for a moment lose sight of a man who had so narrowly escaped a warrant as Yardley had done. Relying on the certainty that very soon Upton would be arrested, it was not to be doubted for a moment but that he would betray his accomplice, if he had one. Criminals in such a plight nearly always do. In the meanwhile, every step of Yardley's would be dogged, unbeknown to himself, even if he attempted to leave the country. As for Upton—"

The man in the corner paused. He was eyeing me through his great bone-rimmed spectacles, watching with ironical delight my evident breathless interest in his narrative. I remembered that Glasgow murder so well. I remember the talks, the arguments, the quarrels that would arise in every household. Was Yardley an accomplice? Did he kill Mrs. Carmichael at two in the morning? Did he tell a lie? If so, why? Did Mr. James Lucas tell a lie? Many people, I remember, held this latter theory, more particularly as Mrs. Carmichael's will was proved some days later, and it was found that she had left all her money to him.

For a little while public opinion veered dead against him. Some people thought that if he were innocent he would refuse to touch a penny of her money; others, of a more practical turn of mind, did not see why he should not. He was a struggling young journalist; the lady had obviously been in love with him, and intended to marry him; she had a perfect right—as she had no children or any near relative—to leave her money to whom she choose, and it would indeed be hard on him, if, through the act of some miscreant, he should at one fell swoop be deprived both of wife and fortune.

Then, of course, there was Upton—Upton! Upton! whom the police could not find! who must be guilty, seeing that he so hid himself, who never would have acted the hideous comedy with the carver. Why should he have wilfully drawn attention to himself, and left, as it were, his visiting card on the scene of the murder?

Why? why? why?

"Ah, yes, why!" came as a funny, shrill echo from my eccentric *vis-a-vis*. "I see that in spite of my earnest endeavour to teach you to think out a case logically and clearly, you start off with a preconceived notion, which naturally leads you astray because it is preconceived, just like any blundering detective in these benighted islands."

"Preconceived?" I retorted indignantly. "There is no question of preconception. Whether Mr. Yardley knew of the contemplated murder or not, whether he was an accomplice or Mr. Lucas, there is one thing very clear—namely, that Upton was not innocent in the matter."

"What makes you say that?" he asked blandly.

"Obviously, because if he were innocent he would not have acted the hideous tragic comedy with the carver; he would not, above all, have absolutely damned himself by disappearing out of the house and out of sight at the very moment when the discovery of Mrs. Carmichael's murdered body had become imminent."

"It never struck you, I suppose," retorted the man in the corner with quiet sarcasm, "how *very* damning Upton's actions were on that particular morning?"

"Of course they were *very* damning. That is just my contention."

"And you have never then studied my methods of reasoning sufficiently to understand that when a criminal—a clever criminal, mind you—appears to be damning himself in the most brainless fashion, that is the time to guard against the clever pitfalls he is laying up for the police?"

"Exactly. That is why I, as well as many people connected with journalism, believe that Upton was acting a comedy in order to save his accomplice. The question only remains as to who the accomplice was."

"He must have been singularly unselfish and self-sacrificing, then."

"How do you mean?"

"According to your argument, Upton heaped up every conceivable circumstantial evidence against himself in order to shield his accomplice. Firstly he acts the part of strange, unnatural excitement, he loudly proclaims the fact that he leaves the kitchen with the fowl carver in his hand, thirdly he deposits that same blood-stained knife and the key of Mrs. Carmichael's room under the mat a few moments before he leaves the house. You must own that the man must have been singularly unselfish since, if he is ever caught, nothing would save him from the gallows, whilst, unless a great deal more evidence can be brought up, his accomplice could continue to go free."

"Yes, that might be," I said thoughtfully; "it was of course a part of the given plan. Many people held that Upton and Yardley were great friends—they might have been brothers, who knows?"

"Yes, who knows?" he repeated scornfully, as getting more and more excited his long thin fingers wound and unwound his bit of string, making curious complicated knots, and then undoing them feverishly.

"Do brothers usually so dote on each other, that they are content to swing for one another? And have you never wondered why the police never found Upton? How did he get away? Where is he? Has the earth swallowed him up?

"Surely a clumsy brute like that, who gives himself hopelessly away on the very day when he commits a murder, cannot have brains enough to hide altogether away from the police—a man who before a witness selects the weapon with which he means to kill his victim, and who then deliberately leaves it blood-stained there where it is sure to be found at once? Why imagine such a consummate fool evading the police, not a day, not a week, not a month, but nearly two years now, which means altogether? Why, such a fool as you, the public, and the police have branded him would have fallen into a trap within twenty-four hours of his attempt at evasion; whereas the man who planned and accomplished that murder was a genius before he became a blackguard."

"That's just what I said. He was doing it to shield his accomplice."

"His accomplice!" gasped the funny creature, with ever increasing excitement. "Yes, the accomplice he loved and cherished above all—his brother you say, perhaps. No, someone he would love ten thousand times more than any brother."

"Then you mean—"

"*Himself*, of course! Didn't you see it all along? Lord bless my soul! The young man—poet or blackguard, what you will—who comes into a boarding-house, then realises that its mistress is wealthy. He studies the rules of the house, the habits of its mistress, finds out about her money, her safe, her jewels, and then makes his plans. Oh, they were magnificently laid! That man ought to have been a great diplomatist, a great general—he was only a great scoundrel.

"The sort of disguise he assumed is so easy to manage. Only remember one thing: When a fool wishes to sink his identity he does so *after* he has committed a crime and is wanted by the police; he is bound, therefore, for the best part of the remainder of his life, to keep up the disguise he has selected at all times, every hour, every minute of the day; to alter his voice, his walk, his manners. On the other hand, how does a clever man like Yardley proceed?

"He chooses his disguise and assumes it *before* the execution of his crime; it is then only a matter of a few days, and when all is over, the individual, the known criminal, disappears; and, mind you, he takes great care that the criminal shall be known. Now in this case Upton is introduced into the house; say he calls one evening on Mr. Yardley's recommendation; Mrs. Carmichael sees him in the hall for a few moments, arranges the question of work and wages, and after that he comes every morning, with a dirty face, towzled hair, false beard and moustache—the usual type of odd job man very much down in his luck—his work lies in the kitchen, no one sees him upstairs, whilst the cook and kitchen folk never see Mr. Yardley.

"After a little while something—carelessness perhaps—might reveal the trick, but the deception is only carried on two days. Then the murder is accomplished and Upton disappears. In the meanwhile Mr. Yardley continues his eccentric habits. He goes out at unearthly hours; he is a poet; he is out of the house while Upton carries on the comedy with the carving knife. He knows that there never will be any evidence against him as Yardley; he has taken every care that all should be against Upton, all; hopeless, complete, absolute, damning!

"Then he leaves the police to hunt for Upton. He 'lies low' for a time, after a little while he will go abroad, I dare say he has done so already. A jeweller in Vienna, or perhaps St. Petersburg, will buy some loose stones of him, the stones he has picked out of Mrs. Carmichael's brooches and rings, the gold he will melt down and sell, the notes he can cash at any foreign watering-place, without a single question being asked of him. English banknotes find a very ready market abroad, and 'no questions asked.'

"After that he will come back to his friends in Glasgow and write dainty bits of poetry for magazines; the only difference being that he will write them at more reasonable hours. And during all the time the police will hunt for Upton.

"It was clever, was it not? You have his photo? I gave it you just now. Clever-looking, isn't he? As Upton he wore a beard and dyed his hair very black; it must have been a great trouble every morning, mustn't it?"

Coachwhip Publications

CoachwhipBooks.com

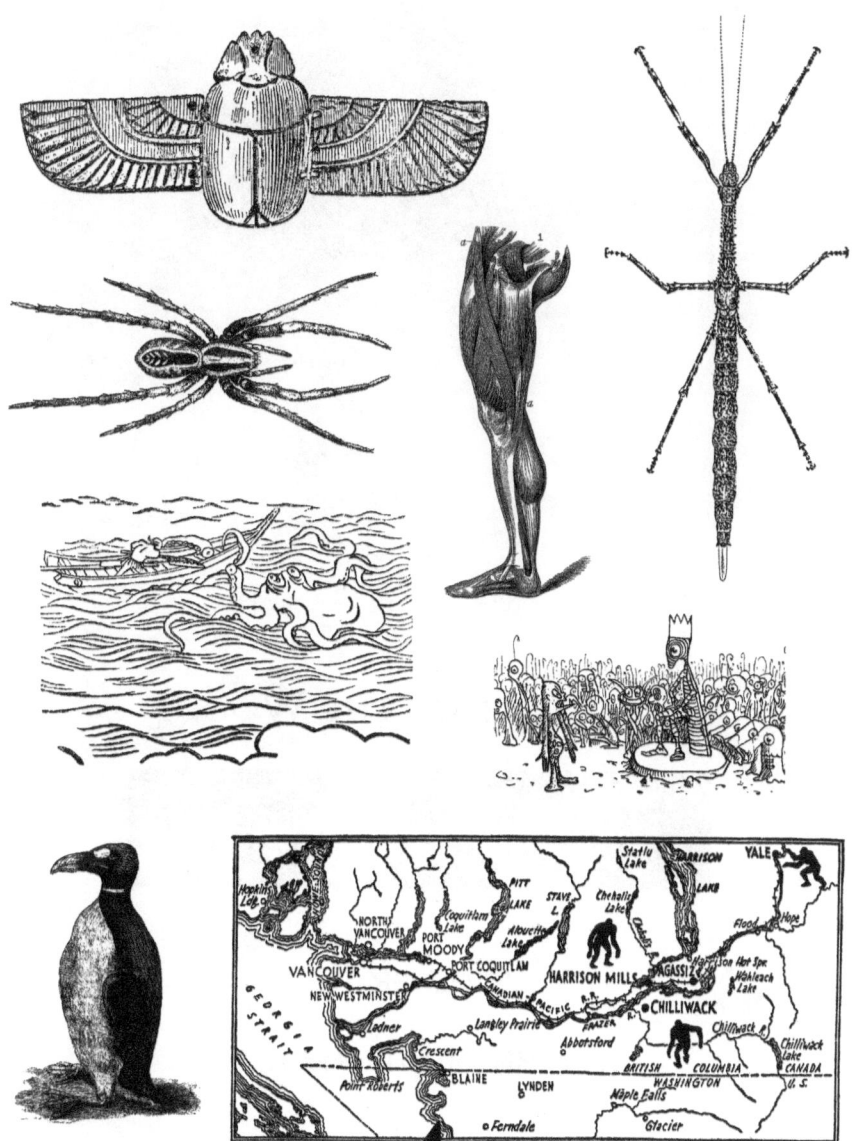

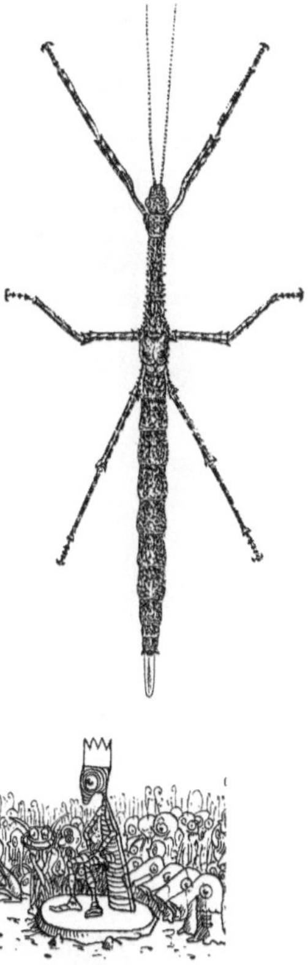

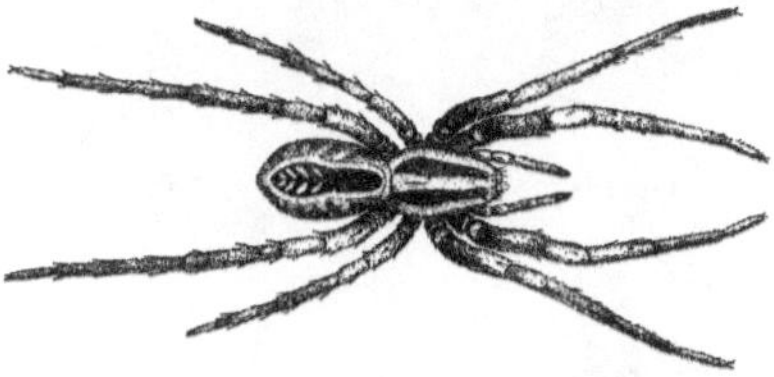

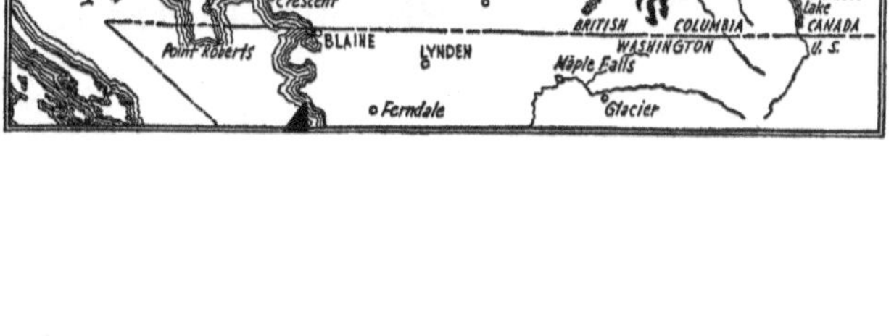

ALSO AVAILABLE

COACHWHIPBOOKS.COM

NOVEMBER JOE

ISBN 1-61646-013-X

ALSO AVAILABLE

COACHWHIPBOOKS.COM

SHERLOCK HOLMES

Volume 1: ISBN 1-61646-006-7
Volume 2: ISBN 1-61646-007-5
Volume 3: ISBN 1-61646-008-3

ALSO AVAILABLE

COACHWHIPBOOKS.COM

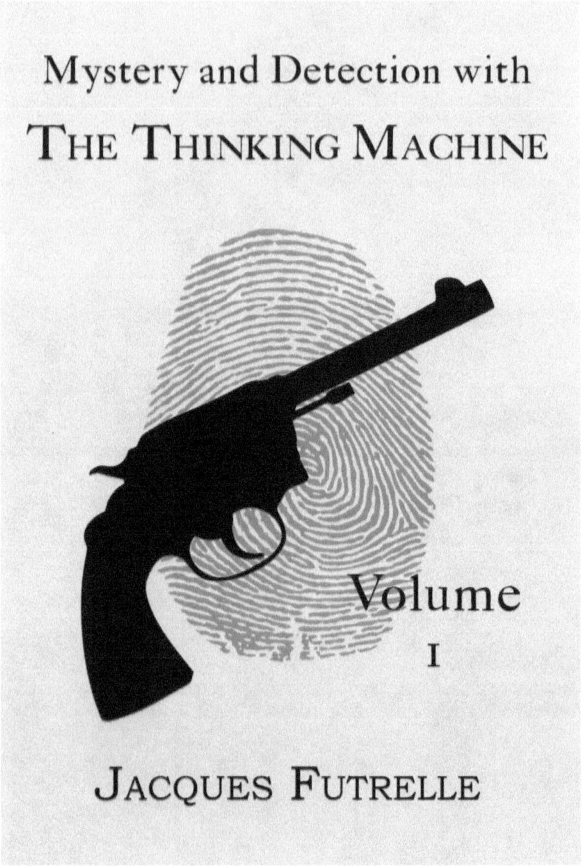

THE THINKING MACHINE

Volume 1: ISBN 1-930585-70-5
Volume 2: ISBN 1-930585-71-3

ALSO AVAILABLE

COACHWHIPBOOKS.COM

CLEEK

Volume 1: ISBN 1-930585-97-7
Volume 2: ISBN 1-930585-98-5
Volume 3: ISBN 1-930585-99-3

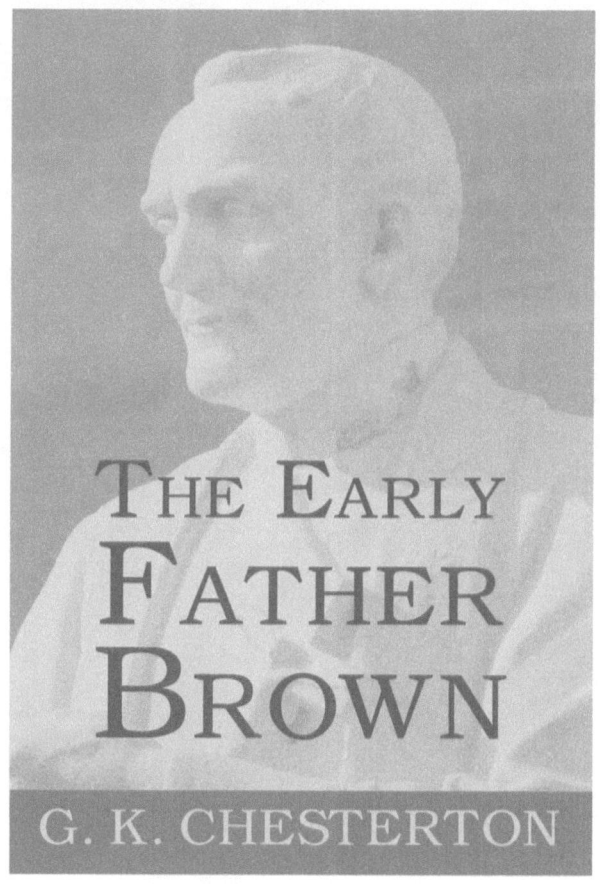